# Forest of the Morning

By

# Emmylou Kotzé

# Book 2

# Maiden of Despair

PINK HYDRA PRESS

2025

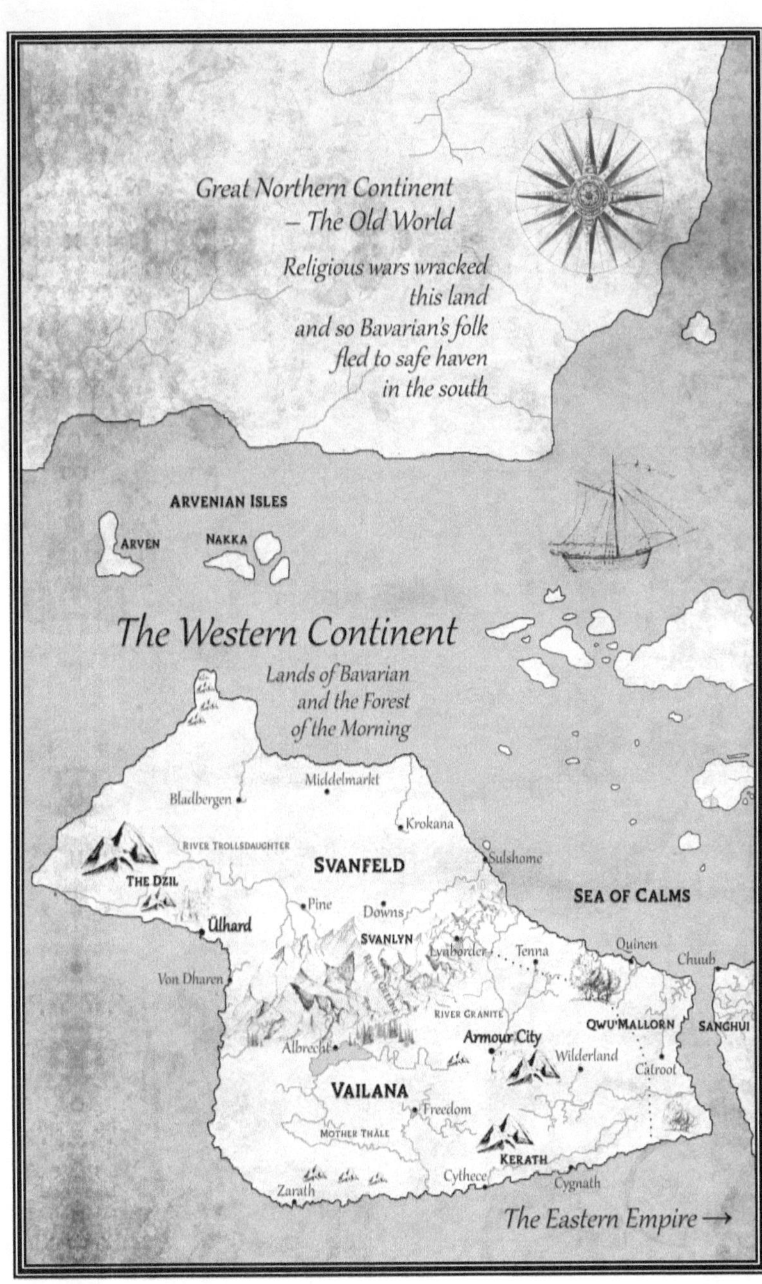

Great Northern Continent
– The Old World

Religious wars wracked
this land
and so Bavarian's folk
fled to safe haven
in the south

ARVENIAN ISLES
ARVEN
NAKKA

The Western Continent
Lands of Bavarian
and the Forest
of the Morning

Middelmarkt
Bladbergen
Krokana
RIVER TROLLSDAUGHTER
SVANFELD
Sulshome
SEA OF CALMS
THE DZIL
Pine
Downs
Ulhard
SVANLYN
Lyaborder
Tenna
Quinen
Chuub
Von Dharen
RIVER GRANITE
QWU'MALLORN
SANGHUI
Armour City
Wilderland
Albrecht
Catroot
VAILANA
Freedom
MOTHER THALE
KERATH
Zarath
Cythece
Cygnath

The Eastern Empire →

# Chapter XXI
# Beerstana Pass

SUNSET BORE DOWN UPON THE MOUNTAINS in a cold haze of sunlight, dying the distant peaks bloody red and orange, the path ahead burnished gold. The cliffs above made mud-dark shadows in the dying of the day. Here and there along the path, pools of snow that had melted with the afternoon sun began to freeze again as it dipped below the horizon in the direction of the beleaguered city they had left far behind.

Hugh Anspeare wound his horn, calling the rest of his riders in, summoning them to assemble for the last stretch of the journey. Behind them, fear and monstrous horror sank away at last, and before them stretched the vast unknown expanses of the spiked mountaintops of Svanlyn.

He brought the horn to his lips and sounded the call again, balancing with the reins in one hand as his horse picked up her pace to a canter. His helmet had been lost in the recent fight, and the westering sun laid a last finger of warmth upon his neat, close-cropped black curls and beard. Dark-skinned but with startling blue eyes, so tall he rode a horse near seventeen hands high, he was an unmistakable figure. That had its advantages, as his riders quickly identified and flocked towards him amidst the burgundy scree of the mountain slope, but of course it could be dangerous too, especially without any protection for his head. He glanced anxiously back, knowing that even a secure victory was not always a guarantee of safety.

Luckily, their foe did not appear to be capable of operating ranged weapons. Still, the possibility remained: a grotesque enemy marksman could be squatting amidst the black cliffs even now, aiming an arrow with deadly skill to pass right into his eye. That was how his mentor, Captain Leiber, had died, fourteen years ago when they had skirmished against Arvenian pirates near the town of Meerheim. Hugh had been right beside him that day, a green cadet still in training, and the noise that stray arrow had made when it hit would stay with him for as long as he lived.

So he kept a weather eye on the peaks around them, hoped that his scouts had done their job. He had no reason to doubt that they had. This handful who rode with him—once twenty men, now reduced to sixteen—were the best of his command. He had sent the rest on towards their destination with the queen and her three young children in tow.

It had not been two weeks since Hugh Anspeare, scion of a noble Vailanan house that now possessed nought but an ancient title, had stood in King Falcon Häger's private chamber in his castle above Ülhard, at the solemn monarch's left hand even as his queen, Bronwyn, stood silently at his right.

*"At least ten thousand." The messenger's voice rang hollow in the silence of the chamber, and the queen was dead-pale beneath her freckles. "Probably more; perhaps up to twenty thousand. Our presence was discovered by their scouts." A hesitation, the haunted look of a man who had witnessed something that would mark him for the rest of his life. "I was the only one who got away, my lord. These walking dead men are not easy to—to destroy."*

*"Cousin," Hugh Anspeare said to the king the moment the messenger was dismissed, "send me there. Send me north with General Vanya. Let us deal with this infestation."*

*"You are the best of the captains under Vanya's command," the king returned. "And the only one I trust concerning the welfare of my family." He turned to the queen. "You, and the three children. Kristina, Lorai, and Patrick. The enemy marches on the capital even as we speak. You must fly away from here."*

*"What of Rolf?" the queen breathed. "And Katrina? What of their safety?"*

*"Rolf is my heir, and the men look to him to lead," the king replied. "He will fight beside me. Katrina will be safe where she is, at your sister's. It's near Von Dharen, their mansion. Close to the moun-*

*tains." He was addressing his soldier, not his wife. "If things go badly here . . . retrieve her." He hesitated. "Hugh, if . . . if things end badly, you may be the only hope for us. I know you have never wanted to involve yourself in the turmoil of politics. Understandable. But if you are—if you are in charge—" He obviously did not want to say, "if I die," and who could blame him? A monarch of Svanfeld had not died from aught but natural causes for nearly three hundred years now. He clasped his wife's shoulder. "—If you find yourself in charge, listen to Bronwyn. She knows all the inner workings of my council and court. She has ruled beside me all these years."*

Hugh had clasped his cousin's hand, reading the king's discomposure in blue eyes that were so like his, though Falcon had the fair colouring of his native people, and the unwavering gaze of a true leader. Though they called each other "cousin," Falcon was really the cousin of Hugh's mother, and was twenty years his senior. Hugh could name no-one who had been more of a father figure to him when he was growing up. His own father had died so long ago that Hugh remembered nothing of him, and upon his death his mother had returned to her native land. That had turned out to be lucky, since it meant that Hugh was nowhere near Armour City when the vengeful blood sorcerer came to power, and had escaped the fate of many of the old nobility of Vailana: summary execution.

His men rode up, flanked and tailed him, the scouts keeping their positions as rearguard, and they rode.

He wondered, again, how their foe had found them in the

mountains. It was far easier to dwell on that, the immediate challenge at hand, than brood over things he could not influence. Whether the army of monsters, marching south from the hill-country of the Dzil, had yet reached Ülhard. Whether the city's defences still stood—or the alternative, which he did not like to dwell on. Whether Katrina, Falcon's eldest daughter, was truly safe. She was not far from him, at this very moment. There was a turnoff along this road somewhere, a steep rocky path, unnavigable with a carriage but doable on horseback, which led down to the town of Von Dharen.

He would have liked to take that turnoff, to ride down to that mansion near Von Dharen, to find Katrina and keep her with him. But that kind of detour could spell disaster in its recklessness, and Hugh was no longer so young as to let his heart do his thinking, if indeed he ever had been. It would be too easy for their foemen to find them again, this time perhaps along an even more winding and easily-ambushable road, and Katrina would be the furthest thing from safe if another fight the like of the one they had just weathered broke out.

He shivered as a chill wind whistled past, his horse going as fast as he would allow along the slope. They had not yet reached the Beerstana Pass, and he did not want to face that famously hostile peak in pitch darkness. Quickly he ran his mind along the road that stretched ahead. There was no proper shelter along the pass itself, only a few places where the road had been tunnelled through rock-wall on either side. Horse and rider could rest awhile in those crevices, but the rest of the pass wound round and round the side of the peak, one side hugging solid rock, the other dropping off into blind nothingness.

It was not a good place to be with night falling, but the alternative—camp before they reached the pass—was even less ideal. There was no shelter out here, on the slope, either, and his men carried only the bare minimum of supplies. They had no tents, no barrier against the wind that was stealing through his layers of armour, leather and wool, finding its inexorable way into the warmth of him. The men who rode with him were veterans, experienced and practical, but he knew from long experience that once they halted their flight, everything would start to slow down. They were moving fast now, riding the strange energy that came after battle. It was his job to try and make as much of that mood as he could, take them as far as possible before allowing them to rest. The moment they stopped, fatigue would set in.

There was also the matter of the weather: only yesterday, the sky above Beerstana had been white, and he knew that a late storm had been howling about the great peak. That storm had broken as fast as it had come up, retreating into the lower cliffs, giving way to a brittle blue day and an insistent, icy wind. Hugh was no weather-master, had no way of knowing how long the clear spell would last. The prospect of getting caught in another storm on the pass seemed even more dismal than tussling with their foes again.

Their foes . . . Hugh scanned the helmed faces of the riders closest to him, but found nothing to betray the thoughts in their heads.

It all seemed like a bad dream. He had seen magic before, but that had been more than twenty years ago, in the days when he'd visited Armour City and other places in Vailana. He had been just a child then. No place had been closed to him in that time, not even the Forest of the Morning. He had spent one brief afternoon, when he was no older than twelve, riding beneath those solemn ironwood trees with a local guide from the town of Tenna, a lovely woman with long hair as black as a raven's wing and the broadest smile he had ever seen. Even as a child, he had not feared what she was, what she could do. He had never seen aught of magic other than wonder. The Morgei used it to create beautiful things, to grow flowers in the dead of winter and to ward the harsh winds of the Vailanan plains from their homesteads and greenhouses.

The name of the blood sorcerer—*Arran Sylvaissen*—had not been mentioned during Hugh's hasty conference with his king. Yet there remained little doubt of their enemy's true nature. What else could be the secret of this strange dead army, if not dark magic?

Hugh was close enough to the king to know some of the doings of his Council, and was aware that Svanfeld had declared its neutrality towards the tyrant of Armour City, as long as he left *them* in peace. He knew that the Council had often averred, in the past, that the mountains of Svanlyn would provide an adequate barrier to protect them against the blood sorcerer's armies, should he ever feel the urge to expand his kingdom. He knew that the Morgei, in General Vanya's words, "kept that bugger quite busy flinging army after army against their magical defences."

But the invasion had come from the north, strange creatures spilling forth in horrific abundance from the caves of the Dzil, and they had fallen upon the nearby villages and slaughtered all of the townsguard and most of the civilian population. The reports from those who had survived and fled to Ülhard were not something he cared to remember, yet it was hard to forget.

When he was a child, war had seemed a distant, abstract concept to Hugh, something he learned of from his tutors, read about in thrilling accounts of the past. Historically, Novlayans from the Great Continent to the north had periodically invaded all the lands within reach, leaving their descendants scattered across Svanfeld and the Arvenian Isles; rogue pirate kingdoms came and went on the Sea of Calms, disrupting the shipping routes occasionally; but Svanfeld and Vailana, the twin lands of Bavarian, lay at peace with each other, prospering on the trade that flowed continually from the Eastern Continent and back around.

The blood sorcerer had changed all that, when Hugh was fifteen, and the world had never looked the same again. Even spared the fate of his peers, he had begun to see a darker future. It had played some role in him wanting to make a military career for himself. The land was becoming more lawless, he remembered Falcon saying, and the people needed to know that their monarch would keep them safe.

The horses crested a rise in the road, hooves skidding over gravel on the downslope, and at last Hugh saw the location which had been foremost in his mind since even before their battle with the dead men that day: the entrance to the Beerstana Pass.

Bracketed by high cliffs to either side, the road sloped down as it approached the great peak. Hugh's riders slowed at his signal. Ahead, an archway had been built across the road, great gates standing open to the coming night. There were guards perched upon the arch, and on the cliffsides around, but none barred the gates. Of course, the rest of Hugh's command must have passed this way earlier, with the queen, heavily disguised, in tow.

The guard captain hailed him from above. "Who goes there?" Flaming torches lit the way ahead, but it was hard to see the guardsmen, shrouded as they were in the dusky shadows above.

"Hugh Anspeare," he called back, "with the remainder of my command."

Grey-browed eyes swept across Hugh and his men as they drew to a halt. "I count seventeen of you. The sergeant who passed this morning said there would be twenty-one."

"We lost the others in a skirmish with the enemy."

A ripple seemed to pass through the assembled guardsmen, though no-one spoke audibly. The captain held up a hand. "Carry you any fresh news from Ülhard?" he called, an unmistakable note of hope in his voice.

"Nothing that the sergeant did not already know."

"And these—enemies?" The man's voice held a tremor, and Hugh wondered what he had already heard.

"We fought them," he replied. "They are not human."

"Then what are they?"

"I do not know. They appear to be dead men, yet the strength in their limbs is double that of any man." There was a collective intake of breath, and the captain's seamed face grew grim. "But they can be killed!" he called, and his men nodded and hollered as he turned round in the saddle towards them. "How many did we fell today, Cedric?"

His lieutenant turned and spat. " 'Bout two dozen, by my estimation."

Hugh knew that it had likely been closer to fifteen, but did not gainsay the man. "When you come to fight them," he called, "aim for the head. They are ferocious, but not smart. They do not ride, and carry no ranged weapons."

The guard captain scowled deeper. "Where do they come from?"

Hugh knew that "the caves of the Dzil" would be no true answer, so he only shook his head. "No-one knows."

"We can guess," one of the guardsmen on the arch piped up. "Who else could create such things, if not that bastard in Armour City?" The others nodded and growled in agreement.

"That's why King Falcon sent us," Hugh lied lightly. He glanced west towards the sinking sun. "We need to get to Albrecht, and quickly."

The guard captain understood the haste in his words, and waved them on. "It's a week to Albrecht from here. Five days, if you ride hard."

Hugh dismounted and led his horse under the arch, knowing that from here on, it was safer to go on foot. "Thank you," he called back, as his men followed after him.

Dusk was falling faster now, and as they emerged from the shadow of the covered arch onto a wide section of grassed cliffside, they had just enough light to appreciate the majesty and grandeur of the Svanlyn mountains.

From where they stood, a narrow causeway wound its way up towards the higher reaches of the Beerstana Peak, an edifice which rose so high and steep that it seemed, towards its tapering tip, like a spike which had been placed there for some fantastical giant god to tread upon. The higher swathes of the peak were limned in ice and dotted here and there with rushing falls of snowmelt, some of them crossing the narrow path which wound around it. That path led all the way down to the roots of the peak, joining up with a road nearly two thousand feet below. As he stood, Hugh fancied he could see the smudge of dusty-pink granite which marked the line of that road, far off in the shadow of the setting sun.

In a roiling abyss of black cliff edges Beerstana stood alone, the rest of the mountains massing far off to east and west, grim and impassable. This was the only way through, the only road which connected Svanfeld to its neighbouring land, unless one wished to backtrack all the way to the foothills and strike out east by northeast, skirting the mountains in a wide loop and coming up south again through the towns of Downs, Wolverton, and Lynborder. There were whispers of smugglers' roads in between, of a path which supposedly began in the town of Pine and snaked up into the inhospitable mountains until it reached the source of the River Greene, but Hugh had never taken such rumours seriously.

He clicked to his horse and stepped forward onto the causeway, his lieutenant beside him, the rest of his men following after. There were the tell-tale signs of exhaustion settling in amongst his riders. He caught snatches of a whispered conversation, and a few of the soldiers had taken out their saddle-rations and were making a meal as they walked. He would need to do the same before long, Hugh realized: exhaustion was a reality for him as much as any, and the will that had carried him through this day was beginning to wane.

The insistent wind tugged at him, swirling his cloak and stirring his hair, setting him to shivering. He thought once more of the ones he was leaving behind: Falcon and his son Rolf, gentle little Katrina . . . At least Hugh's mother, Kristi, was safe, far away on Sul's Isle with her second husband. Hugh had once yearned for a younger half-sibling, after his mother had remarried, but it had never happened. When he had asked her, years ago, she had laughed and asked him when he was going to give her a grandchild.

Relief settled over Hugh as he reached the far side of the rocky causeway and stepped onto the path which hugged the side of the peak. Now the abyss gaped only to his left. Dusk had finally caught up with them, and it was growing difficult to see. He moved some yards along the path, making space for all his riders, then halted and passed the order along. "Halt and light torches."

The horses were well-trained, and there was very little reaction as flint scraped and torches blazed along the column, the flames all seeming very bright in the closeness of the path. He looked back, watching each torch flare, making sure that the men were holding them correctly, left hand for fire, strong right for the halter of the beast he led. He could only hope that nothing would spook the horses; they were light cavalry steeds, obedience a trait which had been bred and trained into each one, but the idea of losing control of even a single beast in the dark, on this cliffside, was nothing short of terrifying.

He began to reach into his saddle-pack for his own torch, but just then he heard his lieutenant gasp, breath hitching in his throat. "Captain . . ."

At once he spun round to face the path ahead, and started. There was a woman there, just inside the circle of light from the torch that Cedric held aloft. No, not a woman, he realized—a girl. She could not be older than fourteen or fifteen. One hand was thrown up over her eyes as if to shield them from the light, and the other held a glinting dagger.

For a moment Hugh could not find his voice. The girl seemed an apparition, as though she had sprung from the vast, bleak mountainside itself. Long black hair was tangled across her shoulders, and the hue of her skin spoke of Vailanan blood. As he stepped forward, she drew back, brandishing the dagger, and he realized that she was afraid.

"I won't hurt you," he called, trying to adjust his eyes to the gloom. Where had she come from? Perhaps she had been coming up the pass from the other side. Perhaps something had happened to her party. Or maybe, this was some kind of ambush. But there was only one way around the Peak of Beerstana, and he had sixteen good men at his back. He held the girl's gaze, and moved another step forward. "We're soldiers, of the royal army." He indicated the twin skirts that hung from his belt, one of them the blue-silver-white tricolour of the Sven royal house, the other striped in his own colours, midnight alternating with pale blue. Behind him, he could *feel* Cedric's hand straying towards the hilt of his sabre, and he stayed the lieutenant with a hand gesture.

The girl gazed intently at the pattern of the royal colours, and lowered the dagger, taking him in. She had set the cliff-face against her back, as if she had intended to fight all seventeen of them with this one dagger. She came forward, moving into the torchlight.

When she spoke, it was with an accent he had not heard in over twenty years, the liquid, singsong tones of Qwu'Mallorn. "Please help us," she begged, and as Cedric lifted the torch higher, he saw two prone figures in the twilight behind her, both of them obviously unconscious.

"My companions—they're injured. They'll die if you don't help us." Tears were slipping down her cheeks, and he realized that her clothes were little more than rags.

"What happened?" he demanded, but she only shook her head, sobbing.

Even as Hugh's heart went out to the girl, he felt some soldiering instinct nudge at him, some sense that all this held more significance than he could unravel through the fog of his exhaustion. Compounded with haste, quickly he made his decision.

"We're taking these three with us," he said to his lieutenant, raising his voice so that all the men would hear. "Bring forward the mounts of our fallen. We'll see about hauling these two injured." He stepped towards the girl, now swaying on her improperly shod feet, and lifted her bodily. Her breath caught, but she did not complain as he carried her to his own mount and arranged her in the saddle.

"It's going to be all right," he soothed, taking her hand.

She did not reply, not even to ask where they were going.

"I'm Hugh Anspeare," he offered his name, and she looked at him through her sniffling.

"I'm Bri—Brialise," she said. "Brialise Grenova."

# CHAPTER XXII
# PUNISHMENT

IN THE SILENCE OF THE LABORATORY, Dannine knelt trembling before her father. The smooth black floor was cold against her bare hands. She was still wearing the armour she had travelled in, all the way from that cursed peak on Svanlyn to the border of Qwu'Mallorn and back to here, where her father was waiting for her to give an account of herself and the catastrophes that had befallen. Dannine was disgraced. She would be lucky to leave here alive, she thought, and there was a certain freedom in that. She did not fear death, not at the hands of the father who had shaped her to become all she was.

Arran leaned back against the low table, his arms crossed, one ankle curled around the other. From her vantage Dannine could not see as far upwards as his face, but she knew he was frowning.

"So Deryck has been found at last," he hissed. Dannine flinched at the name. "Found, and then immediately lost again, and this at the expense of the life of my son."

*The least of your sons*, Dannine thought, but did not dare to speak. The loss of Taunus was still a blow. They had been five once; now only three remained. *Perhaps only two*, she whispered to herself, and somehow found the strength to keep still.

She started as she felt Arran caress the top of her head. "Dannine, my daughter," he whispered, "what am I to do with you?" He moved his hand down her face, lifted her chin. The other hand went to her forehead, caressed her hair. "Now," he continued, "show me, daughter. Show me all I have missed."

For a moment, though all his will and magical being were bent upon her, she did not understand. But then she realized what was happening, and her eyes went wide in pain and horror. She instinctively tried to will him out, struggled against the intrusion even as she told herself to stop fighting. It would only make it hurt more, in the end—

Dannine had used this magic herself, more than once, in the past. When dealing with captives who would not tell the truth, it was the best way. With some, it had the unfortunate side effect of sending them mad, but it was the only way to ensure they were not lying. Open up their minds and take a look inside yourself.

He could just have asked her to tell it all. Dannine was not capable of lying face-to-face to her father. Surely he knew that. He could have asked her to tell him, and expended far less energy.

She could only sob and whimper as her father sifted through the rags of memory, stirring the thoughts inside her mind like vegetables in a bowl of soup. It was the most intimate kind of violation, surpassing anything she had endured in the past. It was a transgression not of her physical body, but of the core of who she was. She could not distinguish the parts that were her own from the invader. She lay naked and gutted like a fish, her most shameful parts dug out and held up for scrutiny under Arran's gaze.

Within a few minutes, she was begging him to stop, but he would not. And a few minutes later, she could not speak a coherent language anymore. All her being had dissolved into grey mush, nothing remaining but the burning of the violation and the sense of something so inherently *wrong* that all of herself tried to expel it.

She did not feel it when he finally withdrew. She came back to herself sprawled on the floor, her stomach churning, Arran's white-bleached leather boots in front of her face. She dimly felt something outside of herself, something she felt she could touch. Great rage, great chaos. Something close, and yet a world away. Pain for her pain—

"This changes everything," Arran muttered, as if to himself. His voice shook with latent excitement. "What you saw, Dannine—this girl who undoes the threads of magic—*she* is the key. She is the sacrificial maiden." He reached down a hand to help Dannine to her feet. "And I will have her."

"Father," Dannine began. There was no visible mark on her, yet the pain lanced through her magical being into her physical body with every breath she took. "I should have captured her. I failed." She bowed her head, her hands shaking. "Strike me down. I do not deserve the life you gave me."

His hand lifted her chin again, cupped it with something like tenderness. "Not today." His eyes were agleam with lust or greed, and the excitement was still in him. He turned away, leaving Dannine to support her own weight on legs that would not stop swaying. He crossed over to his desk, briefly picked up the black empty jar that stood apart from the others. It was still dead and broken; Deryck had managed to destroy the link when he left, preventing them from tracking him. But he had performed magic to destroy Taunus; Dannine had felt his signature, in the mountains, a great surge of raw power that had frightened her at the time. Greater power than he'd had as a child, greater than hers was now. It would be laughably easy for them to find him based on the traces of that surge.

She remembered how numb it had felt, alone in the mountains, feeling the aftershocks of Deryck's power and the emptiness of Taunus's. She had despised Taunus for as long as she had known him, yet he had always been her brother. She had burned for revenge, yet Dannine had never shirked duty in her life, and the first thing she'd done once the storm blew over was to check on the necromes she'd left behind.

She had found a face she'd not expected to see again—the very same half-breed Morgein soldier she had captured only a few weeks ago—and something else.

It had been hard, to realize the extent of her mistake. Deryck lost again, and her two hundred miles from where she ought to be. She had made for the border of Qwu'Mallorn as fast as she could, with the quetzal exhausted and her own magic dangerously depleted, but it had not been fast enough. She had not been able to set a sensible trap to capture Albryan Lana and the girl he had taken up with, and had resorted to a crude attack worthy perhaps of the deceased Taunus. No wonder she had failed. Her head spun. Arran was rummaging through a stack of papers on one of the many shelves of the laboratory.

"Here," he finally said. Dannine came forward, feeling half in trance, not understanding. It took her a long time to focus on the yellow, brittle parchment Arran had unrolled before her.

"Archaic Morgein," she murmured, as if she were a little girl again with her tutor. "Before Bavarian's Landing." She touched the edge of the parchment scroll, which stood up to her fingers without crumbling, as she had suspected. "Parchment magically reinforced, but that spell is wearing out."

"It is good to see you recall your earliest academic lessons," Arran said dryly. "Translate this, then, and we shall see if you grasp the significance of your failure."

She focused on the words. The lines were printed in a neat hand, but the translation kept slipping away from her. She hated these archaic languages. She did not know whether the passage was supposed to be a description of true events, or just some obscure metaphor for something else. Nevertheless, Arran was standing there waiting, so she translated as best she could as she read.

"There comes a time of unrest, of . . . of warfare. Neighbour will turn against neighbour, and sibling against sibling." She frowned. ". . . For the dark one shall be brought through the veil. She who has only known despair will . . . will approach the dark one. Her master will devour her heart . . . and she will birth the darkness. The great goddess requires a final sacrifice. The rose of the Morgei will return to its—to *her* people. She shall be known to all by the thorns which she . . . which she uses to tear apart the works of magic. By her doing the forest of the ironwoods will vanish from the world." She paused. "What lies beyond cannot be seen, for destiny turns upon the . . . the thorned sword?"

"The lone wolf," Arran corrected.

She read the last few words. "When he unites with his"—she hesitated, the vagaries of Morgein pronouns, as always, making it difficult for her translation to find solid ground—"female reflection, the world shall follow the path they choose."

She stood back, tried to make sense of it all, but reason fled before her. "I can't . . . I can't make head or tail of it," she admitted. "I can see that it foretells your coming. It says that we will succeed, that you will bring Qwu'Horya into the world." She felt a queer stirring as she said the name, felt the hand of the shadow reach for her. She shivered. Unity with the dark goddess was not for her; it was Arran who would drink Qwu'Horya's power, who would bring her through the veil. *The lone wolf.* That was her father, no doubt, who had always stood apart from the race of magic. Who was his "female reflection"? And what did it mean to "unite" with her? Blood pounded through her head.

"*She shall be known to all by the thorns which she uses to tear apart the works of magic,*" Arran quoted. His eyes were alight. "It is *her.* The sacrificial maiden. One who possesses an unheard-of gift: the undoing of magic." His hands shook with exhilaration. "She has returned to her people now, as the prophecy foretold. But I will have her, the prophecy confirms it. *By her doing the forest of the ironwoods will vanish from the world.* She cannot escape her fate."

Dannine said nothing. Doubtless her father was correct in his interpretation of the old prophecies. Their victory was foretold, but there was still a long path ahead of her. She cared nothing for roses and lone wolves and maiden sacrifices; her life's sole purpose was as an instrument for her father.

She waited dully until Arran's excitement had run its course, and he turned back to her. "You disobeyed me," he said, his voice gone dangerously soft, and Dannine could not bear to meet his eyes.

"Forgive me, father, please." She bowed her head.

"I have," Arran said, almost gently. He drew closer, close enough for his breath to stir her hair, yet he did not touch her. Something hummed in the air between them, something he had called from the ether.

"I forgive you, daughter, and yet rules are there to be obeyed," Arran said softly. "The price for disobedience is punishment. And it must be done, so that you will learn, will remember." He tilted her chin upwards, forcing her gaze to his. "Yes?"

Had it not been punishment enough, to have her thoughts stripped from her head and dissected inside the burning ruin of her own mind? Had it not been enough to send her to the brink of sanity and make her crawl all the way back?

A hardness came into his eyes as if he had heard what she was thinking, and he moved away, withdrawing his touch. "Take off your armour," he ordered, coldly.

"Father—I—I'm sorry—"

"Which means you *do* understand," he hissed. *"Take off your armour."*

There was nothing she could do. Mechanically, Dannine obeyed. She slipped loose the straps of her breast– and backplate, stowing them on the ground with her white cloak that was edged in silver braiding. The pieces came off one at a time, carefully placed in order upon the stack. Gauntlets, vambrace, rerebrace and pauldrons; the gorget that went across her throat and the faulds that protected her waist and thighs. Cuisses and greaves, after which she removed her short boots and stood in her stockings upon the cold obsidian floor. She glanced at her father, who had drawn away and was watching her intently.

"The padding," he said.

Dannine's face flushed. She had only a single layer of padding, in the form of her arming garments, and beneath those were only her smallclothes. Wordlessly she drew the tunic over her head, pulled the arming breeches down to crease around her feet. The air in the laboratory was cold, and Arran was watching her with an inscrutable look in his seafoam-blue eyes.

"Now, daughter," he said, his words pooling into the silence between them, "now, your punishment begins."

WHEN IT WAS OVER AT LAST, Arran drew her back to her feet and made her dress and neaten her hair. She followed him out of his laboratory, down to the hall where he met with his lesser generals, airy and sandstone-walled. There was still a war going on, and their legions awaited orders. Battle plans needed drawing up, armies had to be hired and amassed. She was nothing more than her father's instrument in this.

She was shaking uncontrollably, but in her mind there reigned a presence of strange calm. She was only a passenger in this body, and she felt only the barest of connections to it. No tears sprang from the moist blue eyes; no pain radiated from the core to pester her. She felt almost safe, as though she had retreated into a stronghold within herself, a place where she could shelter behind high walls from everyone who wanted to see her true being. Perhaps this was only temporary, but she needed it now. She needed it to remain upright, to show the men in this room that she was strong.

She met their gazes steadily and unflinchingly. Reliable and brutal men every one, she had helped train a few, commanded most at some point or other. They respected her strength, and showed deference by dipping their heads and saluting. She acknowledged none of it, drifting past with the cool hauteur for which she was known.

Her body obeyed her promptings: dry eyes, sitting down, scowl on her face, gauntleted hand resting on the table before her. She listened to Arran detail his plans for the future, for Vailana, for Qwu'Mallorn, for Svanfeld. The men around them knew nothing of her father's true plan, of the power he sought. They did not know that their lives were part of the sacrifice.

She answered when it was appropriate, curtly and automatically, feeling nothing. The generals came together in a spat about seniority, and she sat through it all, unruffled, unperturbed, unpresent. She watched them leave at the end, was calm and collected as Arran dismissed her to her chambers.

Alone, in the deep privacy of her bedroom, behind seven different types of warding spell, it all fell apart. Screams ripped from her body even as she tried to rip free of her skin, feeling it—*him*—crawling about all over her, on top of her, *inside* her. The pain was a living thing, nestled like a glowing red snake between her legs and coiled inside her belly. She had her servants draw her a bath, scrubbed and washed, threw a blanket over herself and called them again to empty the water and bring more, so she could attempt to wash herself all over again. It didn't work, and she was still filthy. She tried to vomit, to purge herself, but she had eaten nothing for the past three days on the journey here. Anticipating her own death, she had not been able to stomach the thought of food. She wished she had died in the fires she had called up. She wished that Arran had killed her. She wanted to kill herself.

She halted that thought in its tracks, for even just holding it made the warding spells vibrate with discordance, and if they got too loud then *he* would notice. She was not permitted the privacy of warding spells, was not permitted to have a will of her own. Not even her body was hers. Not hers. Not hers. *Not mine. Not me. Not me. Not me.*

Physical exhaustion overtook her at last, and the vestiges of her overstressed magic bled away into the rogue wards she had constructed. They would be gone by morning. She had spent so much of her magic that it would not be replenished in a single night, not with the battered state of her physical body. She could hardly feel her magic, now, and she tried to imagine what it might have been like had she been born without it. Arran would never have wanted her. She would be someone different, lesser, not a princess, not the blood sorcerer's daughter.

She dreamed of Qwu'Horya.

Darkness ranged about them, the hollow void teeming with death and ordure and fear, yet she was calm. The goddess mirrored her every movement, pointing a hand where she pointed. Killing where she killed.

She took the Goddess's hand, felt Her burn hot as hate and as freezing cold as vengeance. Her skin burned away where they touched, and she stood naked, chest to chest with Her, unafraid. The Goddess kissed her, and she let it happen, let the frozen fire burn away her lips and breasts and all her skin, and at last she felt purified.

*Vengeance*, the Goddess whispered, and she painted herself in blood.

She woke in the small hours of the morning, shivering and sobbing, balled up beneath her sheets and covered in sweat. To her horror she discovered she had soiled herself.

She did not have the courage to go to Qwu'Horya's abode inside her father's laboratory, and so she sat shaking in a corner of her room until dawn painted the sky in a dozen hues of bloodshed.

"I am sick," she announced when her servants awoke and found her at last. "Take all this away and burn it."

She watched them scurry around the stinking bed, and her gaze alighted upon the youngest of them. She could not be more than fourteen years of age, a mousy girl with nondescript hair and lugubrious eyes that watered continually. She was the daughter of one of the others; Dannine's practised mind quickly picked her out. The fat woman named Judy. What had she called her daughter, again? Oh, that was it. She remembered.

"Mistral," she called the girl, whose head shot up in shock. They all were under the impression that she knew none of their names; disabusing the lot of them of *that* comfortable notion gave her a miniscule jolt of satisfaction. What she was about to do would give her so, so much more.

"Stay here with me," she whispered.

The girl nervously smoothed her skirt and adjusted her kerchief. "Yes, Princess." She sounded so young, so small, so naïve and afraid. Yes, this would be satisfying.

Her natural magic was depleted, her reserves gone, yet as a devotee of the dark goddess, Dannine had access to other sources of magic. It was an intrinsic part of the workings of blood sorcery, and it was the reason why servants in Arran Sylvaissen's castle had an improbably high turnover.

She had not done this in a while. Perhaps even over a year. It was high time to avail herself of the energy that came through violent human sacrifice.

Better still, it would bind her tighter to her goddess, bring Qwu'Horya that much closer into her being. The girl's blood would bring her satisfaction, and more. It would bring her vengeance.

# CHAPTER XXIII
# QWU'MALLORN

HE WAS BACK HOME, RETURNED to the world of the living, and all was well, yet when Albryan Lana woke once again in the Forest of the Morning, he knew that something had changed.

The atmosphere around him was as restful and bucolic as could be wished. Straw pricked at him under the blanket, which was woven of wool thick enough that he'd slept cosily all night despite his decision to sleep naked rather than risk soiling his spare clothes. There was a strong smell of horse, and the noises to match, the quiet peaceful rumbling the sturdy farm beasts made in their sleep.

Yet the peace in his surroundings served only to highlight his inner turmoil, and he passed a hand through his shaggy beard as he sat up. As scruffy as he probably looked, at least this morning he was *clean*. He had fallen asleep last night with a full stomach, without any care for standing watch, for the first time in many weeks.

Memory assailed him, and he could hardly believe that it had all happened yesterday. The fire—Hiram's death—Albryan felt it like a kick in the gut once again. As inured as he might be to the loss of comrades and various types of brothers by now, guilt for the old man still stabbed at him. He had promised Hiram safety and surcease in Qwu'Mallorn. Knowing that he would have made exactly the same decision in Hiram's place made it no easier, and he shivered with aftershock, knowing how close it had been for him. For him and Velda...

The thought of her stirred up all the feelings he had repressed into dormancy just to get through yesterday. What had happened with her in the forest had gripped him by the soul and turned him upside-down and inside-out. He wasn't sure what he was going to do, what he should do, what he should say. Duty had been the most important thing... but what was his word worth, now? What kind of man was he, if he continued to keep her at arm's length after this? His justifications all seemed far too feeble now; here, on the other side of fear, he remembered what it had been like to glimpse something unmistakably divine through her.

Her display of power had been absolutely terrifying, yet at the same time the most wondrous thing he had ever borne witness to. Albryan had followed the girl until at last the ringing waves of not-magic had receded and dissipated and she had collapsed in exhaustion. He had set her upon the mule and pressed on, bringing her over the border without incident. He had worried some about that, beforehand—how it might turn out, to bring a creature of anti-magic into the land of magic—but when not exercising her power, she seemed to be nothing more than an ordinary, nonmage woman, and that was how the magical shield had recognized her.

Albryan had immediately sent out a signal for aid, knowing there must be some kind of patrol in the vicinity. Sure enough, a squad of six mage-soldiers had arrived with a female healer, who'd taken one look at his cut and insisted that she had to treat it right then and there. Velda had slept through the whole thing, not even awaking when the soldiers helped Albryan get a message through to Thinas, confirming that he was not missing in action anymore.

The soldiers had then accompanied them to this farmstead, a prosperous place owned by a woman named Andorra Wion. There was no barracks in this area, they explained: the patrols made do with camping, and purchased supplies from the farmers who dwelt here. The farmstead was large but very crowded, since Andorra had at least half a dozen children of her own as well as a huge extended family, but they had found room for Velda in the house. Albryan had not minded being exiled to the stables in the least; the horses were quieter than the children, and the straw was as cosy as any bed he'd known.

He remembered, then, how Velda had looked when the women of the farmstead had bustled her off for the night, and a shard of worry pierced his heart. He should find her, and make sure she was all right. His mind cast back to what they'd done in the forest, and his mouth went dry with something like shame. He had *wanted* that, wanted her more than he could remember ever wanting any other woman, and now he truly didn't know whether he regretted it or not. It ate at him, how quickly it had happened, how completely un-planned it had been. Albryan had always approached the matter of sex rather cautiously, chosen his lovers with care. It didn't feel like he had even chosen Velda at all. There had been no slow seduction from either side, just some power that smashed them together and made them act like madmen and then left them—or him, at least—con-fused and longing for more.

He was no stranger to the arts of love, of course: some level of promiscuity was all but expected of the youth in Qwu'Mallorn, and he had even had a few affairs during his sojourns in Vailana. As he grew older, the Morgein women his age had become more preoccu-pied with their duties, particularly the continuation of the family line, and Albryan did not want to have a child he was not permitted to be a father to. People like Elithan found the arrangement easy enough, somehow, but Albryan had always been wary, mindful of the fact that the child's mother could cut off access any time she wanted, if they were not married.

His last affair had been a brief rebound with a girl who lived in the settlement of Woodsdale, a Vailanan village that had once been the last stop on the trade route that ran from Armour City to Tenna. These days, it was little more than a military outpost, even as Tenna was for the Morgein side. Thinas kept sending him there to spy on the movements of Arran's soldiers along the border, and Albryan had struck up a kind of on-off affair with the little barmaid at Woodsdale's only inn. *Rosemary Fox.* Albryan could not bring himself to refer to her as most others did, as Rose, since that was how he thought of his long-deceased mother. But they had parted in a hard way, more than a year ago, and Albryan had not been sent back to Woodsdale since.

Wincing as stiff muscles made themselves known in the sudden chill, he levered himself out from under the woollen blanket. He dressed quickly, wrapping his cloak around himself, and made for the nearby outhouse before stepping into the yard. Dawn had just broken; the yard was streaked with mist and atwitter with the familiar songs of wood-thrushes and hoop-hoop birds. It was cold, but the blue sky above the green paddocks promised a sunny spring day. The air tasted good; slightly damp, the tang of the forest in it. He smiled a little despite himself and headed towards the large wooden farmhouse.

He had not gone more than two strides when he glanced to his left and saw Velda, fully dressed, leaning against the paddock fence staring out into the west, her whole body poised as if to take flight and drift far away from here. Heavily, he made his way towards her; she turned around, hearing his footsteps, and quickly turned her head back towards the paddock. She said nothing as he came up beside her.

"Velda." Gently, he put his hand on her arm. "Are you all right?"

"Andorra was very kind," she said softly. She looked up at him, and seemed to be trying to smile. "I just—" She shook her head, tears springing into her eyes.

"Hiram?" he asked softly, and she nodded.

"Why did he do—*that*?" she whispered at last, after a long moment. She bowed her head. "I could have saved him. *Would* have saved him. I could have undone any magic she threw at me; I could have just walked in there and plucked him out." She turned an anguished face towards Albryan. "Why didn't he think of that?"

Albryan thought of the flames and the fear of Armour City. He remembered Hiram's face when they had reached the gulley that led out of the city. He thought, too, of when Hiram had first told him about Velda. They'd been sitting at that inn in Lynborder, sipping the excellent ale, keeping to their table in the shadows.

"There's no way of knowing for sure," Hiram had said, picking at his food, his eyes intense even in the gloom of the inn. "But I swear . . . part of me thought I was looking at Lathea again. At my daughter . . ."

"Hiram would never have taken that chance," Albryan said. "It would have put you at risk."

"Me? But what was I—"

"You were the future to him," Albryan replied. "Velda, you *are* the future. Honour Hiram's bravery. Remember him. But do not shame yourself over the choice he made. Many a soldier has made the same choice. It is better to die with honour, better to die knowing that you did all you could, than to live at the cost of something so dear to you."

Velda stirred. "Hiram was not a soldier."

Albryan shrugged. "When our backs are to the wall, every one of us will be a soldier." He sought her eyes with his, resisting the urge to caress her face, knowing somehow that she would not welcome that touch at the moment. "Did you not do exactly the same? You decided that you would rather risk death—or slavery—than stand by and allow strangers to suffer."

"It was the right thing to do." Her voice was constrained. "But if I hadn't gone—if we hadn't—" She broke off and looked away. "He would still be here."

"Or perhaps not," Albryan remonstrated. "We cannot know. Dannine might have surprised us all together, and all three of us might be dead. Or, more likely, on our way to Armour City as her prisoners even now."

He hesitated, gathering his thoughts. "I have commanded men in battle," he finally said. "I have given men orders to go on patrol; I have planned attacks on our enemies. You may feel responsible for Hiram; I have, in some way or another, been responsible for the deaths of over a hundred men."

"That was different—" she began.

"Because they knew they would be going into war?" Albryan shrugged. "Hiram knew what we were hunting, in the mountains.

When we were imprisoned together, it was he who suggested our means of escape. He knew who and what I was from the beginning; he understood that I was at war. He chose to help me anyway."

Velda stood silent, and something in Albryan wanted to keep talking, perhaps to unburden himself, perhaps to make her understand him better. "And do not imagine that they all died clean, in the heat of the fight," he continued. "Four years ago, I led my men into an ambush. Stupid of me; didn't send enough scouts beforehand to check the area. They took me prisoner, and killed my men one by one to try and make me give up the positions of the other patrols. Not quick." He shivered. "Then the next year, they had a new commander, smarter than most of the others. Leroy Rethuen. I was supposed to hunt him down, me and my command. I failed." He grimaced. "Rethuen lived to slaughter hundreds of civilians along the border. He found a way to hop in and out, circumvent the magic somehow. Every time we'd hear of another village struck, we'd have to go and deal with the aftermath. All because I let him get away."

He stopped as Velda suddenly took his hand. An odd expression was playing about her lips, perhaps a smile of commiseration, perhaps only impatience. Whatever it was, Albryan felt the shadows of his memories fall away as he allowed himself, briefly, to be entranced by her beauty.

"I thought I was the one being comforted," she said.

He turned towards her. "The point is, I've had to make peace with a lot of things I feel responsible for. If I had to shame myself every time a man lost his life because of my mistakes . . ." He paused. "I can't change what happened. Neither can you. We can try to do better, that's the only thing we can do. Look to the future."

She looked at him instead, and a crippling guilt stole over Albryan's soul. What was his word worth? He opened his mouth to begin to tell her, to finally share with her all the things she didn't yet understand, but there was a shout from the farmhouse and Velda turned away. Andorra Wion's husband Liamus was waving them over, shouting of breakfast.

*Later, then*, Albryan thought, even as he was now aware of how badly he truly wanted to keep the girl.

AS KIND AS THE FARMER'S WIFE—*no*, Velda corrected herself, *Andorra is the farmer here, she owns the lands, her husband only works the fields*—had been, and how comfortingly familiar their hospitality was, so much the same as any farm she'd been in the mountains, Velda did not feel truly at ease until she was finally alone.

It was no fault of theirs. Velda liked Andorra, with her curling chestnut hair and dark laughing eyes, and found the company of her eldest daughter, Tirena, as pleasant as she'd found the friendship of the orphan girls at the monastery. But there was grief in her heart, and guilt, even after what Albryan had said to her that morning. She had to think about it alone, and so later that morning, when the men of the farmstead had gone to their planting and Andorra was absorbed in a list of accounts and figures, she slipped off on her own.

Knowing what lay in the west, she ranged towards the east, following a narrow dirt path hemmed in by exotic woodland. She wandered for a while, turning off the main path to admire wilder groves along muddy tracks overgrown by flowering bushes. There was a scent of honeysuckle in the air, the sound of a spring flowing through the woodland. She did not know the names of most of the trees, though she recognized a few old friends: pines bushier than those that grew in the mountains, swordferns, wild cherries, some kind of star chestnut that grew smaller than the ones she knew. She startled a lamb-sized antelope that bore a strong resemblance to the rock-springers she had once helped hunt, and balked at a bright green snake as it slithered up one of the ubiquitous black-barked forest giants. She watched it, fascinated. Snakes were not totally foreign to the mountains, but she had never seen one before.

A strange barking chatter startled her, and she turned wide-eyed to see a totally unfamiliar creature sitting on a high branch up the tree. *A monkey*, she realized in delight. Its fur was almost bluish, its face a black mask ringed with silver. Leaves suddenly rustled all over, and she watched as the rest of the tribe swarmed across a long branch towards another tree, appearing only briefly before vanishing in the dense green ocean of foliage. Some of the monkeys were carrying their young on their backs, the babies securely clinging on as the parents effortlessly swarmed from branch to trunk, from trunk back into the leafy canopy.

She sniffed the air. The day was beginning to grow warmer, but the cool scent of wet mud and moss and distant water still hung upon the breeze. Something in her felt suddenly too light for grief.

She chose a track that ran alongside a little stream, twisting up and up until she reached its source, a waterfall that sprang from a crack in a sheer cliff only about as high as Albryan was tall. The water was cold as ice when she ran her hand through it.

She wandered, losing track of time, until she realized that the dappled sun was shining from directly above. The woods had warmed so gradually that she hadn't even noticed at first, but now she was perspiring in her one remaining dress.

She sighed. She would have liked to remain here for the rest of the day, but there were certain realities she needed to face, and sooner was better than later with these things, she'd been told in the past.

She had had Albryan for one wonderful moment, felt an intimacy with him she'd been afraid to feel again. There had been desire and ecstasy in his arms, and release—for him as much as for her. There had been hard evidence of that.

As wonderful as that had felt at the time, and as much as she had loved her son and wanted to be a mother, her life was currently far too unstable to entertain the thought of another child.

She mentally ran through the available options on the way back, and finally decided that she would talk to Andorra. Her daughter Tirena might be technically closer to Velda's age, but was only fifteen and probably full as innocent as Velda had been just four years ago.

She had more in common with Andorra now, despite the older woman being well into her thirties.

Her instincts were good: Andorra was curious to hear where Velda had come from, and over continuous mugs of tea Velda regaled her with details of life in the mountains.

The conversation drew naturally towards her husband. "You must have loved him very much, to marry so young," Andorra remarked, and Velda could not but agree. Andorra had been twenty at her own marriage, she confided, and madly in love. There were those who waited, however, she said, and those who had their children long before settling down with a husband.

The conversation then naturally turned towards their own children. Andorra was sympathetic to Velda's story, and told how she had lost two of her own, one in miscarriage, another in stillbirth. She had never lost one to disease, luckily; thanks be to the Goddess and the healers in Algorthar for that. She had thought about having one or two more, before she got too old; but the house was already crowded and the last baby had been difficult in coming.

Velda then craftily circled the conversation towards the thing she wanted to ask in the first place. Andorra immediately guessed the situation.

"The captain?" she asked Velda, and at the hesitant nod she giggled like a girl. "Well, I don't have any of what you need, at the moment," she said at last. "Tirena might, but me going to her and asking, at her age . . . that wouldn't do. Be a bit too much motherly interference." She grinned, dark eyes mischievous. "They'd be able to sort you out at the apothecary, but that's in town." She tapped a finger against her earthenware mug. "Let me go out this afternoon and see what I can do. Need to see Filla anyway, about her damn goats."

After she left, Velda wandered into the little walled garden that ringed the house. She had a view of the yard from beneath an arched doorway, and noticed a knot of people. The soldiers they had met with yesterday had returned to the homestead and were talking with Albryan. There was one woman amongst them—the healer.

Velda felt curiosity stir, yet some shyness kept her watching rather than going over to join them. The people of Qwu'Mallorn seemed incredibly varied to her eyes, and this group were no exception. The eight of them had very few racial characteristics in common, not even the so-called almond-shaped eyes that were supposed to be typical of the Morgei. The young healer was tanned chestnut-brown, with a thatch of curly hair that seemed dark brown but turned to auburn when the sun glinted upon it. Two of the men were darker than Velda, one with long straight hair as black as a raven's wing flowing in a tail down his back, the other possessing a beaky profile to match her own and hair so curly that it coiled in a dark cap about his head. Their eyes did have a certain slant to them, but she thought they seemed more like half-moons than almonds. Not a single one of the young soldiers came within a handspan of Albryan's height. He stuck out in their company like a hawk amongst crows. Fair-skinned, blue-eyed, and ginger-haired, Albryan had not looked too far out of place in Lynborder—at least, not for his face.

*I look more Morgein than he does,* Velda realized with some surprise. Looks could be deceptive, though; that much was obvious. She had entered the magical forest and thus far had seen no magic. The farm folk seemed perfectly ordinary. Perhaps there was some difference in the way men and women seemed to approach their respective roles in society, but otherwise, they were really quite disappointing to one who had expected exotic magic and mysterious foreigners.

That very evening, however, she realized that Tirena used no flint striker to light the cold hearth in the bedroom; she simply stared at it for a while until a crown of tiny flames began to flicker amongst the kindling. It was such a little thing, so commonplace that Tirena clearly thought nothing of it, and yet it made so much difference to the daily difficulty of life.

The next day, Velda began to notice still more. Andorra picking up a mug of tea, making a face at it, and staring at it until suddenly steam began to rise from its surface again. Tirena muttering something over the bread as she sprinkled it with flour, and her assurance that it would not mould if left on the shelf. The men of the farm lifting and carrying just a bit more than Velda thought they should strictly be able to. The way the pumpkin patch near the back door was flourishing this early in the season. And when one of Andorra's male relatives, brother or uncle Velda wasn't sure, showed her around the orchards, she noticed plants that she wouldn't have believed could be properly cultivated this close to the mountains—cinnamon, with its distinctive fragrant bark, and rows of glossy-green vanilla vines twining up the trunks of cocoa trees.

She saw these small magicks every day, as they ended up spending over a week at the farm, taking them into Thirdmonth, which marked Velda's nineteenth year of life. The twenty-first of this month marked the famous siege of Armour City, when the Morgei had been expelled from Vailana. It was scarcely unusual to not know one's exact day of birth, yet Velda had always wondered how close hers was to that fateful day. It was a point which seemed to link her to Albryan, for he had lived in Armour City as a child. They hailed from the same place, despite the fact that they had been reared in different worlds.

She wondered, all that week, what sort of link still remained between them. Amidst preparations for their journey onward, Albryan barely said two words together to her. He spent most of his time with the soldiers. Apparently the border post was due for a change in garrison, and a hundred fresh soldiers ought to be arriving any day now. The hundred who currently occupied that post would be relieved of duty, and most of them would be travelling to the town of Tenna, where their commander-in-chief had his headquarters and Albryan had his home.

Albryan had not spoken of what would come after that. Not to Velda, at any rate. There seemed to be a lot that he needed to discuss with his fellow soldiers, and he rode back and forth between the farm and the guard-post nearly each day, retiring early every night. Part of Velda wanted to go to him and corner him in the barn, but she held back. There would be no way of hiding where she was going from Tirena, and even though no-one seemed to care about such things in Qwu'Mallorn, she felt none too comfortable with everyone *knowing* about it.

She had never been one to sit idle, so she helped Tirena with her baking, learning the recipes and techniques of Qwu'Mallorn, and she observed Andorra's manipulations of her plants and crops, delighting in what she called "earth-magic." She visited the nearby town, Algorthar, to purchase fabric for new clothing. At first the merchants squinted suspiciously at her silver pawns and copper pennies, decorated as they were with the likeness of a foreign king, but once they had weighed them and verified that they were the same as coinage minted in Qwu'Mallorn, they were happy enough to accept her money and to exchange the silver for copper pennies of their own, bearing the likeness of a bushy tree on one side and some inscription in letters she could not read on the other.

The beauty and variety of fabric in the town's market overwhelmed her, even as Andorra bemoaned the prices and told of how much more choice she would have in Tenna. All her life Velda had been restricted to plain earthy shades in different weights of wool, but in Qwu'Mallorn, it seemed, bright dyes were cheaper or easier to come by, and she was bewildered by the sheer variety of oranges and blues and greens to be had. More expensive were fabrics of purple and yellow, and she spent at least ten minutes admiring a bolt of deep golden silk that was far beyond her price range.

In the end, she followed Andorra's advice and purchased summer-weight linens for tunics in three different colours, with a dark wool for the breeches that seemed to serve both sexes for everyday wear in Qwu'Mallorn. Belted tunics seemed to be the thing to wear over these, although she did notice a few men wearing the type of puffed blouse that was common in Svanfeld. A handful of colourful silk ribbons she was unable to resist would serve as decoration, and finally the heat of the day, the mugginess they seemed unable to escape in the forest, along with Andorra's assurance that the weather would only get warmer the further she travelled from the mountains, persuaded her to dabble with a new type of footwear: sandals.

Before she knew it, the eve of their departure arrived. Albryan had been gone all day, as usual, and excused himself to bed after dinner. Velda spent the evening with a book of poetry she had borrowed from Andorra, her eyes moving from page to page without taking in a word. She only looked up when the door opened and Tirena came into the bedroom. "Lights out?" the girl asked.

"I—" Inspiration struck. "I think I may have forgotten to pack my sandals," Velda said. It was true; she had been wearing them in for the past few days, and they now lay on the floor beside her bed. Tomorrow it would be back to boots, since she was going to ride a horse provided by the military, and that promised to be its own kind of adventure. Velda had never ridden anything more intimidating than a plough-horse, and had never used stirrups in her life.

"I'd better go and pack them in now. Make sure I don't forget them," she continued. It could have waited until tomorrow morning; she knew that full well. But for the past hour, Velda had been unable to think of anything other than the fact that she and Albryan would be travelling with fourscore other people tomorrow—several days' journey, and after that who knew what would happen? There would be no opportunity to speak with him alone, not with so many others about. It had to be now, for only Vermayn, trickster god of chaos, knew when they might actually be alone together again.

"You can turn out the lights," she said at Tirena's wide-eyed look of protest. "I'll take a lantern. I'm going to double-check I didn't forget anything else, so I might be a little while." The girl finally nodded. "I promise I'll be quiet," Velda whispered.

The deserted farmyard seemed very dark, despite the moon. Trepidation welled up in Velda's chest as she pushed the stable door open, but she did not falter. Holding the lantern high, she stepped inside.

There was a smell of fresh straw and horse and the familiarity of all farmyard barns. Albryan was already awake when she espied him, squinting against the light with his hand shading his eyes.

"Velda," he said, and his other hand eased off the grip of the sword that was lying sheathed beside him. He sat up, drawing his knees to his chest. It looked like he was naked underneath the blanket, and for a moment she felt embarrassed before she remembered that she truly had no reason to be. "May I ask why you're here?"

She hung the glassed lantern on the bracket that was set in the wall for that purpose, and advanced towards him. She dropped down next to him, setting the sandals aside. Albryan did not move away, though puzzlement was plain in his blue-green eyes. Despite herself, she hesitated. Albryan did not look away from her.

"I know why you're here," he finally said. He made a grimace. "It was I who should have come to you."

"I need to know one thing," Velda said quietly. "Before we set off again, and gods-know-what comes between us. You and me, Bryan—I can't stop thinking about it. What happened between us—do you regret it? Is that why you've been avoiding me?" She kept her gaze level, not looking away. Disappointment or joy, at least she would have clarity.

Albryan cleared his throat. "I don't regret it," he replied hoarsely, "and that is why I haven't spoken to you. I—I didn't want to lose you." He reached for her hand, but she moved away and it only brushed the bed of straw between them.

"Lose me?" she whispered. "What do you mean?"

For a moment Albryan seemed at a loss for words. Then he sighed deeply, as if at last coming to terms with something painful.

"I have been so, so stupid," he whispered, "about you. About all of this. The Goddess holds that we must keep to the promises we make each other. And you unselfishly promised to come here, to make the journey with me. And I haven't lied outright, but I have

deliberately kept certain truths from you so you would not understand, not completely."

"Understand what?" She searched his face for the answer, but
Albryan dropped his gaze and stared at the straw for a long time
Velda bit her lip to keep from asking again. Albryan seemed to be
struggling with some other part of himself. At last he looked up, eyes
darker and greener than usual in the deep shadows.

"Things are more complicated than what I let on," he said. "I was
going to discuss this with my commander, Thinas Sovaya. But my
heart tells me, now, that isn't right." He shook his head. "I have been
a soldier, Velda, since I was seventeen. A good soldier follows orders
and keeps his duty foremost in mind. But a good *magician* is a bastion of independent and creative thought, and obeys none but the
voice of the Goddess in his heart." He lifted his eyes at last. "I have
no doubt that She *meant* this to happen. Qwu'Kiya. If I don't trust
my gut on this"—he shook his head again, and ran a hand through
his hair—"it's Her I'll have to answer to."

Velda was about to remark that *she* had never seen any evidence
that the gods, whichever ones you worshipped, held any sort of sway
over the mundane world. But she halted the words when she realized
just how ridiculous they would sound coming from *her* mouth—
from someone who had *felt* some kind of outer force move through
her, who had reduced fierce foes to nothing more than motionless
corpses with a thought, who had broken both the necromes and their
mistress and brought herself and Albryan to safety despite all that

had stood in their way. She recalled how it felt to be in the grip of that power. Something that was aligned indelibly towards good, yet powerful and distant and immeasurably strange. Was that what he called the Goddess? She shivered.

"Let me explain to you," Albryan was saying, quietly, "what my people are like."

"Your people?" Velda refrained from asking, *Are these not your people?* She had already begun to sense that there was a subtle difference between Albryan Lana and the farm-folk. They spoke the common language less precisely and more liquidly than he did, sometimes distressing the vowels so that Velda barely understood what they were saying. And when the men yelled orders to underlings on the farm, they spoke in a different tongue altogether, which Velda was learning to recognize as the native Morgein language. It was everywhere around, spoken by labourers and young lovers and children at play, yet Velda had not heard Albryan use it once, not since that single time she had lain in his arms as he whispered endearments, stroking her hair and kissing her face. *Ki'jaya.* Beloved.

Albryan seemed to have guessed her unspoken question. "People like these farm folk," he said, making a gesture that took in the entirety of the homely barn, "they are not like me. Not quite. I don't mean just that we were born of different families, different blood." His demeanour became different; he almost seemed to glow with what seemed a sense of pride, and the air shifted subtly around him. "They can nurture plants and grow food, care for the earth, but they cannot draw fire and lightning from the air. It's the difference between what we call low and high magic."

"And that's because you're highborn?" Velda asked.

"Somewhat," Albryan replied guardedly, and she noticed that he did not deny the fact of high birth. "Strong magical ability—it's a rare thing. Over the years, the noble families have preferred mates with stronger Gifts, and this has the tendency to concentrate the ability." He paused. "But it's not a sure thing. My older brother barely has any Mage-Gift to speak of. And I've trained enough soldiers to see the brightest ability crop up in someone who was born to the lowest of stations. Added to that, ability isn't everything. A moderate Gift with strong discipline and focus—that's more valuable than the most powerful of Gifts with no control."

Velda tripped over her questions. If stronger mages were more marriageable, why wasn't Albryan married? *Was* he married? Was this what he was finding so difficult to tell her?

"Dannine Sylvaissen," Albryan continued, and Velda's stomach lurched even as the speculations running through her mind screeched to a halt. "She was born of the most powerful and influential family in Tenna, before Arran took her as his daughter and trained her in blood magic. She has a Gift the equal of mine—at the very least." He paused, and fixed Velda's eyes with his own. "And *you*—you just shrugged off her deadliest attack like you were swatting a fly."

Velda blinked, confused by the drift in subject. But Albryan went on without waiting for an answer.

"Velda, do you know how terrifying that was?" There was a strange timbre in his voice now, and she gazed at him wide-eyed. "For *me*? Do you have any idea of the kind of powers that are involved in that sort of magic?" Albryan drew a deep breath. "You've never seen war-magic in action, so I'm guessing you have no idea. And that—that scares me so much."

The words fell between them. Velda was silent for a long moment. Then she finally asked, softly, "You were . . . afraid?"

Albryan snorted a sudden, startling laugh. "Was I afraid? Velda, all the way back to the Border that morning, I was ready to cack my smalls." He stared at her as she burst into giggles. "Do you not believe it? Can you not imagine how terrifying it is, to know that you could undo any of us with a snap of your fingers? That you could break all our military defences with a bare minimum of effort? Destroy the very thing that makes us who we are?"

The giggles died immediately, and at last, Velda understood. "I . . ." she began. She felt suddenly cold inside. Had she been mistaken? Had someone—some*thing*—perhaps gifted her this ability for the wrong reasons? Was she certain that the unknowable power was truly aligned with good?

*No, I felt it. I felt it, and I've never been surer of anything before or since. It wanted me to heal Albryan, that night by the Dreaming Water. It wanted me to destroy the necromes, and they were evil. Mindless creatures who knew nothing but slaughter. And it protected us. And when I came through the magical Border, it didn't break . . .*

"I'm not sure it's up to me," she said at last. "This Gift . . . it's not mine. It exists outside of myself. But for my part, Bryan, if it were . . . I couldn't use it to hurt people."

Albryan looked away, for a moment seeming as if he were holding back a question of his own. But finally he said, turning towards her, "Tenna is safe whilst the Border holds. But it's where our high command is, and it's a strategic target for a whole host of reasons. If the blood sorcerer ever does make it through the Border, that is where the invasion will begin." He spoke more softly. "If you'd rather I took you elsewhere—or perhaps stay here—"

"No." The answer came quicker even than Velda would have guessed. "Where you go, I'm going too." She felt her cheeks heat as Albryan raised his brows. "For now, at least. You got me here; the least I can do is keep you company."

Albryan leaned forward, and this time she let him take her hand. "Promise me something," he said. "I've learned better than to try and command you, but it isn't safe for others to know what you can do."

"I'd surmised that for myself," she returned.

"Don't tell anyone," he said, "and don't call on it for any reason."

She nodded. "I won't."

"We have scholars in Tenna," Albryan said. "Clerics, libraries . . . I know a man, a fellow soldier, who reads all the old texts he possibly can. If a Gift like yours has appeared before, I'm sure we can find out."

She nodded again, distracted by the way his hand encompassed hers and how the blanket had fallen into his lap with the forward movement, confirming that he was indeed naked underneath it. Albryan followed the direction of her gaze, caught her staring, and started to grin as she quickly averted it.

She began to mumble an apology, but he reached out and cupped her cheek, bringing her towards him yet stopping short of the kiss. Their breath mingled in the twilight, and his lips were so close she felt it when he whispered, "May I?"

She arched her eyebrows. "You didn't ask before."

"A regrettable oversight." Something boyish sparkled in his eyes, so close to hers now, and she could not stop a soft giggle from escaping. Moving back, he brought her hand up to his lips. It was the lightest of brushes, a smidgen of the bruising contact they'd had before— and yet she trembled. "My lady. Say what you would have me do."

"I'm no lady," she whispered. Her head was spinning. Ladies certainly did not behave like this, or so she'd always been taught. The holy brothers of the monastery did their utmost to ensure their orphaned charges lived moral, chaste lives, yet it was difficult to tame the wild side of someone whose station at birth had left them nothing to lose.

"Nonsense," Albryan whispered back. "You are in Qwu'Mallorn now. Here, women command men." He suddenly lay back, pulling her with him. The blanket slid down to the straw. She hadn't seen all of him before. The heat of his bare skin was like a furnace through her clothes. "What do you wish?"

Andorra had presented her with a different package of herbs that morning, telling her with a huge wink, as Velda blushed darker than she ever had done, that *this* concoction was intended for daily usage. Strong arms encircled her, and Albryan laughed at the intense lewdness of her words when she told him.

# Chapter XXIV
# Monastery

FISH AWOKE IN AN UNCERTAIN TWILIGHT and stared up at the ceiling.

Familiar sounds came to his ears: Nico's steady breathing as he slept, the crackling of the fire, muffled movements in the room below theirs. It was hard to tell what time it was, whether it was dawn or dusk. The room was brighter than could have been expected from the firelight alone, so it wasn't night.

When had he gone to bed? He frowned, trying to remember. Maybe he'd been drunk. It certainly felt like he had been drinking, bones aching and fur in his mouth, but there was an odd smell about. Medicinal, not the kind of cheap-beer-and-stale-sweat smell that usually resulted from a night out drinking with his partner.

There was something in the back of his mind, something he felt he should remember, but he was relatively comfortable despite the aches, and still sleepy. He put out his arms for a long stretch, then winced in pain as cramps shot all along them. He gasped as the cramping continued in sudden bursts of agony. He tried massaging his wrists and muscles with each hand, and sat up in bed, feeling pain in his shoulders intensify sharply as he moved. He was a bit worried now. Had he gotten into some kind of fight? Was that what he couldn't remember?

He moved sideways, reaching for Nico, and froze in shock.

This was not his room in Ülhard, the cosy home he'd shared with Nico for the past year. He was in a narrow bed, the fireplace behind him and not in front, the wavering light coming from an oil lamp that someone had carefully made fast in a bracket against the opposite wall. There was one small, narrow window in the room, with an outside view of total blackness; it must be the middle of the night.

Fish's guts roiled with the disorientation of not knowing where he was, how he had come to be here, nor even what day it might be. He sank down onto his stomach, breathing hard, cramps firing along his shoulders and back now. Ülhard—they'd left Ülhard at the beginning of Secondmonth. Him and Nico. Climbed steadily into the mountains . . . they'd been tracking slavers, and then—

It all came back upon him in a rush, and he clenched his hands against the pain as his body stiffened in renewed fright. *Taunus.* He remembered the rage and despair, the desperate choice he had made. Remembered how the berserk magic had filled him, burning everything away, his fear and his sense of self-preservation. There had only been him and his enemy, the murderous man he had once called brother, and Fish had visualized the face of his father even as he struck at Taunus with all of his anger and the last of his strength. No-one else had existed to him in that moment.

Fish had fully expected to die there, after Taunus broke the hold of his power. The magic had rushed back in on him; he'd deflected, reaching too hard, and lost control. The backlash had burned through him like a red-hot dagger through a pat of butter. *No wonder I feel like I have the world's worst hangover.* By all logic, he should feel worse. He trembled with the effort of warding off the pain.

He remembered Arran and his lecturing voice, calm and even-toned. The sunlight in his father's garden glinting in the white-gold highlights of his hair. Remembered looking up at him, a small boy wanting the respect and affection of his father.

*"Your magic is like a muscle, Deryck," Arran said. "Just like any part of your material body. If you twist your ankle, you cannot walk on it afterwards. If you wrench your arm and take no rest, you will wind up injuring yourself. If you overreach your magic, you will experience backlash. Do you know what happens when lightning strikes?"*

*The boy shook his head, wide-eyed, and his father leaned forward.*

*"Lightning is pure energy, like magic. And when it comes down from the sky, it seeks to enter metal, or living flesh. But magic is attracted to the living flesh of its master. If you call up too much magical energy—if you cannot control the flow—it will dissipate back into the*

*easiest path. Which is always back into you."*

*The boy shivered. "I could hurt myself?"*

*"You could roast yourself," his father replied. "These are the risks of high magic, Deryck. This is the risk we take to gain power. So before we practice, we must have control. And that is what I am to teach you today."*

Fish wept, for how long he did not know, whether from relief to be alive or delayed terror or some deeper grief that was beyond him to define, he could not say. He wiped his eyes on his shirtsleeve, noticing that it was the same shirt he had been wearing for days now, since Taunus had captured them. He closed his eyes, trying to gather his magical senses to him, trying to see whether he could still sense Taunus, but everything was far too raw. For eight years he had completely abstained from magic, and the pathways had become quiescent. Now they had suddenly been burned open again, scorched and forced, the lid torn off like a torturer might rip off a fingernail.

Something told him that Taunus was dead, though he could not substantiate that feeling. Certainly he had been expecting to die at Taunus's hand; his last memory was of his cruel laugh, his unsheathed sword, advancing upon Fish even as he lost consciousness. *I would not be here if Taunus were still alive.* It had to be one or the other, or neither. Both of them could never have walked away from that confrontation.

And where was "here"? No place he recognized, that was certain. It could not be in the village; the walls around were all of stone. And what . . . what had become of Nico? His heart was pounding loudly all of a sudden. He'd told Nico to escape without him. To go on . . . but Nico had refused. Fish remembered the troubled blue of his eyes, his resigned scowl. *We go together.* Nico had fought some henchmen of Taunus's, he remembered that . . . he was sure that he remembered seeing Nico alive. *Just before I went to sleep . . .*

Carefully he levered himself up again, now taking into account the toll that had been inflicted against his body. The room was larger than he had first thought. Neat rows of beds, about a dozen—must be some kind of infirmary. They'd put him in a bed near the fire. Only one other was occupied: his next-door neighbour, the bed on the other side of the fireplace.

Fish started, recognizing the sleeping profile. "Nico!" he called softly, voice high with relief. There was no response, just the quiet breathing that had been there since he awoke. He called again, louder, and again nothing.

Forgetting completely about his own weakness, he swung out of bed and gave a cry as he collapsed to the floor. His legs cramped too badly to stand back up. There was still no sign of awakening from Nico, despite the cry and the loud thump he had made. Fish crawled across the oiled wooden floorboards, propelling himself by his elbows. He reached the low bed, gripped it, pulled himself up slowly and painfully to perch on the bedside.

"Nico," he whispered, stricken, and his hand hovered. He had been going to clasp his partner's hand, or maybe caress his face, but he was not sure if it was safe to touch him anywhere. He took it in with horror. Nico was fast asleep, breathing too shallowly, as if he were only catnapping, yet he had not woken throughout all of this. Fish remembered times in the past, when they were on a job together, when Nico had woken at a telltale creak of floorboard or whinny of an unfamiliar horse, and dread tightened its serpentine coils about him.

Nico's face was bruised and bloodied as if he'd been beaten, and there was dried blood pooled below his nose, in his moustache. His injured arm was wrapped in so many layers of bandage that it looked immovable. There were more bandages around his hands, and wound over his chest. Though he'd been divested of his shirt and armour, there was not much bare skin to see.

Fish reached for the nearest hand, the left one, and gently inspected the bandage. Blood had seeped out from some open wound across the palm. His gaze went to the chest-bandage, recognizing the technique for trying to stabilize broken ribs. He swallowed hard. He could not remember how Nico had gotten like this—how these injuries had come to be.

He shook Nico gently by the shoulder, called his name again. The big assassin did not awake.

"Nico." Fish felt panic rise. He clasped his partner's hand as tight as he dared, shook him a little harder. Nothing happened. There was only stertorous breathing and closed eyelids.

He tried a third time, fair yelling his partner's name. This time there was a grunt, and his heart leapt for a moment, but Nico's eyes did not open. Fish stared at him for minutes afterwards, poised to catch the minutest movement, any sign that said that Nico was going to wake up.

He jumped and turned at the sudden sound of an opening door behind him, and stared uncomprehendingly at the stranger who entered the room. The middle-aged black-robed man gaped for a moment, then beamed. He had a homely, angular face, and the type of wide-eyed stare that was totally free of guile. Despite this, Fish was instantly on guard.

"You're awake," the man said excitedly, and Fish knew at once that wherever they were, it was still in the mountains. He had never heard a more concentrated highland brogue. "I am Brother Jakob Corder," the man continued, approaching Fish and holding out a hand for him to shake.

*A monk.* Fish had never actually met any of the men who devoted themselves to Svanfeld's largest religion; the breed was practically unknown in Vailana and he'd never had cause to visit their temple in Ülhard. Nico had been raised by monks but generally said very little about them, except once or twice that they were passing good healers. "Benjamin Fisher," he introduced himself, "but everyone calls me Fish." He hesitated, realizing that the monk was looking down at Nico now. "My partner in business," he said, the words catching slightly in his throat. "And my friend. Nico Klavbert."

The monk nodded sympathetically. "It is good to know your

names at last. I had hoped that you would both wake quickly—but in *his* case, there is still some healing to be borne. I have done what I can; I must leave the rest to nature."

"What happened to him?" Fish demanded.

Brother Jakob raised his brows. "I had rather hoped that you would be able to tell us."

Fish said nothing, averting his eyes to gaze back down at Nico. The monk hesitated.

"As far as I can tell," he said at last, "your friend is suffering from a head injury which has not resolved. There is, luckily, no bleeding on the brain at this stage. However, the very fact that he has not awoken for so many days . . ."

"How many days?"

"After you were found," the monk said, cautiously, "they managed to bring you both here in four days' ride. You arrived here this morning, and now it is nearly midnight."

Fish was silent for a moment, digesting this news. It was little wonder that he felt like hell. *Five days gone, in the blink of an eye.*

"The men reported that you seemed at least partly conscious," the monk was saying, "though perhaps you do not remember. You would take water on command, though they could not get you to respond to any questions. I myself found today that you seemed nearly alert. You tried to speak to me a time or two, before you fell asleep this evening."

Fish marshalled his thoughts, putting questions born from hysterics firmly in the back of the queue of things he sought to know. The whys and wherefores, he told himself, were not truly important. They were here. The only thing that mattered was Nico's recovery. From all he'd heard of the Sven monks, it did not seem likely that they were in any danger here. Yet, there was clearly something that Brother Jakob was not telling him.

"Where are we, exactly?" he asked.

"The monastery above Lake Mountaindale." The answer came quickly, honestly. Fish nodded, recalling seeing the place marked on the map. A stiff distance from where they had begun little more than a week ago, but it had been a week like none before in Fish's life.

"Brother Jakob," he finally said, "tell me: am I and my partner free to leave this place if we wish?"

The monk looked at his feet and grimaced. Fish gave a mirthless chuckle.

"Found none of my weapons so far." He ostentatiously checked the pockets of his trousers and the folds of his shirt. "Don't think Nico has his, either." He turned back to Brother Jakob. "So we're prisoners here. Passed from one captor into the hands of another."

"Master Fisher," the monk said hesitantly, "would you be willing to answer any of our questions—give an account of yourselves—before your partner wakes up?"

This time it was Fish who grimaced. "You knew the answer to that already."

"I guessed," the monk admitted. "From what I could deduce

from your appearance, and from the little that Bree has told us."

Fish's head snapped up. "Bree?" He tightened his grip on Nico's hand.

"The young, dark girl," the monk clarified unnecessarily. "It was she who saved both your lives."

"How?"

"She brought you," Brother Jakob replied, "from where you both were injured, down the mountain towards the Beerstana Pass. All on her own." He hesitated. "Is she kin of yours? You have a similar look."

Fish shook his head. "No." He looked down at Nico's hand, taking this in. *Brialise.* He remembered his unreasoning anger at the girl. He hadn't cared what might become of her after he got to his brother; he had figured she would escape somehow, and leave them behind. *She came back for us.* There was an odd feeling in his guts, surprise mixed with something else. "I need to speak with her," he told the monk.

"She is asleep now, but I can bring her to see you tomorrow." There was a long silence, and the monk fidgeted until Fish looked at him again.

"Is there something else?"

"The . . . the child that she is carrying." The monk's eyes flicked between Fish and his partner. "I need to ask . . ."

*Dear gods.* Fish tightened his grip on Nico's hand. "We only met the girl a few days ago," he growled. "Has she not told you that?"

"The truth is, she has not said much," the monk countered, "and given her condition . . . We have not wanted to distress her without good reason." He turned towards the door. "I will fetch you something to eat," he announced, "and then you must sleep again. Your body needs to recover its strength."

Fish was certain he would not be able to eat anything. But when Brother Jakob arrived back with a loaf of bread and a pot of honey and cajoled him into trying at least one slice, his appetite suddenly awoke and before he knew it half the loaf was gone. His legs still hurt too badly to support his own weight, and the monk transferred him back into his own bed, helping him easily across the stretch of floor. He made sure that the bedpan was within Fish's reach before taking his leave, extinguishing the lantern and leaving Fish with the firelight.

Fish curled up in a ball under the bedclothes, certain that he would not sleep. His whole body ached dully, as though he had been practising sword-drill all day, or been sent out for the kind of exercise they gave new recruits in the townsguard. Remembering the townsguard, remembering Zarath, gave him a chill in the guts that he could not shake. For a few years, there, he'd tried to build a life that did not belong to his father. The old woman had taken care of him. Old Delly, they'd called her, but her real name had been Delourien Luzerna, a Morgein name if ever there was one, and she had loved him without any reason, any ulterior motive. Until inevitable death had snatched her away, and left him alone in the world again. If Nico should die . . .

Fish worried at the thought until he fell asleep at last, waking around midmorning from troubled dreams in which his past was mixed all together, old Delly hunting thugs with him in the streets of Ülhard, his sister Dannine jesting with him as they watched a ship approach the seaward watchtowers of Zarath. Brother Jakob brought him a bowl of porridge, then went about feeding Nico. To Fish's surprise, Nico moved his head and swallowed water and honey willingly, even opening his eyes, but did not appear to be aware of his surroundings.

"This is a good sign," the monk said, even as Fish was thinking the opposite. "I have seen many head injuries in my years. Any sign of awakening usually means that recovery is taking place, no matter how small it may seem."

With the monk's encouragement, Fish stretched out his aching muscles as best he could and hobbled around the room, leaning heavily on a cane the monk had brought. His shoulders ached as badly as his legs, and it was only a short while before he sank down again in agony, all his limbs cramping so badly that he could only sit and gasp for breath. Brother Jakob made him get back into bed then, and mixed him some kind of draught that helped ease the pain somewhat.

"How exactly did you injure yourself?" the monk asked in concern.

Fish's only response was to start laughing hysterically, the pain somehow fuelling the laughter even as it made him hurt more. Brother Jakob only shook his head over him, asking no more questions.

He dozed again, seeking a refuge from pain. It was past midday when he finally roused again, ate some more porridge, checked on Nico (still no change) and moved around the room, more carefully than before. The monk left him alone again, after Fish managed to propel himself into a comfortable chair that stood just beside the lone narrow window.

It was overcast outside, the window showing nothing but greyness. The chair was too low and the window too high for Fish to look down to whatever might be in the yard, so he sat there and stared at the unmoving clouds, tried to piece together all that had happened.

When he was a young boy, Arran had often spoken to him of "the war," and hinted frequently that Fish himself was meant to play a significant role in it. He had always assumed that the war would be against the Morgei, who were, after all, his father's enemies. Now he wondered. His memories of those days were not so clear as might be wished; there were blind spots, scenes that filled him with dread yet could not be wholly recalled, and he wondered if perhaps he had forgotten them out of some kind of instinctive self-defence.

The door behind him creaked, and Fish turned his head quickly. He relaxed again as he recognized the slight figure creeping into the room. Brialise had come at last.

Her lot in life seemed to have improved rapidly: the monks had obviously fed and clothed her, and her new garments were warm, if plain. Her long, curly black hair had been washed and neatly braided, coiling far down her back. Her pregnancy was quite obvious in the plain woollen shift that was common wear here in the mountains, and she was still every bit as shy as she had been that day when he first saw her in the village. Even as she made her way towards him, he got the impression that she was but one fright away from bolting like a wild hare.

She took a seat on the empty bed opposite him, crossing her legs awkwardly underneath herself. Fish consciously adjusted his demeanour to appear less threatening before he spoke. "I'm glad you came," he said in a low voice. "Brialise, I—I'm sorry I got angry at you. None of it was your fault."

She smiled. "You killed Taunus," she replied. "You and him." Her gaze flicked briefly towards where Nico lay. "I thank you for that."

Fish got the whole story out of her in fits and starts. How she had gone back into the caves and decided to prevent the necromes from following their master's call with a ridiculously simple bit of magic. "A sticky gate," she explained. "We put it between trees to keep livestock from wandering. Simple enough, in the tunnel. Necromes don't think to go *around*." How she had then made her way back to find Taunus dead, Fish and his partner unconscious. Her voice was low, but steady when she described the wound that had killed Taunus. Nico's silvered dagger in the throat, which explained what had befallen Nico. The storm had mostly blown itself out by then, but Brialise had moved them both inside the caves and waited until the snow stopped falling. There were wooden sleds in the caves that Taunus's men had used to move supplies, and she had bound them to two of those, using a bit of magic to move them out once the snow started to abate. Hoping to find help from travellers on the mountain road below, she had moved them out of the valley and straight down onto the Beerstana Pass, an expenditure of magic that had left her quite exhausted. That was where a passing nobleman, Hugh Anspeare, and his retinue had found her and rescued them all.

Fish was stunned. "You could have gotten away clean, on your own," he said at last. "Why did you stay behind? Why save us?"

She was about to answer when suddenly she gave a little strangled gasp, clutching at the side of her belly.

*Oh gods.* Fish got to his feet as quickly as he could manage, even as the girl remained doubled up in pain. "I'll go find someone—"

Brialise caught his hand and pulled him back towards her. "Stay with me. Please, *janara*."

Fish started back. The girl's liquid brown eyes were wide with fear. She didn't seem to have registered what she'd said, and doubtless she didn't realize that Fish understood her native tongue perfectly well. *Brother*, she'd called him.

He sank down next to her, wincing as the movement bent his limbs in ways they did not quite want to, not yet. "All right," he promised. "I'll stay with you."

Brother Jakob found them there less than an hour later, examined Brialise and then vanished, reappearing with a middle-aged woman who quickly rearranged everything in the infirmary to her liking. A corner of the room was partitioned off with a thick curtain, and several monks and other women—girls, really, no older than Brialise herself—came and went from the room for the next few hours. Fish, having no idea what to expect, was on tenterhooks throughout all of it, half expecting the child to appear spontaneously at any moment.

By late afternoon, things were moving a bit faster, though he was still uneasy at how long it all seemed to be taking. Brialise had been trying to push the baby out for several hours now, yet very little seemed to be happening. No-one had tried to remove Fish from the girl's side, and he was still next to her, ensconced in the same chair. It was his hand she clutched for when her body contracted in pain, and it was he who smoothed the sweat-soaked hair from her face and muttered soothing nothings to calm her, trying not to let her see his true thoughts.

There was a muttered conference between the midwife and Brother Jakob. The midwife turned and addressed both Fish and Brialise.

"We're going to help the babe out," she said bluntly, without outlining exactly what they were going to do.

Brialise was trembling not only from exhaustion, but from real fear. *She has no-one here*, Fish realized. *Mother and father, brothers, sisters, friends: all vanished, dead or far away. No-one here for her but me, and I'm no kind of brother.*

He turned her face towards him, keeping his hand on her cheek. "Look at me," he said. He held her so she could not look away, and clasped her hand tightly. "It's going to be all right."

The next fifteen minutes were pure hell, and he did not blame her in the least for her screams and sobs, the string of Morgein curses she gabbled off in the manner of one reverting to the language they had been taught as a child. From the corner of his eye Fish could see what was happening. *That's a lot of blood*, he thought absently. As much as there had been every time Arran had a sacrificial victim under his obsidian knife in the bowels of his palace.

Brialise had stopped screaming, and her eyes were fluttering shut, the hand that had gripped his falling limp on the bedspread beside her. Fish started, coming back to himself. He felt the pulse beneath his fingers slow, becoming faint. Panic shot through him, spurring something inside him to rise in response.

Sharing magic was one of the most basic, child-level things a magician could do, and though Fish had never had much occasion to practise it, natural reflex took over and directed his movements—left hand entwined with hers, right hand on her forehead—willed his strength through the right conduits. He was a lot stronger in magic than she was, a Gift that had outshone all others early on. Even in his depleted state, he had more strength to share, the power to boost her fast-waning determination and will to live. It hurt; all the pathways in Fish's magical being were still scorched raw, and the power flowed jerkily at first, in fits and starts, before momentum took over and the channels opened fully.

No-one else even noticed what was happening, for just as Fish felt Brialise begin to revive beneath his hands, felt vigour return to a depleted being and the pulse in her wrist begin to beat steady, there was a sudden wail, and a relieved exclamation from the midwife's two young assistants.

And as he carefully released her to lie exhausted yet now out of immediate danger, it seemed to him as though the sun suddenly came up and shone inside the room, filling the dreary infirmary with a sudden blaze of radiance.

Fish had been aware, his whole life long, that he would always be able to sense whenever another magician was about. As a child, the presence of his father and siblings had been an everlasting background to his existence. Sometimes wavering, waxing and waning, yet never absent. The severing of that bond had taken a lot to accomplish, of willpower and planning and ironclad determination. He had become gradually used to the emptiness, afterwards, the sensation of being alone. *It is better that way,* he remembered Delourien saying to him, even as he tried to reach out and only barely sensed the tiny spark of magic inside the old woman, her secret from the rest of the world. *This is how you will survive. You must make yourself so small that no-one can sense you, even if they are close.*

Yet he had never really wondered how it felt, to have a new source of magic come into the world right before his eyes. The sheer beauty of the sudden glimmering power stunned him. Magic burst into the world as though it had been freed from bondage, coalesced and flowed into the tiny, bloody, screaming bundle that the midwife cradled in her arms.

He looked about him, his heart beating fast, wondering that no-one else seemed to have noticed. It was hard to believe, when the sensation was so powerful and overwhelming that Fish could not even focus his eyes properly. Outside the narrow window, evening had begun to fall, along with a penetrating rain that spattered against the cloudy glass. Inside, he felt that he was basking in the heady glow of full summer sunlight.

They handed the babe to Brialise, who was too exhausted to do very much but blink at it, and then somehow Fish found it passed over to himself. *A boy*, he noticed absently as the last of the new, miraculous magic swirled about him and subsided slowly into the tiny, infant being. Had it been this way when Fish was born? Had there been someone about who could sense the newborn power, who had sat there as stunned as he was now, unable to do anything but grin down at the small red face scrunched up in confusion?

For a moment, as he had oftentimes in the past, Fish tried to picture his own parents, his true parents. But the face he envisioned for his father kept crumbling into piercing blue eyes and the smirk of the blood sorcerer, whilst he could not imagine for his mother anything further than his own reflection in feminine. He pictured his mother, as he often had, the same face as his and about the same age he was now, holding him as a baby, kissing him softly on the forehead before she slumped back in exhaustion, dying even as she brought him into the world.

It was an idle fantasy, and one Fish should have outgrown long ago. No-one knew who his true parents had been, save perhaps the slavers who had sold him to Arran as an infant, and Arran had never asked. He had always told Fish that it was more than likely his mother had sold him so she might buy safe passage away from Armour City in the wake of the great siege. Fish had never wanted to believe it, and as a child he had clung to the idea that perhaps the slavers had captured her and she had died giving birth to him, or maybe they had killed her, or sold her someplace else.

The babe was still crying, wanting comfort of a kind Fish could not provide. Fish got in a light kiss on his forehead before one of the girls came up to take him away, cooing over him and promising milk. Brother Jakob was bending over Brialise, who had fallen asleep, a look of puzzlement on his face.

"She must be stronger than we know," he muttered to Fish. "So much blood lost, yet her pulse is perfectly steady."

"We should leave her to rest," the midwife said firmly. "I shall return shortly, to watch over her."

With babe and bloody rags and midwife and helpers all gone, the infirmary sank into a deep silence, broken only by the soft sleepy breathing of the girl who was now a mother. Fish got awkwardly to his feet and left her in privacy, returning to his own bed. He sank down heavily, feeling the stress of the day, the sink of expended magic, course through him. Then he went rigid with shock.

On the bed opposite, Nico was sitting up, supporting himself with one trembling arm, blue eyes wide as they cast about the room and landed at last on his partner.

"Fish," he whispered, and his voice shook with relief. "Where are we?"

# Chapter XXV
## Armour City

Indigo-and-violet twilight descended in a slow haze over the squat stone buildings of Armour City, the dust of the day coalescing in a sunset that glowed in a dozen hazy hues, passing slowly over the faraway western horizon. The disappearing sun seemed like a bruising kiss across the endless rolling landscape.

Poppy Proudfoot watched the sun sink into the approaching night, the high hills with their mining adits and the smelters' district in deep shadow just behind her. There was the usual metallic, smoky tang on the evening air, the confirmation of a day's work done and wages earned. The workmen of the foundries and refineries were slouching down the hills, as were the miners who had drawn the day shift. Adolescents leading tired ponies hitched to now-empty charcoal carts offered an informal transport service, for those in a hurry who didn't mind coming out the same colour as the inside of the cart. But the majority of the workmen were in no great rush, whether they were returning to cosy slate-roofed cottages nestled in the feet of the hills, or to establishments such as the one by whose front door Poppy lounged, boarding-houses for single men that also functioned as inns.

The earliest of the foundry workers had already begun to creep in for the night, and Poppy could hear the creak of benches and low murmur of voices in the room behind her. She straightened her pose, smiled broadly at an oldster who doffed his floppy hat at the sight of her. This side of Armour City, a suburb just beneath the granite bulk of Brockton Hill, she was probably one of the most distinctive sights to be seen. A hair under six feet tall, she was bigger than most of the dusty workmen, and all who had reason to know her knew that she was proficient with the great battle-axe which she sometimes wore over her shoulders, not to mention the daggers at her belt. Her short brown hair was shot with strands of grey, now, but Poppy had not yet lost any of her strength to old age. For the past sixteen years she had been a fixture at the door of this inn, occasionally sorting out fights, more often running off petty thieves and would-be rapists.

As languidly as she draped herself against the doorpost, Poppy was filled with tension. She anxiously scanned the dusty road that led down to the city proper, ran her eyes along the violet stripe that marked the last of the daylight. It was Thirdmonth at last, and the strength of the sun was finally beginning to outmatch the cold that lingered in the nights. It had been a warm day, and Poppy had left off her cloak, donning her worn leather armour over a lighter tunic and trousers than usual. Her scuffed boots scraped against the stone doorstep as she shifted her position. Spring celebrations had come and gone in Armour City, the exhausted populace too spent to summon much hope for the coming summer. Yet Poppy, old campaigner that she was, could taste something new in the air tonight, over the flavour of foundry smoke and copper ore dust.

The young Sven messenger quietly finishing his meal in a corner of the inn's taproom had not brought good news; in fact, most would surely call his news dreadful. Yet despite that, despite the bleakness of it all and the many lives that had been lost, there was a sliver of hope, an offer of alliance.

She leaned back to cast a surreptitious glance at the young messenger, as she had been doing nearly all afternoon. Nothing had changed; he was chewing his way slowly through Armour City's modest workman's fare, sipping often at the mug of watered wine on the table. Conversation in the room was perhaps a little louder than usual; there was a Zammùkian miner drinking in there today with the other labourers, and Poppy leaned a little further inside the door to hear what he had to say.

"That caravan was *not* just carting silver," she heard. The Zammùk's accent was harsh, his whole face drawn into a scowl beneath his floppy hat. His tufty black beard and narrow, hooked nose made his face seem as pointed as the beak of one of the ibises that fished on the mudflats of the river. "I spoke to them bastards myself. They wouldn't let me near the wagons and horses, and there was the stink of blood and piss on them. I'm telling you, that was a slaver's caravan." He made as if to spit, then seemed to remember that he was not at home in his own mine.

A low murmur ran through the assembled workmen at the bar; no-one would doubt a Zammùk's word, least of all Poppy. At least *she* was trying to do something about it.

"Wouldn't let my daughters out of my sight," the man continued. "The little sons, neither. World's all going to shit." He slugged back a great swallow of whatever it was they were drinking; it looked more than a mite stronger than the watered wine they had given the Sven.

"At least you lot can crawl down into the mines when things get hot," one of the workmen grumbled. "More than what *we* can do. We're stuck with that bastard—" He lifted his mug to gesture, and there was a sudden silence. The speaker himself trailed off, no doubt remembering that people had been hanged and slashed and slaughtered for less.

*For less than saying that Arran Sylvaissen is a bastard.* Poppy's mouth twitched, and she swallowed hard, remembering her husband, Joseph, who had done nothing.

*Oh, for sure, he never approved of our tyrant king, not after all the slaughter and slavery, but he wasn't doing anything. We weren't doing anything.* Somehow, they had believed that if they kept their heads down far enough, they would not be lopped off. They were just ordinary city folk, after all. A woman who made her living as a wandering mercenary and door-guard, and a man who had been born in the stews of the city and knew these streets better than the back of his hand. They were not the stuff of heroes.

A shape appeared against the violet stripe of the setting sun, the first of the figures she was waiting for, and Poppy grinned in recognition. Even from a distance, Josephine's swaggering gait was distinctive. She wore no armour today, just a loose tunic tucked into coarse hessian trousers. A long knife hung on her belt, and as usual she had adorned herself with the portable treasures of her mercenary trade, golden bracelets and glass beads and all kinds of gems. She halted at the foot of the inn's stone steps. "Good to see you here, Ma."

"Josie." Poppy hopped down and hugged her daughter, not because it had been long since they had last seen each other—it had been this morning, in their house—but simply because she *could*. Since Josephine had turned seventeen eight years ago, she had never stayed home for long. Poppy, of course, had done much the same thing in her youth, but never wandered as far as her daughter had. Josephine's latest foray had been to the Eastern Empire, to the fabled capital city of Bassah itself, and there she had done more for their cause than Poppy would ever have dreamed possible.

Mother and daughter looked nothing alike; Josephine had inherited her father's mist-grey eyes, his slender build, and the cool-toned teak complexion that marked her as a quarter Eastern. Joseph's parentage had always been a bit of a mystery; he had been raised by his mother, but his father had clearly been of foreign blood, a dashing trader of exotic goods, or so his mother had always told it. Josephine had only been nine when they lost him, and it had been just the two of them ever since.

"Magda's busy with someone," Josephine said in a low voice. "Said she'll probably be late."

Poppy frowned. "What kind of someone?"

"Sounds like someone wanted to escape the palace." Josephine gripped her knife casually. "I'd better go watch out for her. And make extra sure we don't have any tails after us."

"Sure." Poppy had never been much good at subterfuge, preferring to face all of her problems head-on with her fists and a good blade, but her daughter was a natural at this sort of stuff. Despite her stunning looks and general penchant for showy dress, Josephine could sneak through the city without a single person ever having noticed her, if she wanted to. It was a knack she had for blending in whilst standing out, something Poppy had never known anyone else to master.

The tension inside Poppy had subsided a trifle, and she was calm and composed as everyone else began to trickle in one by one.

Wurald Wolfsson was already here, seated a sensible distance away from the Sven messenger and in deep conversation with two men who looked to be fellow prospectors. He had been boarded here for the better part of a year now, ostensibly doing nothing more than poking around the mountains in search of silver deposits on behalf of the Miners' Guild in Svanfeld.

Mitch Zenfielder, a captain of the Guard, left his men to their carousing at the brothel down the street and sauntered in for a mug of the innkeep's famous pear brandy. Resplendent in his uniform of oiled leather and sable silk, his dark hair close-cropped and face neatly shaven, he drew nasty looks and inaudible mutters from many of the workmen, few who had reason to love Arran's City Guard.

Richard Madden drew far less attention, though by rights he was many times more notorious than any mere guardsman. Former high commander of the City Guard of Cythece, his support for Arran Sylvaissen's rule had earned him many bloody sobriquets, most of which Poppy thought were probably justified. However, five years ago he had defected from the Guard and fled, and now counted himself as one of Arran's most implacable enemies.

The man gave Poppy a chill between her shoulder-blades every time she saw him, not because his appearance was sinister, but in fact the opposite—for a man who had been so notorious, who had slaughtered his Morgein liege lord and so many others, he looked horrifyingly *normal*. Sixty-five years of age, squat and creased and bald, he looked quite at home in the shabby company of Armour City's workmen. It would have taken an astute observer to notice the sword-calluses on his hands and the muscles underneath his accumulated stoutness, and *those* seemed to be in short supply. So far, no-one had gotten wind of the fact that the Butcher of Cythece was alive and well and living quietly in Armour City under their tyrant king's very nose. Poppy supposed it helped that Cythece lay at least three hundred miles away, by the path of the crow flying due south.

As darkness fell, the district was getting busier; this was, after all, where many workmen went to spend their pay. On the street where Poppy stood, public-houses, inns, coffee-shops and brothels were all opening for the night, and the lamps were being lit in the temple to the Goddess Qwu'Kiya, casting a warm glow upon the lush foliage of its gardens at the crossroads where it stood. Poppy craned her head to see the temple entrance, timber fronting giving way to the same grey stone that comprised the rest of Armour City, for trees had always been in short supply here. The temple was an oasis of calm in the bustling night, casting an aura that spoke of peace, of remembrance.

Many religious creeds were practised in Armour City, where tolerance had always been the order of the day. It was said that the non-mage folk of Vailana were descended from those who had fled the ancient religious wars of what was now the Zemlyan Empire, half the world away in the great continent that lay across the sea to the north of Svanfeld. The people who had built Armour City never wanted to see such a war again, and so had decreed that all could freely practise the faith of their choice. There was a mercenaries' religion, dedicated to the deities known as the Twins; the little gods of the land who found worship amongst the farmers of the plains; the strange singular god of the Zammùk, whose temples were to be found only in the underground deeps of Armour City's mines. The Sven church had a presence, of course, but none of the secular power they wielded up in Svanfeld. And some people worshipped the Great Goddess of the Morgei still, a religion that had been widespread and celebrated in the days when mage-folk sat on the Council and mingled in the streets with those of nonmage blood.

Most of Her temples in Vailana had been abandoned, fallen into disrepair over the years with all the mage-priests gone and the mage-gifted congregation vanished. But a few held on, the one in this suburb the only outpost of Qwu'Kiya's worship in the whole of Armour City. There were not many followers who passed through the timber doors anymore, particularly not on a working night like tonight, but some few drifted through the verdant gardens and the butter-yellow glow of the lamps nonetheless. Most of them would be ambivalent about religion, Poppy knew, coming simply to enjoy the peace and beauty of the gardens. But there would be a few of Her faithful still, hooded figures muffled head-to-toe in grey robes of mourning, their faces often covered as a gesture of remembrance for the fallen who had once filled the temple.

One of those grey robes was approaching the temple right now, face completely hidden in a heavy swathe of fabric, hands tucked away into sleeves that were far too long. The figure was attended by a single companion, an ordinary guard-for-hire by the looks of him, yellow-haired and weather-creased.

As soon as Poppy recognized the face of the guardsman, she

knew it was time. One did not keep the sister of an emperor waiting, not even when she was travelling incognito.

She leaned inside the door of the inn, searching for her employer. The inn was bustling, and it took her a few tries to catch Ivy's eye. A stout woman past sixty, Ivy Palm's golden hair had turned half silver with age, but she was still possessed of the strange and beautiful pale blue eyes that had done her such good business in the days when she was the colleague and fast friend of Joseph's late mother.

Ivy noticed Poppy's frantic gesturing at last, and yelled for her husband, Noah, to take over the position of door-guard. Poppy could feel eyes from three disparate corners of the room watching her, though she dared not acknowledge them. Wolfsson, Zenfielder, and Madden would make their own ways towards the temple, in their own time, Wolfsson bringing the messenger from Svanfeld with him.

Poppy made her way across the bustling road and through the timbered gate, turning off immediately to wind her way into the silent garden. Sounds from the busy street were muffled here, and only the moon lit her way as she moved beyond the welcome warmth of the yellow temple-lanterns.

A black-limbed milkwood tree marked the place where she needed to turn off the path. Poppy hesitated, making sure that no-one had chosen this spot for quiet meditation or a private tryst before ducking beneath the gnarled branches and striking out for the side of the temple. She came to a narrow doorway, half hidden in an angle of the stone wall, and slipped a key from her pocket, letting herself inside. Closing the door behind her, but leaving it unlocked for her compatriots to follow, she descended a set of narrow stone steps to come at last to the temple's vast storage cellars, now mostly empty.

Indoor lanterns had been lit down here already, the chairs and table were in their usual setting, and Sirandah of Bassah was waiting, her thick grey hood let down and the mask that had concealed her face now discarded upon the table.

"My lady." Poppy fell into an instinctive lowborn's pastiche of manners upon seeing her, and the dark-skinned woman smiled.

"It has been far too long, Poppy." As always, Sirandah's manners were impeccably refined and polite, her words well enunciated, barely any trace of her natural accent. Poppy supposed she had been born to her high role in society, probably schooled in etiquette and languages since she had been a little girl. They were stark opposites of each other, the lowborn, freckle-faced, rough-spoken, middle-aged, barely lettered Vailanan mercenary on one side, the elegant young Eastern princess on the other, her face like a carved profile of jet shot with undertones of blue amethyst.

They were interrupted by the sound of footsteps coming down the stone stairs, and Richard Madden entered the room, shook both their hands in brusque greeting, then settled himself upon the nearest chair.

"So, a messenger came from Svanfeld," he said to Poppy, going straight for the point as usual. He tapped on the worn table. "Good news, or bad?"

Poppy hesitated.

"Oh, all right—I know. Best to save it for when we're all gathered in one." He tapped again at the table, impatiently. "Where's your daughter? And Magda?"

"Delayed at the palace," Poppy replied. "Josie's gone to scout the area."

"Good work." It sounded like a military commander giving praise to one of his men, a manner Poppy did not much care for. Madden turned his head as two pairs of footsteps scraped upon the stone above, and Poppy frantically motioned for Sirandah to replace her mask and hood. The messenger would never guess the identity of the others massed around this table, but the Bassan princess was one-of-a-kind, the imperial family known for being uniquely dark even amongst their own race. If the messenger turned out to be a traitor, or even just rather loose-lipped and stupid, it would not do for him to have seen a young woman of true black complexion at their secret meeting.

It took a little longer for Zenfielder to arrive. The young captain had managed to lose his guardsman's uniform sometime during the evening, and was carrying an open bottle of red wine which he placed ostentatiously upon the table as he entered. "Refreshment?" he asked the others with a grin.

Madden scoffed, but Wolfsson accepted, and so too the young Sven messenger. Poppy was wondering just how late Magda would be, and whether they should begin the meeting without her and Josie, when the door creaked open once again and the murmured voices of two young women carried down to the storeroom. Josephine descended the stairs, Magda hard on her heels. Poppy spared a moment of scrutiny for her. Magdalene Kotman, longtime confidante and special friend of her daughter, was fully as Zammùkian as the miner who had been in the common room that evening, yet had a lighter shade of hair and a softer, less pointed visage. In Armour City, amongst a thousand other brown-haired brown-eyed girls, she had the perfect face for someone who did not wish to attract undue notice. That face was paler than usual, the quiet demeanour even more subdued. Poppy wondered what had happened at the palace that day—nothing good, it never was—and squeezed the young woman's shoulder as she passed to lock the door up top, earning her a tight smile from the drawn face.

Zenfielder was already bantering with Josie when she came back, apparently trying to foist some of his wine on the two girls, but quieted down soon enough when Poppy took a stand at the head of the table, motioning the Sven messenger up from his seat.

"I'll not waste your time with preliminaries," she said to the assembled group. "We all know why we've come tonight. Go on"—she motioned to the messenger—"tell 'em what you told me."

The messenger stepped forward. Beardless and freckle-faced, not a day older than nineteen by Poppy's estimation, he was younger than anyone else in the room. Yet he had managed to travel here, all the way from beyond Lake Mountaindale, in less than two weeks, showing a rare commitment to the officer who had sent him. He stood with a proud, confident military bearing, and his demeanour was solemn.

"My name is Bjorn Schoenmaker," he said quietly. "A junior soldier in the army of Svanfeld." He bit his lower lip, hesitating, then came out with the blunt words. "The city of Ülhard has been sacked. King Falcon of Svanfeld is dead, along with his son Rolf."

The words fell like hammer blows into the sudden, stunned silence. Wolfsson had gone pale under his beard, and seemed to be biting back an exclamation. The three younger people around the table looked more confused than upset. Madden's face had merely gone a shade or two grimmer than his accustomed expression.

Wolfsson, unsurprisingly, was the first to speak. "H-how?" he stammered. "Who has done this? What army?"

"There is a long story behind this, Wurald," Poppy interjected softly. "Will you let Bjorn tell it?"

"Of—of course." The Guildsman subsided, his hands trembling. Zenfielder reached past him for his cup, refilling it with wine. "Drink," he commanded softly, and Wolfsson did not argue.

"It began but a few weeks ago," Bjorn continued. His gaze was fixed upon the table, but his voice rang clear. "The king and Council received reports of a hostile force massing in the hill-country of the Dzil, north of Ülhard. The Council was slow to make a decision, and this army, when it was massed, moved fast. They attacked several villages in the area, slaughtered most of the inhabitants. Even civilians. Then, they marched straight for Ülhard.

"The king sent General Roald Vanya up north to deal with them, and sent the queen and their three younger children away with a military escort. I was part of that escort. Our commander was the king's cousin, Captain Hugh Anspeare."

"Anspeare?" Madden scowled and shifted in his seat. "I know that one; he's from Vailana. Family held a lot of land around the Lonely Water. The patriarch died, years ago. Before *our king* came to power."

Early on, the whole company had decided that they would never mention the name *Arran Sylvaissen* in their secret meetings, lest some magical power alert him. Poppy was fairly sure that magic did not actually work that way, but she had agreed; it never hurt to be too cautious.

"This Hugh," Madden was saying, "he was still a pup, back then. I had no idea he survived the purges. I do recall his mother came from up north, though."

"I remember a Councilman Anspeare," Poppy interjected. "When I was young. An old man."

"That would be Guy Anspeare," Madden said. "This one's grandfather. There was a Councilman in almost every generation, the family was that powerful." He subsided and sat back. Bjorn continued.

"We took the queen into the Svanlyn mountains. Shortly afterwards, the attack on Ülhard happened, though we did not know for many days how the battle fell out. We fought an advance guard of the enemy army in the mountains." He shivered suddenly, and took a deep breath. "We saw the truth of it. The army that took Ülhard was not made up of men. They were something else—something monstrous and terrible. Captain Anspeare—he said that they were *magical constructs*. Things created by dark magic."

Into the silence that fell, Zenfielder voiced what they all were thinking. "Our king," he muttered, and took a great swig directly from the wine bottle.

"Captain Anspeare sent me here, after we received word of—what happened in Ülhard," Bjorn said.

"The Guild representatives would likely have shared the broad details of my mission here with King Falcon," Wolfsson murmured. "It would seem that he has passed his command to Anspeare."

Josephine stirred. "Bjorn, do you know who commanded this enemy army? Its general?"

The messenger shook his head. "Captain Anspeare was trying to find out himself when I left. Unfortunately, these magical constructs do not have the power of speech." He hesitated. "Just before I left, he asked me to share with you one more piece of news. Taunus Sylvaissen is dead."

Poppy had nearly jumped in the air at that, the first time she had heard the young soldier's message, and the reaction was, once more, quite predictable, with many cries of "How?" from her compatriots.

But the messenger only shook his head.

"It seems there was some internal fight at a secret stronghold in the Svanlyn mountains," he said. "We do not know the details, but just before I left, the captain recovered his corpse and so confirmed his death. We rescued three survivors from this fight, but none of them were in any state to be questioned before I left."

Poppy cleared her throat. "And the reason why Anspeare sent you to us . . ."

"Yes." The young soldier stood a little straighter. "You have a common enemy with the land and throne of Svanfeld now," he declared. "My captain asks to send any aid you can. He has a hundred men in an easily defensible position in the mountains, but we are cut off from the main part of the Sven army. He vows that if he can stabilize the situation in Svanfeld, he will come south and join you here."

The entire room fidgeted, and Poppy could almost hear their thoughts as clearly as if they were all shouting together. A military leader. Alliance with the throne of Svanfeld. Somehow the dreadful news of what had happened in Ülhard paled before the sliver of hope they were being offered.

Sirandah leaned forward on her elbows. "We have much to discuss amongst ourselves," she said, the liquid tones of her voice muffled by the mask. "Thank you for bringing us this message, Bjorn Schoenmaker. It may make all the difference."

"I'll be around, later tonight, to tell you what we decide," Poppy assured the young messenger. Before she could let him out, though, Wolfsson stirred.

"Bjorn," he began. "The situation in Ülhard—what is happening to the people? Are they being—mistreated?"

The young soldier flushed beet red, and stared at his boots. "Sir—" he began. "The captain—he would not tell any of us such things. If indeed he knows. The reports that have reached us are very few. The captain only said—we must not lose hope. That our people may be spared."

The Guildsman nodded and sat back, and Poppy, unable to look at him, shepherded the messenger away.

When she returned, Magda was sharing details about the servant woman she had smuggled out of Arran's palace that day. The woman's daughter, also a servant in the palace, had vanished, and she feared for her own life. Magda's theory was that the daughter, like all of the servants who simply vanished inexplicably from the palace, had been murdered in some sort of dark magic ritual. *Magic doesn't work that way*, Poppy thought again, but Arran Sylvaissen had upturned most of the rules of the world she had known, and who was to say that he had not done the same with the rules of magic?

"So," Madden said, the moment she resumed her seat. "Alliance with Svanfeld."

Sirandah had removed her mask and set aside her hood again. "If indeed this nobleman speaks for the whole of Svanfeld."

"With Falcon and his son both out of the picture," Madden said, "the chain of command is unclear. By the law of paternal succession, the throne of Svanfeld passes to the younger son, but he is a boy of ten. His mother, Falcon's queen, will speak for him, but she knows little of military matters."

"What of General Vanya?" Poppy asked. "Wouldn't she take advice from him?"

"Vanya is not with her," Madden reminded her. "Since the boy did not say, he is likely lost, his fate unknown. At any rate, Queen Bronwyn cannot contact him. And if Hugh Anspeare is half the military man his father was, she will not need to." He gestured with his hands on the table. "Anspeare is now the only hereditary royal with the capacity to fight a war against our king," he declared. "Being a military leader already—that is another point in his favour. He has the authority, the lineage. The land will follow him if he steps up."

"Then there is only one question," Sirandah said. "What aid can we send him?"

"It's a pity none of us have armies," Josephine mused.

Zenfielder shook his head. "It's not like my boys can just desert from the Guard," he said. "They will declare their loyalty to Anspeare if I tell them to, but we cannot join him unless he comes to Armour City."

"And most of *my* people are in Kerath," Madden growled. "Even so, they are not soldiers. Not the kind who can fight pitched battles."

Sirandah stirred. "I could possibly spare a few of my guards—"

"No," Madden said immediately, in a tone that brooked no argument. "You need every one of your swords with you, in case something happens here. We can't lose you. We can't lose the support of your brother."

"I suppose we could send him money?" Magda piped up, glancing at the Bassan princess.

"Yes," Sirandah said, and Madden nodded this time in agreement. "Not gold, perhaps, but I have brought plenty of trade goods with me. These are rarer in Svanfeld, and will be even more valuable there."

"Fat lot of good your jewels and silks will do him, stuck up in the middle of the mountains," Zenfielder said curtly. "We don't even know who commands this magical army! He needs men. Failing that, he needs *intelligence*. He knows nothing of our king." He glanced at Magda. "That's your department."

"Our king had five children," Magda responded. "Taunus was the eldest. Can we truly believe that he is dead?"

Madden shrugged. "Mages die the same as anyone else, when you stick a blade in 'em."

Poppy shuddered, and the rest of the table grew quiet. *I'm sure you know from experience, Richard.* "There was one that died young, though," she said aloud.

"Deryck, the youngest," Magda replied. "I knew him; they had me mind his books and equipment when I was younger. He was only a child." There was a sudden haunted look in her eyes, and she shook her head. "I don't know what happened to him. I tried to find out, but no-one has even the slightest suspicion."

"I told you," Madden said, almost gently, "that our king most likely got rid of him. Maybe he was acting a bit different from the others. Maybe he wasn't as easy to control."

Magda sighed. "Then we should have rescued him."

"That was long ago, and beside the point," Zenfielder said impatiently. "Who are the other three?"

"There is Dannine, whom he keeps here in Armour City," Magda said. "The worst of them all, by any account. The other two, Baukin and Ceazyn, have been gone for a long time. More than a year each."

"Our mystery commander, then, must be one of those two," Madden said.

"Or both together," Zenfielder cut in.

"Maybe."

"You are the most valuable source of information around this table," Zenfielder said to Magda. "You should go to Anspeare."

"I can't—" Magda shook her head. "I can't leave so abruptly, there'll be questions asked—"

Josephine laid her hand on her friend's knee. "Everything Magda knows, I know," she declared to the room at large. "I'm a mercenary; I know of warfare, I've fought in pitched battles, all things that Magda hasn't. *I'll* go to Anspeare."

Poppy sighed, knowing that her daughter was right. "Very well," she said. "You'll return with Bjorn, and take whatever Sirandah can give you that's portable and valuable. Perhaps you'll be able to hire a few more mercenaries." She hesitated then, and drummed her fingers on the table. "As for potential allies," she began delicately, preparing to brook a subject that had caused much contention in the past, "there is still the obvious question. What of the Morgei?"

"What of them?" Zenfielder asked flippantly.

"In the past, we have voted not to contact them," Poppy said. Magda and Josephine had been the only ones who had voted on her side. Sirandah had been the tiebreaker between the three men and the three other women at the table, and she had sided with the men in the end, believing that such a mission would carry an unacceptable amount of risk.

"We have talked so much of armies tonight," Poppy continued, over Madden's scowl and Zenfielder's chugging of the remainder of his wine. "The Morgei have armies. They have successfully resisted our king's military advances for nineteen years."

Madden scoffed. "Neither have they been able to throw him off for good."

Madden, Poppy knew, could never be swayed in this; she could not even say that she condemned him for it. Very few Morgei had ever lived in the regions of Kerath and Zarath along the southern coast of Vailana. Zarath was said to be the oldest nonmage settlement on the continent; tradition held that Bavarian Lana, first and only High King of the West, had come ashore there with hundreds of ships in tow, refugees all from the religious wars of the Great Continent. If Zarath was truly the oldest, though, the Kerathi cities of Cygnath and Cythece were tied for second and third place. They were bulky, rugged cities both, originally built for defence against pirates from the sea and—depending to whom you lent your ear—either Arvenians or Morgei from the land. Occupying a strong position, protected by a famously inhospitable mountain range as well as a cold, deep river, the region had been the first bastion for the nonmage settlers to hold out against both hostile wilderness and ravening barbarians. Its inhabitants were fiercely proud of their history, of their ancestors' achievements, and were implacably loyal to their own. Yet the Council in Armour City had given them a wealthy Morgein liege lord with no familial ties to the area, and allowed him to operate more or less freely as long as he delivered the capital their annual tax. It had been the source of much contention between the Council of Vailana and the people of Kerath, and it had turned ugly when Arran Sylvaissen arose as a warlord with the stated aim of freeing Vailana from the tyranny of the Council. Poppy tried not to remember that the man sitting across the table from her right now had probably not only participated in the sack of her city on that night nineteen years ago, but been one of Arran's chief commanders and advisors during the battle.

It was, therefore, to the others around the table that she directed her words. "It would be the simplest thing to sneak an army from Qwu'Mallorn into the mountains," she said. "All they'd have to do is cross the delta-valley. Or sail around to Sulshome. They can help

Anspeare more easily than they could ever help us."

"They could," Madden said quietly. "I do not believe that they *would*."

"And which of us would go *there*?" Zenfielder demanded. "There's a war happening along that border, or have you forgotten?"

Poppy turned to Sirandah, who shook her head.

"As I have said before, they are too insular to trust," she said. "The Morgei sit in their forest, even as your king sits in his castle. The Empire trades with them, as we trade with everyone. They take coffee and spices and ebony, sell us their fine wines and crafts, their fruits and jewels, but they do not part with their secrets. They will not give us a phalanx of mage-soldiers, nor any weapon that can provide an advantage over our enemies. They are"—she paused, meaningfully—"different. In their thinking, and in their nature."

"Differences in colour and creed can be overcome," Madden declared, glancing between the inky-skinned Bassan princess to his left and the thatch-haired Guildsman to his right. "But the mage-kind are *not* the same as us. Can any of us around this table give a true account of their powers?" He spread his hands as all remained silent. "They have no interest in Vailana any longer; they've made that clear. Let them have their forest; they'll owe us a favour when we finally crush our king and remove the thorn from their side."

There was loud assent from Zenfielder, slightly muted assent from Sirandah and from Wolfsson, who had been all but silent the entire meeting long. It was rare enough for Zenfielder and Madden to agree so wholeheartedly on anything. That it happened to be *this* filled Poppy with a sense of dismay.

"All right," she finally said. *It's not all right.* They were supposed to be building something new here: a future for her country. Without the magic of the Morgei, they could never hope to fight the dark magic of their tyrant king. Richard Madden was all bluster, still riding that high from nineteen years ago when he had executed a single liege lord who had been a pretty feeble magician to begin with. Arran Sylvaissen was anything but feeble, and there were at least three of his spawn to contend with, still loose in the world. Poppy listened to Magda's stories from the palace, and probably had a better idea of what Arran was truly capable of. The man possessed a terrifying amount of power, and showed irrational tendencies in his behaviour. Should his defeat ever seem a likely possibility, there was no telling what he might do. What he might unleash. There would be no freedom for any of them if he reduced Armour City to a smoking wasteland.

Perhaps the memories of the Vailana of her youth were a touch rose-tinted these days, but Poppy remembered when there had been magic. Now, there was only darkness, and it seemed like the light of morning would never come. She remembered a cradle-tale from the old days, something she had used to tell Josephine when she was only an infant. *It takes magic to defeat magic.* The story had told of darkness, of an evil bear who arose to block out the sun and chase all the good magic away. In the tale, it could only be defeated by a wolf, a creature of equal violence and power.

The others filed away one by one, leaving Poppy as the last, the one to put out the lanterns and close the door upon the darkness. Despair nestled in her heart, and she wondered suddenly whether she would live to see the morning rise again.

# Chapter XXVI
# Tenna

B Y THE TIME HE HAD ARRIVED in Tenna, found a room for Velda at a boarding-house in town, made his way to barracks and arranged the return of their mounts and the drop-off of their meagre baggage, it was night and Albryan was dead on his feet.

Dinner would already be concluded in the mess-hall, and he took a shortcut to officers' quarters through a grove he remembered visiting just before he left. The woods were transformed all in spring blooming, the trilling songs of late doves sounding in the far branches as the black silhouettes of bats swooped overhead. He took a few spare trail-biscuits from his pocket and ate as he walked, not truly hungry but knowing that food was necessary.

He was dog tired: exhausted from four days' worth of riding, unsettled in mind, magically drained. Any respite from the cloud of anxiety that seemed to have attached itself to him was brief, and he had started experiencing nightly flashbacks to the worst parts of his journey, usually some scenario involving Dannine Sylvaissen, sometimes reliving things that had happened to him, sometimes scenarios that had never actually occurred. Sometimes he would dream of armies of necromes, dream again what it had felt like to die. Velda had pulled him back from that deadly poison, just as Caras had pulled him back from what he'd done to himself ten years ago. Back then, he had experienced similar dreams for months afterwards, and he dreaded the thought that they would last that long this time.

A preliminary report, carrying details of Albryan's physical health along with the condition he was in when he reported at the Border, had already made its way through magical means to Thinas. Included in that report would be the healer's recommendation that Albryan was to have two weeks' leave from duty starting the day he arrived back in Tenna, a recommendation Albryan himself supported wholeheartedly. Part of his officers' training had included the means of assessing fitness for duty, be it his soldiers' or his own, and Albryan knew perfectly well what his symptoms—nightmares, flashes of dread and paranoia—meant.

A trip to the mind-healer was in order, as much as he hated the idea and the wastage of time it would mean. Albryan argued back and forth with himself about it as he went. *Would you consider the time you'd spent recovering from an arrow in the gut a waste of time?*

*You can't fight and ride when your belly gapes open every time you move, and you can't look the enemy in the eye when you're still fretting about what happened last time you faced them.*

Before the anticipated rest and the sojourn with the mind-healer, though, Albryan would have to visit Thinas and give his own report in person, and that was something he dreaded more than anything else at this moment.

There was no-one else about when he arrived at the officers' residence, which was just how he would have preferred it. Albryan unlocked the door and slipped inside as quietly as possible, making his way silently across the corridor to his own room. It was, blessedly, just as he'd left it. None of his friends had had the idea to welcome him back, probably because Albryan had failed to inform them of when he was due back. As much as he had missed Elithan and Gardan and the rest of his brothers-in-arms, he knew their reunion would be much fonder once he was in a state of mind to welcome it.

Albryan tossed his pack into a corner of the room and settled down upon his own bed with a sigh of relief, all by himself at last. He stretched out and pulled his feet up, cradling the pillow under his head. *Just a moment to relax*, he told himself. Then he would get up, go have a wash, maybe eat something more, prepare himself for bed—

When he awoke, morning sun was streaming into the room, a clatter of recruits were arguing loudly down the far end of the compound, and he was gritty with road-dust and eye-gunk and rotten sweat. Sleep had come so quickly that he'd not even taken off his boots, and his cloak was wrapped around himself the way he'd been sleeping on the road.

Wincing at the stiffness in his limbs, he unbuckled the cloak and stripped off the rest of his soiled clothing as quickly as possible, kicking the hobnailed boots aside. *Good soles, those, to have carried me all the way to Svanfeld on foot and then back here. But thank the Goddess I'm expected to wear something else today.* He squinted out against the light. Thinas, ever the earliest riser, was probably already ensconced in his office, yelling at messengers and waiting impatiently for him.

There was no time to draw a bath in the communal washroom, so Albryan carried out the necessary with the water from the pail under the washstand, gasping at the cold. He wet his face, ran his hands through the patchy beard. It would never do to appear in front of the general with two months' worth of bristle on his face, so he picked up the razor which still lay in its place by the washstand, inspecting the sharp, thin blade. He sighed and unrolled the stropping leather. On the wrist of his right hand, his old scars looked deeper and whiter than usual, the surrounding skin tanned golden.

Albryan didn't wear short sleeves as a rule, not even in summer, but the heat of the sun had been blazing when he and Hiram had departed Armour City. He recalled long afternoons with nothing to do but walk and talk, feeling so relaxed with the old man that he rolled up his sleeves in the midday heat. The thought of Hiram unsteadied him for a moment, and he clutched at the edge of the stone basin, the metal razor clattering.

It took Albryan a while to stop shaking, leaning heavily on the edge of the basin, taking slow deep gulps of air as he had learned from the mind-healers so long ago, till the clenching in his guts subsided and he could breathe normally again. Then he picked up the soap and lathered his face with his left hand, keeping his right firmly upon the basin's edge, and cropped at his cheeks and chin until they were as smooth as a dewy-eyed recruit's, making him look younger than he felt he should.

The uniform of the Morgein Guard stood out in its stark simplicity and lack of colour. The Morgei loved bright dyes and varied colours, but the guard uniform was designed for camouflage and subterfuge, the tunic the green of forest foliage, the breeches the dark grey of tree-bark. Not being on active duty, Albryan was free to forgo his armour. As often as he had wished to have it during his recent adventures, that was a relief today. The room around him was warm with the sun already, though a light breeze rippled through the leaves outside his window.

Albryan neatened the ends of his breeches into his boots, arranged his sword and dagger on his belt, and slid four shining bronze rings over the left sleeve of his tunic, signifiers of his rank within the army. He attached leather cuffguards to his wrists, ensuring that the sleeves of his shirt would not move nor flap open.

It was too late to think of having breakfast, even if his stomach had been able to stand the thought, so he avoided the mess and peeked in the back of the kitchen, where Lissia the cook welcomed him back with a cup of coffee, drunk hastily as he stood at the back door, watching a troop of blue monkeys inch their way along a thorn-tree branch towards the dining deck.

Then there was nothing for it but to find his way to the winding path that led up Triaan's Hill, as he had done so many times before, and climb. It seemed to take an inordinately long time, the sky blue and clear, the wind insistently chapping at his bare face. But at last he entered the familiar wooden room, nodded at the general's new secretary, who saluted him enthusiastically, and was ushered into the general's tiny office.

"Albryan." Thinas moved out from behind the desk, clasped his hand around Albryan's arm, smiled with relief crinkling the corners of his dark eyes. "I am glad to see you." He was matter-of-fact, as usual. "For a while there, I feared you lost. I sent out a patrol to your last known location. They found only bloodstains on the grass, along with your discarded armour." He grimaced. "Sit down. Report. Tell me what happened."

It took Albryan a long moment to find his tongue, and he sank down slowly upon the worn chair. Where to start?

"I found no armies near the swamplands," he finally said, "but I did find Dannine Sylvaissen."

Thinas was instantly alert, though he said not a word.

"I found that they have a faster mode of transportation," Albryan continued, speaking easier as he went. "Arran has imported quetzals from the Pirate Islands, long-distance fliers. Dannine—and I imagine, by extension, all the rest of them—can control these creatures through magic. I made the mistake of leaving my horse in an open place." Albryan hesitated. "Dannine found it, and almost found me. The quetzals eat meat—it devoured the horse. Hence all the blood. I had to escape quickly; left my armour and supplies behind. I realized that I could not use magic, or she would surely track me down, so I did not try to communicate." Thinas nodded. "I marked the direction in which Dannine flew afterwards, and decided to follow her."

"She did not simply fly back to Armour City?"

"No, she flew northwest, towards the Svanlyn mountains. I fetched up in a small town just over the Svanfeld border—Lynborder." Thinas pushed a map forward, and Albryan easily indicated the isolated town. "And there I did find something important. Our enemy is breeding necromes in the mountains."

He paused, and was not disappointed by Thinas's reaction. "*Necromes?*" the general hissed, his face twisted in disgust and disbelief. "But those—that type of construct has not been seen in at least three hundred years. Albryan, are you *sure?*"

"I fought them," Albryan said. "All the descriptions fit. The spellbase is a human corpse, twisted to develop fangs and claws. There is no mental function save an all-encompassing hunger to destroy the living. They are controlled from afar, by a sorcerer—Dannine Sylvaissen, in this case. Their blood is poisonous, and can kill if it enters a wound." He hesitated. "I saw this happen. Dannine is unleashing these creatures upon isolated farmsteads in the mountains. Even in the delta-valley just beyond our border."

Thinas tapped slender fingers on the wooden desk. "This will provoke Svanfeld," he finally said. "Arran will find himself another war before long."

"With these creatures in his arsenal, he can *win* that war," Albryan said. "If he takes Svanfeld—"

"*We* stand that much more alone. I know." Thinas tapped his fingers again. "You have done well, Albryan. Knowing of this sooner rather than later may make a difference. And we have never sent patrols into Svanlyn. You made the right decision, to follow her."

Albryan swallowed heavily. "You'll be meeting with the Council?"

"Certainly. I fear that we must set aside our distaste, and prepare ourselves for open war at last." Thinas's gaze roved over his desk, settling on a piece of paper in front of him. "But you, at least for the moment, have earned a reprieve. You have been injured?"

"There are bands of Vailanan soldiers roving the delta-valley," Albryan said. "That's the fastest route back, so I came that way from Lynborder, but I wasn't aware of how bad the situation has become."

Thinas grimaced again. "*That* I am aware of, but can offer no help for it. When the blood sorcerer wants to make war on his own people, what can we do?" He paused. "You say you fought with necromes?"

Albryan shivered. "It was . . . an unexpected encounter. They are strong, more ferocious than most men, and cannot be killed by any means other than a direct blow to the head. I . . . I have nightmares about those fights, sir. Still."

"You do seem more subdued than usual," Thinas returned. "Two weeks, then, and we'll have you back here. There's a lot that needs doing. As always." He paused, his finger now tapping on the piece of paper before him. "There was a message for you, about a month ago, from Catroot. Not by messenger; they sent it by echo, so probably took about three days to arrive here. I told Elithan Dorad to handle it. Don't know what the message said; I told him to inform your family that you were still away. When you contacted me again, I told him to let them know you were back."

As blunt as Thinas always was, Albryan felt yet another anxiety grip his heart. The "echo" was a public messaging system that worked by magic, designed so that people living in different towns could get urgent messages to each other quickly. Since the transmissions were public and could be intercepted by anyone who wanted to expend the energy to "listen," people tended to use it for emergencies alone. *Something must have happened in Catroot.* His heart set to pounding. He was suddenly worried for his brother, and for his sister-in-law, who had been expecting their third child. He quickly tried to reckon up her due date. Was that what the message was about? They would not have bothered just to inform Albryan that all had gone well; an echo message was for when you needed your brother at once. He swallowed hard. Caras loved his wife with all his heart; if something had happened to Iselma, Albryan needed to be by his brother's side.

Thinas's hand tapped again on the sheet of paper. "I am told you vouched for an immigrant at the Border? A young woman?"

"I . . ." Albryan collected his scattered thoughts. "Velda Davidz." He shifted in his seat. "She was the survivor of a necrome attack. I . . . I swore to protect her."

Thinas lifted the paper. "You put in a request to have her listed as a dependant of yours. Says you have adopted her as blood-kin."

Albryan nodded. "That's right."

Thinas arched an eyebrow. "You have that right, Albryan, same as anyone else . . . yet why not secure this, and marry the woman? That would be a simpler legal status."

Albryan could feel himself colouring. "That's—that's not how it is."

"If you say so." Thinas scrawled something on the paper. "I don't suppose it's worth me interviewing this woman about the necromes?" he asked offhandedly.

Albryan's mouth went dry. "It would be traumatic," he said immediately, trying to keep his tone even. "In my opinion, any information she could give you would not be worth the cost in mental recovery. She knows very little of magic." He hesitated. "And given that she is kin of mine . . . I would not support that request."

Thinas cocked an eyebrow again, but said no more save to bid him goodbye. There was nothing left for Albryan to do but leave the office, egress onto the top of the stony hill, wonder whether Thinas had noticed anything amiss in his demeanour, wonder whether he would do anything even if he had noticed, or ascribe it to the stress Albryan had undergone during his interrupted mission.

And bear the fangs of his military conscience gnawing at him, the sickness roiling in his gut, the knowledge that he had, for the first time, *lied* to his commanding officer. Lied about something so important that it could be construed as treason, no less.

Albryan quickly stowed thoughts of *that* ilk away. What he truly needed right now was someone he could trust, who would trust him unconditionally in return. He had long been familiar with the notion that if you couldn't settle on a sound strategy yourself, it usually helped to run your ideas past your lieutenant.

As luck would have it, back at barracks he ran almost immediately into Gardan Féa, who had once been a corporal under Albryan's command. He was off-duty, by the looks of it, and clasped Albryan's hand warmly as he welcomed him back.

"Where would I find Elithan?" Albryan asked him, and Gardan was helpful as always, knowing as he often did what everyone else's business was.

"He's gone off to the hills today, taking a company of new recruits to the training grounds. Should be back around sunset." There was a confidence about the young lieutenant that seemed new, and Albryan set a mental reminder to visit him sometime. Gardan seemed to already have his off-day planned out. "It's been rather peaceful around here since you left," he remarked as he took his leave.

"Peace is always broken by something in the end," Albryan shot back as the black-haired young man set off again.

He returned to his room, having some idea of continuing his sleep. The cleaning service had been in there already, and the soiled clothes had all been taken away, the mess he'd made with the water pail mopped up. He doffed his uniform and lay down on the neatly made bed, but could only think about Thinas, about Velda, about the family situation in Catroot, and how he should be talking to the mind-healer sooner rather than later. But soon enough all of that was eclipsed by his growing hunger.

In the end he rose and dressed again, this time in civvies, and went to fetch Velda from the boarding house—where he found that she had already inveigled herself into a sewing circle with three tailors who boarded there—before stopping at a bakery he knew for fresh coffee and rolls baked with dried fruit. Velda was fascinated by everything yet seemed a bit intimidated by the more crowded parts of Tenna, so he offered to show her around the barracks, at least the part where the soldiers lived and were allowed to bring their families. Some of his tension eased as she asked him a thousand questions and smiled brightly at all the intrigued comrades he introduced her to. It was a pleasant feeling, to for once be the one with a pretty girl on his arm. Albryan had never quite gotten to this stage of easy friendship with any past lover, where he felt comfortable enough to bring her into the space he inhabited.

He showed her the woodlands around Tenna, brought her down paths he knew like the back of his hand. Like any settlement which had been inhabited for centuries, there were extensive ruins in the forest beyond, walls and defensive structures from when their ancestors had built in stone. These had been abandoned more than five hundred years ago, after the Morgei and nonmage settlers had banded together for the last of the wars against the Novlayan invaders, who had settled most of Svanfeld and attempted to subjugate the entire continent. Warfare had been different then, the weapons of choice for the Morgei being arrows tipped with sorcerous poison and evil little blades impregnated with magic. Knowledge of the making of these weapons had disappeared from Qwu'Mallorn with the last of the blood sorcerers of old, and nowadays the Morgei fought with honest steel and cavalry like everyone else, though of course they had not foregone *all* the advantages their magic granted them.

Velda could not fail to notice Albryan's preoccupation, his brooding over the message from his family, and before he knew it, he found that she had drawn him into conversation about his fears, his brother, the situation with his father. He recounted knowing Iselma since childhood; she and Caras had gravitated together since the moment they'd met, and had married when Caras was eighteen, she a year older.

"We have a lot of advantages when it comes to healing, with the magic," he said, seated next to Velda on a low cliffside that looked out over a densely forested valley that had once hosted an extensive compound of residential buildings. Little remained of that ancient compound save a crumbling tower directly in their line of sight. The forest had crept back and covered the rest of the ruins, tangled wild fig and olive growing just below the level of the cliffside, the great yellowwoods towering overhead like spindly green parasols. Here and there Albryan could discern the paler foliage of domesticated fruit trees, apple and quince and cherry, that provided silent evidence that once humans had lived here and cultivated these slopes.

"But it's not always enough," he continued, dangling one leg over the edge of the cliff. "Sometimes things happen so quickly—go so severely wrong—that not even magic can remedy them."

"If she hadn't pulled through," Velda said softly, "wouldn't your friend Elithan have told the general? It's been a month since, after all."

Albryan grimaced. "I hope you're right." He cast around for a change of subject. "I feel like I'm always talking about myself, these days," he teased. "Isn't there anything about *you* that you feel I should know?"

"There's nothing about myself to tell," she said with a smile and a shrug. "Sometimes"—she hesitated, and looked down at her swinging feet—"sometimes, I wonder what it is you see in me, Bryan. By comparison to this life you've shown me, I seem so ordinary, so simple."

He looked dubiously at her for a moment. "And who says I don't yearn for a simple life?" She laughed, and he started laughing too. "Besides, you're not simple, even if you had a simple life before. You have a wild heart, like me."

"Well," she admitted, "I did use to sneak out at night all the time. And go hunting whenever the boys would take me. So I do know how to use a bow, at any rate. And pick a lock. Which actually came in useful when—well, that night you saved me."

"You freed all those captives with your skill at lockpicking?"

"Well . . ." Her cheeks glowed. "Not exactly . . ."

He listened in incredulity as she told him the full story, how their madcap plan to escape had come together, how she had been recaptured after making sure that everyone else had won free.

When she had finished, he cleared his throat. "Velda . . . I've heard many tales of courage, from various soldiers. I'm not sure any of them come close to this. I doubt I know any of our civilians who would remain as focused as you did. No matter how *ordinary* you think you are in comparison to them."

She shook her head. "It's like I just . . . forgot to be afraid for a while. It came back in the end, the fear. And worse than before. But in the thick of it . . ." She shuddered. "I've had nightmares about it since. About what could have happened, if just a single thing had gone differently. I don't know how I made it through."

She entwined her hand in his, and for a while they sat in silence, looking out over the forest canopy where it met a sky as blue as the faces of the little wildflowers that grew along the cliffside. She leaned against him, nestling into his shoulder, and he put an arm around her, drawing her close.


IT WAS PAST SUNDOWN WHEN he finally knocked at the door to Elithan's room. His heart leapt as he heard a muffled call from within, followed by five brisk paces, and then the door flung open and his best friend was standing there, dark eyes hooded with fatigue and jaw shadowed with stubble yet full as handsome as Albryan remembered him. By the look of it he had been interrupted in the middle of divesting his armour, for he was stripped down to his padded tunic yet his weapons-belt, silvered steel tassets and boots were still on, his golden-hued face and hands darkened with dirt and sweat. His eyes went wide, but he gave no more than the startled greeting— "Bryan!"—before Albryan flung himself upon him.

It was like finding a raft in a storm-tossed sea. It felt incredibly good to clasp Elithan again, to feel the warmth and solid comfort of his truest brother-in-arms. He didn't even mind the stink that told him it had been a hard day's worth of soldiering in the field. When he finally let go, Albryan realized that his eyes were wet and self-consciously passed his sleeve over them.

"What happened to you?" Elithan looked him up and down, gripped him by the shoulders, inspected his face as carefully as any concerned grandfather. "You've lost weight, but you don't seem nearly as dead as we all thought." He ushered Albryan inside, forced him down upon the most comfortable chair. He stood in the middle of the room, arms akimbo, shaking his head.

"We were just about to declare you missing in action, did you know that? I was going to have to tell Caras—"

Albryan immediately seized upon the name. "What happened in Catroot? Is everybody all right?"

"Everyone's alive, don't fear." Elithan made a calming gesture with his hands. "Your sister-in-law delivered early. There were complications, and for a while it looked like either she or the babe wouldn't make it, so they sent you the echo message." He rested his hands on his sword-belt. "I contacted Caras directly. Tried not to alarm him too much, made it sound like you were expected back any day. Luckily, you came through." He grinned broadly. "Iselma and the babe came through as well, so we both had good news to relay each other the last time I spoke to him. Both are out of danger now, and on their way to a full recovery."

Albryan sighed in relief. "Thank you." He hesitated. "So—a brand new niece."

"Nephew," Elithan corrected. "Apparently they plan to name him after your father."

Albryan grimaced. "A gesture, to be sure."

"You need to talk to Caras, yourself," Elithan reprimanded him gently. "He was asking me if you could get an extended leave soon, to go see him. How long has it been since you were last there, anyway?" Elithan screwed up his face with the reckoning. "It's been only once since you arrived here, hasn't it?" he said, slowly.

"Best part of five years ago," Albryan admitted, feeling ashamed. "When Ankara, the eldest, was born."

Elithan folded his arms again. "You see? She won't even recognize you. Her own uncle by blood."

"Speaking of babies," Albryan said, seeking to wean Elithan away from the subject of *his* family, "I seem to remember that I missed a naming ceremony, whilst I was languishing in mortal peril."

Elithan grinned fondly. "She was named Elissa."

"For you, I presume?"

"Perhaps so." His hazelnut-brown eyes sparkled. "She knows who her father is. As do they all. Little terrors that they are." He looked down at Albryan. "Something tells me that this is going to be a long story," he said, "and you'll have so much more of my attention once I'm no longer starving and covered in road-dust. So why don't you come with me, we'll get a wash, grab something to eat, you'll tell me all about this lovely nonmage girl you've been trailing around with—"

"By the spirit guardians—" Albryan had forgotten just how fast gossip could travel in the army.

"You speak to Gar, Gar speaks to his friend Erastes, Erastes happens to be my staff lieutenant."

"Gar was out all afternoon," Albryan countered. "Wait—Thinas appointed Erastes to you?"

"Two weeks ago. None of us felt much like celebrating, what with you still missing, but I suppose we still have the opportunity . . ."

"You bet we do." Albryan was grinning broadly despite himself.

In the end it was many hours before they arrived back in Elithan's room. Word had spread that Albryan was back at last, and he was touched to find that every one of his fellow officers wanted to welcome him "back from the dead," as they put it. Even the ones he didn't usually get along with that well. There was a lot of excitement in the mess hall that night, and Albryan found himself at the centre of it. A few were injudicious enough to ask what had happened to him, but he easily warded them away with the short phrase "classified."

Elithan was his usual self, quipping and teasing Albryan with the best of them, nothing in his manner betraying any impatience or undue curiosity. Yet one who knew him as well as Albryan did could see the tension in his affected languor, the way he stuck close to Albryan's side, rocking his cup back and forth on the table. When they finally made their way back, he latched the door securely, retrieved a bottle of clear brandy from its place on a high shelf, and handed Albryan an earthenware cup before sitting down next to him and filling it. "Now talk," he said, stoppling the bottle and stowing it at his feet, "and this better be worth the wait."

An hour later, he sat flabbergasted, his own cup forgotten next to him, staring at Albryan.

"You didn't tell Thinas any of this," he repeated.

Albryan shook his head, and Elithan reeled with disbelief.

"What would you do if you were the general?" Albryan asked in a low voice.

"I—" Elithan shook his head. "Bryan, I don't know."

"I know what Thinas would do. He would report faithfully to the Council." Elithan lifted his eyes as Albryan spoke. He thought he could see understanding dawning in them. "And then what would the Council do?"

Elithan rubbed at his stubbled jaw in thought. "Depends whose faction managed to carry the day," he said at last. "Some of the families—" He hesitated.

"Some of the families would have her put in chains for being a threat to our way of life," Albryan said bluntly. "I fooled myself, at first. Told myself I could prevent that from happening, if Thinas was on my side. But after what she did in the delta-valley—" He shivered. "That scared the piss out of me, El. How much will it scare *them*?"

Elithan shifted in his seat. "Set that aside for now," he said evenly. "She's a person, not a weapon; there's some argument for making sure she gets treated like one. This blight—" He tapped his fingers against the side of his cup. "I'm not convinced it is what you thought it was. The Border doesn't work that way. You know that it recognizes your intrinsic signature. To try and control you or access your magic—that would mean that Arran's signature was in there with yours. The Border wouldn't recognize him, and by extension it then wouldn't allow you to pass back into Qwu'Mallorn." He regarded Albryan's incredulity. "Maybe he thought he could recruit you to his side, if only you were prevented from coming back home."

Albryan shook his head. "He had me as a helpless prisoner—what better way to try and 'recruit' me? And you're guessing at what the Border's capable of, anyway."

"It doesn't fit," Elithan argued. "To take control of you—*some-how*—would mean communication across the Border. That's the whole *point* of the Border: to keep outside communications *out*. Even if you managed to pass the Border with this thing inside you, there's no way Arran could contact you once you were in."

"You *can* get outside communications past the Border. You know I've reported to Thinas from Vailana before."

"That's different—the Border recognizes you as one of its own. It wouldn't recognize Arran."

*I hope that's true*, Albryan thought as he subsided, but did not say so out loud.

"I've talked to Mialiné about this before," Elithan pressed his point.

Albryan groaned. "Pray don't forget who it was that chased me across half of Vailana," he said acidly. "You shouldn't trust that family."

Elithan shrugged. "Mia's not so bad. Nothing like her mother."

*Mia?* Albryan wondered, but supposed he was hardly in a position to lecture Elithan on his choice of female company.

"At any rate, the blight is gone; the problem we have to deal with here is the girl," Elithan said as if he'd sensed Albryan's thoughts.

"Bryan, if it were anyone else telling me this—I think I'd send them to get their heads checked immediately."

"Well, lucky for you, I've had my head checked plenty," Albryan snapped, and Elithan raised his hands in a conciliatory gesture.

"I was just saying—it's something that doesn't seem possible. Seems to defy all the laws of nature."

Albryan subsided. "I wouldn't believe it if I hadn't seen it for myself," he finally admitted. "But it's real, all right. She's real." He stared into the clear depths of his cup, then took the last swig. It was good stuff, Elithan's own brew, and it put him at ease almost as much as the presence of its maker did.

"Maybe this is some sort of . . . of response to the resurgence of blood magic," Elithan said thoughtfully, after a long silence. "I mean—you found her at the exact same time and place you first found the necromes."

Albryan stirred. "I never considered that," he said. "If it is some kind of natural reaction, magic trying to balance itself out—"

"And if it's happening now, when the blood magic is coming back, it must have happened in the past," Elithan said excitedly.

"Over three hundred years ago, at any rate." Albryan frowned. "What we need is a complete collection of histories—" He broke off, seeing Elithan's expression shift to smugness. "What?"

"As it happens," Elithan said delicately, "I know a very bright student of history. One who has access to her family library, famed as one of the most complete collections in the area."

"I've a feeling I know whom you're speaking of," Albryan said with trepidation. He sighed. "It's Mialiné, isn't it?" When Elithan did not deny it, he continued. "Dammit, El, we can't trust someone like that! Not with secrets I haven't even shared with the Commander-in-Chief!"

"But Mia may be all we have," Elithan pleaded. "Look, Bryan, we don't have to tell her everything. We can tell a half-truth. Concoct a complete lie if necessary. The most important thing is that we have access to those books. We have to start *somewhere*." He hesitated. "Do you believe Dannine Sylvaissen is dead?"

"Not for a moment," Albryan said bitterly. "Someone with her kind of power—I wouldn't believe it until I'd burned her up myself and scattered the remains." He clenched his fist.

"And she saw what this Velda can do; ergo, we must now assume that Arran also knows."

Albryan felt a sudden chill cross his heart. It was proper and logical, that deduction, and extremely obvious now that Elithan had put it into words, yet somehow, the thought had not crossed his mind before. *But Velda is safe here*, he told himself, wishing he could fully believe it.

Elithan sucked in a breath. "That hadn't occurred to you?"

"You forget, I've met him face-to-face now." Albryan shivered. "El, I felt things in that place—such power, such darkness—" He broke off, overwhelmed with dread. Since escaping from Arran's dungeon with Hiram, Albryan had not allowed himself to dwell upon what he had seen there, what he had sensed. He had come within a handsbreadth of the blood sorcerer's inner sanctum. *The thing behind the door.* Magic burned, but whatever had lain hidden there *smothered*. Albryan clapped his hand over his mouth as suddenly his stomach lurched with the memory. The immediate horror, then, had been whatever it was Arran had done to him with his set of surgical silver blades. But the smothering magic—the looming power—something far greater and darker than any of them, even Arran Sylvaissen himself—

"Are you all right?" Elithan clasped his shoulder.

"It's so much bigger than us," Albryan choked, his hands shaking with the aftermath of that memory. "You're right; we can't afford to sit idle. Arran Sylvaissen is dabbling in powers that none of us can even imagine." He took a deep breath. "I trust you. If you say that you trust Mialiné enough for this, then that's what we'll do. I'll even do my best to settle things with her. I'm not sure it'll work, since she did call me 'half-breed' in front of the general—"

"She *what?*" Elithan made a disgusted face. "Bryan, I'm sorry—
"

"Thinas keeps on saying that rather than *be sorry*, we should all *do better*." Albryan held out his empty cup. "Refill this, would you?" He gave his best friend a half smile. "I should be used to it by now. Truly. I've been called far worse, by better people."

"Have this." Elithan handed him his own untouched cup. "You know, you're not responsible for what others say about you," he said softly, as Albryan took a huge swig.

Albryan's head swam from the alcohol. "I know. Doesn't stop me from wishing, sometimes, I'd never been brought into this world. If all I am is an inconvenience—"

"You're much, much more than that." Elithan touched his arm. "If anything had happened to you, I'd be out a best friend, the true brother I never had. And frankly, I feel like we could all do with a bit of inconvenience from time to time. Stops us from getting complacent."

# Chapter XXVII
# Hugh Anspeare

FISH LOUNGED AGAINST THE FIREPLACE, taking in warmth from the rough bricks that made up the chimney, whilst the monk checked over Nico's arm.

"Try stretching a little," he advised. Nico obeyed, making a small sound of discomfort.

"Pain?"

"Not the same as before," Nico replied. "Stiffness."

"Try moving it about, like this."

Fish rested his shoulder against the mantelpiece, a residual soreness in his body soothed by the heat that made its way through him. He had recovered enough to stand and move around, so long as he didn't get too excited. It was morning outside; he could hear birdsong from the narrow window, but the day was overcast as only these mountain spring days could be. There was hardly any light in the room, certainly not enough for Brother Jakob's inspection, so the monk had brought a lantern with him. Nico was perched on the rumpled foot of what Fish supposed was technically *his* bed; they had decided several days ago that it would be convenient for them to simply move their separate beds together, rather than try and have a conversation across the room between. And there were other reasons, ones perhaps neither of them wanted to admit to, but which transcended the simple excuse of wanting to have a conversation.

That first night after his partner had finally regained consciousness, Fish had perched on the edge of his bed to say good-night, and been taken aback when Nico had suddenly wrapped his arms around him and pulled Fish into the bed beside him, holding him tighter and closer than any previous time he could remember.

It had not been a sexual embrace but a desperate, brotherly one, and Fish had been in far too much pain to have felt the slightest stir of excitement anyway. Both of them had been in pain, the embrace a strange sharing of two mutually bruised bodies. He had held Nico close, buried his face in his shoulder. He remembered the smell of camphor and dried blood, the catch of pain in Nico's breathing close to his ear, the almost defiant, steady warmth of the man who held him. Neither of them had said anything, words seeming too small to convey the weight of comfort and gratitude that was locked between them.

Somehow they had both fallen asleep like that, and slept soundly until morning, when the monk's entrance into the room had woken them. Fish studied Brother Jakob as he in turn studied his partner's damaged arm. Gods alone knew what the monk thought of them, but if he had anything on his mind, he had yet to voice it.

The monk let Nico shrug his woollen shirt back over the arm, and turned his attention to the bandages that bound Nico's hands. The cuts were deep, and until a few days ago had still opened up and bled daily, but by some miracle Nico had avoided serious infection. Fish could almost believe that the monks truly had some sort of divine aid for their healing, but Brother Jakob himself had laughed at that suggestion. "The goddess Finantha is with me, I believe, but Her ways are more mysterious than that," he'd said. "Thank your friend Bree, who knew to pack snow around his wounds, and Captain Anspeare, who listened when she gave suggestions regarding his treatment."

*Captain Anspeare.* Fish scowled. Their rescuer, protector, and captor, he was the one man Fish and his partner both wanted to see the most. But when they had both been pain-ridden, hobbled to bed, the monk had insisted that they needed to recover first; and now, when they were recovered at last, he had vanished into the mountains on some secret errand.

"I'm going to leave the bandages off now," Brother Jakob said. He gave a broad smile. "You did well. Healed up good as new."

Nico grimaced, though Fish had noticed that his partner always gave the monk a measure of respect, something like what he imagined a nephew might give his uncle. "I'll be good as new when this arm can swing a sword again."

The monk *tsk*ed. "Think of this as a respite from all of that. You can go get yourself cut up again when your wounds have finished healing." He stood, gathering up used bandages. Nico forestalled him.

"Brother, do you know when Hugh Anspeare is returning?"

"As I've said before, either today or tomorrow." The monk glanced towards Fish, who had moved from the fireplace to stand next to the lantern. "But there is a chance he will be delayed, particularly if the weather worsens."

Fish waited until the monk had left the room, then flopped down next to his partner. "Breakfast?"

"Gods, yes." Nico stretched carefully, supporting his injured arm with the other, and reached for his boots even as Fish did the same. The clothes they both wore were hardly stylish, but Fish was grateful that they were *clean*. Brother Jakob had rustled up garments from the monastery's common stores: simple woollen tunics, plain shirts and hessian trousers. He had also returned their old clothes, their boots, and their leather armour, all of it in dire need of a wash.

The hobnails on their bootsoles clacked loudly against the wooden floor when they left the room, alerting anyone in the vicinity to the fact that they were abroad, and Fish cringed a little at the noise. These were their outdoor boots, intended for camping and marching, not the kind of thing you would wear if you were going to assassinate someone. But those days, it seemed, had been left in the past. As had many things.

They took their breakfast, as they had this past week running, in the dining hall of the monastery. It was always noisy there, in a sort of homey way, the tables crowded with orphan children of all ages, dotted with the monks who watched over them. There was no high table; even the Supreme Father of the monastery, whom Nico had pointed out in his distinctive black-and-white habit, sat amongst the small children as casually as any grandfather.

Nico and Fish took seats towards the edge of the hall, where the older children tended to coalesce. Brialise, the same age as the very eldest of those children, arrived so smartly that Fish could believe she had been waiting for them in the wings. She sidled up and took a seat next to Nico, her son absent, probably with the wetnurse. Yesterday she had told Fish that she would be naming him Berton, if he survived the prerequisite three moons.

Five military men in the uniform of Svanfeld's army sat by themselves at a corner of one of the long tables: the officers Captain Anspeare had left in charge of his soldiers. He had evidently left them with some specific orders, for they would not talk to Fish and his partner beyond a word of casual greeting. Brother Jakob had made the two of them pledge that they would not leave the confines of the monastery and its gardens, and Fish suspected that he had set one or more of his orphaned urchins to watch them and make sure they kept that promise, so they had not been to visit Anspeare's camp. They were not even quite sure where he had made it: the mountains around here were densely wooded, and could have hidden a whole army from sight, let alone the hundred-odd men that Nico estimated Anspeare had brought with him.

Conversing casually with the officers was a mystifying figure—a small, dainty woman no older than fifty, with eyes the same attractive Sven blue as Nico's and chestnut-brown hair that had not yet turned fully grey. She had three children with her, obviously *her* children: two girls not far from Brialise's age, and a boy who was but ten, if Fish was any judge. She was soft-spoken and friendly, and had introduced herself as Wynne Huntersson, yet had not given a reason why she was sojourning here. Fish knew that the monks had provided her and the children with lodgings in private quarters of their own, whilst Brialise had been put in a cramped room with a clutch of orphan girls.

Nico was more unsettled by the woman and the mystery she posed than Fish was, and as they sat down with their bowls, he could see his partner's eyes shift again towards Wynne as she smiled politely at something one of the officers had said. Fish sighed and shook his head, applying himself to his food. Breakfast was a plain, but filling affair: oatmeal, milk, butter, a bit of honey.

"There's something familiar about her," Nico muttered, not for the first time.

"Your long-lost mother perhaps?" Fish teased, and his partner turned to scowl at him.

"Guess we'll figure all this out when that bastard nobleman deigns to speak with us. If he ever does." Nico quit staring at the woman at last, and began to eat.

The days of enforced lassitude had begun to chafe at them both, and after breakfast Fish suggested that they tackle the thing they had both been putting off: cleaning and sorting out the gear Brother Jakob had returned to them.

Fish could not say, in the end, whether remembering or *not* remembering was the worst part. He remembered quite well how his own shirt and jerkin had become soiled with dried mud; he could not remember how Nico's had become soaked in blood. Nico separated the cotton shirt from the leather with a grimace of disgust, the dried powder of old blood sticking them together. "Do you think either of these will ever be any good again?" he asked.

"The shirt's done for," Fish opined softly. "The leather—you can't afford to throw that away. It's the only one you've got now."

"We could go back to the village," Nico muttered, and Fish sighed. Most of their gear and money had been with the donkeys, where they'd been staying in the house of Friedma Smit. The idea of returning there, knowing what he had brought upon them, filled Fish with a sense of dread and shame too terrible to bear.

"We should leave the gear for their trouble," he said softly. Nico lowered his head and said nothing more. By a small stroke of luck, both of them had the hire-sword's penchant for hiding money in unlikely places, and Taunus's henchmen had not found all of it when they'd been frisked of their weapons. Going through the secret pockets of their trousers, boots, stockings, drawers, undershirts, jerkins, collars, and vambrace, they turned up seventeen gold pieces, twenty-five silver pawns, and thirty-one copper pennies between them.

"Tell you what," Nico remarked as they regarded their tiny pile of treasure, "we should convert this lot into bracelets and rings. Carry it with us easily, and it's better for trading than coin."

"Like mercenaries?"

"Way I see it, we *are* mercenaries. And I don't intend telling this nobleman Anspeare any different."

They took their soiled gear down to the washing-room, which to Fish was one of the most wonderful things he'd ever seen, a mystifying arrangement of copper piping carrying the water from where it was heated by the kitchen ovens all the way here, where wooden tubs and wide stone basins stood for washing bodies and scrubbing laundry, respectively. He suggested a bath before they began on the laundry; the room was empty, which was rare enough, and the hot water was always plentiful.

Brialise turned up, as she was apt to do around them these days, and for reasons known only to herself, elected to bathe herself and the babe whilst they were washing, going behind a thin muslin curtain for privacy as she sang to him, a rather gloomy song in her native tongue that rose and fell in pitch like the waves upon the sea, or possibly the branches of the forest in the wind. The Morgein waif still kept largely to herself, saying very little to Fish in regular conversation, but he was growing accustomed to her ways.

Nico and Fish had already begun with the bloodstained leather at the stone laundry basins by the time she finished her bath and wandered past. They stopped and duly made a fuss of the to-be Berton. The spark of magic he possessed had receded to a small but brightly flickering flame, from what had felt like the whole of the sun the day he was born. Even Nico, unaware that the boy was in any way special, seemed entranced by him, leaning over Fish's shoulder when he held him and grinning like a loon when the babe stared up at him.

Brialise left them to their laundry, humming to the babe in her arms, and Fish turned to regard his partner. They were both shirtless, having elected to spare the clothes they still owned from the harsh soap they were using on the leathers. Nico was scrubbing the filthy leather jerkin with his left hand, every sure stroke squeezing pinkish foam from the garment. Despite the fact that he moved mostly without pain, he heavily favoured his uninjured arm. He was still covered in bruises, the livid colours fading now to yellow and mauve but starkly visible against his pale skin. The bruising was worst over his chest where he had cracked that one rib, though there was a large one on his stomach next to his hipbone, and another on his shoulder that had gone an incongruous greenish colour.

"We're in rather bad shape, aren't we?" Fish said in a low voice. "Seventeen pieces to our name, waiting the mercy of some puffed-up nobleman with not a single blade between us."

Nico paused in his scrubbing, the hard knots in his shoulders going slack. He dipped his hands in the hot water, washing away the bloody foam. Fish absently admired the curve of the muscles in his milk-white arms as Nico turned and took him by the shoulder. "At least we're still together," he said.

That woke a grin from Fish, the first of the day, and lest things turn too serious, he splashed Nico with his washing-water. It ended, predictably, with him doubled up in laughter, leaning over the basin with Nico trying to rub soap into his hair, until the scrape of a footstep in the corridor outside alerted them both to the fact that there were other people about, and they broke off, trying to keep their faces straight as they resumed their task.

It was much later that day, when night had already fallen and they had crawled into bed, Nico squeezing his hand as they whispered goodnight, that they heard hooves pounding up the dirt road outside, the holler of a soldier, gates squealing as they slid open. Nico got up and squinted out the narrow window into the darkness. "Looks like our puffed-up nobleman's back at last," he said.

THERE WAS A MURMUR OF VOICES in the room around him, but they stilled before they could awaken any more than a mild curiosity. Fish was warm, the bedclothes were comfortable, and he had no intention of opening his eyes. Drifting on spiderwebs of dream, he thought he felt Nico's hand brush through his hair before it tightened on his shoulder and shook him gently.

"Wake up, Fish."

He stirred, mumbling an incoherent protest. Nico was on the edge of the bed, and Fish's body snaked towards him, snuggling into the hand that was on his shoulder, before he remembered that he was not supposed to do that.

Nico leaned over him, giving him another gentle shake. "Brother Jakob was just here. We're having our audience with Anspeare after all."

"When?" Fish gasped, coming alert all of a sudden.

"Now."

Fish pushed off his blanket, disoriented. The room seemed almost pitch-dark, only lantern-light illuminating Nico's solid form. Far away in the darkness, a single rooster crowed. So it was morning after all.

Nico was slowly stripping off the smallclothes he had worn to bed, and Fish could hear the usual catch of pain in his breathing.

"Fish," he finally said in a low voice, "can you help me? Completely stiffened up during the night."

It took a few tries, working together, for them to get both undershirt and tunic over Nico's head. Fish could tell that his partner was biting back curses of pain all the while. He could probably have managed the rest by himself, but Fish misliked the idea of leaving him to struggle. So he helped Nico get the trousers on and buttoned up before making him sit back down and sorting out his boots for him, tucking the ends of his trousers in and lacing the tops.

When he was done at last, Nico seized his hand. "Thank you."

Since they had both woken here, battered and exhausted and thinking of little but recovery, Nico had sought to touch him more often than usual, perhaps simply needing the human comfort, the assurance that he was not alone. Fish tried not to make too much of it, in his own mind. They'd both had a horrible experience, nearly hadn't made it out alive. It was to be expected, that Nico might take a while to come round to his normal self.

"Don't mention it," he said. "Are you going to take anything for the pain?"

Nico shook his head. "Should have all our wits about us." He got up heavily, and reached for the thick cloak that he had worn out of Ülhard. There had been a few bloodstains on it, too, but they had managed to dry-scrub them out. "There are soldiers waiting for us downstairs. They're to take us to Anspeare's camp in the forest."

*That's ominous.* Fish pulled on his own shirt and trousers, laced up his boots feeling a twinge of his own muscle-stiffness, and shook out his own cloak. He passed his hands through his hair, feeling off-balance, scruffy and itchy. He could not help a slight limp in his gait, and he noticed that Nico had folded his arms very carefully across his chest, left arm covertly supporting the injured one.

There were four soldiers waiting for them in the predawn just outside the front door to the monastery. *At least Anspeare hasn't un-derestimated us.* All four were dressed similarly, plain steel helmets and breastplates over light blue tunics, though the degree of arm and hip protection varied between them. Their thick woollen cloaks were dyed in a tricolour pattern of blue, silver and white, making them painfully visible in even the slightest amount of light. They carried the short sabres that marked them as horsemen—light cavalry, Fish guessed.

In all his time in Svanfeld, Fish had never paid much mind to its government nor military. The Guilds hired their own private units of militia when necessary, mismatched collections of mercenaries who seldom fought under a unifying banner. Like most cities, Ülhard had its own Guard—or watchmen, as they called them—and it was to them that Fish had devoted his attention, their methods and weaknesses. Fish could not recall even having seen a soldier of Svanfeld in uniform before this; the king's palace was some distance from the city, overlooking it from a high hill to the north, and the army was more often deployed to small towns along the coast, trading ports likely to become the prey of pirates and other outlaws.

For a year Nico and Fish had avoided the slightest interaction with Ülhard's watchmen. Now, Fish thought, as they were hustled through the gardens and out the gates, along the rutted road flanked on either side, they had fallen into the hands of a much more implacable authority. And their mission this time had even been perfectly legitimate and legal, when they'd started out. He'd ribbed Nico several times about "going straight." It hurt him, now, to think of how flippant he'd been, the days before that morning when he had woken to find himself adrift in a sea of mountain mist.

He wished he'd thought to speak to Nico before they left, find out what was in his partner's mind, what they would do if things rapidly disintegrated. The guard to his left was very close, and when they turned from the main road onto a narrow path carpeted with last year's leaves, he put a hand on Fish's elbow to turn him. Fish shrugged off the hand with more than a touch of disquiet, reminded that he was a prisoner in truth.

The forest was dense along the path, dawnlight just peeking through the interlaced trunks of trees here and there, birdsong floating on a light breeze. They seemed to walk for a long time, the path winding amongst gently sloping stands of birch and pine.

At last, cresting a rise, they saw a clearing with tents, sentries standing guard, the rising sun slanting in from the north. The guard by Fish's side took hold of his wrist to halt him. Fish glanced angrily at him, an older man with grey in his beard, taller than Fish—as most men were—but the soldier was not even looking at him, intent upon the man waiting for them at the end of the clearing.

Fish did not need his guard to salute this man and name him "Captain" to guess who he was. Nor did he need to see the obvious markings of rank: the immaculate segmented armour, the family colours at his belt paired with the livery of the Sven royals. The man had a quiet ease about him, a confidence that could have matched the languor which Arran Sylvaissen had always displayed. He wore command like a light garment, gesturing without a word for his four guards to fall back, which they did at precisely the same pace and distance.

"So. We are well met this morning." The man's arms were folded across his chest, his bearing nothing short of regal. Fish wondered what his story was: he looked nothing like most men from Svanfeld. His dark curly hair and amber-toned skin were reminiscent of Vailana, particularly where Fish had spent time in the south. He looked up at the nobleman with the same disquiet he had been feeling all morning. Fish was used to other men being taller than himself, but this man was an inch or two taller than *Nico*, and that he was not accustomed to.

"I won't waste any of our time with preambles." The man's voice was deep and quiet, and up close, it looked likely that he had not slept since the previous day. His eyes were a darker blue than Nico's, heavily lined. "Both of you must know who I am by now: Captain Hugh Anspeare, of the Royal Army. But I know precious little of either of you, save the names you've given the monks."

Fish heard his partner shift beside him. Hugh Anspeare might feign relaxation, languor—but Fish could feel the tension beneath the surface. The nobleman held himself as tightly poised as a mountain panther just before it pounced.

Nico shrugged. "We're just mercenaries," he said, and Fish saw a glimmer of wry amusement in the nobleman's eyes. His heart sank. *No way does he believe that.* "We live in Ülhard. Came out here on a job for the Guilds."

Anspeare reached for a silver-edged dagger tucked into his belt, and for a moment, Fish snapped to guard, but he reversed the blade and held it out.

"Brialise had this, when we found her. It must belong to one of you." He proffered it hilt first, and Nico reached out, automatically it seemed, to take it. Fish's heart was suddenly beating very loudly. *That's the dagger that killed Taunus.*

"You'd trust us with a weapon?" he asked in a low voice.

Anspeare raised an eyebrow. "Should I not trust you?" He stepped away and regarded them for a moment, the amused glint back in his eyes. "Besides, should I need to fear for myself against a beardless boy who was too weak to walk a couple of days ago, and another who still nurses his sword arm in his lap?"

Fish felt the flash of anger, the jolt of scalded pride, and let it flow through him without outlet. Better that Anspeare think them no more than a pair of boys, he knew. Better that his picture was of a pair of young flash-fire hire-mercs on their first job out of Ülhard, too city-bred to plan their escape from a mountain storm. Beside him, Nico became still as a chunk of granite yet said nothing.

Satisfaction flashed in the nobleman's eyes, and Fish had the sinking feeling that they'd failed some sort of test: of course, if they really *were* a pair of inexperienced boys, they'd have flared up at the insult. *Why is he playing this game with us?*

"Do you have any proof of that Guild association?" Anspeare was asking, and Nico passed him the crumpled, folded and re-folded letter that Fish had last seen in Harold Velman's hands. Thinking about the man gave him a queer chill between his shoulder-blades; he could not but picture the vast hordes of Taunus's newly harvested, slowly transforming dead, the faces of the men who had gotten mixed up between Fish and his brother and died for it.

Anspeare examined the letter carefully. "And your objective was . . .?"

"To rout a group of slavers they believed were getting people across the Beerstana Pass somehow."

"And how did that go wrong?"

"The slavers caught us," Nico replied shortly.

Anspeare arched a brow. "You would not be the first pair of mercenaries to come to grief in the Guilds' war against slavers," he said, folding up the parchment and handing it back to Nico, and for a moment Fish just dared to hope that they might have gotten away clear after all. But then the nobleman gestured to both of them. "Come with me for a moment, if you please."

There was no real question of what they pleased to do, not with four guardsmen behind them and many more dotting the entire campsite around, so Fish and his partner followed the nobleman further down the clearing towards where it ended in a forested rise. A long table had been raised there and draped in a white linen sheet, and as they drew nearer, Fish realized with dread anticipation that the shape beneath the linen was probably a corpse, the linen itself a shroud.

Anspeare drew the sheet away, exposing the face of the deceased, and Fish could only stare at it as a multitude of conflicting emotions coursed through him. Foremost amongst them stood relief; despite the accounts of the battle that both Brialise and Nico had given him, it was good to have the proof of his own eyes to show that *he* really was dead after all. The corpse looked half-frozen still, as though it had been recovered recently from the snowy valley where it had fallen. The blood along the death-wound had dried out, and no-one had thought to close his eyes; they stared open, even harder than they had been in life. His nose had been smashed half into his face, the blood streaked across it turned black, yet it was still recognizably his brother.

Anspeare stepped away, watching them both closely, and dread coiled in Fish's stomach. *This is what he went away for*, he realized, *this is the prize he wanted to retrieve. But why?*

"Who was this man?" the nobleman asked.

Nico's voice was steady as he answered. "The slave-trader who captured us."

"What was his name?"

Nico shook his head. "I don't know."

"And you?" Anspeare turned towards Fish, who dragged his eyes away from his dead brother's face. "Can you give me his name?" He stepped closer, and suddenly his hand was on Fish's shoulder. "You know who he was," he whispered. "This wasn't just a job to you. This was something more. *He* was more." Fish was aware of how loudly he was breathing, how much the sight of that corpse had shaken him.

Ferried him back to their duel in the snow, the knowledge that he was to die by his own brother's hand . . .

"Just tell me his name," Anspeare whispered, and Fish couldn't look away.

"Taunus Sylvaissen."

No surprise appeared in those dark-blue eyes, only satisfaction, and Fish realized with a sickening swoop in his stomach that he had already known. *Damn you, Brialise*, he thought sourly. There was no knowing what else the girl had told him, nor how much she truly knew of Taunus and what he had been to Fish.

The nobleman stepped back, glancing again between Fish and his partner. "And which one of you killed him?"

"I did," Nico replied, glancing covertly at Fish, who could feel his cheeks flushing. The trap was sprung, and he had walked them right into it, although he did not yet know exactly what it was that Anspeare was hoping to catch.

"Quite the achievement," Anspeare breathed. "A young mercenary—ordinary as can be—getting close enough to the son of Arran Sylvaissen, mage-king of Vailana, to drive a dagger into his throat." He clasped his hands behind his back and paced to the left, gazing into the trees. Following that gaze, Fish realized with trepidation that they were surrounded on all sides. The four guardsmen who had brought them here lurked behind; more had come up whilst they'd been talking, arranging themselves so casually that he had barely noticed, and still more, a dozen at least, had been stationed in the trees beyond the clearing all along. Covered on all sides, and yet still he could not guess at Anspeare's intentions.

"This whole situation makes very little sense," Anspeare said, still looking into the trees. "Am I to believe that you achieved this feat without any magical aid?"

"Brialise helped us," Fish threw out, desperately. A glimmering of Anspeare's purpose was making itself known at last, and suddenly he wanted to be anywhere in the world but here.

The nobleman turned to him with a sardonic smile. "Brialise has untold amounts of kindness, determination, courage," he said, "but these are not things that would avail her in a duel against a blood sorcerer. Her Mage-Gift is small; her abilities are nowhere near what someone like Taunus Sylvaissen could conjure." His eyes fell squarely on Fish, who felt his heart hammer in his chest. *What precisely did she tell him? That I have the Mage-Gift? Or more? Why is he looking at me that way?*

"Another thing that confuses me," the nobleman continued, "is how a pair of ordinary hire-mercs from Ülhard would be able to identify Taunus Sylvaissen in the first place. *I* did not know the man's description, only his father's. Did the Guilds send you two to assassinate him?" He looked between Fish and his partner, who both stood dumbstruck now. "Without any magical aid? How would the Guilds know that he was here, when king and council did not? What am I to make of all this?" He paused, and spared another glance between the two of them. "If either of you can possibly assuage my confusion, now would probably be the time to do it."

Nico said nothing, and Fish felt his guts lurch as he realized that the two of them had run out of things to say. Still, it wasn't like Anspeare could force them into talking. Unless he decided to torture them. And what could possibly compel a straight-laced army captain like this one to torture people for information, Fish could not guess.

"We can't, I'm afraid," he said flippantly, and saw the nobleman's eyes darken. "So are you going to let us go our way?"

"Back to Ülhard?" Anspeare almost whispered, something unreadable sparking in his eyes.

"That's where we live." The nobleman didn't need to know that they had resolved not to return there. "And our pay's waiting."

"And may wait a long time yet," Anspeare said softly.

Nico stirred. "What do you mean?"

"You left Ülhard over a month ago," the nobleman replied. "Is that right?"

Nico nodded.

"A stroke of luck for you." There was a strange, desperate emotion behind Anspeare's eyes now. "Ülhard has been taken, occupied by an enemy army," he said flatly. "I received word of this only yesterday, though the battle was fought over two weeks ago. It appears that our king and crown prince were both killed during the battle."

Fish could not have cared less about which members of the royal family had survived or not; the stirring in his guts was for the people he had known. He'd never spared a great deal of thought for the folk he associated with in Ülhard, besides Nico, but suddenly he felt fear for them rise in him. For Stonetooth Skimmer and his brother, widely regarded as fixtures of their particular community. Their landlady and their neighbours, the girls who worked at the bath-house, the boys who sold papers of news every day in the streets. Ordinary people, none of them with the means to flee the city. He flicked his gaze towards the deceased Taunus. *Father has three more children. No shortage of battle commanders there.*

"Wh-what kind of army?" he heard himself ask, almost incoherent with shock. Beside him, Nico was not faring much better; he seemed unable to put words to anything that was going on in his head.

Anspeare's countenance was as still as any deep lake of the mountain valleys. "I think you already know that, don't you, Benjamin Fisher?" he said, and Fish started at the use of his full name, his full alias.

"I—I don't know what you're saying."

"I ask you two again," Anspeare said coolly, "to tell me who you are and how you killed Taunus Sylvaissen." When neither of them answered, he turned upon his heel and began to pace back and forth. "So, since you both refuse to enlighten me, I must draw my own conclusions. And one thing is painfully obvious: the pair of you are no ordinary hire-mercs. Despite what you may believe, I have met all kinds of scum in my life, the dregs of the underworld, the bruisers of Svanfeld's alleys." He turned to face Nico. "I know an assassin when

I see one, Nico Klavbert."

Nico was still holding the dagger he had taken from Anspeare earlier, and for a moment it seemed like he might spring at the nobleman and use it. But Anspeare turned away, showing not the slightest trace of fear, and folded his hands behind his back again.

"But whomever you've murdered, it's in the past now, in a city that is no longer under the rule of any land's law." He shrugged, and resumed pacing. "I do not care about that. *You*, on the other hand..." He came to a stop directly in front of Fish. "You're no common hire-muscle from off the street. Vailanan name, Morgein looks, a certain manner that marks you as being born into the noble class, though you do of course try to hide it." He met Fish's defiant gaze, eyes boring into him as if he could open his skull and pry the truth loose. "It took a sorcerer to defeat Taunus," he said softly, "a magician as powerful as himself. Are you that magician, Fisher? Tell me about your family. Tell me your *real* name."

Silence fell sharply, neither of them giving any ground, till suddenly it was broken by Nico.

"Are you trying to imply that Fish is in some way—magical?" Nico guffawed loudly, and Fish felt a rush of affection towards his partner. "That's the stupidest thing you've said so far."

Anspeare stepped back, brought two of his guards forward with a snap of his fingers. "Restrain this man," he ordered, indicating Nico.

Fish stepped forward, having some thought to intervene, but

quick as a snake, Anspeare's hand closed on his arm, forestalling him. Fish briefly tried to pull free, to no recourse. The nobleman was much stronger than Fish, in his currently depleted state. Fish glared up at him, but subsided as his guards pinioned Nico between them. His heart was beating loudly now, and he could feel Anspeare's grip through both his shirts.

Anspeare looked at Nico with distaste. "I've seen a hundred of your ilk in the alleys of every town I can name," he said. He released Fish, retreating to stand an equal distance between him and his partner. "And I have no use for you." He gestured to his guards, and his voice was steady. "Take this man away. And for the crimes he's committed against this country, hang him."

Disbelief rushed in on Fish. "You—you wouldn't do it," he sputtered. "It's not the law, you've no proof—"

"The *law*?" There was something deranged in the nobleman's bright eyes now. "My cousin is dead, and his son into the bargain. Svanfeld has no king. *I* am the only law that remains." He turned back to his guards, who had already begun to drag Nico towards the forest, with little success as he was struggling mightily against them. "Get him up there right now!"

Fish had no weapon on him, had run out of time to consider any of his options. But instinct stirred in him as it had before when Nico was in danger, and this time he did not lose control in a fiery blast.

The wave of magic throbbed through the camp, stirring tent canvas, sending every guard to his knees. The moment it radiated from Fish, snapping through reality like a windswell along a cliff, everything happened at once.

Anspeare staggered back from the magic, throwing both hands up, turning his face away, his wrists crossed, glinting silver from his vambrace. Fish felt the magic stutter around him, felt the connection break in the presence of the silver.

Nico tore loose from his captors, the dagger he was still holding flicking scarlet. Rather than grab for him, both guards fell back in apparent terror, one of them bleeding. Nico seized the hilt of the sabre at that one's belt, pulling it free as the man fell to the ground and crawled precipitously away. Nico was still several yards away from Fish; he gripped both sword and dagger, and made straight for Anspeare. But before he could move more than a few paces forward, the nobleman recovered, steadying his feet. His hand went to the back of his belt, and drew out—of all things—a long whip that charioteers might once have used to bewilder their competition.

The whip cracked, and Fish's eyes widened in horror as silver coils flew out in a blinding arc—no greyish paint this, but *real* silver, and some part of him had to pause to wonder at the resolve of a man who would have *a whip* dipped in molten metal just to gain the edge in a fight. Magic recoiled, snapping wildly along the ether, and frantically he recalled it before he lost control and had it rebound on him again—

And then Anspeare was on him, quicker than he would have believed for such a big man, or perhaps it was just that his own reflexes were still sluggish after his injury. In one fluid movement, he cannoned into Fish, twisted both his arms together behind his back and wrapped the hardened coils of the silver whip around his wrists, cutting off the flow of the magic, and wrested him down to the ground, his knee landing in the small of Fish's back, his full weight behind it, pinioning him as securely as a trussed-up lamb for the spit roast.

Fish landed facedown in the dirt, spitting out pieces of bark and earth, trying to turn his face upwards to see what was going on, almost screaming aloud as pain twisted his shoulders and knifed upwards into his spine. Anspeare was panting loudly, and Nico's hobnailed boots slid to a halt just a few yards ahead, a curse tripping from his lips along with a low call of his partner's name.

"Drop the sword, or you know how this ends," Anspeare said harshly, and Fish realized that there was a blade at the back of his neck: Anspeare's own sabre, the cold steel kissing him in a fine line just above his collar. He squirmed against his bonds, and was rewarded with a harder dig from that heavy knee. Pain arced along his spine, and he sobbed into the dirt.

"You don't think I'd do it," Anspeare hissed. The unyielding steel pressed down a little lower, making Fish gasp at its coldness, then suddenly was lifted and gone. Anspeare straightened his pose a little, and Fish heard the whisper of steel sliding into leather as the sword was sheathed. "And you'd be right."

"What are you playing at?" Nico whispered.

"No game." Anspeare settled his weight easily, still restraining

Fish. "Apologies for pretending that I was going to hang you. But I needed to get a reaction. I *had* to know whether my suspicions were correct." Fish could hear the smirk creeping through his voice. "As it turns out, they were. Spectacularly so." He leaned over Fish, brushed just enough leaves and dirt away from his face so he could glare up at his captor. "You fought Taunus, matched him in magic, weakened him so your big friend here could take him down with a dagger. Working for the Guilds—hiding your true identity—consorting with assassins and the like—I'd wager my name that you're one of Arran Sylvaissen's brood. That man you killed was your brother."

Fish was pressed to the ground so hard he could not have answered even if he had wanted to. He could practically feel Nico's stance wilt.

"If you two had only been honest with me from the start," Anspeare declared, "this might have gone easier. Now, Nico, the way I see it, you've got three options right now. Option one: you attack me like you want to. I can't say for sure how far you'll get, but you can see for yourself how many soldiers there are surrounding you. Maybe you'll kill a few, but you'll never touch me, because the moment you move, I'm retreating and dragging your young friend out of here. And you've seen how fast I am."

Nico said nothing, and the nobleman continued, "Option two: you turn around and walk away. You have the sword, the dagger, whatever else you're carrying on you right now. My guards will let you go. You never have to see my face again."

Fish squirmed in incredulity, wishing he could see Nico's face. *There's no way he's serious. He can't be trusted. And there's no way Nico would ever take that option . . . Would he?*

"And option three?" Nico demanded quietly.

"Three: you put down that sword. You stay. I've a place for you too, Nico, together with your partner. Brother Jakob Corder has told me how close you two are: true comrades-in-arms. You defeated the blood sorcerer together. A mage and a fighter, working together with that level of trust—that's rare, and useful."

"You'd just let me go, though?" Nico's voice was low, but steady. "Let me walk away?"

Anspeare straightened a little more, and Fish could feel the weight shift down even harder upon his back. "You have my word," he said. "As a prince of Svanfeld, on the name of my late cousin, King Falcon Häger. You can go, and live whatever life you might choose."

"Me," Nico said. "But not Fish."

Anspeare sighed. "I am sorry, but no. The very future of this land is at stake. More may depend on your friend than what you can imagine. Even if he will not co-operate, his life may yet buy safety and survival for many more."

"Co-operate?" Nico repeated.

"I want a mage working for me." Anspeare was looking down at Fish now. "I need magic to fight magic. Svanfeld is at war now, and we haven't a hope of victory unless we can find some way to counter the dark sorcery that has been unleashed upon us. And if you refuse"—his voice darkened—"perhaps Arran Sylvaissen will pay a rich ransom for his defected son."

"If I put down this sword," Nico said, "I want you to swear you will not do that. That no matter what, you won't ransom him. Make him your prisoner, or kill him now, but you wouldn't keep a man with that hanging over his head. Not unless you have shit for honour."

"Lectured by an assassin on the meaning of honour," Anspeare remarked wryly. He was silent for a long moment, as if considering. "But you have the right of it," he finally admitted. "Very well. I will not sell him to Arran."

At last, the sword clattered to the ground. Nico kicked it a few yards away from him. Craning his head upwards as far as it would go, Fish could see his partner tucking his silver-edged dagger into his belt.

Anspeare breathed a long sigh of what sounded like relief. "I'm going to let you up now," he said to Fish, and suddenly the crippling weight on his lower back was gone. Fish felt almost as limp as he had the day he woke from unconsciousness, and could only whimper with pain as a pair of seemingly disembodied hands tried to lift him from the ground.

"Fish." There was an unexpected note of concern in Anspeare's voice now. "If I release these bonds, do I have your word that you will not try to use magic on me again?"

Painfully, Fish twisted sideways, looking up at his captor. "I doubt I'd be able to even if I wanted," he spat, which was not quite true. He cocked his head. "Perhaps if you'd been honest with us from the start, you wouldn't have to worry about me roasting you the moment you let your guard down."

Anspeare coloured visibly, and Fish allowed himself a small measure of satisfaction. The way it had fallen out, Fish felt a grudging respect for this man that he'd never have had, had it not come to a physical trading of blows. Arran had never taught his children to deflect attacks on their magic, and Fish had always blithely assumed that there was little that could be done by a nonmage to counteract magic. Now, he knew that wasn't true.

"You have your wish," he growled, knowing defeat when he saw it. "You have your *ally*. There's no-one hates Arran Sylvaissen as much as what I do, and you have my word that I won't fry you *and please now can you get this damn thing off?*"

There was a grunt of assent, and Fish felt himself drawn back onto his face, the bonds picked loose. His shoulders were finally freed of tension, and he felt as though he could have cried in relief. Strong hands gripped him by both arms and pulled him back to his feet. Still unbalanced, he vainly tried to disengage himself from the man who held him, but to his surprise he saw that Anspeare had drawn away and it was Nico's hands that had come to support him. He leaned back against his partner, accepting his assistance and strength. The sun had finally risen across the clearing, hailing in a warm spring day at last, and Fish's head was surprisingly clear.

"So where do we start?" he asked, regarding the sombre nobleman before him.

Anspeare crossed his arms. "Let's start at the beginning, Fish. How about you tell me your real name?"

# Chapter XXVIII
# Brothers in Arms

FOR A PEOPLE LIVING IN FEAR of imminent attack by some deranged sorcerer who commanded living corpses, for a land now at war against a murderous despot with untold dark powers, the monastery was surprisingly peaceful, noticeably calm.

It had been this way even with the monks who had raised Nico on the other side of the Svanlyn mountains. Rather than panic, the Sven brethren prayed. Whether that would save them in the end, Nico had no idea, though he knew from experience that prayer was not the only resource available to the holy men.

After prying the whole story of Fish's complicated past out of him, Hugh Anspeare had simply sent the two of them back to the sick-room. "Until you're both fully healed," he had commanded, and Nico had been tempted even then to flick out the dagger at his belt and hurl himself at the man who dared command him anything.

But since then—absolute quiet. Even Fish had said little, seeming resigned to what they had promised the damned nobleman, and reluctant to discuss anything further. The only talk he showed any true interest for was of what might have happened to their old friends in Ülhard, grim as such talk might be. News of the city's fall, of the king's death, had spread since that morning, and the atmosphere of the whole monastery had collapsed into cheerlessness. The news had been particularly hard on "Wynne Huntersson." Once Nico had seen her with Anspeare, the two of them obviously more than just companions of circumstance, he had finally read the riddle before him. He had muttered to Fish, who was as usual right beside him: "It's her. Bronwyn. She's the queen of Svanfeld."

Fish had just looked puzzled, and for a moment Nico had wondered if his young partner had ever even deduced that the country he currently resided in had a queen in addition to its king. But Fish had finally muttered back, "I suppose that makes sense."

In one of those grim ironies of life, the weather had begun to turn that very day, galloping into spring with blue skies and golden sunlight, happy notes of birdsong in budding green branches, in stark contrast to the gloom that Nico now found wherever he went.

Truth was, things were stirring in Nico too, things he found hard to put a name to, and his frustration with the whole situation that lay before him had been mounting for some days now. He was tired of the sickroom, fed up with its medicinal smells and silences, weary even of the attentions of the kind-hearted monk who tended to him. So the moment Fish had made the tentative suggestion of taking a walk downstream to a small lake that Brother Jakob knew, Nico had pounced on the idea. Anspeare was allowing them to go, reiterating that they were not his prisoners but *operatives*, and probably well aware that it wouldn't be easy for them to escape him anyway. His own men were deployed on the road north; south, along the river, a single bridge that was watched over by the local militia connected the only road to the monastery with the main road that ran down to the town of Albrecht. East and west lay only impassable forest and mountain peak; high cliffsides rose in both directions, and would turn them either north or south before they got very far.

As usual, this morning Nico had awoken early, and was now moving about the room as quietly as possible, checking the travel-pack they were taking along. One way or another, he and Fish had gathered all they needed for a short camping trip. It was the ground coffee that had been the hardest. The monks of Svanfeld famously did not drink coffee, but Nico had managed to make the acquaintance of a particularly scholarly young brother who kept his own private supply.

It was too early for breakfast, yet the sun was already streaming into the room from the open window. Nico turned and looked at his partner, still outstretched beneath the sheets and snoring softly, and those barely-identified feelings fluttered inside him.

Fish had always been good to look at. Back when they were sharing a small room in the city that was now fallen, it had been commonplace for Nico to wake before he did, and he had liked nothing better sometimes than to prop himself up on an elbow and simply gaze at his young partner's slumbering face. It was nothing more than pure physical admiration, he remembered telling himself. If he sometimes thought of sliding his hand into those dishevelled curls, of gently tasting the boy's slightly chapped lips—well, that was nothing Fish needed to know about, and Nico was perfectly capable of controlling his own urges.

It was the same now, yet different. Fish still slept in an untidy sprawl, one hand flung out over his head and the other resting on his stomach; his face had not changed noticeably, even if the curls had grown a little longer and perhaps some more peach-fuzz had started to come in around his sideburns and upper lip.

But there had been a sweetness about those bygone days, an innocence that was not there anymore. In the past, Nico had been able to tell himself that his feelings for Fish indicated nothing more than a strong brotherly bond between the two of them. He'd had plenty of "little brothers" in the past, after all. He'd shared a small room with five other orphan boys for most of his life. He had drifted to sleep at night to the sound of their breathing, woken when one of them would have a nightmare and comforted him, tussled with them the way he did with Fish.

That pretence had shattered inside him now, and he wondered if he would ever be able to resume it. Nico remembered feeling a certain protectiveness towards his younger friends; he remembered the camaraderie with the boys his own age, even the budding feelings towards one particular boy who had changed his whole outlook on himself. Those feelings paled before the bond he felt between himself and Fish. There were times he thought he might not survive losing him.

That was a hard thought, and every time it came, Nico felt a deadly fear take hold of him. *Better to lose a brother than a lover*, he told himself. To deepen his relationship with his partner was a treacherous path. Had he not realized that, once again, just a week ago? Nico had read Hugh Anspeare, correctly, as a man with high moral limits and standards, but would still have said anything to get him to lift his blade away from Fish's neck. The fear he'd felt in that moment was not something he was likely to forget in a hurry, and every time Fish had taken off his shirt since, the mauve-black bruises that Anspeare had inflicted had been there to remind him.

Fish stirred in his sleep, mumbling something incoherent, and Nico, having endured enough of his own lonesome feelings this morning, decided that it was time to wake him.

Less than an hour later, they were outside, and Fish was fiddling with the straps of the heavy pack, adjusting them to suit his short stature. The air was already warm, and he had rolled the loose sleeves of his blouse up over his elbows.

"Let me know when it's my turn to carry that," Nico said as his partner hoisted the pack onto his shoulders. Fish snorted.

"According to Brother Jakob, there's still a chance your ribs and shoulder haven't fully healed," he said bluntly. "So I'm carrying it alone. I'm not even sure you ought to be walking this far with me."

"I'm not the one who was hurting too badly to even walk at all," Nico returned. He paused as his partner set off, boots crunching on the gravelled path. "Why was that?" He caught up to Fish easily enough. "Was it something that—he—did to you?"

Fish glanced towards him but did not answer immediately, and Nico struggled to make out the expression on his face.

"If we're still partners after all that's happened," Fish finally said in a low voice, "I suppose it's time you began to learn. About—about my magic."

"Of course we're still partners," Nico said impatiently, and the boy smiled.

"Well, before this, I hadn't used any magic in nearly eight years." He glanced at Nico's slightly incredulous expression. "I mean it. Never. Not even in situations where it might have saved the day. You see, anyone who uses magic can also detect it." He rubbed the back of his neck, as if in remembrance of an uncomfortable feeling. "It's— it's like the wind, or the sun. You can't disguise it." He looked away. "But it did become easier, over the years, for me. Not using it. I was at a point where I didn't even think to touch it, didn't have to guard myself against that. Until . . ." He drifted off, gazing around at the trees to either side. Beams of sunlight fell across his face as he walked.

"Until we met those creatures," Nico muttered at last, when

nothing more seemed forthcoming.

"Until I needed to protect you." Fish sighed and quickly looked away, as if he regretted the words. "Well, then it all came out at once. Even more powerful than before, but with less control. And I was trying to hurt Taunus—but the user of uncontrolled magic is a bigger danger to *himself* than anyone else." He moved closer to Nico again. "I was trying to wield lightning, and it got away from me. I lost control for just a moment." He stopped, so abruptly that Nico nearly cannoned into him on the path, which was beginning to lead steeply downhill.

"Nico, I—I don't actually know how much control I have," Fish confessed, looking earnestly up at him. "Now that it's loose again, I don't think there is any putting it back, and it scares me. Knowing how strong that power is, and what it could do to me."

This last was delivered in nearly a whisper, and Nico felt his own throat go dry. "Is that the real reason you wanted to come out here?" he asked. "To regain this control?"

"I certainly can't unleash this anywhere other people are about," Fish replied. "Nic, I hope this doesn't alarm you—"

Nico put a hand on his shoulder, forestalling him. "I may be alarmed, but I'm still here, aren't I?"

Fish rolled his eyes and struggled to hide his grin, resuming the walk. "Gods only know for how long yet."

"You may find I'm harder to get rid of than you thought."

"Oh?" Fish fell easily into the banter. "There's a lake up ahead.

Pulling you to the bottom ought to do it."

"You could try," Nico returned, and for a while they traded mockery back and forth, relieving the tension of that too-honest conversation. The path wound ever more steeply downhill, finally coming out of the forest to meet a rushing, stony brook. Long grass and ferns fringed the banks, sombre pines standing sentinel on the opposite bank. Fish stopped to dip his hands in the water, exclaiming at the cold but even so proceeding to wipe the sweat from his face and the back of his neck. Nico stood beside him, casting an eye over the brooding trees, wishing that the stream and the pines did not remind him so strongly of the place he had called home as a child.

The path grew rougher as it followed the water downhill, narrowing to little more than a goat-track even as the stream grew wider and noisier, sending up a fine mist as it thundered down ochre-tinted boulders on its way toward the bottom of the mountain. The moisture-tinged spring air was as fresh as sparkling wine, but it turned out to be a taxing walk for them both, newly recovered as they were. The going was steep, the gravel underfoot treacherously wetted by the spray, and a few times Nico thought he might misstep and send them both tumbling towards the bottom of the trail.

But his fragile balance won out, and soon enough the path abruptly levelled, the river alongside rushing through a last steep ravine to fall a dozen feet into a deep pool which formed the mouth of a small, arrow-shaped lake cradled amongst the forested hills. The path wound away from the river, snaking through the woods, which at this height were less pine-dominated, oak and ash and star chestnut making their appearance, new growth of ferns providing a lush carpet. They followed the trail around until it led out upon the quiet lakeshore, a comfortable distance away from the thundering of the ravine, cool water rippling over beds of river-smoothed pebbles and fine grey gravel.

Nico sank down beneath a large star chestnut tree, sighing in relief for the respite. Fish dropped the pack beside him and moved towards the lakeshore, seemingly not tired at all. There was a pent-up, fiery energy about him now, and Nico watched him covertly.

Fish looked far more like himself than he had for weeks; they were both wearing what they could of their old clothes from Ülhard, which were more suited for wandering through the mountains. Fish had not had to scrub bloodstains out of his shirt and jerkin, yet to Nico's eyes he looked quite a bit shabbier than when they had started out, a few weeks that might as well be a lifetime ago. His leather jerkin was scuffed and scratched, though luckily not ripped.

Anspeare had restored the weapons that Taunus had taken from them: their daggers, the slim curved sword that Fish favoured and Nico's own short blade. Without discussing it, both of them had buckled their weapons at their belts this morning before leaving. Small chance of needing them in the wilderness, yet Nico had felt uneasy leaving anything precious behind at the monastery.

A sudden breeze lifted Fish's hair as he stood by the edge of the lake, and the tension around him increased almost palpably. Slowly he lifted his face to the sky, the sun at its zenith shining full upon him. Nico had thought he knew his partner's face as well as anyone could know another, but the vacant, yet focused expression with which Fish stared at the sun was new to him. He leaned backwards, seeming almost weightless, unfazed by its glare. Nico could have sworn that his boots were no longer connected to the ground.

Fish moved slowly, shifting into a new position, head still thrown backwards, movements languid, eerie in their deliberate strength. Another position, and then another, muscles flowing with a palpable sense of rightness even as the strange apprehension continued to build around him. It was like a sword-dance slowed right down, and Nico thought he could recognize some of Fish's distinctive style of fighting in the movements. The tension built steadily, like the nervous energy of a thunderhead before the storm, until Nico could hardly bear to look at him, yet he knew he could not look away.

The dance stopped all at once, Fish coming to rest on one knee with his arms outstretched and his head thrown back, and *something* crested, overflowing through and out of him. Nico could not contain a gasp of fright. Lightning, bolts of it, blue and fierce, flashed and danced around his partner's prone form, across his outstretched hands, along the skin of his face, which was still and calm. Nico watched with bated breath as the lightning arced forth, soundlessly exploding outwards towards the sky, branching out in a great glowing tree over the surface of the lake. It fissured and glimmered, a nest of silent blue snakes as cold as stone. It was beautiful, yet Nico felt a primal fear arise deep within him.

Fish curled in on himself, appearing to push through something as sticky and unyielding as cold tar to bring his wrists together crosswise, palms of both hands spread and facing outwards. He moved his right fingers into a complicated, deliberate gesture, and the lightnings flickered and glowed and then dispersed, vanishing so silently and suddenly that Nico blinked and wondered if perhaps he had been imagining things. Tension drained out of the air as if a plug had been pulled somewhere in the ether. Fish gave a groan and collapsed to a crouch with none of his usual grace, his hair hanging limp with exertion. Nico wanted to go over to him, but was held back by apprehension. Fish had not warned him away, yet he could sense the danger around his young partner, thick as pea soup fog.

For just a moment, Nico understood precisely how his distant nonmage ancestors must have felt, coming to land on this wild shore a thousand years ago and seeing a display like *that*. He shivered, thinking of the fireside stories people in Svanfeld told, of the slender dark Morgei with their inscrutable almond eyes, watching from the primaeval forest as the men of Svanfeld and Vailana stumbled through their hunting grounds.

Yet the eyes he imagined were the same as Fish's eyes, deepset and golden, and Nico had never feared what lay in those eyes, not until Fish had flung a sizzling cloud of red-hot energy a few feet over his head and made it rain body parts around him. How dangerous was he, truly?

Fish got to his feet, moving cautiously as if to contain pain, and had never looked less dangerous. The face he turned towards his partner was the old familiar face: his lovely, expressive eyes, his crooked nose. He massaged his shoulder as he slouched towards Nico.

"Like working an overstretched muscle," he muttered, as he reached his partner and sat down heavily in the shade of the same tree.

Nico cleared his throat. "Fish—that was—" He broke off. "I don't have words to describe it."

"You're easily impressed." Fish chuckled darkly. "That was me just trying to relearn how to hold a sword."

*A sword of fire and lightning.* Nico shivered despite himself. "In a fair fight, there's no way someone like Anspeare could take you," he said in a low voice.

"Most fights aren't fair." Fish looked over at him with his usual crooked grin, sardonic this time. "What are you thinking?"

"Where this lake narrows," Nico replied, pointing, "a man could swim to the other side."

"Or roll a log down to the water and paddle behind it," Fish said. "And then he'd be alone in the wilderness beyond." His eyes met Nico's, and the grin faded from his face. "You could go, Nico, but I can't."

"I told you already, I'm not going anywhere without you," Nico bit back. "Why can't you go? Why can't we escape? None of those soldiers would be any match for your magic—you could raise your hand and sweep them away like—like ants!"

"And the moment I did raise my hand"—Fish's tone was cold, and his hand was in the air as if to demonstrate—"the flare of magic would signal *anyone* else. They would know *exactly* where I was, and who I am. I told you, anyone who can use magic can also sense it. The more powerful you are—the more of it you use—the stronger the impression you leave behind. It would not even be a day before some other member of my family tracked us down, and once they could sense me, they'd just keep coming. Taunus was the weakest of my siblings, the least disciplined, and I couldn't even take *him* in single combat!"

A ringing silence fell, and Nico subsided in dismay. "I'm sorry," he finally muttered. "That's why you had to hide it so deep, isn't it?"

"Yes." Fish was looking down at his hands, his knuckles clenched into fists, and Nico wondered briefly whom it was he wished to hit.

"Are we . . ." Nico hesitated, wondering how to phrase the question. "Are we in danger here?" he finally asked.

"Probably not." Fish looked up, and the anger had subsided from his eyes. "They've got to know where I am, more or less, after what happened with Taunus. But I doubt they'd come here." He glanced towards the sky. "At any rate, I would know they were coming, since I'd be able to sense them in turn. But none of them has been around; no-one came to investigate Taunus's death. That's Arran's way." He seemed almost lost in thought. "Devote your whole life to him, but one misstep and you're no longer in the fold. I guess he has more pressing matters at hand than mourning my departed brother." He folded his arms across his knees and leaned his head against them. "Figures I'd have the strongest Mage-Gift to be found," he sighed bitterly, "only for it to be completely useless."

"Not completely useless," Nico rebutted softly. "You got rid of Taunus."

"*You* killed Taunus."

Nico shook his head. "I just finished him off. It was you who fought him." He moved closer to Fish, touching his shoulder cautiously. The boy responded by sinking into his embrace, closing his eyes as Nico's arm encircled him.

"Have you had enough exercise," Nico murmured, "or shall I beat you a few times at some *real* fighting?"

Fish's eyes flew open, and suddenly the grin was back, all the mischief that Nico loved to see in his face. "You never beat me."

"When you're at your best," Nico countered, mussing his hair. "You're not at your best now."

"Oh, I'll show you which one of us is doing better," Fish growled, getting to his feet.

They spent the rest of the daylight dancing back and forth across the forest floor and the pebbled beach, landing in the water once or twice when the sparring was particularly intense. Nico's arm was too stiff, his fingers shorn of their accustomed dexterity, their grip so compromised that Fish managed to swat his sword out of his hands at least half a dozen times. Fish's own agility was not what it normally was, yet Nico judged him to have come out of their ordeal a lot sounder than himself. He was aching by the end, when the sun set in a golden blaze over the mountain behind them as they lay stretched out, panting, on the stony shore of the lake.

"I'm famished," Fish managed at last. "What did you pack for food?"

They shared a simple meal of bread and sausage and cheese as the sun disappeared and the waxing moon rose out across the surface of the water. They had fallen back into their usual style of easy friendship, himself and Fish, and neither of them had to say anything; their silence was comfortable, companionable. It gave Nico a sliver of hope. Perhaps things could return to how they'd been before. If he wanted them to.

"Did we bring any booze?" Fish asked. The world around them was quiescent. Somewhere in the distance, Nico could hear the clanging cry of a nightjar, underscored by the constant deep rumbling of water across the steep ravine at the far end of the lake. Closer by, there was only the lapping of the nocturnal tide on the waters, and the soft noises they made breathing and moving.

Nico grinned at his partner's question. "That is not something that the monks would think we needed," he said mock-admonishingly.

"Yet Brother Jakob gave you *something* to help you sleep."

Nico gazed at him. "Fish, do you really believe I'd stoop so low as to pinch a bottle of medicinal alcohol from the good monk who has taken so much care to heal me and make my nights free of pain?"

Fish said nothing, just looked at him and raised one expressive eyebrow. Nico gave in with a dry chuckle.

"Alright—it's wrapped in my cloak."

"I knew I could count on you," Fish said as he got to his feet. Returning with the precious bottle, a flask of golden glass filled with a paler golden liquid, he popped the cork and took a sniff. "Whoa! What is in this stuff?"

"It starts out life as apple cider in the autumn," Nico explained. "The monks then take it outside in the winter, where it will freeze. Or at least, the watery part will. Throw the ice away, keep what's left, and you have *that*. After a few cycles at least, but that's the gist of it."

Fish grinned and took a swig before Nico could stop him. The result was predictable: choking, coughing, exclamations and curses as the fiery liquid ran down his throat and melted the wax in his ears. Nico rescued the precious bottle from Fish's grasp and carefully sipped at it. His partner flopped down unsteadily on the pebbles next to him.

"I'm not sure you're cut out for life in the mountains, partner," Nico teased.

"Gimme a bottle of *that* e'ery day and I'll be happy."

Nico took another careful swig from the bottle and lay back on the gravel. The drink burned some of his tension away, and he drifted for a moment, light-headed. The sky above them was carpeted with stars.

"They say that down at the big lake"—Nico fumbled with the words, and began again—"by the shore of Lake Mountaindale, that's where the holy saint Svanos once stood looking out over the water, and saw there reflected the faces of all the gods in the stars."

Fish creased his brow. "Must have been a pretty crowded sky."

"Oh, it was. So many gods he could not even name them all. No-one could." Nico leaned over to gaze at his partner. Fish, as often, was the very picture of relaxation. One arm pillowed his head, his hair tousled into a soft curly mass, his eyes fixed on the stars. Nico pulled his gaze away reluctantly, not daring to test his own resolve.

"Some of them he did name, of course," he continued unsteadily. "Like that one." He pointed. "See that little triangle over there? That's the hat of Minori, patroness of tutors and scholars."

"Where's the rest of her?"

"It's just the hat."

"Oh."

"And *there*," Nico continued with self-satisfaction, "is the lord of chaos, Vermayn himself. Those two, they're his two eyes, and that little line over there is his long nose."

"Should you be saying such things about Vermayn?" Fish queried.

"That's not an insult. In the world of the *gods*," Nico said with conviction, "having a long nose is the very height of style."

Fish began to laugh. "*By the sly eyes of Vermayn,*" he mocked gently. "What other sayings are there? 'By Vermayn's crooked nose'?"

"By *your* crooked nose, you silly lout."

"Give me that bottle again." Fish sipped more carefully this time, but Nico noted that he held on for longer, imbibing more than he had on the first sip. When he was done, he flopped backwards, and Nico could tell that nothing more that was sensible would come out of him tonight. The boy had half Nico's capacity when it came to drink, yet he had twice Nico's thirst.

Well, perhaps that was for the best. Nico remained where he was for a long while, finding every constellation he had been taught as a boy, until the rasp of a snore alerted him to the fact that Fish had fallen asleep where he lay.

"That won't do," Nico sighed, getting heavily onto all fours and thence to his feet. Gazing down at his partner, helpless and languid in the moonlight, awakened all the usual longings and more.

*I could have this.* Was that the drink whispering to him, or something deep down inside himself, something festering and rotten, a permanent corruption implanted there? *Look at him. He wouldn't resist, not tonight, not when he's like this.* Nico was fairly certain that Fish was still completely innocent when it came to the realm of passion and desire. He could show the boy a good time no matter what breed of longings nestled in his heart. It wouldn't have to hurt. Not like Nico had been hurt.

A stab of guilt awoke inside Nico, so red-hot and painful and raw that it translated into a physical twist of his stomach. He turned away from his partner, dazed with self-disgust. These feelings were nothing new, but he was stunned now with their resurgent violence. It was as if something that had lain dormant inside him had at last awakened fully, and now it was battering itself like a wild animal against the cage of his heart, desperate to be released.

He paced away, breathing deeply of the cold evening air, and gradually began to sober up. Fish was still asleep at his feet. He poked the boy in the side with his toe, perhaps a touch harder than he normally would have, and Fish started and groaned.

"Come on, you," Nico said harshly. "Move yourself."

"Make me."

"C'mon," Nico repeated, stooping down and clasping his hand around the boy's wrist. "Can't sleep here." He dragged Fish to his feet; the boy clung to his arm, reeling.

"You've had far too much," Nico admonished. Fish's breath smelled of spirits, although at least he did not seem likely to retch.

"I'll be all right," Fish mumbled, leaning on his partner. He was warm, very close, and Nico knew his own cheeks were flushed. Not that Fish would notice. He half-carried, half-dragged the boy up the beach to the shelter under the trees where they had laid their bedrolls.

Guilt washed over him like a cold draught, a confusing stab of anger at his partner mixed in with the ugly nest of emotions. At times these confused Nico so much that he barely knew what he wanted. Did he love Fish for being his friend, or hate him for being so beautiful, so tempting, so desirable? Nico wanted to be close to him, wanted the boy's friendship, his regard and yes, his love. But how could that ever be possible when Nico himself had been damaged beyond repair? The physical wounds had healed long ago, but the wound to his spirit went on and on, never quite closing up, never completely healing. And having to half-carry the boy he was fair obsessed with to bed and having him pressed up so close and so warm—well, that was like opening the wound all over again and letting it bleed freely.

"Nic . . ." Fish mumbled, indistinctly, and Nico felt himself bleed out. It was too much. He rubbed his sleeve over eyes that had suddenly become wet. Fish was already snoring again.

"Gods," Nico whispered, "I wish . . ." He could not speak it aloud. *I wish this had happened differently. I wish I was a different person when I met you, someone undefiled and easier to love.*

Ruminating had never helped him, and neither had the gods. Nico wiped his eyes one last time and put himself to bed, knowing that he would feel better in the morning. Guilt tore at him as he curled himself into a ball, and the cold earth below was a stark reminder of his loneliness.

# CHAPTER XXIX
## QUETZAL

NICO AWOKE THE NEXT MORNING to grey skies and a drizzling rain, with the occasional flicker of real lightning out over the little lake. He was cramped and cold, and his arm ached, but he felt better than he had for a long while, cooped up in that stuffy upstairs room with no proper window, which was somehow still never warm enough. The morning was chill with the rain, yet it was a *good* chill. The sharp mountain breeze spoke of antelope and pine trees and the black basaltic buttresses of upper Svanlyn.

The rain was as yet too light to wake Fish where he slept in the hollow of the star chestnut tree. Nico's violent longings of last night had, thankfully, dissipated with the morning rain, leaving only the usual affection tinged with a touch of yearning. He sighed in relief and went to search for deadfall under the trees. Soon he had gathered a generous pile, and he dug out flint and firesteel from the pack, building a small campfire in a rocky indent half-sheltered by the reach of two black-barked evergreens. In due time he had a measure of coffee going in a small pot, the sharp bitter smell snaking through the trees. Fish stirred, sitting up with a groan, passing his hand over gummy eyes and through tousled curls.

The rain began to fall in earnest when they were halfway through breakfast. Dripping water from the ends of branches spattered in the fire. They drew beneath the shelter of the trees, making a comfortable couch of both their bedrolls, drawing their cloaks tight against the chill.

Fish produced two battered cigarillos from his trouser pocket, telling how he'd managed to bum them from Anspeare's second-in-command. They lit them from the guttering campfire, both letting out exclamations of contentment as the smoke wreathed around.

"How long were we planning to stay out here for?" Nico asked, taking sips of his coffee in between smoking.

Fish shrugged. "*A few days* is what I told His Lordliness back there. He said, *You'd better be back within three*, but I doubt that was a threat with much bite to it." He grinned at Nico. "Much nicer out here, isn't it? I'm inclined to stay as long as we can make the food last."

Nico gave his partner a measuring look. "There's antelope around here. Found their spoor this morning."

"A lot of effort, antelope," Fish returned, carefully flicking tobacco ash from his trousers, "when the lake's probably full of fish."

"And what are you going to catch them with?"

"My hands." Fish spread them wide. "Come on, Nic, how are *you* going to take us a whole damn antelope? You don't even have a bow."

"You can set snares for the rock-springers," Nico insisted. "I don't believe that you could catch a fish with your hands."

"How do you think I got my name?" The boy's grin was his usual dazzling variety.

"As to that, I've no idea, since you've kept it secret along with everything else."

Fish's grin faded, and Nico felt guilty all over again as he recalled that in fact, Fish had been unusually forthcoming lately, if a trifle hesitant. And who could blame him for that?

"It's not some great secret," Fish said softly. "I was just a child when I ran away from my father, you know that. Well, after a winter on my own, I got pretty good at living off the land. Managed to avoid starving to death, anyhow. Turns out following a fish through the water is a deal simpler than handling the magicks flowing through the ether. Fish are slower." Nico made a sceptical noise, but his partner just shrugged. "Well, in the end I got caught stealing fish from this old woman's garden, and she took me in."

"What, just like that?"

"Well—she could tell that I had magic."

Nico took a moment. "Which means that she had magic too, right?" He shifted his position to see Fish's face better. The boy was breathing in the last of his cigarillo, his gaze fixed somewhere in the rain past the fire. "This was in Vailana?"

"Yes. The town of Zarath. It wasn't a place where many of the Morgei lived, but this old woman—Delourien Luzerna—she married a nonmage, and he was of that area. He died years before I was born—they had no children—she'd been living in that house on her own for over twenty years by then. Her Mage-Gift wasn't very strong to begin with, and she didn't often exercise it. By the time Arran took over, everyone had forgotten that she even had any magic at all. She helped me hide." A fond smile was playing about the boy's face now. "Gave me my name, that day she caught me. Stealing *fish* from her river."

Nico had to laugh. "That story's far too sweet for someone like you."

"Why do you think I've waited till now to tell it?" Fish cocked his head. "Would've ruined my reputation in Ülhard."

"What became of her?" Nico asked. "Why did you leave?"

"She died." Fish flicked the stub of his cigarillo into the fire, and stood up. The rain had ebbed substantially, only a thin curtain of gossamer remaining to mist the landscape and spiderweb the trees. "I'm going down to the lake," he announced. "Bet you I could get at least five fish before you catch anything in your antelope snares."

"You're on," Nico returned, getting up himself and scattering a handful of dirt over the remains of the fire.

True to their name, the diminutive antelope that Nico knew as "rock-springers" frequented high cliffs and stony places, just the sort of terrain that surrounded him at the moment. He searched the area where the forested cliffside dipped to the narrow end of the lake, where the animals would come down to drink. Soon enough he found what he was looking for, the tracks of small, pointed hooves imprinted in the mud by the water. He backtracked towards the cliff, making out fainter markings of the same hooves leading upwards, and carefully began to set snares at likely places along the trail. He'd learned to make these as a child, from a fellow orphan boy who'd elected to join the Sven brethren when he came of age. Stay in the family, as it were. Brother Edwin had lived his whole life in the mountains, and become a woodsman second to no other. Were he here now, Nico might have entertained some further idea of escape into the wild expanses of Svanlyn.

He lifted his eyes to the mountain that bulked beyond the little river. Fish kept talking as if his magician siblings had some way of tracking him across even the most impassable terrain. As if they had wings and could fly on demand.

He shook his head and stooped to set the last snare along the lower trail. The path was heavily overgrown, the small prints neatly outlined in the mud underfoot. He turned to look up the edge of the rocky cliff. It was not more than eight feet high, and he picked out several places for likely footholds. There might be another trail along the top, more places to set snares, so he climbed up the cliff face, wincing a little whenever he used his injured arm. But it needed exercising, and the stretch felt good despite the twinge of stiffness.

As he swung himself up into the long grass that grew over the lip of the low cliff face, there was sudden movement about ten yards away, accompanied by a mighty creaking reminiscent of wicker and dry paper. Alarmed, he lifted his head, still in a prone position, half of his body over the cliff and the other half supported by his right foot on a slippery ledge of rock.

The thing unfolded itself, wings creaking like the snapping of high wind in a galley sail, twin swords connected to the body of a feathered serpent. Nico yelled loudly in shock and sudden fear, and flinched instinctively backwards. He lost his footing and toppled back down the cliff, just having the presence of mind to tuck himself close together and shield his face with his arms. He hit the ground with his left shoulder, thankfully not the injured one, and sprang to his feet.

He looked up with horror as a shadow loomed over him. The thing was on the edge of the cliff, and its sinuous form blotted out the sun. He could see now that the brightly feathered serpent was its neck, the two swords the two halves of its gigantic beak. Momentarily paralyzed with shock, he watched as the sharp halves parted and a piercing scream arose from that overlong throat, so loud he clapped his hands over his ears until the echoes over the surface of the lake died away.

The thing sprang from the cliff, landing in front of him with great wings outspread four yards to either side, crunching saplings under its splayed feet. Nico backed away, wanting to turn and run yet unwilling to take his eyes from that deadly sharp beak which he judged was big enough to snap him in half and devour him in two bloody mouthfuls. He drew his sword.

The muscular neck snaked out towards him, the two halves of the beak coming together with a ringing snap that would have decapitated him had he not sprung precipitously backwards. It reared back, coming around for another strike, and he brought his sword into position.

Hasty footsteps thudded between the trees, and suddenly his partner came into view. "Fish, careful!" Nico shouted in warning. The boy had obviously just come from the lake; he was shirtless and weaponless, barefoot and muddy, trousers rolled up to his knees.

Fish ran heedlessly up the slope towards the monster. "Nico!" he yelled back, gesticulating frantically with one hand. "Nico, drop the sword!"

The massive, bulbous head turned towards the half-naked boy. Nico hesitated, and gripped the blade tighter.

"Drop it!" Fish repeated loudly, desperately. There was a fish in his right hand, a large speckled trout that must have weighed almost as much as the antelope Nico had hoped to snare. Slowly, Nico lowered his sword. Fish waved the trout back and forth, captivating the monster's attention, motioning with his left hand as if to soothe and pacify it.

"You want this?" he breathed, holding the fish aloft. "You do, don't you?" The monster's head followed his every movement, the sharp tip of its beak inscribing small circles in the air as it watched him.

Fish threw the trout overarm, and the great beak opened and snatched it from the air, swallowing it down in one quick gulp. The creature leaned closer, regarding the boy, and silence fell save for Fish's still-belaboured breathing and the rustling of the leathery wings against the battered undergrowth. Its head was poised sideways, a single round black eye turned upon Fish, who returned its gaze without blinking.

"I won't hurt you," he panted, and slowly raised his hand. The creature was perfectly still now. "I won't try to coerce you." He took a step closer, and Nico bit down on a frantic yell that bubbled unsought-for up his throat.

As if it had heard, the monster flinched away from Fish's outstretched hand. It turned abruptly, flattening still more undergrowth, and lumbered away on all fours, crashing through the trees.

Fish's bare chest heaved up and down with his breathing. "We have to follow it," he said, tones of awe and wonder dripping from his voice.

"And be devoured?" Nico's hand was shaking, and he sheathed his sword rather than drop it. "Fish, are you mad?"

His partner turned and lavished a dangerous grin upon him. His eyes blazed gold, and Nico wondered now that he had never suspected that the boy possessed strange powers. "Stark raving. Are you with me?"

Nico let out a deep, shuddering breath and closed his eyes briefly, shaking his head. "Mother Thäle help me," he muttered. "*Yes.* Do you even need to ask?"

NICO HAD PARTICIPATED IN MANY HUNTS in his time. Going after hares as a small boy, antelope when he was older, one unsuccessful time they'd attempted to trap a panther in the mountains. Later on, he'd hunted men, stalked an unaware quarry with as much patience and persistence as any forest predator. He and Fish had hunted together more times than he could count, but this hunt was to be different: his partner had promised that there would be no blood at the end.

*Not its blood, anyway*, Nico thought privately. If the creature chose to turn berserk, there would be little defence they could mount against it. Fish refused to entertain the idea of using magic to pacify it, telling Nico as they followed its all-too-obvious trail through the brush of how his father had brought these creatures—quetzals, as he named them—to his castle and tamed them by magical coercion.

"If it's tame, then why are we hunting it? Why's it acting like a wild creature?"

"Maybe I shouldn't say *tamed*," Fish returned. He floundered for a moment in the rich mud that the creature had turned up in its passage. The quetzal had made its way around the densely forested slope of the low bluff. There were no paths save for the one it had now created, pushing trees aside and uprooting thorny bushes in its wake. It was a ridiculously easy trail to follow, but the terrain slowed them down. They were just above the far end of the lake; silver-green water shimmered between the tree-trunks if they cared to look down, and they could hear it rushing through a narrow canyon where the mountain sloped downhill.

Fish stopped for a moment, panting, leaning heavily against a half-uprooted sapling that Nico would not have trusted with his own weight. "The better word might be *controlled*," he continued. "Arran didn't care whether these things obeyed him willingly. The method he used was an imposition—an erosion of the quetzal's own will. Making it obey without question, even if its own life should be in danger."

Nico shivered. "I hope he can't do that to people."

"No, luckily not. Not so easily, anyway." Nico shot him a horrified glance, but Fish did not elaborate. "The quetzals have a kind of magic of their own, a connection with the forces of the earth. It's that connection which makes them vulnerable, and they're not as complex as a human being. But it's that connection makes me think that his way isn't the only way." His eyes shone when he looked at Nico. "I felt it, back there; I felt some sort of magic pass between us. Some kind of bond."

Nico raised his eyebrows. "We're going too slowly," he said. "This thing can fly, right?"

"Yes, but it needs a pretty long run to take off. And it goes fast on the ground; it's perfectly comfortable on four legs. I don't think it'll attempt to fly away."

"Where do you think it's headed?"

"Back to a safe place, probably. They prefer warmer weather, so it wouldn't surprise me if it was going towards shelter."

Nico nodded, and gestured up the slope. "We should try to get higher. We might be able to see which direction it took, and cut off some of the distance."

The top of the hill was as densely forested as the slope, and they could not see past the treetops. Fish climbed the tallest tree, a great greyish-green highland pine that had spread its needles and cones for yards around, creating its own miniature clearing in the sea of shorter, bushier trees that encroached around it. Halfway up, he startled a red squirrel in its nest, nearly fell out of the tree in surprise when it came out to chitter at him.

"Be careful!" Nico hissed up, his heart in his mouth, but Fish only laughed and confidently scaled the upper branches.

"I can see it!" he called down excitedly, in a hushed voice.

"The trail?"

"No, the quetzal!" Fish lowered his voice even more, to the point where it was barely a loud whisper. "It's stopped. I think maybe it's hunting."

"Figures that trout wouldn't be enough," Nico muttered to himself. "What's the plan?" he hissed up to his partner.

"I need to get close to it." Fish hesitated. "Alone."

"If things get out of control—" Nico paused. "You'll use your magic, right?"

Fish did not answer, but carefully dislodged himself from the high branch. He made his way down in a quiet and controlled fashion, making so little noise that Nico could scarce credit it.

"You didn't use your magic to get down, did you?" he asked suspiciously, as the boy's boots thudded into the pine needles beside him.

"What?" Fish frowned and shook his head. "I don't need *magic* to make a climb." He turned towards Nico. "I'm going to head straight towards it. Through these trees." He indicated a direction ahead of where they stood. You go—" He hesitated, licked a finger, tested the wind. "Downwind. That way. You shadow me."

"*Downwind?*" Nico repeated. "You sure of that?"

"Sure." His partner fished out half a dried sausage from his pocket. "Take this. I want it to smell you. Know that we're not trying to sneak up on it. That we've got food."

"Or perhaps we *are* the food," Nico growled, accepting the sausage all the same.

"It's not acclimated to eating humans." Fish stopped, something crossing his face. "At least I hope not," he muttered quickly, then shook his head. "No, it was trying to chase you away before, not eat you. Things got ugly when you took out your sword." His eyes travelled towards the blade at Nico's waist. "Maybe . . . maybe you should leave it here."

"No."

"Then you've got to promise me you won't draw it." Nico hesitated, and his partner whispered, "Nic, do you trust me?"

*I used to.* Nico's heart hammered against his ribs. No, that wasn't fair. Fish might have obscured the details of his own past, but he had never given Nico any reason to believe that he would gamble with his life. Fish had always watched his back. He had never been anything less than a true friend.

"Alright," he replied at last. "I won't draw my sword. I promise."

The boy beamed, flashing him that dazzling grin that Nico should be used to by now. It still shifted things inside him.

"Then let's go," Fish said in a low voice. "You start off that way, across the trees. Keep your eyes on me."

Nico could barely see his partner through the trees between them as he walked, and was hard-pressed to keep up with him. Fish's legs were a lot shorter, yet he seemed to slip easier through the thick underbrush, whilst Nico struggled against thorn-bushes that raked at his calves and tripped on tendrils of strangler vines laced between the tree-trunks. A wickedly long white thorn from a yellow-blooming bush caught in his trousers, threatening to rend them if he kept walking. Biting back a curse, he bent to coax the thorn out. It was well stuck. He lifted his head and could not see where Fish was. He tried to inch his other leg forward to crane around the bush. His foot slipped, and the thorn ripped through the fabric of his trousers, tearing a long scratch in the flesh beneath. But he barely registered the pain.

Just ahead of him, through a gap in the trees, waited the quetzal. It had come to rest at the summit of a low hill crowned with a broad pavement of black rock. Its pose was uneasy, as if any moment it might suddenly take off into the air like a giant bat. Its great, dangerous beak was outstretched, and just outside of its reach, Fish crept forward, hands held high as if to show that he was unarmed, eyes intent upon the creature.

The quetzal shifted, the point of its beak circling towards where Nico stood, and he knew it had seen him. He stood his ground, afraid to move any nearer, not wanting to unduly startle the creature. A shaft of morning sunlight broke through the clouds and shone down upon the iridescent green and blue feathers that grew along its neck, and for a moment Nico forgot his fear. The creature possessed a certain savage beauty, something that seemed right out of the hero-tales that Nico had loved as a child. Something fully as magical as the storied Forest of the Morning.

The great beak returned towards where Fish had stopped, patiently waiting. The black eye, outlined in red, was wide open. This time, Nico read no fright in the creature's pose. A sudden breeze from the water ruffled the quetzal's neck feathers as well as Fish's curls. Nico held his breath, watching his partner take a step forward.

There seemed no sound but the soughing of the wind in the trees.

For a long moment neither quetzal nor man shifted position. Then, smoothly as any girl bobbing before her dance partner at a harvest festival, the great feathered lizard inclined its gigantic beak and bowed its head, letting Fish reach out and touch the gleaming green feathers.

Relief broke out like a fever over Nico, and a broad grin came to his face. The quetzal seemed all but tame of a sudden, and Fish laughed in delight as he touched the azure-crested shoulders, standing on tiptoe to reach, and caressed the delicate wing-membrane which arched high over his head.

"Nico!" Fish turned, scanning the forest, and hesitantly Nico stepped forward, now only a few feet away from the creature. It came upright again, head bobbing into the air, and Fish kept a hand upon its wing as if to reassure it. "He's all right," he said soothingly. "He's with me." He turned to Nico. "I don't think he fully trusts you," he called. "Maybe you look a bit too much like Taunus."

Nico stood rock-still. "You think it belonged to—"

"My brother," Fish confirmed, stroking the soft leathery surface of the wing under his hand. The creature had jerked at the mention of the dead sorcerer's name, and Nico found himself wondering what sort of intelligence hovered in those keen eyes, black and hard as the rocky pavement it stood upon.

He cleared his throat. "What are we going to do with it, now?"

"It?" Fish turned towards him, grinning. "He has a name, you know." The creature bobbed its beak as if to confirm his words, looking almost comical in its malformed proportions.

"A name?" Nico repeated. "You've given it a name?"

"No, it has its own name. *He* has a name. Brightfeather, he's called."

Nico gave a short chuckle, startling himself. "Fitting," he conceded.

"And as for what we're going to do with him—" Fish tapped the quetzal's wing-joint, and the creature sank down to its knees, stretching its overlong neck horizontally along the pavement until the point of its beak touched the ground. For the first time, Nico saw that it had some sort of leather apparatus attached to its humped back. Something that looked remarkably like a—

"Is that a saddle?" he breathed. "They *flew* these things?"

His partner turned back to him, grinning so wickedly that Nico instantly divined his intentions. He took a step back, going cold all over at the thought. "You're not going to—"

Fish approached the quetzal's shoulder, looked over a few straps and buckles, then took a deep breath and gripped the horn of the saddle, placing a foot between a pair of straps and pulling himself up onto the creature's back.

Astride the great shoulders, feet cushioned against the corded muscles of the creature's wings, Fish looked as nonchalant as though he were taking a filly out for a trot to test her paces. He cast around for Nico, found him standing just on the edge of the trees. "Well, what are you waiting for?" he called out, his voice trembling with suppressed excitement. "He can carry two easily enough! There's a seat behind me, as long as you hold on."

Nico retreated further back, and found that he had gone as far as he could without actually cowering underneath the forest canopy. "Tell me you're not serious," he said, trying not to sound as nerve-wracked as he felt.

Fish stared wide-eyed at him. "What do you think the point *was*, of taming these?"

"I don't know," Nico replied lamely. "I don't have any magic—"

"I've never known you to be scared of anything before," Fish said.

Nico said nothing, at least not aloud. *I am scared of some things, Fish. Not a clean death, but something that might leave me maimed and crippled. And you. I'm scared of what I would do without you.*

The quetzal's long beak was resting near Nico. Slowly, it motioned towards him, and its visible eye locked upon his gaze, transmitting only calm.

It was as though the quetzal had read his very thoughts, and suddenly, Nico did not feel nearly so afraid anymore. And there it was, a clear invitation—though how he knew this, Nico could not say. One thing was for sure, this was no dumb beast of burden to be equated with a horse.

He reached out his hand, touched the silky-bright neck feathers and suddenly wanted to laugh. His partner watched avidly from where he was seated, as Nico made his way down the sinuous neck, reaching the muscled shoulders, noticing now that the massive wings were covered in down-feathers so fine they felt like silk beneath his hand.

Fish bent over the saddle, and reached out a hand to help him up.

If this was madness, so be it. Nico was shivering in excitement now, and he could feel Fish shiver as well as he swung a leg over the saddle and settled himself behind him. There was more space than he had thought; the creature's back was longer than it had seemed from the ground.

"We have to crouch down when it takes off," Fish said. "Put your hands here, and here—keep your head down—see what I do." The quetzal brought its neck horizontal, and Fish crouched low against it, settling his feet securely against the edge of its wings.

The quetzal began to stand, straightening its forelegs so that its back sloped at a precipitous angle. Nico quite forgot about looking foolish as he scrabbled for the right hand- and footholds, and clung on for dear life. The quetzal turned, facing the long, rocky pavement.

Suddenly, vividly, Nico recalled once having watched a black swan take off from a lake near the monastery where he had been raised. He could not have been older than ten. The swan could probably have made a satisfying meal for the quetzal, yet it had seemed to require an incredible amount of determination just to lift its relatively much smaller body into the air. He remembered the loud slapping of its wings against the water, the lengthy path it had required before gaining purchase against whatever it was that allowed it to remain aloft in something as insubstantial as air.

The quetzal faced the rocky pavement, began to gain speed, and Nico broke out into a cold sweat. But if indeed there had ever been any possibility of him refusing this adventure, it was far too late now. The forest passed by in a verdant blur. The speed took his breath away, even as it terrified him.

"Have you ridden one of these before?" he yelled up at Fish.

"No!"

Nico heard but couldn't react, forgot to be terrified, forgot everything but the flight which seemed a dream yet more real than anything he had experienced before. There was a sudden lurch, a jerk, a moment of weightlessness and a swoop in his stomach as though he were falling, though he knew he was rising higher than he had ever been.

The bright-feathered quetzal streaked out over the forest, spreading wide its leathery wings, casting a running bat-shadow over the treetops as it flew with its back to the sun. It flapped hard to climb higher, then angled out gently. The trees grew smaller and smaller, and they could see the mountain stretched out below like the spine of a gigantic mythical monster. Fish sat up as the quetzal righted itself, and Nico mirrored him, gazing down towards an endless vista of green hills and black cliffs and icy-white distant peaks, the river trailing through the green like a silken ribbon affixed to the hem of a dress.

The wind whipped icily across their faces. Fish made a small gesture with his right hand, and it subsided, seeming to flow past an invisible barrier he'd placed in the air around them. Brightfeather stretched out his serpentine neck and uttered a squawking call of delight, and suddenly Nico found that he was laughing. His partner turned his head.

"See, I can't imagine what you made such a fuss about!" His voice was muffled in the wind racing past, but Nico could hear him well enough.

He was about to answer when the quetzal gave a sudden lurch as it banked to the east, turning. Nico clutched for his partner's waist, drawing himself close against his comforting solidity, and now it was Fish's turn to laugh.

"Easy there," he murmured, and Nico realized that he was addressing the quetzal. "I think he's quite impressed by you. No need to show off."

The sinuous body beneath Nico slackened and straightened out, and for a while neither he nor his partner said anything, simply taking in this new and strange reality, gazing out south to where the clouds over the mountain terminated in a blaze of gold that Nico knew must be the Vailanan plains. He felt slightly alarmed, wondering how far they were from the country border. They had been flying for only a quarter of an hour, and already it seemed that they had covered a distance that would have taken them the better part of a week to walk.

The mountain fell away beneath them, the slender ribbon of the little river widened out and began to meander, and Nico gasped as suddenly the great blue mass of Lake Mountaindale shimmered unmistakably ahead. They were facing due south, and were on course to leave Svanfeld behind. Fed by two great torrents that flowed down from the mountains and a third, the Bluestream, which meandered west from the highlands surrounding Armour City, the great lake which marked the border between the two lands glittered like a carpet of diamonds and sapphires under the bright sunlight that bathed the plains. Nico could see just a suggestion of the large market town that was Albrecht, nestled in a valley at the calmest point of the lakeshore.

Nico's arm tightened about his young partner's waist, yet he felt he dared not ask what Fish was thinking. He felt the boy stir and sit forward, saw the shape of a frown form across what he could see of his face. Fish gazed out into the golden glow of the plains for a long moment, then reached out and touched the quetzal's neck.

"We need to turn back," he said decisively.

The quetzal's wings continued to beat all around them, and Nico sensed uncertainty.

"No. I'm sorry, but we can't go that way." Fish paused, stroking the quetzal's beautiful neck-feathers, looking for all the world like he was receiving a reply in a half-silent conversation. "I know, but it's not home anymore. It can't be for either of us."

They tore both their gazes from the horizon at the same time, the young man and the bright-feathered beast, and again Nico felt that he sat astride something he could not rightly dismiss as a mere animal.

The quetzal banked, more gently this time, inscribing a broad circle in the air, and looking down, Nico suddenly saw it directly below him. The road, brown and arrow-straight and broad enough to follow from this height. The Lynborder road. The road that led to Sulshome and beyond, to the port where ships set sail for shores far beyond the reach of any tyrant in the lands of Bavarian.

Brightfeather completed his circuit, straightening out as soon as he faced north, and Nico watched the road fall away below. He followed its course with his eyes, east and east and slightly north, snaking away into the foothills, until it faded from view alongside the glittering lake.

He turned his head. They had exchanged the view of the lake for that of the mountain. The entire impassable line of Svanlyn stretched out before them, distant peaks soaring higher than they flew, rows upon rows of grey-and-black spires ranging from east to west, filling the whole horizon, brooding over their eternal secrets.

He shifted his grip around Fish's waist. The boy's shoulders were tense, and he faced into the north, angular features showing nothing but composed concentration.

Nico did not know where they were going, but one thing was for certain. Already he was a world away from where he thought he'd be this morning, and whatever was to follow promised to be no less surprising. The path behind and the path ahead swept him up between, and the mighty mountain cast its shadow over him as they hurtled into its heights.

# Chapter XXX
# Safe Haven

They had been flying for over an hour, and the novelty, for Nico at least, was definitely beginning to wear off, when he saw the slender peak rise before them, and knew that they were over the Beerstana Pass.

His mouth was suddenly dry. They had been heading due north, only banking very gradually, and Nico had not realized they'd managed to turn so far west. They had passed the monastery, a stout whitewashed blur on the mountainside, ages ago, and Nico had thought that perhaps his partner was simply testing out the flight, seeing how high he could go into the mass of peaks and ridges of the wild mountain range before he needed to turn back. There was nothing so vague in Fish's intentions, he now realized. The boy had a plan.

"Fish." He was no longer holding onto his partner's waist; the quetzal's flight had evened out considerably, and he had eased into a position that was relatively comfortable, to watch the forest and rivers pass by below. Now, his back was stiff from the inactivity, his arm was complaining as if he'd strained it once again, and he would dearly have liked to feel the familiar steadiness of earth beneath his feet once more. But whether he truly wanted to land *here*—

Fish looked back. "We're landing," he said brightly, and Nico scowled.

"*Here?*"

Fish did not reply, and Nico's stomach lurched as suddenly the quetzal began to descend, folding its wings to drop dozens of feet all at once. He held grimly to the saddle as they spiralled down towards a niche in the side of the tall peak, a little valley that was all but inaccessible save from the air—or from the caves that he could see yawn wide even from this height.

The quetzal came to an ungainly landing, hitting the damp ground with four splayed feet, rending great gouges in the thin mountain grass as it stumbled on for a few dozen yards, finally coming to a standstill, wings quivering, head horizontal, facing the dark hole that was the entrance to the caves.

Nico was rigid with foreboding. The bodies had been cleared away, and the snow had all melted, leaving only sticky black mud interlaced with long fibres of grass which had not yet begun its summer growth. The quetzal's bright feathers were spattered with it, and it shook its great head in annoyance. Nico shivered; they were in the shadow of the peak, where the sun had not penetrated today.

Fish dismounted without hesitation, and there was nothing for Nico to do but follow, shouldering the pack they had luckily remembered to bring with them. Fish was waiting for him, eyes fixed upon the cave mouth. The mud sucked at Nico's boots as he approached his partner.

"Looks a bit different now, doesn't it?" Fish said conversationally.

Nico halted. "Fish, what in the name of Vezzat are we doing here?" *We should be going forward, not back*, he wanted to say. *We should have kept going, south and then east and around the mountain towards the sea.* There was no way anyone could track them now, not when they had a mount that could fly with the speed of the wind and seemed to have the endurance of fifty horses.

They'd made promises to Anspeare, sure enough. *Promises, when he had a blade to the back of my partner's neck.* Nico wanted nothing so much as to be taking the long route east with Fish, breaking those promises.

It was what a man who made a living killing people for money would do, and were Nico on his own, he would have done it without a second thought, saving his guilt and other complicated feelings for later when he was far away. But there was no way he was going to leave without his partner, and the boy seemed to have something else on his mind, something Nico could not rightly fathom. This was a different side he was seeing of Fish, something that had lain beneath the surface all the time Nico had known him. Buried along with his magic, which had burst forth like an adder out of the long grass and now had its coils woven securely around them both.

"I'm collecting information," Fish replied shortly, and shivered, rolling down the sleeves of his shirt. "Pass me my cloak from that pack, won't you?" He watched as Nico grudgingly obeyed, crouching in the mud to keep the pack clean. "I should carry that," he said.

Nico hoisted the heavy pack with a grunt, holding Fish's cloak out to him. Fish's lips quirked and he turned away without a word, heading across the muddy plain. A curious sense of foreboding overtook Nico as he trailed in his partner's footsteps. Behind them, the quetzal made a forlorn, chirping noise deep in its throat. Fish turned briefly, made eye contact, gestured towards the caves. The quetzal shrank back, looking nothing short of woebegone, and made for a relatively dry patch of nearby rock. There it curled itself serpentinely over the ground, in much the same pose it had been when Nico had first disturbed it that morning.

"We shouldn't be long," Fish promised, striding away.

Nico looked for signs of what had happened here. But the traces had melted away with the snow, leaving only a feeling of intense isolation trailing on the wind. The caves were familiar enough, though, dank and rocky and pitch dark inside. Without saying a word, Nico dug out a torch from the pack and lit it. Fish took it from him, the yellow light casting a harsh glow over his angular features, and Nico remembered how he had looked, last time they had been here. The madness and desperation on his face, the searing flames of his magic. There was none of that there now, but still Nico was full of apprehension.

"Fish . . ." The boy was heading straight down the tunnel, as Nico recalled, where Taunus and his necromes had made their habitations. His voice sounded hoarse in his own ears. He cleared his throat. "Anspeare's been here already," he said. "What could we possibly find that he hasn't?"

Fish turned for the briefest of moments. "Magic," he replied shortly, and did not pause in his stride. The tunnel sloped sharply downwards, burrowing deep into the earth. The going was rough; the floor was sharp with jutting rocks, and they had to navigate carefully in the light of the single torch.

After a while Fish stopped to catch his breath, looking sidelong at his partner. Nico was glad for the reprieve; the pack was heavy, and it seemed now that it had been a very long time since breakfast.

"I know this seems—odd," Fish said abruptly. Nico glanced at him; the boy's features were outlined in the torchlight, making a deep-red glow of his skin and golden flames of his eyes. "But I need answers, Nico, and there's only one way I can get them." He clenched his hand about the torch. "I don't like this place, either. Even less than you do. It smells of death in here, and blood. Reminds me far too much of my father." His voice faltered, and he hesitated for a moment. "Even if Anspeare searched all the caves—and I doubt he did—he couldn't have found anything that Taunus hid magically.

*I* can." He crouched down, and shone the torch upon the rocky wall opposite. "See that blood?"

Nico frowned, and leaned closer. "I can't see anything," he replied.

"But there is blood there, nonetheless." Fish now wore an inscrutable half-smile. "Taunus's blood. He must have scratched himself there, at some point. Months ago. Maybe he didn't even notice. But the memory of him is here. Everywhere about. Because of his magic, I can locate his private quarters. I can find whatever he kept there."

Nico shivered. "But he's still dead, right?"

Fish smiled a little more at that. "We saw the proof with our own eyes," he reminded Nico. "No sorcerer has ever managed to come back from the dead, at least as far as I know."

"Good to know," Nico muttered as they set off again. He heard Fish chuckle, and felt reassured.

They continued down the tunnel for a long while. Nico began to settle into a steady rhythm as he walked, not noticing much beyond the distance. They rounded a corner, and a dark shape uncoiled itself from the shadows cast by the torch.

Nico had just enough time to recognize a necrome, to realize that he had completely forgotten about the possibility of these monsters still lurking within the caves where Taunus had created them. It sprang at Fish without hesitation, claws raking for his face, teeth gnashing against blood-foamed lips. Nico had no time to react, so taken aback was he; but Fish seemed to have been expecting something of the sort. He leaped backwards, colliding with Nico and in the same movement throwing off something from his free hand that flared like fire in the darkness.

The sudden magic, flared off whilst Fish was touching him, rang through Nico like a weight striking a brass gong, setting his whole body alight with uncontrollable aftershock. He cried out, and felt himself fall to his knees, pain ringing through them as he landed on the rocky floor. Something was burning in the cavern. The sickening smell of seared flesh choked him.

"Nico!" He had just enough wit left to recognize his partner's voice. "I'm sorry. You were touching me. Didn't realize." The glare of the fire faded to nothing, and the smell of burning flesh receded. Nico was still reeling, but at least now he could see. Fish was holding the torch aloft, and there was concern in his eyes as he crouched over Nico. He made as if to take his partner's arm, then seemed to think better of it. "Best stay still for a moment," he said. "It should wear off soon."

Nico leaned forward, letting his hands come down to support his weight on the rocky cave floor. "By the sly eyes of Vermayn," he managed.

"I'm sorry," Fish repeated, and leaned the torch against the wall. He smoothed down the sleeves of his shirt, flicked something from his hands as if he'd been handling soapy water, then reached for him. Nico flinched, but the magic had evidently dissipated, and he felt only the steadying force of his partner's usual grip. Fish took the pack from him, and without its weight Nico felt a lot better.

"I think you'd better eat something." Fish handed him a dry travel-biscuit, popping one into his own mouth before shouldering the pack. "Are you all right to stand?"

Nico manoeuvred himself to his feet, using the rocks protruding from the wall as handholds. He nodded cautiously.

"That particular necrome might still have been carrying out my brother's orders: to guard this tunnel," Fish said, thrusting the torch forward. "I've found his living quarters."

Nico squinted into the darkness, but saw nothing save the same rocky walls that had hemmed them all the way here. Fish laid his hand upon a section of wall much like any other, and it shimmered beneath his touch and faded away, uncovering the entrance to a circular chamber.

Eyes wide in amazement, Nico followed his partner inside. Fish lifted the torch high. The room was not large, and most of it was revealed in the flickering light. A narrow bed, wooden shelves strewn with clothes, racks for weapons and armour—all of it deplorably ordinary. But in one shadowy corner stood a desk, and Fish immediately stepped towards it. The light danced across the objects arranged upon it: a selection of blackened jars which looked strangely ominous, an oil lamp, a neat pile of books.

Fish passed the torch to Nico and lit the lamp, providing them with a steadier source of light, then gazed at the pile of books. Cautiously, as if fearing that Taunus might have set a trap for him, he reached out and took the first book from the top of the pile. Neatly bound in dark leather, it resembled some of the journals Nico had seen monks use to keep their personal writings, their daily prayers and observations of medicine, history and the natural world.

Fish flipped the pages of the book. They were quite blank, and Nico felt disappointed. "Try the next," he suggested.

Fish scowled. "This book isn't empty. Its messages are hidden."

"Messages?"

"A simple magic." Fish raised his eyes to Nico's. "You can exchange messages over long distances, and keep them secret."

"Can you reveal the messages?" Nico asked excitedly.

"If this is the usual spell Father used,"—Fish paused, and an oddly blank expression came over his face—"then yes. I can break it."

Leafing through the empty pages, he came to the middle of the book, and carefully laid it upon the desk. Then, to Nico's bewilderment, he took a dagger from his belt and held up his left hand to the light.

Without hesitating for an instant, Fish slashed a deep cut across the palm of his own hand. Nico's eyes went wide in shock; he stepped back, horrified, his heart suddenly beating very fast.

Fish whispered several harsh syllables that Nico could not quite make out. It did not sound like any language that had been developed for use by human voices, and a chill rippled up his spine. Fish was silhouetted by the lamplight in the dark little room, and the shadows seemed to crowd closer around him than was normal. He clenched his bleeding hand into a fist, held it directly over the blank pages of the book. Blood dripped between his fingers, but just before it spattered onto the pages, it vaporized into smoke and wisped away. Fish made a small noise deep in his throat, as if in pain, and suddenly words shimmered into being on the page, shining brightly as though they had just been inked into existence.

"Taunus wrote this, all right," Fish whispered, leaning over the desk. "It's a message to my sister Dannine. Telling her of our capture. *I have Deryck, sister.*" He gave a harsh laugh that was rather unlike him, and Nico eyed him cautiously.

"This book contains every communication that Taunus exchanged with my father and the others." Fish's voice shook, with excitement or with something else, Nico could not tell. His hand was bleeding, leaving dark spatters on the desk as he leafed frantically through the pages that still stood blank. Randomly, he stopped paging, and reached for the dagger again.

Before Nico could say anything, the blade was back in the wound, bringing more blood, deepening a cut that had already been deep to start with. Nico flinched away, finding the sight disturbing. The lack of hesitation in Fish's desire to hurt himself was unsettling. A chill realization centred inside Nico: this was dark sorcery. What was that term Anspeare had used? *Blood sorcery.* This was nothing like what Nico had fondly imagined magic to be, long ago when the monks were teaching him his letters and the tales from afar, of the Morgei. This was different even from the magic that Fish had done at the lake, which was beautiful in its own way. There was no beauty about this, and a madness glowed in Fish's eyes as the blood ran through his mutilated fingers.

"Details about his necromes," he muttered, looking at the writing that had appeared on the page. "Useless." He flipped through the pages again to arrive at another blank junction.

"Fish, stop it." Nico reached out, decisively, and shut the book with a clap. Fish started, and looked up at him as if he had forgotten all about his presence. The dagger hung loosely from his hand, and Nico reached out and took it from him.

"Let me bandage this," he said, taking Fish's unresisting left hand. He burrowed in the pack, found a clean cloth that had been intended to dress his own wounds should they reopen, and tore a ribbon from it.

"You've only just recovered from what they did to you last time," he continued. "Give it a while before you hurt yourself again. I'm sure there isn't anything in that book so urgent that you need to open your own veins to get at it."

Fish watched as Nico carefully bandaged his hand, looking bemused. "It's just blood," he said at last. "It doesn't matter."

"And if you got wound-fever from that cut?" Nico's voice came out harsher than he had intended, and Fish's eyes seemed very young and wide as he looked up at his partner.

"Thank you," he whispered, unexpectedly. Nico still had his hand; he was applying pressure to the cut, which threatened to bleed right through the flimsy bandage. "It's just—it's driving me crazy." He shook his head. "All those promises Taunus made. What Father was going to do to me. What *Dannine* was going to do. I keep expecting to look up and see their faces somewhere in the shadows." He gestured into the corners of the chamber, and Nico had to resist the urge to look over his shoulder himself. "This isn't how you run a conquest," Fish continued, a deep crease appearing between his expressive eyebrows. "Why attack so sporadically? Why try and start a war with Svanfeld when you've not yet conquered Qwu'Mallorn? It doesn't make any *sense*."

Nico shifted uncomfortably. "Some people think your father's mad," he offered.

Fish laughed sardonically. "Oh, that would certainly explain it. If you didn't know the man as I do. Trust me, Nico, there isn't anything he doesn't do for a *reason*, even if it's not immediately obvious. If the necromes are running helter-skelter around the countryside, it's because he wants them to. If my siblings seem sluggish in their retaliation, it's because he ordered them to be. If I'm still at large—" He hesitated, as if suddenly struck by a revelation. "It's because he *wants* me to be. Or because it helps his cause in some way. Even if I don't realize it."

He fell silent. Nico was still holding his hand, and he took a deep breath and drew closer. "Fish," he said, "we could escape him. If they're not looking for you, so much the better. We could get away clear."

Fish blinked. "What?"

"We have a quetzal." Nico faltered, seeing his partner's eyes brim with something that looked like temper. "That thing flies so fast, no-one would be able to catch us. Not Anspeare, not your father, not *anyone*. If we wanted, we could be out over the Sea of Calms before they even noticed we'd gone."

Fish said nothing. He slid his hand out of Nico's grip, and tucked it into his elbow, folding his arms, frowning as if he were marshalling his thoughts.

"The quetzals," he whispered at last, raising his eyes to Nico's. "Did I tell you where they live? Not on this continent. There are desert islands on the Sea of Calms, and that's where my father first found them. I don't know how old he truly is—no-one does." He crossed his arms more tightly, as if holding himself together. "But I remember him telling me of a time long ago, when he was but a boy—of watching the wild quetzals bank and soar over the sea, and knowing that someday he would tame and fly them."

"I thought your father was one of the Morgei," Nico said hesitantly. "Only the Morgei have magic."

"Only the Morgei, and Arran Sylvaissen." Fish shrugged. "Where did Arran come from? Nobody knows. He has no ties to Qwu'Mallorn, no family, no home there. He just sprang up one day, or that is all anyone knows of him. Amassed himself an army and rampaged through Vailana."

"He didn't tell you where he hailed from?"

"Not directly. But he always spoke of being an exile," Fish replied. "From all he said, I think he grew up somewhere on the Sea of Calms. But the last people to be *exiled* from Vailana—that was three hundred years ago."

Nico was silent, digesting this for a moment. "They banned dark magic in Vailana," he said at last, remembering. It was just a snippet from history to him, something learned by rote long ago when he was a young boy.

"They banned blood sorcery," Fish returned. "The Morgei carried out a complete sweep, rooted out the families that practised the forbidden magicks. Killed most, burned down their strongholds and mansions, set the rest upon the Sea of Calms and called up a tempest to destroy their ships, betraying promises they'd made that the exiles could leave and start somewhere anew." His scowl deepened. "Or at least, that is what Arran taught me. That story—he used to tell it like he remembered it."

Nico swallowed. "So what you're saying is—"

"How far do we need to go to outrun my father's influence?" Fish's eyes bore into Nico's. "The Sea of Calms won't do, I'm afraid. Nor Arven; that's too close. My father trades with the Eastern Empire, sends them copper and steel and slaves in exchange for silk and ivory. Should we go to the old world, the Great Continent?" Nico's heart sank into his boots, and he stared at the floor as the boy continued, "Zemlya? Limojenga? How safe will they be, once Arran has conquered the whole western continent and allied with the Empire in the East?"

Nico fell silent, and remained that way for a long while. Fish turned away, gathering up the pile of books that sat on the desk.

"That's how it is," he stated at last, putting a hand on the oil lamp as if anxious to get going. "If you didn't know before, Nico, now at least you do. I've had enough of running from my father." He took a deep breath. "I'm tired of a life under his power. To live in fear forever—that's no life at all." Nico swallowed hard, and turned away from the boy's eyes, shining golden with courage. "If I'm destined to die by his hand, then so be it," Fish continued quietly. "I can't ask you to die with me, but I can ask you to make up your mind." He paused. "Are you going to do this with me, or not?"

Nico caught his shoulder. "Fish, I—I have to tell you something."

Fish turned fully towards him, studying his face, and the resolve Nico had felt for just a moment frizzled away into nothing. He stared at the floor, muttered a disclaimer, looked back up just in time to see disappointment pass over his partner's face.

"We should go," Fish said at last, lifting the lamp from the desk. "Tell me in out in the daylight, perhaps?"

Nico nodded, and when his partner had turned his back, brushed a hand across his eyes. He stayed close to Fish and the light as they crossed the threshold of the chamber. Perhaps he really would tell Fish this time, as soon as he mustered his courage again. Then, with no more secrets between them, where would they go?

Something strange happened as Nico's feet crossed the threshold between the room and the tunnel beyond. A swoop in his guts as if he were falling, an eerie echo of the feeling he'd had when Fish performed magic too close—and the boy swore loudly, holding the lamp aloft.

"Does any of this look familiar? Nico?"

Nico turned in the lamplight, horror rising within him. They were not in the rocky tunnel by which they'd come, but in a different part of the caveways entirely. Dozens of entrances led from the dark rocky wall beyond, but when he pivoted and looked behind, Taunus's chamber had vanished.

"What happened?" he demanded, clutching at Fish.

The boy groaned. "I should have suspected something of the sort. Protection spell, a simple one, but I'm surprised it lasted this long after my brother's demise. It's transported us to a different part of the cave system. Gods alone know where we are." He paced about, scowling towards the various criss-crossing entryways and side-passages. "I guess he figured that if someone intruded in his room, he could catch them after the fact when they were trying to make their way out. Or his necromes would find them."

Nico felt a chill in his gut. "Will the necromes find *us*?"

"I think they've mostly been killed or dispersed," Fish replied quietly. "That doesn't mean there aren't a few stragglers—like that one we found earlier. But the greater danger for us—that's all too simple. Trying to find our way out before we starve to death."

They both fell silent, and when the echoes died away there was nothing in the world to be heard save their own breathing, louder than it felt it should have been. Fish stirred, and angled the beam of the lamp towards a narrow passageway on their left.

"I can feel *something*, away down there," he said softly. "Some kind of magical residue. Might be from Brialise, from the ways she used. If it is, we could be close to someplace familiar."

Nico sighed. "Well, gods know I've no better ideas," he admitted, and Fish stepped forward without any more delay.

They spoke little as they strode through the tunnels. The caveways were more of a maze than Nico had ever suspected, and as the hours crept by he began to feel more and more despondent. Fish was heading, as he said, towards a suggestion of where Brialise had been, but they seemed no nearer a way out than when they'd started. They made their way through tunnel after tunnel, all of them similar, some sloping uphill, some back down. Nico was tired, but the creeping dread upon him would not allow him to stop lest he sink down under its full weight and never manage to get back up. After all he had been through with his partner, wandering forever through a crazed tangle of passageways was *not* how he'd expected it all to end.

Just as he felt he was reaching the end of his tether, Fish suddenly gave an excited exclamation and sped up. Nico moved with him towards where the narrow tunnelway terminated in a wide, level drive, and gazed out in the lamplight to a sight that seemed familiar at long last.

Fish lifted the lamp, gazing left and right. "That end," he said, pointing to where the level tunnel began to descend slightly, "I'm sure that's the way down towards the village. Brialise brought us down here."

"You're right." Nico felt he could breathe freely at last. "We've gone past the place, I think, where you—you—" He glanced askance at Fish, not knowing what to say.

"Where I had a flare of temper," the boy admitted dryly, and gave something that might have been a soft laugh. "It's a long walk down, but at least we'll know where we're going. I can call Brightfeather from the other side."

The relief that rippled over them both felt almost like a celebration. They stopped for a moment in the tunnel, Fish setting down the oil lamp with a sigh of relief, and nibbled some biscuits and dried fruit, ate the last of the hard dried sausage. They set off, and Fish finally consented to let Nico carry the pack again. The walk was a long one, and Nico had plenty of time to dwell on his thoughts, to imagine what he would say to Fish when at last they reached daylight again. One thing he knew for sure, striding beside his best friend and gazing every now and then at his expressive, beautiful face: he wasn't going anywhere without Fish, nor would he let the boy throw his life away. For now, there was nothing for him to do but fight by his partner's side. Should the fight look hopeless, however, it would be up to him to persuade the boy to walk away. And if it truly came, in the end, to what Fish had suggested—the tyrant of Armour City coming to destroy his errant son by his own hand—Nico would engage swords as readily with *him* as he had with Taunus, for Fish's sake.

Daylight began to show at the end of the tunnel, and at last they emerged out into the brilliance of a dazzling afternoon sun. "How long were we down there for?" Nico asked, as they both waited for their eyes to acclimatize to the light. Low hills rose all around them, and the air was fragrant with spring. The cliff that marked the edge of the village could only just be seen from the high rise where they stood.

Fish only shook his head. "Feels like most of the day. I wouldn't have been surprised to find it was evening out here, really." He wandered down the rise and stood looking away at the cliff. "I wonder how they've been doing since," he said quietly.

Nico moved to stand beside him. "We can always go and ask—"

"For our money and gear back? Come on, Nic, that would be a terrible thing to do."

Nico scowled, but said nothing more. Fish turned to face south, where his quetzal waited upon command.

A sudden scream rent the air, muffled with distance, yet carrying a world of urgency and desperation in its timbre. Nico stiffened, and Fish whipped his head back around, eyes wide. It was a woman's scream. They both stood motionless and silent for just a moment, and the mountain carried further sounds up to where they stood: metal clashing on metal, yells and cries.

"The village," Fish said breathlessly, and without any more preamble they raced down the slope, down the face of the low cliffside and through the green copse beyond, until they stopped to take in the scene that unfolded before their eyes.

The enemy force seemed to have come straight through the main gate, which lay hacked into bits strewn across the muddy road. About two dozen villagers were holding off the attackers, fighting with axes and pitchforks and scythes, no proper weapons between them. The enemy numbered at least as many as the villagers; perhaps more, for dark shapes were still moving through the ruined gates as Nico and Fish looked on. Most of the attackers were necromes, Nico realized, but not all. Small fires burned here and there in the wooden structures that stood athwart the road; a man armed with a bow was firing off flaming arrows towards the defenders, standing a safe distance back from the combat.

One of the villagers went down as they watched, screaming in pain, and Nico involuntarily stepped forward, moved by something he could not explain.

"Wait!" Fish held him back. "Don't fight the necromes." He flexed his right hand. "I can get them from here. Not the men, though. Can you take all of them?"

Nico attempted to count: there were four men he could see, including the archer, amongst the dark shapes that flailed and clawed at the desperately battling villagers. If there were more that he hadn't noticed, so be it. He nodded frantically.

Fish released him, bringing both his hands together to make a strange crackling noise that Nico barely heard. He made straight for the archer; nothing else existed, only the feel of the blade in his hand and the man he was about to kill.

None of the attackers had expected anyone to come around on their flank. By the time the archer noticed Nico, it was much too late. He was only a few yards away, and there was no way he could fire his bow in time. He drew a short sword from his belt and brought it up frantically to meet Nico's.

Last time Nico had been in the midst of a fray, he'd had very little to eat for several days, on top of a badly sprained arm, and his only weapon had been a little silvered dagger. The arm was still healing, but he had a sword in it now, and had been resting and eating well for the better part of a month. The archer fought fiercely, but Nico had a substantial reach advantage over him, and he was nowhere near Fish's equal when it came to speed and agility. Nico cornered him in a few moves, striking his sword deep into the gap below his helmet, pushing away and searching for his next quarry before the corpse hit the ground.

The next man was closer to Nico's size, but laboriously slow. Nico allowed him inside his guard, risking a hit on his leather armour. The ensuing cut was shallow, not even leaving a mark. Before his enemy could recover, Nico had shoved his blade point-blank through the man's leather vest. He felt the shock ripple up his injured arm with the man's weight, bit back the ensuing pain. He was nowhere near finished.

The third man was struggling with a woman who had dressed herself in some kind of leather armour; she did not draw back when Nico approached, but kicked her assailant in the shins, loosening his grip on her arm, and buried the head of the axe she wielded in his chest. Panting in effort, she looked up just in time to see Nico salute her before he collided with the last enemy fighter.

This man was faster than the others, and wild with battle-anger; he was big, and swung his sword at Nico with a bellow of rage. Nico danced out of reach, not finding an opening. The man gained ground fast, driving him backwards, and Nico could not see where he was putting his feet. If he stumbled, he knew, he was done for.

Out of nowhere the same female fighter appeared; she brandished her short-handled axe and hewed at the enemy soldier, who frantically windmilled his sword to block her attack. Nico took advantage of the distraction and pressed forward immediately, landing a blow to the man's thigh that downed him, then coming back for his head.

The man fell, and all sounds of battle stilled. Nico and the woman stared briefly at each other then looked around, both panting. The ground around them was strewn with necromes who appeared to have burst; Nico had not even seen them fall, but now Fish came forward, moving slowly, ashen-faced under the dusky bronze of his complexion. He poked one of the fallen necromes with his foot, nodded at the axewoman, then turned to Nico.

"They have a magic that links them all together," he said in a low voice. "Required a bit of focus to follow it, though."

Nico swivelled, letting it sink in. Near twenty necromes lay motionless upon the battlefield. "Well done," he managed. Fish began to grin, but they were interrupted by a sudden loud cry, and a flurry of activity between the houses. Nico deciphered the cry, even as the woman turned. *Fire!*

Of course, the archer had done his best to start his many small fires before Nico slew him. Whilst he had been busy with the other fighters, one of those little fires had managed to spread fast and had engulfed a large house, now spreading to the cottages beyond. There was a great commotion as the villagers ran to and fro for buckets, trying to draw water from the well fast enough.

Fish stared at the scene for a moment, then moved towards the fire with his hands held out, as though trying to calm an unsteady horse. Nico was beyond surprise by now; his partner had done so much today that was totally alien to him. It had brought home to him that Fish was truly different. His powers seemed dangerous, yet he had saved them all from necromes, led himself and Nico out of the underground, and tamed a creature that could take him places in a fraction of the time normally required for overland journeys.

The fire flickered uncertainly, burned a little lower for just a short moment, then suddenly spread outwards with a great roar and a sickening rush of dry, hot air that raced towards where Nico stood, burning his eyes. Fish was standing a lot closer, and Nico called desperately for him. The boy stumbled back, raising his arm across his face.

"Fish!" Nico shouted. "Fish, get away!" The conflagration was keening like something tormented, black smoke roiling, flames rising higher than Nico would ever have thought possible. Sweat ran down his forehead, but he would not move. Not without his partner.

Step by step, Fish made his slow way backwards until he stood only a few feet away, yet still far too close for Nico's comfort. The boy gazed at the fire with desperation, swore under his breath, then unfocused his eyes and raised his hand a second time.

"No—" Nico began, his cry cut off as suddenly the mud shifted beneath his feet. A great hissing sound rose from the burning house as Nico stumbled to one knee. Mud from the ground rose up to pelt the flames, smothering them. As Nico watched, the fire receded, yet Fish did not manage to damp it completely. His focus broke palpably; he swayed dangerously on his feet, and would have fallen had Nico not moved forward to catch him.

"Are you alright?" he asked in a low voice. Fish was even paler than he had been before, and beads of sweat had broken out across his forehead. Some of the villagers were just standing about, dumbfounded and confused; the others had kept their heads, and were dousing the remainder of the fire.

Fish nodded and managed to find his feet, keeping a cautious hand on Nico's arm. Nico looked around. The fight was over; the surviving villagers were gathering together behind the axewoman, who seemed to command some sort of presence.

"You have magic," she stated, looking directly at Fish. He nodded, and a smile appeared on her face. "Thank you," she said simply. "If you hadn't been here, it would've gone ill for us."

The woman's accent, somehow, didn't sound quite like the people they had met here before. Nico swept his eyes across the group, and saw nobody he remembered. It had been such a small village to start with, and now there were fewer than two dozen standing here before him.

"Do any of you remember us?" he asked, and was startled to see how blank their faces went. "We were here just a few weeks ago. Before the—the trouble started."

"We're not from here," the axewoman said. "We found this settlement and thought we'd hide here for a while. We're survivors from the massacre in Von Dharen."

*The what?* Nico stared at her dumbly.

"Where are the village folk, then?" Fish asked quietly. The woman shrugged.

"We never met 'em. Reckon they fled; it didn't look like there was a fight. The houses were fine, so we've been using 'em. We were gonna hide out here a few weeks, rest and get our strength back, then try and get across the pass. If the whole world hasn't fallen, that is." She tossed her head, throwing back her straw-coloured hair, for a moment almost noble with a kind of homely defiance.

"We can help with that," Fish said. I'm Ben Fisher, but you can call me just Fish. This is my partner, Nico Klavbert."

"Embeth Lach," she returned, and a few of the others murmured their names as well. Nearly all of them were women, Nico realized. There were two older men who looked much like stout farmers, and a sprinkling of teenage boys. The youngest of the group was a girl of about twelve who had padded herself with leather and stood with a pitchfork in her hand and a frown on her face. The eldest was a thick-set, balding man who limped on his left leg, untidy beard shot through with grey.

One thing Nico felt quite sure of: none of these folk had taken up a weapon in their entire lives before now. The absence of young adult men from their group spoke volumes. Von Dharen was not a small town; it had a standing militia, as well as a coastguard. Under ordinary circumstances, none of these people would ever had had to concern themselves with self-defence.

Nico himself was no stranger to violence, had dealt death in a multitude of savage ways. Yet the things he had done—brought death to powerful men and the fighters they in turn hired to protect them—seemed somehow fairer than this. This was Nico's first glimpse of true war, and he hated it already.

If the world made any sense, then he would continue to operate from its margins, keeping to himself, never coming into the light. But the world was mad, the boy he had fallen in love with was a runaway prince with terrifying magical powers, and nothing looked the same as it had just a few short weeks ago, when he had dreamed of the life of a wandering mercenary with Fish by his side.

"We'll take you across the pass," he heard himself say, as the refugees looked to him with their faces stained by soot and simple clothes spattered with necrome blood. "There's safe haven beyond. King's men who hold the monastery above the lake."

# Chapter XXXI
## Forest Song

THE FACE IN THE WATER SANK BACK with a cry . . . and the dream faded, and Velda was awake, blinking in the dazzling sunlight that shone through the half-shuttered window.

She was with Albryan, crushed up against him in this bed that was really only fit for one person, both of them still nude from last night, limbs tangled together, hair unbound. This was the first time she was waking up with him in the morning. She hadn't meant to stay the night, but somehow she hadn't been able to keep awake. Perhaps it was the lousy quality of sleep she was getting lately, what with her days spent adapting to this new life, these strange people—and the haunting, unsettling dreams she was having whenever she closed her eyes.

She remembered some sort of sleepy conversation from last night about her staying, remembered Albryan warning her that every foot– and mounted soldier in the vicinity of Tenna would know for sure that they were sleeping together if she emerged with him from the barracks in the morning. "Don't your soldiers have more pressing things on their minds than gossip about who's sleeping with whom?" she'd asked, and he had shrugged under her caressing hand.

"Junior soldiers love to gossip about their officers. You'd be surprised, but on a day-to-day basis, their lives are actually rather dull. Life-or-death encounters don't happen every day, and most of your time is spent preparing for them, training and waiting and fixing your gear. And talking, spending time with the men who are going to risk their lives for yours once battle comes. You've got no secrets from the men in your squadron, nor the men you command."

She squirmed free of Albryan's grasp, sitting up, and he came awake, stretching out with a wide yawn, squinting against the sunlight.

"Is it morning already?" he muttered. He lay back and gazed sleepily at her, as if going over something in his mind.

"Why are you here?" he mumbled, then blinked. "Oh—you never left last night, did you?"

"I fell asleep," Velda admitted, and he laughed softly.

"It's not funny," she protested. "I'm getting hardly any sleep at all—I'm having nightmares—"

His face turned apologetic. "Sorry," he said sincerely, reaching for her hand. He yawned again, then rolled out of bed, leaving her still wound up in the sheets, and dug around for a set of fresh smallclothes in an open drawer. He stopped by the door, catching sight of a paper envelope that someone had clearly tucked under there whilst they were sleeping.

He sighed, and picked up the envelope. "Well, the general never wastes any time. My leave runs out tomorrow, and right on schedule, here are my orders." He strode over to the bed, sitting down and drawing out a piece of paper.

"It's not confidential?" Velda asked tentatively.

Albryan shrugged. "If it were confidential, they wouldn't have shoved it under my door." He examined the document, and his face darkened for a moment. "As I expected," he said with strained lightness, looking up. "I'm to report for duty first thing tomorrow. They're giving me a squadron and orders to bivouac at a classified location." He looked at her. "I'm not sure what this is about, and I probably couldn't tell you if I knew. But it looks as if I'll be leaving Tenna tomorrow. I don't know for how long."

"We've talked about this," Velda said, swallowing down a sudden sadness. "That's what a soldier's life is like, right? You often don't know where or when the fighting is going to break out, do you?"

"Too right." He shifted closer to her, and lifted a strand of her tousled hair. "Well, since you're here today, and I won't be tomorrow, how about I do your hair in those braids you were coveting?"

Velda smiled. For the past few days, she had been admiring the intricate hairdos sported by fine ladies in Tenna. She acquiesced, and

Albryan settled himself on the bed behind her, fishing out a comb and a vial of oil that smelled faintly of lemongrass and roses from his bedside cabinet.

"Do you want to tell me about these nightmares you're having?" he asked, as he carefully divided her thick hair into sections and ran the greased comb through each. "Are they about—the things that happened to us? Hiram?"

"No," she replied, feeling the usual leadenness in her gut thinking about Hiram. "I'm afraid they don't make much sense."

Albryan's hands were gentle as he drew together a strand and commenced braiding. "Do you want to talk about them?"

She drew a deep breath. "Well, they're not really nightmares— maybe more like gloomy dreams. I'm always in a cave. Underground. There are ruins in the cave, with some kind of—of inscription. Somehow they feel very, very old. Older than any place I've ever been."

Albryan paused in his braiding for a second, but he said nothing, so she continued, "And then, somehow, there's a lake. Inside the cave. I can see it so clearly, yet I've never actually been anywhere like this before."

Albryan stirred again. "In the east of Qwu'Mallorn there are such places," he said softly. Underground caves with lakes in them. I've seen one, but only a small one. They say there are huge ones further into the wilds, and some of them do contain ruins. Goddess-worship sites from long ago." He ran his fingers through another section of hair. "Is there anything more?"

"Yes. In my dream, I always go to the edge of the lake. I'm looking for something, but I can't say what. I can see my reflection in the water, but . . ." She paused, trying to find words to put to the feeling. "It's strange. It's me, but at the same time I know it's—not me. And it's even stronger, this feeling that I need to find—something. Or some*one*."

Albryan was silent for a long moment, though she could feel the tension in his pose as he worked on her hair. Finally he asked, quietly, "Can you recall the inscription?"

"It's not in the common tongue," Velda replied. "I *think* it might be the same language that's embossed on all your coinage."

"Well, that's archaic Morgein, so it fits with the ruins and Goddess-worship."

She sighed. "Please don't tell me we have to go back to Mialiné and the library today." Velda had never felt more like an outsider than she did in the house of the Ebraskaia clan. It wasn't only that it was far, far above her station, that everything was expensive and fancy and seemed somehow too delicate for her to touch, but Mialiné was apt to treat Velda as if she were a servant come in from the basement. Worse, whenever she was there, Velda *felt* like a servant, even though she'd never actually *been* one in her life.

Albryan did not answer immediately, and she continued, "I've nothing against books, in general, but her collection's particularly gloomy. I think they gave me these bad dreams. It started with something I read . . ."

"Oh really? What was it?"

"I'm trying to remember," she replied. "Oh—that's it. It wasn't even something meaningful. I was bored and picked up a book of fancy-tales. Written for children. Mialiné laughed when she saw me reading them." She could feel her cheeks heating. "She said: *That's a book I remember reading with my sister when we were little.*"

Albryan made an indistinct noise. "Her sister," he muttered, and then asked aloud: "So which tale was it that gave you the nightmares?"

"Something called *The Thorned Sword*," she admitted. "Even though it was just for kids, I found the tale oddly—fascinating."

"Really?" Albryan asked as if he was dissecting something of note. "How so?"

"Well—it's all about a woman who undoes magic. Like me."

"No, it's not," Albryan said, as if she had just told him that trees were red rather than green. "You must have mixed it up with something else in that book. *The Thorned Sword* is a lone hero's quest to restore magic to the world after it's all eaten by a monstrous bear." He chuckled. "Every child in Qwu'Mallorn has read it."

"Well, perhaps you should read it again," Velda said tartly. "Your lone hero fights with a magic-undoing sword by his side, and it's obviously a metaphor for some sort of lady love—a woman. The story is named after her, for Vermayn's sake!"

Albryan went silent for a long moment. "I haven't thought about that story in years," he finally admitted. "Don't think I even took note of the symbolism when I was little. I remember enjoying all the blood and guts—"

"The exhaustive descriptions of gory battles, the two rivals taking bloody mouthfuls out of each other," Velda completed wryly. "A bit much for a children's tale, *I* thought. I couldn't get it out of my head that night, and kept thinking of wolves and walking dead bears and gloomy underground crypts."

They were both quiet for a while, and at last Albryan spoke again, as he tied off the last braid. "Well, you don't have to beg when it comes to *not* spending the day with Mialiné, *ki'jaya*," he said. "It's my last day free, and I'll be damned if I'm spending it in the company of someone who annoys me as much as she does." He turned her to face him. "Let's go see the underground ruins outside Tenna today. At least we'll be alone."


OVER THE PAST TWO WEEKS VELDA'S LIFE had settled in Tenna, at least as much as one could reasonably have expected it to. She had settled comfortably into the boarding-house Albryan had found for her, and to her own surprise was actually enjoying the independence that such a life offered. She had never truly been on her own before. Now she had her own rooms, and was tentatively starting to earn her own money doing little jobs for which there was a shortage of workers in Tenna—basic sewing and weaving, things like knowing how to pluck and dress a chicken, mending boots and other leathers.

Tenna's status as a military outpost was a relatively recent development, and as such had created an enormous demand for things that soldiers liked or couldn't provide for themselves. The army had drawn off many of the local leatherworkers, cooks, shoemakers and so on, leaving relatively fewer of those who plied these trades in town.

To Velda's surprise, the list of things that soldiers liked in Qwu'Mallorn apparently did not include prostitutes; she had not detected a single brothel nor street-walker in the entire town. She remembered bringing this up with Albryan, who had then pointed out that if any of the soldiers wanted a woman for the night, there were literally scores of women in Tenna—young, old, maiden, matron—who were more than willing to oblige.

She had begun to ask a thousand questions, then realized that none of them made any sense. Amongst the Morgei, family lines were matrilineal. The consensus amongst most people she met was that a child needed a *mother*; fathers were largely optional. Every woman she met in Tenna plied her own profession and earned her own living. The Ruling Council of Tenna, presided over by the heads of the five most powerful families in the area, currently counted four women to one man. Sometimes when she was about in town with Albryan, women would make remarks about his appearance that were nothing less than brazen. She had almost been ready to make a scene once or twice, but every time Albryan himself had laughed it off. "At least you know the quality of what you've got," he said to her.

The ruins Albryan wanted to show her were a stiff walk from the barracks, on the opposite side of town. They stopped along the way for a quick breakfast, coffee and baked rolls, and by the time they reached the abandoned city in the forest, the sun was high in the sky and Velda was feeling rather baked herself. Though it was still early in the year, Tenna was already hotter than she found comfortable.

"We have to visit the temple on the way," Albryan told her. "The ruins aren't always safe, and we need to check first."

Velda had been to the great temple once before, when Albryan had taken her along to one of the evening observances he often attended. It was not that much different from the way the Sven monks worshipped their native gods, save that everything took place outside, half the clergy were female, and there was magic involved in the prayers. Nothing she could define, but it was as though the priests of Qwu'Kiya worked some spell to make the atmosphere the way they wanted.

There was no magic in evidence today, although the usual sense of calm pervaded the temple grounds. Albryan found an acolyte, a pretty young woman with curly auburn hair and wide green eyes, and questioned her regarding the ruins. She assured him that all was well, then leaned up and whispered something in his ear that had him grinning and shaking his head.

"Not far now," he said to Velda, taking her arm as they set off again. For a moment she wanted to ask what the young acolyte had whispered to him, then thought better of it.

THE RUINS WERE A MAZE OF TUNNELS and rocky chambers, reaching deep into the cliff where she had sat with Albryan a couple of weeks ago.

Velda wandered back and forth, overawed by the impression of vast age and grandeur, yet this was nothing like her dream. There was no water, for one thing, and none of these chambers were near big enough to house the kind of vast empty space she had dreamed of. The entrance to the ruins, a natural cave which had been carved into pillars and alcoves decorated with symbols and lettering, was enormous, but completely different from the silent, eerie place she had dreamed. In her dream, there had been moss everywhere, phosphorescence glowing from dripping cave walls, a strong smell of damp and decay. This place smelled only of dust; the ancient inscriptions were brushed clear of moss and lit by flickering torches set into the walls. She examined the inscriptions as they walked.

"I think this one's similar," she finally said to Albryan.

He squinted down. "Well, I'm no expert," he said, "but I think that's something generic about this being a site of worship for Qwu'Kiya. I could ask the priestess, I suppose. Or maybe Elithan. He knows more of the archaic tongue than I do."

"I'd certainly prefer that you asked Elithan," Velda said dryly. "*He* doesn't make bedroom eyes at you any chance he gets."

"Are you jealous again?" Albryan took her sleeve. "Flirting

doesn't mean anything. I've told you before, people do it on principle, to show they're available. I haven't reciprocated anything, you know that."

She sighed. "I know. I'm sorry."

Albryan put his arm around her shoulders, and for a while they meandered through the caves in silence. Velda finally worked up the courage to speak.

"Do you—do you think we should talk to your commander after all?" she asked in a low voice. "All this doesn't seem to be getting us anywhere."

Albryan frowned. "All this was a long shot to start with," he replied. "It hasn't been that long, though, and you're still getting used to things here. Let's give it a little more time, at least. I'm leaving tomorrow, but I'll be back—"

*Hopefully.* Velda's heart constricted. "Bryan, what if you—what if something happens?" She could see by the look in his eyes that he understood what she was asking.

Albryan pulled her closer to him in the gloom of the torchlight. "If I *don't* come back," he said slowly, "Elithan will still be here. But by that point, it'll be up to you to decide what to do next." He hesitated, and his eyes glittered oddly. "I'm not sure the best place for you is here," he whispered. "The place you dreamed of—it's far more likely to be somewhere around Catroot, or maybe even further into the wilds."

"Catroot is where your family lives, right?" she asked.

Albryan nodded, looking sombre. He put a hand up to neaten his hair, causing the long sleeve of his tunic to droop and show the three thin white marks which striped his wrist. They resembled old, deep knife wounds. Velda had noticed them before, and had wanted to ask, but the look he'd given her a few days ago when she touched them had forestalled her.

"I haven't been back home in ages," he was saying now. "Perhaps, if things quieten down here—" He shook his head and ran his hand through his hair. "Try not to worry about things for the next few weeks," he said.

She fidgeted. "I wish I could be of more use, though," she said quietly.

"Putting yourself in danger isn't useful to anybody," Albryan returned. "I believe you have a greater purpose, Velda. I don't know what it is yet. But given that we've gone through that entire damn library and found *nothing* that relates to your abilities—that only strengthens my conviction. I may not know if you're quite where you're meant to be, but I *do* know that you don't belong on the frontlines. You're no common soldier."

THEY MADE THEIR WAY BACK TO BARRACKS in the late afternoon. Velda was dusty with the walk, sticky with the heat, and wanted a wash, but there was no time to stop. They had already agreed, ages ago, that tonight they would attend a small gathering of Albryan's fellow officers, an expression of their delight at his safe return and celebration of a few significant promotions in the ranks.

They met the group at yet another ruin in the forest, this one's origins seemingly completely unknown, a great roofless stone edifice close to the barracks compound. They built a campfire in the ancient pit, grilled flatbreads and sausages, and passed around a bottle of some kind of clear alcohol that burned all the way down her throat when she took a swig. Velda had met only about half the people there; many of the men had brought female company of their own, and after the food and drink had run its course, the party quickly scattered into smaller, more intimate groups. There was a large pond on one side of the ruins, fed by a chattering streamlet, and various couples peeled off to wander along the edge of the water.

Many of the other officers had received their own orders to deploy that very day, and the mood was subdued. Everyone seemed quite determined to have a good time, yet the uncertain future hung like a wisp in the air, casting a dampener over all. Even Elithan, who had so long as she'd known him been a walking repository of ribald jokes and good humour, kept to himself, strumming idly on an eleven-stringed lute that looked like it might have cost him a month's wages to acquire. He was a good player, and half the women who'd turned up for the occasion were enraptured by him, which Velda didn't mind in the least. She stayed close to Albryan, who was more attentive than usual.

Unattended, the fire smouldered to embers. Elithan, who had

been wandering back and forth doing something to the lute, now sank down upon a stray brick of stone, struck a chord, and began to sing. He was better than most minstrels who had ever passed through Lynborder, though the song was far from the simple, catchy folk tunes they'd had in their repertoire. The music was so mournful that Velda felt a lump rise in the back of her throat, and the lines didn't even rhyme, though they had a sweet singsong mesmerisation all the same.

*Forest of the morning, watched over by nighttime peaks,*
*Why do the fitful ibis cry as they sail across*
*Your verdant canopy of ironwood and pecan,*
*as the streams sob through wild stands of rosemary and mint?*

Albryan put a hand on the small of her back. "I think this gathering is completely tuckered out," he whispered. "Want to sneak away?"

Velda shivered to his touch, smelled a whiff of the alcohol they'd been drinking on his breath. The night was almost over, and she didn't know when she was going to see her young captain again. She nodded and got to her feet, and they slipped off into the forest.

They found their way to a secluded patch of trees near the pond without disturbing anybody else, and there Albryan pushed her against a tree-trunk and began to kiss her as insistently as they'd done the very first time. The moon was rising above the trees, casting a golden glow across the surface of the pond, and they could barely see each other in the shadows. Velda could just hear, in the distance, Elithan finishing his mournful song.

*Forest of the morning, song of the elder race,*
*Where now is the music of your forgotten people?*
*No comfort lives for me in your feral orchards*
*watered by this downy fall of early rain.*

The last strains hung like motes in the air, the delicacy of the music at odds with the urgency in which they moved together. Clothes came off like petals to be shed from a late rose, and she gripped Albryan's broad shoulders as he gathered her into his arms. When they sank to the ground, she ended up on top, moving eagerly against him, taking him into her even as he brought her closer, until they were connected so deeply they could have been one.

She arched into his chest, aching pleasure welling from where their bodies met, gripped his hair as she cried out in passion, determined to make this something he would remember in the lonely weeks to come, the nights he was camped out waiting for battle. He was totally immersed in the moment, clasping her firmly to him as their gazes remained locked. The heat of his breath was on her lips, yet she did not lower her head for a kiss, wanting his eyes to remain open. She reached the peak of ecstasy in his arms, allowing him to see it all, giving him the sweetest song without any restraint. At last she let him kiss her, the two of them tightly locked together as he rode out his urgency. She felt his body tense as he released hard inside her, swallowed the moan of pleasure that he gave in her mouth.

He slumped bonelessly to the ground, half pillowed on the pile of clothes they'd left there, and pulled her close as she rolled off him. "Now this was a night I'm not like to forget soon, *ki'jaya*," he murmured, breathing hard.

She traced the line of the scar that ran along his chest. "I hope you don't."

SHE AWOKE ALL OF A SUDDEN to the noises of the night, a cicada chirping somewhere in the bushes nearby, and felt the discomfort of having fallen asleep on nothing more substantial than a bed of forest grass. Next to her Albryan was still fast asleep, snoring gently, his face lit softly by the risen moon.

She got to her feet and smoothed back her hair, aware of how sticky she was. The pond rippled invitingly before her, and she remembered summer nights in the mountains, a place where the rushing river pooled in a silent valley, the water clear and cool as ice even on the hottest summer night.

Naked in the moonlight, she walked down to the still pond. There was soft mud under her feet, between her toes, the substrate of growing things. Brown, slimy leaves, still left from last year's fall, lay scattered around the edge of the water.

The moon was high above her, silvering the surface of the pond into velvet. Velda stepped forward, feeling the water lap over her ankles, washing the mud away. The face she saw reflected upon the shimmering surface of the water was her own, a deep well of darkness pooling beyond the reach of the glowing moonlight.

The eyes of the reflection in the pool were shafts of amber light, following her face even as she followed every ripple upon the surface. A wavelet crooked her nose, and the rest of the reflection was cut off as the water stirred in the wind, leaving only the two eyes like glowing coins, and the impression of a face hidden within the shadows of dark, curly hair.

# Chapter XXXII
# Leavetaking

NICO SHOOK HIS HEAD VEHEMENTLY. "No. No, Fish. No way. You and I, we—"

He broke off, staring at the face of the boy before him. The boy he shouldn't have started loving in the first place. What had he been about to say? *We belong together. Fish, don't you see? I haven't come this far with you just to let you go. I can't let you go. It would hurt too much.*

A fine rain was falling in the forest near Hugh Anspeare's camp. Nico had arrived back at the monastery only yesterday, leading the refugees they'd saved last week beyond the pass, but Fish had gone on ahead with Brightfeather to tell Anspeare of all that had transpired. The past week or so, he'd been flying patrol over the mountains between Beerstana and Von Dharen, reporting his findings directly back to Anspeare and no-one else. The first thing Nico had noticed yesterday was how drained his partner looked. After hearing how much he'd been doing and how far he'd been flying, he no longer wondered why. And now Fish was planning to leave him behind for a lot longer . . .

"Brightfeather can't carry more than two," Fish whispered, "and Brialise doesn't belong here. Her home is in Qwu'Mallorn—"

"I understand that," Nico interrupted, "but why does she need to go with such urgency all of a sudden? Why now? When her son is still too young to travel? And why do you have to go with her?"

Fish looked away, arms folded tightly around himself, and with a leaden weight in his gut Nico felt the distance between them, the things left unsaid, and Fish's own feelings, things that Nico, as a penniless orphan from the sticks who'd never had a family nor a proper name of his own, struggled to understand.

Perhaps, if Nico could only find the right words . . . but gods only knew what his partner truly held in his heart, even if Nico had been in any frame of mind to sort through his own tangled feelings and say something that was plain and true. What to do when you wanted someone so much you felt like a wild animal was tunnelling its way through your ribcage? How did you avoid being hurt when the beast was already tearing off bloody shreds of your heart?

"It's not really about Brialise," Fish replied at last, which came as absolutely no surprise. He took a deep breath. "It's *me* who needs to get to the Forest of the Morning. Now that Arran has proven an enemy to both lands, it makes sense for us to ally our forces. And it makes sense for me to go. I'm the only one who can fly, but more than that, I have something they need in Qwu'Mallorn. All the knowledge I possess of my father and his doings."

*And this puffed-up nobleman is giving you over, like so much chattel, a piece to be traded between two players, to obtain the assistance he wants.* Nico felt sick. "Fish—" He struggled to breathe around the shape of his fear. "Your father's been their sworn enemy for as long as—as you've been alive. What if they imprison you? What if they *execute* you?"

Fish glared back. "I don't intend to allow them to do anything of the sort," he returned, "and why would they? We're on the same side. I'm Arran's enemy as much as they are."

"Do *they* know that?" Nico demanded. "Will they believe it when you say so?"

Fish scowled, glancing away, and Nico sensed uncertainty. He took a step forward, touched Fish on the shoulder. "Partner—" he began.

The sudden crunch of cavalry boots on the forest floor made them both turn their heads, and Fish moved away from Nico's hand.

"There you are." Cedric Leibsson, Hugh Anspeare's second-in-command, strode towards them, biting off a wad of chewing-tobacco as he came. Nico could not quite tell which of the two of them was being addressed. He drew his arms back around himself.

This was, of course, the reason why he and Fish found themselves having such a heated discussion this early in the morning, this close to the soldiers' camp. Fish had woken today much earlier than Nico had ever known him to, and immediately set off along the path into the woods. There had been nothing for Nico to do but tail after him, if he wanted any time with Fish at all. Along the way, Fish had begun, hesitantly, to tell Nico of how he was leaving in just a few days, and gods only knew when he would come back—if he came back.

Events were closing in on Nico with alarming rapidity. On their way up to the Beerstana Pass, he and his group of refugees had met with several dozen more ragtag travellers, all of them seeking safe haven where they hoped the invaders would not seek them out. But that hope had rapidly proven false: they had arrived at the pass just ahead of yet another raiding party, men and necromes, and this time Fish had not been there to take care of the latter. The guardsmen at the pass had helped fight their attackers off, taking concerning losses themselves. The necromes turned out to be more deadly than Nico had even imagined: their blood was poisonous, and the slightest amount of it in any open wound would quickly paralyze and fell any human soldier. But that was by no means the worst of it: after a few hours of apparent death, the afflicted person would rise once more and join the ranks of the necromes, throwing themselves with raucous bloodlust upon those they had once called comrade. Nico was still shaken by what he had witnessed, that night at the pass after they all thought they'd reached safety at last.

"Where is he?" Fish asked without wasting a single moment on preliminaries. The grizzled cavalryman made a grimace.

"He's not talking. The boys have been trying to beat it out of him since yesterday."

"Has it occurred to your boys," Fish asked in a deadly soft tone of voice that Nico had never heard him use before, "that he probably doesn't even know the name of his overlord?"

Cedric shrugged diffidently. "He's a traitor. Admitted to being one. Says they plucked him off the streets of Ülhard and made him commander over a dozen necromes. He went along with it for the plunder and the glory. For that alone, they feel they've a right to punish him a little."

"You know your captain wouldn't allow it if he were here," Fish said. Anspeare was gone yet again; this time, he had taken the queen and her children with him, and no-one seemed to know where to.

Cedric grunted. "Captain Anspeare understands, sometimes, a man's got to do *something* to keep himself from exploding into steam. We've all got families, down there. In Ülhard, in Varya, in Von Dharen. Mothers and fathers, wives, sweethearts. Some of us have children." His face darkened. "Someone like that, who's admitted to being a traitor—"

"If you beat him to death," Fish returned icily, "there's no way *I* can extract anything from him."

"How are *you* going to—" Cedric began, then broke off, no doubt seeing the same strange glow in the boy's eyes that Nico just had.

"I don't need names," Fish said quietly. "I just need to know who he saw."

The cavalryman seemed to consider this for a moment, then turned. "Come on, then."

The atmosphere around the camp was tense, the soldiers on edge, and Cedric made them wait outside the perimeter as he barked out orders to bring their prisoner forward. A face peeked out from a nearby tent, but was gone before Nico could ascertain what he suspected—that it belonged to a woman. He wondered about that. Many of the refugees were women who had lost everything. And of course, the monastery housed a number of teenaged orphan girls who could well be tempted to bed with gifts and gentle treatment.

Before long a pair of young cavalrymen appeared, dragging a battered prisoner between them. Nico recognized the pair: they were the same two who had restrained him that day during their confrontation with Anspeare. One was still wearing a bandage on his forearm, and spared a moment to bestow a cold glare on Nico.

The young man hanging between them looked no different from any other boy Nico had known. Perhaps he could have been Nico, in a different life. He had been about the same age when he first arrived in Ülhard. Nico had never had such bad pimples, nor neglected to wash his hair for that long, but they were very similar in height and build, and under the bruises on his ruined face the boy glared defiantly around at his captors with deep blue eyes. Blood dripped in slow globules from his shattered nose as the guardsmen drew to a halt.

Nico fought to restrain himself, to swallow down the bile that rose in the back of his throat. One would have thought that a man who'd made a living out of killing people would have a stronger stomach, but Nico himself had never *beaten* anyone to death. He remembered what Anspeare had said to him. *All kinds of scum, the dregs of the underworld.*

The people who had beaten this boy more than half to death were ordinary soldiers, honest men, counted by many as heroes and defenders of their homeland. Nico knew that if things had gone differently, that day with Anspeare, these two would have killed him without a shred of hesitation.

There was something very disturbing in that knowledge. Nico could hardly imagine ever owing such obeisance to someone else. When he'd killed men, it had been in situations where it was their lives or his, or where he, himself, stood to gain immense personal profit from their deaths. Some thugs he'd known enjoyed it, of course. Some of the men who had hired Nico would gladly have had men beaten, tortured, worse. But Nico realized now that he had never developed a taste for blood. Perhaps he was still, in truth, an innocent orphan boy at heart. Perhaps he was nowhere near as hardened as he had imagined himself to be.

Fish stirred beside him. His golden-brown eyes were hard with anger, and Nico thought for a moment that he was going to say something, but he did not. The two guards released their grip on the prisoner, who stumbled to his knees, barely having the strength to keep himself from falling the rest of the way to the ground.

Fish took a deep breath and knelt down, putting out one hand to keep the young man steady. He took in all of what was before him without flinching, then reached out and brushed the lank hair back from the boy's forehead.

"I'm sorry about this," he whispered, so softly that Nico could barely hear him. "They've done this to you, but what I'm about to do—" He lifted the young man's chin, so that the defiant blue eyes met his. "Listen. You can make this a little easier on yourself, if you don't resist. Try to go someplace else, in your mind. I'll just be in there for a little while. Take only what I need, and then it's over."

"Go bugger yourself." The boy made as if to spit, but only bloody froth spouted between his lips. Nico shifted uncomfortably.

"Fish, what are you going to do to him?"

Fish did not answer, cupping the young man's face with his hand.

It was as if, suddenly, lightning struck. The prisoner screamed, long, loudly, painfully, though Fish had not done anything but stare at him intently. Nico stepped back in fright. The air smelled burnt, though it was a damp day. The scream went on, wordless and horrible, then suddenly trailed off into incoherent sobbing as the blue eyes rolled back into white. Fish disengaged himself as if he'd been burned, stumbling to his feet. There was blood on his hand where he had touched the prisoner.

The boy no longer seemed sane. He continued to moan wordlessly, and was completely limp when his guards took hold of him again. He was drooling now, his jaw hanging slack, and there was not a shred of comprehension in the eyes that had been bright and defiant just a moment ago.

Fish was breathing heavily, as though in exertion, and his eyes followed the prisoner as they dragged him away gibbering.

"My brother Baukin," he whispered, and his voice shook. "That's who they have in charge."

Cedric grunted in satisfaction. "See that you tell Captain Anspeare all about him, when he arrives back."

IT WAS THE DAY THAT FISH WAS DUE to leave, and the fine rain had started again, which was fitting. Nico lounged under a tree in the monastery yard as he watched Brialise and Fish both take leave of the infant who was too young to accompany his mother to his rightful homeland. From what Nico had seen, the child seemed more attached to his wet nurse than to his mother, at least for now. According to Fish he had the gift of magic, though Nico had not seen any evidence of that himself.

Without the backdrop of the monastery, Fish and the girl looked remarkably like a young couple fussing over their first child. Perhaps the girl was a little *too* young, by most folk's standards these days, but

Nico was well aware that life could happen fast sometimes. He chewed on that for a while, scrutinizing his young partner's face for any indication of his true feelings. Fish had never before shown the slightest interest in women, and Nico had wondered from the moment he met him which way his affections lay.

The child was stowed safely back in his wet nurse's arms, and Nico joined the two of them on their way down to a remote field where Fish had been keeping his quetzal, well out of sight of any unsuspecting onlooker. It was a silent walk; Brialise had never been in the habit of speaking overmuch, and Fish's face was closed off, his eyes elsewhere. Nico and the girl both pulled the hoods of their cloaks up against the rain, but Fish did not seem to notice it spiderwebbing in his curls.

All too soon Nico laid eyes upon the hulking form of the flying serpent that was Brightfeather, standing high above the lower trees, silhouetted in the soft rain like some sort of gargantuan stork pricking about for its prey. Hugh Anspeare and his escort were already there, waiting a safe distance away below the forest canopy.

Anspeare exchanged some last words with Fish as Brialise approached the quetzal almost as if she were greeting an old friend. She reached up and caressed the bright neck-feathers without fear. The rain glanced off those feathers like it would with any waterfowl. Brialise ducked her head, and stood expectantly waiting under one of Brightfeather's gigantic wings. Fish clasped Anspeare's hand in farewell, then turned towards Nico.

It was time for him to take leave of his partner, and Nico had in no way prepared himself for this moment. He had planned no private goodbye between himself and Fish. The things he had wanted to tell him still lay unsaid between them. Nico had not had the courage, and now, he doubted that he ever would.

Fish approached him, expecting a hug, and Nico drew him into his arms without hesitation, holding him as tightly as he dared. He could smell him, smell that Fish's shirt hadn't been washed since that day before Anspeare arrived, that he had recently bummed another cigarillo from somewhere, and for a moment he wanted to laugh. *I hope they treat you better in Qwu'Mallorn, partner. Clean shirts and the vices of life whenever you want them.*

Still, he had never minded the smell of other men, not even in his own living space and on his sheets, and he felt a pang in his guts as he realized how much he would miss it. Nico had never been truly easy with sleeping alone, not even when he was younger.

Fish broke the embrace, his eyes bright, and Nico had never felt more like an older brother than he did just then, his partner gazing up at him, looking years younger than his almost-nineteen, eyes brimming with some emotion that Nico could not even begin to dissect. He placed his hand on Fish's shoulder, as close as he dared get to touching the boy's face.

"Come back," he whispered.

Fish took the hand and squeezed it, his eyes never leaving Nico's. "I will."

And then he turned and approached the quetzal and the waiting girl, and there was nothing for Nico to do but watch, arms folded tightly trying to hold himself together.

Once he had arranged himself in the flying-saddle and settled Brialise behind him, Fish did not look back. The quetzal gained the air, swooped low over the forest, and disappeared into the horizon in a grey-green blur, lost amongst the clouds as it travelled in the direction of the morning sunrise.

HUGH DREW HIS EYES AWAY FROM the retreating form of the feathered flying beast, and turned towards the young assassin. He was gazing desperately after his partner, arms folded tightly about his chest. His face was stricken, and Hugh had the sudden, absurd thought that he ought to apologize for sending Fish away, something he'd never felt towards a soldier before.

Still, the pair of them were not soldiers—at least not in the traditional sense. Neither of them had any love for authority, and despite his common birth and uncouth demeanour, Nico Klavbert was smarter, more independent, and much more inventive than the majority of men one was likely to meet in the livery of the Crown Army. That, of course, was part of the reason Hugh had wanted so badly to recruit them both to his side in the first place. His heart pounded in the back of his throat. For what he planned to do—what he *had* to find someone for—an ordinary soldier would not suffice.

"Nico," he began, and the young man deigned to look his way at last, dragging his eyes away from the empty clouds. There was no more sign of the quetzal nor its rider. The day was becoming more overcast by the minute, the rain falling more insistently. It was mid-morning, yet it seemed close to dusk.

"The Morgei have always been an honourable people," he said. "I wouldn't send your partner there unless I had confidence that this could work. That they would treat him fairly."

He could not tell what impact his words made; Nico said nothing, only nodded absently and looked away again. Every movement and bearing of his demeanour told Hugh that the young man would rather be left to brood on his loss in solitude.

Perhaps it had to do with their youth, but Hugh had never before met a pair who were as painfully obvious as Nico and his partner, and he was not sure what to make of it. Experience had taught him that it was generally best to ignore that sort of thing completely; soldiers of their persuasion tended to be very defensive against any kind of interest that could be construed as interference. From his own experience, it had never once interfered with a soldier's competence, nor were men like that any worse-behaved than the average Sven soldier, who drank, whored, and traded his small arms for tobacco whenever he got the chance.

Hugh steeled himself, knowing that he must be behaving oddly; Nico was regarding him now with a kind of mild curiosity, as if wondering what strange thing he would do next.

*When it comes to those we care for*, he thought desperately, *I suppose all of us come across a little strange sometimes.* Hugh checked behind him, to make sure that his men were staying out of earshot as he'd instructed. He and Nico stood alone in the middle of the field. Raindrops pattered against the hood of his cloak.

"I have a task for you," he said at last, in a low voice. "Nico, I don't want to have to command you to do this, but—"

The young man shrugged. "Do I have much choice?" he asked quietly. "If I want to live to see Fish again?"

Hugh sighed. "I have never gambled with the lives of any of my men," he said. "This . . . I wouldn't send a regular soldier on this kind of job. I don't think they'd survive, nor succeed."

Nico laughed harshly. "Enough with the flattery! Just tell me what it is, Commander. Either I'll come back covered in glory, or I won't come back at all." His eyes were hard beneath the hood of his cloak. "Never have I been afeared of death."

*It is not death at stake here.* Hugh recalled Fish, just three days ago, standing in his tent with his usual irreverent manner.

*"There's no doubt about it,"* Fish said, *flicking aside the stub of a cigarillo which looked like he might have picked it up from the gutter. "The one they have in charge of the invasion in Ülhard—it's my brother, Baukin. I saw him in the captive's mind, clear as day."*

*Hugh's men had told him all about the captive. A young man who had been taken prisoner when he attacked the guardsmen at Beerstana Pass as part of a band of men and necromes. Fish had interrogated him by magic, and somehow that had killed him, and they had buried his body forthwith. There was a lot that Hugh found fishy about this story, but what had really happened to a young prisoner who stood traitor to his country didn't truly matter. What mattered was the information that Fish had extracted from him.*

*"Now, with Baukin there won't be any of the dumb bravado you'd have found with Taunus," Fish continued. There was a haunted, feverish look in his eyes. "Expect the underhanded, when it comes to this one. But he's cautious. Won't commit too many of his troops at once, which is probably why we've seen only these small raiding parties. If he's taken Ülhard, expect him to dig in his heels and not budge very far."*

*"They took Von Dharen," Hugh reminded him. Panic blossomed in his heart. Von Dharen had fallen, and he'd had no news from Katrina, and battle lines were rapidly building beyond the pass.*

*Fish shrugged. "Von Dharen is small potatoes, less than a week's range from his home base." He hesitated. "Now, I don't think he would mistreat people at random. Baukin's very, very cruel, but restrained where he exerts his cruelty. And he wouldn't engage in wanton destruction. The people of Ülhard are—most likely—safe, so long as they don't rouse his ire. But if, say, he should capture the queen—"*

*Hugh went rigid, and took care not to show it. This was no moment to divulge weakness.*

*"All I can say is," the boy continued blithely, "I wouldn't let it happen if I were you. But you already know that, don't you? You've moved*

*her someplace even more secret than this."*

*It was disquieting that the boy had somehow guessed the queen's identity, but perhaps it had been a bit too obvious from the start. Bronwyn never could disguise her royal bearing, her impeccable breeding. That was why she was safer with the hermit-nuns, further up the mountain. She and her children.*

*Her* remaining *children. Rolf was dead. Katrina—*

*"May I go?" Fish asked, when the silence began to linger, and Hugh unconsciously gestured him out. Katrina . . .*

Nico listened silently as Hugh explained the situation. Reports from anywhere had been spurious, and Hugh had to fill in the gaps with a lot of guesswork.

After he'd taken Ülhard, the blood sorcerer Baukin Sylvaissen had sent auxiliary armies down the coast to subdue the towns of Varya and Von Dharen. With the Dzil already ravaged, he now controlled a full third of Svanfeld. Hugh kept receiving conflicting reports about the fate of General Roald Vanya; either he'd fallen fighting beside his king, which was good and proper yet terrible news for his country, or he'd made a miraculous escape and was now massing the remnants of the Sven army somewhere near Pine.

Katrina had been visiting her cousins in Von Dharen when the crisis had struck. The king had gone so far as to order Hugh to "retrieve" her if the situation worsened—but the situation had deteriorated so far beyond what any of them could have predicted, that Hugh was hard-pressed to defend himself and the queen, if it came to that, and had almost nothing and no-one to spare.

No-one but a young assassin, a common bruiser from the streets of Ülhard, whom he was about to entrust with the safety of a princess. Still, if Hugh was any judge of character—and long years of commanding men had given him a keen sense of these things—Nico was more trustworthy in this regard than any other man he currently had.

Nico listened intently, and a scowl crept across his face. "This mansion," he said at last. "Was it in any way suited for defence? When the fight came, would they have stayed there, or would they have fled?"

"Fled is what I would have thought," Hugh answered heavily, "yet if they had, they'd have turned up *here* by now."

"And he likely would not have killed her," Nico said, softly as if to himself. "You know this means that she is almost certainly his prisoner. This Baukin."

Hugh nodded, surprised and yet pleased by the young man's quick grasp of the situation. "That's why we need to act, and act quickly," he said. "Once Von Dharen settles down, he might have her transferred to him in Ülhard. But if you get there in time—"

"Alright, I understand." The young assassin regarded Hugh with something like dark amusement. "I'm to take myself into this war zone that Von Dharen has become, find out if the princess is still alive, figure out where they're holding her if she is, come up with a way to extract her, and bring her back through this war zone safely to you—all on my own."

"Not on your own." Here it was, the singular piece of good news that Hugh Anspeare had received since he'd come beyond the Pass of Beerstana. "There'll be a second going with you. An experienced mercenary."

# CHAPTER XXXIII
## BOUND

THE CONTINENT STRETCHED OUT BENEATH him, brown and green and golden yellow, and Fish flew, staying one step ahead of his confusion and sorrow, speeding towards an uncertain future. It was all in his hands now, the path they would take, and he felt almost dizzy with nerves and guilt and the twinge of regret that assailed him whenever he thought of Nico left behind.

The dense cloud cover dispersed once he was past Lake Mountaindale, and he directed Brightfeather to turn northeast, high above a twisting river and the trade road which led back into the mountains. He made sure to keep the line of the mountains to his left, the sun safely shining out in front of him. The last thing he wanted to do was veer too far east, and wind up within reach of Armour City.

As the time passed and Brightfeather gradually settled into a long-distance glide, Fish fell into a reverie that was almost like a dream. Brialise was quiet, studying the landscape below, her hands resting gently on his back. The quetzal was calm, focused on their destination as Fish had relayed it to him, and today at least there was no desire to ride the air currents down to Armour City, where he had been taken as a hatchling, raised with his nestmates, then trained and controlled and bound to Taunus's will.

Fish had run away before his father had allowed him to train his own quetzal, and he felt an immense joy at the thought that at least one aspect of his magic had remained free of the blood sorcerer's taint. He had never learned how to dominate the will of another living creature, and so had approached Brightfeather with a bond based on mutual trust instead—the promise that Fish would not punish him to make him obey, nor drive him to fly till he was on the verge of collapse from exhaustion, nor make him go places where he was totally unwilling. All things, as Fish knew from the images and feelings that passed down the magical link between them, which Taunus had done to him.

It was a long distance to the border of Qwu'Mallorn, and Fish wanted to cover most of it today, but after four hours, neither he nor Brialise could stand it any longer. So he directed Brightfeather down towards a cliffside overlooking a rushing mountain stream and the plains beyond, and they both dismounted gratefully. The quetzal looked down upon them almost with disdain, and Fish caught an impression of disapproval at their lacking endurance.

"We're people, not great flying serpents who were made for this sort of thing," he shot back. "Go catch some fish in the river, or something."

Brightfeather, however, was not hungry, having dined on a substantially sized sheep last night, courtesy of the arrangement Anspeare had made with the monks. He shuffled off and perched on a boulder, stretching his wings out to catch the sun. Fish recalled once having seen a cobra near Zarath doing much the same thing, expanding its hood to bask. Next to him, Brialise giggled at the sight.

Fish watched her covertly as they unpacked food and water to make a picnic on the sunny slope. He'd had several tense conversations with Brother Jakob the past few days, with the girl maintaining that above all she wanted to return to Qwu'Mallorn, and the monk trying to insist that they wait until he was fully convinced that she had recovered from the childbirth. But despite having left her son behind, Brialise seemed lighter and happier than any time previous. She stretched a lot, winced a little and complained that she was crampy and stiff, but nothing that Fish felt presaged anything serious. She giggled at butterflies, sent little magical messages of her own to Brightfeather, ate more of their lunch than Fish did.

Fish studied the map yet another time before they set off again, going over landmarks which were already firmly memorized. If they stayed on course along the mountains, they should soon intersect the confluence of the Dreaming Water with the River Granite, and there Fish planned to camp for the night.

They flew again, this time for what felt like twice the length of time, yet Fish knew from the position of the sun that it had only been half. An arrowhead-shaped lake appeared to their right as the sun began to dip into the shadowy cradle of peaks ranged upon their left. He banked Brightfeather towards it, putting the mountains behind them at last, and a swathe of dark green appeared in the not-so-far-off distance.

Brialise gasped into his ear. "There it is," she breathed.

*There it is, indeed.* Fish's heart jumped into his throat.

The view of Qwu'Mallorn was lost as they descended towards the lakeshore, and exhaustion assailed Fish as he stumbled off onto the soft grass. Swans glided upon the still surface of the water in the rays of the descending sun, and the air smelled of soil and grass that had been baking all day in its radiance. It was so different from where they'd started that morning that it felt disorienting.

They watched the swans in the sunset light, talking quietly as they ate some more trail-food. "Are you missing Nico?" she asked.

"I am." Fish did not elaborate on how complicated his feelings towards his partner had become in the past few weeks. It had seemed almost as though Nico were trying to take a step towards him, to share something with Fish that might change the nature of their friendship . . . but then they had been separated, Fish had been so busy he'd barely had time to breathe, there had been that horrible affair with the benighted young prisoner and everything had been so muddled afterwards. Nico had sat with him the rest of that day, his hand on Fish's shoulder as he explained in a broken voice what he had done to the captive, how he had extracted the information they needed by a technique Arran had taught him. To Fish's surprise, Nico had still accepted him afterwards, hugging him tightly and speaking nothing but soothing words.

*Nico comforted me. Who was there to comfort that boy before they decided to finally dig him a shallow grave?* If Cedric and his brothers-in-arms hated everyone who had ever worked alongside a blood sorcerer, then there was no-one they should hate so much as Fish himself. Were it not for the fear that drove him to run away when he was still a child, it might have been *him* leading an army of necromes to invade Svanfeld.

Fish put thoughts of this ilk aside, and turned to Brialise. "Are you missing your son?" he asked back.

She toyed with the end of her long braid, and levelled her gaze at him. "No."

Fish looked away, feeling foolish and embarrassed. "I shouldn't have asked that."

She took his arm. "I apologize, Fish. It's just . . ." She looked out over the water. "I do not know what to do. The great monastery . . . there is nothing like that in Qwu'Mallorn. We do not produce unwanted children . . . Even if, sometimes, the mother isn't ready, there is always a family . . . parents, sisters and brothers, aunts and uncles. But of my family, I am the only one left."

"The boy has a Mage-Gift," Fish said quietly. "The monks of

Svanfeld can't raise him. Not properly."

"He will have a stronger Gift than mine," Brialise confirmed. "My mother would have said that was a blessing." She looked away, still fussing with her braid. "Have—have you ever thought of raising a child?" she asked, diffidently. "You and Nico?"

For a long moment Fish stared at her, not comprehending, then his whole body grew hot with the force of his discomfort as he realized what she was saying. Brialise caught sight of his face.

"I—I thought you and Nico were—"

"No." Fish shook his head vehemently. "We're not. Nico's not—"

"But you are?" she asked, carefully, into the pause as he broke off.

Fish grimaced. *What a sticky question.* And yet, he sensed that there was no dishonest motive behind it.

He'd been a little older than she was now, around sixteen, when he'd joined the Townsguard in Zarath. He had been living there, with Delourien, for the past four years at that time. The old woman had civilized him a little, accustomed him to spending time with normal people, and he'd even had friends his own age, not close friends, but still. He'd already been half-trained in true swordsmanship, having been drilled by the best armsmasters Arran could retain, and he'd figured the Guard was as good a place as any to start earning some money of his own.

As a child, Fish had not spent a lot of time with either of his brothers; the only sibling he could be said to have been close with had been his sister Dannine. Crammed, for the first time, into close living quarters with a group of other young men in the barracks of the Guard, he had quickly come to a startling realization about himself.

Those feelings, directed as they were towards other boys, had frightened him at first, making him worry that perhaps he had been permanently damaged, that the fear he felt regarding the sexual ritual of blood sorcery had somehow translated itself into something twisted inside him. That anxiety had driven him, at last, to tell Delourien about them.

To his vast surprise the old woman had only nodded and taken his hand sympathetically, then explained to him that some people were simply made that way. *Born* that way. Fish had been astonished to hear that he was not the first to experience such desire, nor was it as strange and unnatural as he'd thought. There was no shame in it, at least not according to what Delourien's Goddess taught, but she had stressed that he should be careful about whom he chose to tell. *Goddess knows, Fish, I don't have to tell you to be cautious to trust. I'm glad you trusted me. I fear that life will always be a hard road for you, and this won't make it any easier.*

"Am I what?" he asked now in a low voice, wanting Brialise to make it clear before he ventured any answer.

"*Ak'a'jana.* One who—who loves the same sex."

Delourien had called it the same thing. "Yes," he whispered.

"But you do not want it known." She leaned forward. "Why not?"

He caved to the easy answer. "In the lands of Svanfeld and Vailana, it is not—encouraged. Not forbidden, not exactly, but if other men knew—" He shook his head. "They might hate me. Hurt me."

"Other men?" She frowned. "Even Nico?"

"Exactly." He forced himself to speak past the lump in his throat. "Nico's not—he can't be—" He broke off what he had been about to say. *Nico can't be trusted?* Or was the impulse holding him back a much more selfish one, the fear that if Nico *knew*, he would lose the closeness of their friendship, the physical affection, the easy rapport? Would Nico still be comfortable sharing close living quarters if he knew that Fish craved his touch, his close proximity, not just from brotherly comfort but romantic longing?

Yet there was also the way Nico seemed to approach him sometimes, to initiate something he never quite went through with. It had happened weeks ago in the mountains, that night when he'd rubbed liniment all over Nico's injured arm, and it had happened again just that morning, when Nico bade him farewell. Fish had no idea what to make of the intense way Nico had looked at him, the way he had hugged him.

Fish had always had a vivid imagination, and it would be all too easy to fantasize that perhaps Nico was coming to feel the same way he did, that despite his liaisons with the opposite sex he harboured some hidden desire that Fish as yet had no inkling of. Could it even work that way? Could someone shift their romantic longings from women to men? Fish had no notion of how other people regarded these things in their private lives, and the workings of love were completely mysterious to him. He had no framework for what a love affair was supposed to look like, only a confusing jumble of longings and half-formed wishes. How did people—particularly those like him, where there was no initial assumption of romance—even begin to find one another?

"Are you all right?" Brialise asked softly. "I am sorry that I assumed—"

"Don't be." Fish touched her shoulder. "They say that in Qwu'Mallorn, these things make no difference, am I right?"

"That is true." Her face brightened. "Perhaps you will meet someone to your liking!"

Fish did not have the heart to gainsay her. "Perhaps."


THE NIGHT PASSED WITHOUT INCIDENT, and early the next morning they were in the air again. A low, wispy mist had come to hover late the previous night, and it was clearing slowly before the sun, filling up hollows in the scrub forest as they winged across it. Fish kept Brightfeather positioned over the scrub, riding that narrow corridor between rolling plain and real forest, aware that any moment now—

He felt it, or rather, didn't feel it. An interruption in the natural flow of the world, a storm-dyke holding back untold power behind itself, causing the energies of the earth to shift and flutter around it. It loomed large in his magical senses, like a sudden shadow cast over the sun, and he shivered.

"The Border," Brialise breathed.

To the naked eye, nothing was amiss; the Forest of the Morning stretched out wild and verdant before them, dotted with the occasional hill-slope and cultivated fields. But on the eldritch plane, where Fish could sense magic, it was as if the whole forest had been muffled in a blanket, cutting it off from the rest of the world. There was a sense of innate power, of age and grandeur. It clung close to the ground, much like the receding mist; Brightfeather could fly above it, though he did not like it one bit, and kept winging higher when Fish directed him over it. Fish wondered what would happen if they fell from the sky onto this muffling thing, and with that thought he was no longer keen to fly above it either.

"It's as if the whole forest is simply—dead," he whispered, and a chill rippled up his spine. "I can't see—or feel—*anything*." The land of Qwu'Mallorn was home to at least half a million souls, the majority of whom possessed the gift of magic. All of that was hidden, completely invisible to Fish's senses. It unsettled him more than he cared to admit, and he directed Brightfeather back towards the unblanketed scrub, which the quetzal definitely preferred. They winged along the forest's edge, Fish keeping a sharp eye on the ground below.

The two settlements appeared at almost the exact same moment, one on the plainsland directly below, the other a little way off in the midst of the verdant green that was the forest. *Woodsdale, and Tenna.* He needed to pass the first well before he thought of landing; this was Arran's military outpost. *I hope Dannine and Ceazyn aren't nearby.* The thought of his sisters made Fish's heart beat faster, bile rise in the back of his throat. But no, he would *know* if they were anywhere near; he would have enough advance warning even if they arrived on their own quetzals.

They flew over a wide, blue river. *The Tenna Vey.* Once, there had been a bridge here, and a trade road had connected the Morgein town with the capital of Armour City. Fish could just see the wooden bridge-supports that remained to either side of the river, anchored on the high banks; the rest had been broken away nineteen years ago, sent to float downriver so that Arran's armies would have no easy crossing. The road beyond was overgrown, but it was broad and had once been paved, and Fish felt Brightfeather's desire to land even before the thought occurred to him.

He spoke over his shoulder to Brialise. "We're going to land on the road. Hold on."

She nodded vigorously, and they descended, coming to a halt that was a little more graceful, on the flat surface of the paving-stones, than what Brightfeather's landings normally were.

Fish dismounted and strode, mesmerized, towards the Border.

Now that he was on the ground, he could actually see it: it towered high above him, a rippling wall of distorted light, an implacable barrier between two wildly differing worlds. He could sense its power, almost a live thing, a cold entity with a will and loves and hates of its own.

Brialise strode forward, reached the shimmering barrier, and vanished from existence.

Fish resisted the urge to call to her, not wanting to seem quite as overawed and anxious as he felt. The girl strode out again, looking curiously at him, as nonchalant as though she were on a holiday outing. Fish blinked, abruptly sensing her presence as if she had simply been dropped back into the world.

"You know I can't follow you in there," he said.

She nodded. "I know." There was a pause between them, and then she spoke again, "But—others have broken through it. The veil. How, I do not know."

Fish stood a moment, considering, then took a dagger from his belt. Like most valuable weapons, all of his daggers were silver-edged, so that they would repel magic. Carefully, he reached out and drew the blade of the dagger across a section of the Border, the shimmering magic parting as the silver approached.

For the briefest of moments, Fish thought that perhaps he had succeeded, using only the simplest possible onslaught to this mighty edifice; a break shone through the veil, like the sun peeking from behind a dark storm-cloud, and he reeled for a moment with the massed power he could feel beyond, with the essence of thousands of beings who carried the gift of magic. But before he could even begin to react, something stirred in the great barrier, rippling along the surface of the dense magicks; the tendrils he had slit with the dagger found each other and re-formed, weaving themselves into threads that were just a little longer and thinner, beyond the reach of its point. Startled, Fish drew the dagger back. The magic beyond the veil vanished as though it had never been. The barrier smoothed itself out, presenting again a cold, unbroken surface, and Fish could have sworn he sensed a new hostility.

He stood in awe of the strength and inventiveness of this creation. Yet he could also see a way to outsmart it; one little dagger was not sufficient, but if there were a silver object large enough, he could force the barrier past the limits of those tendrils and tear a hole that lasted longer than a moment. It was the weakness common to all things of magic.

He turned to Brialise. "Do you think that will have alerted someone?"

She nodded. "I believe so. There is a border-patrol."

"Then all we need to do," Fish said, trying to settle himself, "is sit here and wait for them to find us."

Brialise sank down upon a convenient fallen tree, looking for all the world as though she were picnicking. Brightfeather once again spread out his wings to bask, his long neck stretched along the paving-stones. But Fish was still restless. He wandered a little along the Border, keeping girl and quetzal both in his sights. He turned his head, sensing something new. Yes—unmistakable. Sudden firings of magic some way away, like someone letting off a volley of attacks. An edge to the ether; Fish could almost smell it. Conflict. Battle magic.

He turned and moved back towards Brialise, running through the available options in his mind. Brightfeather had turned alert, and was gazing steadily at him in that sidelong manner he had, regarding things on the ground with a single beady eye.

Brialise stood up, looking worried. "Something's happening," she said.

"A fight, by the feel of it."

She looked at him. "You—should we go? Go to help?"

"I could certainly help," Fish returned, and felt the raw excitement of battle stir under his skin. "Will you wait here?"

She shook her head vehemently. "No. I won't be left alone. If you go, I'm going with you."

Fish knew that the girl had been abducted from *inside* the Border, and could not blame her for not trusting in it now. "I don't want to take you into danger," he said cautiously. "We'll go, but you stay with Brightfeather. Don't leave him for any reason. He'll protect you."

The quetzal fidgeted as they mounted back up, stretching out his great beak to give a loud squawk that Fish could only interpret as battle-excitement. He patted the glossy neck-feathers, taking a deep breath himself to keep his magic contained. That had been a problem too often lately. Whenever he touched his Gift these days, it responded with a lightning-fast surge of power, a thousand times stronger than anything he needed. It was hazardous, Fish knew, not only because he was doing his own body harm by having to contain the backlash every time, but because the uncontrolled power radiated from him and spilled over into anyone else who happened to be touching him or even standing too near. This was particularly dangerous to the unGifted, and Fish had spent the past week or so brooding on how it had hurt Nico, that day in the caves, and how much worse it *could* have been.

Quickly he checked himself over. He was wearing his jerkin and vambrace, which were only leather and would not protect him from magical attack, yet better by far than nothing at all. Anspeare had let him have a spare cavalry pot-helm, complete with the lobster tail at the back, in case he got himself into just such a situation, and he retrieved it now and put it on. His sword was attached to Brightfeather's flying-saddle at such an angle that he could have pulled it out to strike against an opponent in mid-air, and his various daggers were in their usual places, belt and boot and others.

"All right," he breathed, and Brightfeather tensed beneath him, ready to fly. "Let's go."


THEY CAME FROM THE WEST, BEARING down upon the battle like a brightly feathered dart thrown from high above. It was a proper battle, this one: no skirmish of untrained villagers, no necromes. The combatants were men, on one side an impression of dirty white and dishwater grey, silver-plated armour of Arran's nonmage troops; on the other, the men seemed almost to meld into the forest behind them, lightweight uniforms of brown leather and dark green fabric. The Morgein troops were mounted, but heavily outnumbered; Fish could tell that by a glance, though he wasn't sure how many men were involved. It seemed like a lot, but he had never actually seen warfare on this scale before.

Despite their low numbers, the Morgein cavalry seemed to have a solid plan; they cut in neat lines through the nonmage foot-soldiers, leaving them in disarray. However, Arran's foot-soldiers carried long pikes, and as Fish watched were already starting to form lines of their own, forcing the horsemen to have to veer off-course or risk impaling their mounts.

Against this, however, the Morgein soldiers could work magic. The foot-soldiers were armoured, albeit patchily, with steel that was silver-plated, and Fish could feel the shimmer of all that massed silver from where he soared above, but that did not stop the magicians from interrupting their lines with sudden blasts of magic that rent the ground asunder, causing them to stumble, the formations to break. But just as Fish was admiring the way the Morgei had come up with this tactic, he saw that Arran's soldiers had come prepared for it after all.

Though the larger part of the nonmage force was on foot, a small wedge of cavalry held back from the battle, and now they took out their own weapons, bringing them into position. Fish recognized the unmistakable shape of the long-barrelled musket, a weapon of gunpowder that hitherto had been virtually unknown in the lands of Bavarian.

Gunpowder had been around for several centuries now; Fish himself had spent time with sailors, and had actually handled a gun a few years back. In the Great Continent, it was said, in the quarrelsome lands of Zemlya and Limojenga, handguns and cannons were as common as swords and spears, and had been a vital part of warfare for at least the past century. Svanfeld and Vailana, on the other hand, had not been involved in any substantial wars until Arran Sylvaissen had arisen. Firearms here were a bit of a curiosity, owned mostly by nobles to provide more sport when hunting. They were not even issued to the army of Svanfeld; Hugh Anspeare and his men carried no guns.

But now, the mounted nonmage soldiers lined up, sighted down the barrels, and a volley went off, adding the crack of powder and crunch of bullets to the already horrible noises of death-cries and blades clashing, screaming horses. The Morgein cavalry, standing as they did well above the heads of the pikemen, were easy targets. Horses and men alike fell screaming, breaking their advance, interrupting their magic. Fish felt Brialise shudder, bury her face in the back of his shirt.

And with that, he knew what he was going to do.

Of one mind with him, Brightfeather spiralled lower, coming in over the musketeers. They raised their heads without fear, one or two of them even waving and saluting, and Fish was taken aback until he remembered that the quetzals belonged to Arran, after all. Taunus had ridden Brightfeather; Dannine had her own quetzal, as did the rest of the blood sorcerer's children. These men believed that Fish was coming down to fight on *their* side.

A savage thrill gripped Fish as he called forth his magic and fed it into the shape he desired, allowing himself to concentrate on nought else. There was fire in his hand, hot and terrible, and the ether sang around him, rippling in the wind of his passing. The quetzal swooped down and down, until he could see faces of individual men, turned up half in confusion, some of them holding their muskets uncertainly, the others already reloading for the second volley.

Without hesitation, Fish released the magic burning in his hand.

The resulting fireball ripped through the ranks of the musketeers. Brightfeather was already swooping back up, and Fish had to turn in the saddle to behold his handiwork. The confusion was devastating. The horrible fire unique to magic ripped through men and fleeing horses both. Something like guilt twinged in Fish; he'd never aimed for the horses, but it was probably inevitable that the poor beasts would get the worst of it. Some of them had managed to win free, and fled careening into the battlefield, picked off easily by the Morgein cavalry.

As Fish watched, a man who had been standing ahorse on the very edge of the battlefield, likely Arran's commander by that position, rode forward and began to yell loudly, plucking a heavy musket from his own saddle-bow and aiming it into the air. Those few of the musketeers still standing, who still had their weapons and the wit to load and aim, did the same.

Fish went cold, and acted by instinct alone. He threw a quick magical shield down, scattering the lead balls even as the crack of gunshots resounded once again. He was not quick enough for a few; a bullet that might have belonged to the commander himself zipped past, narrowly missing Brightfeather's wing-joint. The quetzal shied, lurching sideways, and it was all Fish could do to keep the bullets away, building shield after shield in the air as the musketeers continued to fire.

*This is too dangerous.* Brightfeather winged up and away, putting desperate distance between himself and the battlefield. He kited sideways, over the Morgein soldiers. Fish had given them some respite, but many had fallen already and they were still struggling with the pikemen, still outnumbered. A good many had lost their horses and were fighting on the ground, attacking the pikemen with swords and axes. After their initial energy, they seemed to have given up on magical attack. Fish spotted only one soldier who was still sending intermittent fire: a young man who seemed to be the Morgein commander, judging from the way he was yelling orders as he laid about him with his short cavalry sabre. He had lost both horse and helm in the fight, and his long hair glinted copper in the morning sunlight. He and two other horseless men were making a stand, keeping the enemy before them at bay, but even as Fish soared overhead one of his companions went down, skewered on a pike, and more enemy soldiers circled around to come up behind him.

In that briefest of moments, Fish made up his mind. "Stay with the quetzal!" he yelled back at Brialise, and reached out to grasp the hilt of the sword affixed to the flying-saddle. He sensed a slight protest from Brightfeather, the feeling that the quetzal thought that Fish was putting himself into far too much danger, but he obeyed Fish's prompting and went low once again, coming down so close to the ground that foot-soldiers tripped and flailed away before him. There was but a moment for Fish to move; he had to time it right, but the incredible partnership he had cultivated with Brightfeather paid off.

He took a deep breath, hefted his sword and leapt the ten feet down to the ground, using a bit of magic to cushion his fall. The quetzal winged away, taking to the sky, bringing himself and Brialise far away from the battle. Fish scrambled to his feet, found himself surrounded by foemen. He did not hesitate; his advantage had always been his speed, not his reach, and he dashed back and forth, meeting their blades even as he drew a sizzling swathe of magic around himself.

These soldiers wore a lot more silver than Fish himself ever had, though, and they hardly batted an eyelid even when Fish caused the wooden handles of their pikes to go up in flame. They simply cast away the magicked weapons and drew silver-chased shortswords from their belts, now well-nigh immune to his magic.

Gunfire sounded again, intermittently; horses neighed, men screamed; Fish fought back his assailants even as they came at him from all sides. Hazy smoke hung in the air, casting the confusion in shades of dull grey. Morgein horsemen charged back and forth, scattering groups of foot-soldiers before them.

A man rushed at Fish out of nowhere, musket in one hand, cavalry sabre in the other. He stopped and fired the gun before coming onwards. Fish flinched and ducked down, and the bullet missed him by more than a foot. But the man was almost on top of him, and there was no time to get away. The sabre whacked him across the forehead; he felt the edge connect just above his eye, and his helmet went flying. He stumbled, trying desperately to regain his balance, knowing that he was done for if he didn't straighten up in time.

But someone else rushed into the gap, connected with the sword arcing down towards Fish, shoved the assailant away and caught him a blow under the helm that opened his throat. Fish straightened to meet the gaze of the young Morgein commander. He had regained his helmet, and now he grabbed Fish's from where it had fallen and shoved it at him, yelling: "We've got them on the run!"

Fish rocked backwards, and realized that it was true. The horsemen were no longer dashing wildly back and forth; they were in pursuit now, driving the hapless foot-soldiers before them, ululating a wild battle song as they mercilessly cut the fleeing men down. The young commander stepped forward, raised his hand in an arcane gesture. "Kill them all!" he shouted, and with a great *crack* the very earth split open in a ragged line before the fleeing men.

Fish hung back, reluctant to join the butchery. Hate and exhilaration still coursed through his veins, but he felt suddenly exhausted, ready to drop where he stood. The moans and screams of the last enemy soldiers lingered for a while, then slowly died away. The air stank of blood and gunpowder and the sulphurous residue of magic.

"We've wiped them out," the commander said hoarsely. "Let them chew on *that*, next time they want to have at us again." He paused and turned to look at Fish, who met his gaze. His face became still.

"I don't know you," he said quietly. "But—this victory is yours. If you hadn't—"

He broke off, looking suddenly supremely confused. Fish started to smile, trying to think of something to say to put him at ease. Battle-excitement was warring with exhaustion inside his veins, and he could not seem to figure out how to string words together. But then, the commander caught sight of something behind him; his eyes went very wide, and he stepped backwards. Fish turned. There in the distance stood Brightfeather, with Brialise hovering by his side.

"You came in flying on that thing," the young commander hissed, and his sword curved out in front of him. "That's what feels off about you. *Blood sorcerer.* You're one of—of *his* children." He stared at Fish, who stood his ground. "Deryck Sylvaissen."

Confusion swept over Fish, and shock, and a touch of fear. How had this common soldier guessed his identity so quickly? He steeled himself; the young commander held a sword, but had not used it against him—yet. *I must remember what I came here for.* "If you know my name," he said at last, evenly, "then you must know that I haven't been seen for the past eight years."

"Now you have been seen." The commander shrugged, then narrowed his eyes. "But you joined the battle on our side. Your magic is—off. Not quite like ours, but it doesn't have the taint of blood sacrifice about it either." He lowered the sword. "I have a feeling, now, that you're about to say something amazing, Deryck. That you've defected from your father and come to join us."

Fish managed a weak grin. "That's the essence of it," he managed, noting that the commander's expression was still hostile. "I don't go by that name anymore," he continued. "Don't call me Deryck. It's Benjamin Fisher, or Fish for short. And there's more. I'm offering not only myself, but an alliance with Svanfeld against our common enemy."

The young commander blinked several times, looking rather as if he had just been clubbed in the back of the head. Before he could reply, one of his men came riding up, a grizzled veteran by the looks of him, with grey in his long black hair and scars on his face.

"Captain!" he called. "The enemy has been annihilated. I estimate about thirty of us are still walking, thirty wounded too badly to walk, another thirty-something dead. We're gathering all the horses we can find. Are we to collect the wounded, and the slain, and make for camp?"

"Thank you, Erion," his captain returned. "Do as you suggest. I leave you in command. Make sure our slain are accounted for, and pile the enemy bodies into the ditch." He waved a hand towards the abyss he had opened with his magic. "Don't burn them; I want this new general to *know* how many we slaughtered." He paused. "I have urgent business in Tenna. I don't know when I will return. Proceed as usual, without me."

The grizzled lieutenant glanced curiously at Fish, gawked briefly at Brightfeather in the distance, but did not question his orders. "As you say, Captain."

The captain turned back to Fish. "The girl," he said, gesturing towards Brialise. "Who is she?"

"She was abducted from the west of Qwu'Mallorn, some time ago," Fish replied, and saw the captain's face darken even further. "Her name is Brialise Grenova. I found her in the mountains of Svanfeld, and now I'm returning her back home."

The captain was silent for a long moment, looking as though he were chewing something over. Fish gave him time. At last he said, "If you're real, and not just something I'm hallucinating in the fumes of after-battle, I need you to know something." He looked directly at Fish, put a hand on his shoulder. "You can trust me," he said, deeply, earnestly, and Fish was so taken aback that he almost gaped. "If you're who you say you are—if you are truly the son of Arran Sylvaissen who has turned against him—you have my friendship, my enduring loyalty, for that alone." He drew away, leaving Fish reeling, and slid his filthy sword into the scabbard at his hip. "My name is Albryan Lana," he said. "I'm going to bring you before my superior officer—the general who commands all the troops in Qwu'Mallorn. But I have to speak with him first, so I'm going to leave you with a friend in Tenna. Brialise will have to stay here, with my men."

"And the quetzal?"

"Stays here too," Albryan Lana replied firmly, and Fish detected something in the glance he cast towards Brightfeather that looked suspiciously like fear. "We'll ride. Horses. Tenna's not far from here. I'll bring the quetzal over the Border, but you have to swear that it won't cause any mischief."

"He won't," Fish said immediately. "Albryan—" He stepped forward. "You can trust me too," he said, quickly, and wondered for a moment at his own feelings, the way he meant every word.

The captain only nodded. "I would like to," he returned. "I would like to believe that this is true, that you're for real. But if it's not—if I bring you over the Border only for you to wreak destruction . . ."

A silence fell between the two of them. Fish did not know what to say, and resorted to flippancy. "You could always cuff me."

Albryan frowned. "I don't have any silver cuffs. And if I did—" He broke off. "I'm not bringing you in as a prisoner," he said at last, decisively. "I'm bringing you as an envoy."

# CHAPTER XXXIV
## REFLECTION

IT WAS HIGH AFTERNOON BY THE TIME they arrived in Tenna, and Fish privately thought, but did not say out loud, that Brightfeather could have brought them there in much better time. Their horses, two enemy steeds they'd taken from the battlefield, were too tired for anything faster than a light trot, although that seemed to suit Albryan just fine. He had made Fish talk to him the whole way, tell his entire life story and more besides, and the young auburn-haired captain had a rather self-satisfied expression on his face now, as if he were pleased with his purchase.

They had come through a long stretch of wild and beautiful forest, up a road that looked as though it saw a lot less traffic these days than when it had originally been built, and finally into the middle of Tenna, which was a quaint, mid-sized market town. They dismounted and led their tired horses onwards, towards a quiet residential street lined with buildings that looked like boarding houses, each one of them three stories high, constructed—as was everything in this town, it seemed—out of timber. Although hazy clouds obscured the sun, the air was hot, and muggy. Fish's hair was soaked with sweat, and he would have liked nothing better than a cool mountain stream, or some of the fine rain that Nico had complained of at the monastery just yesterday.

They tied up their horses, and Albryan led the way towards the front door of one of the three-storied buildings. However, before they could reach it, the door opened from the inside and a young woman hurtled out, made as if to throw herself upon Albryan, then caught sight of Fish and seemed to think better of it, freezing almost mid-step in front of him.

She made as if to speak, but Albryan took her by the arm. "Stay here," he said to Fish, who drew back, bemused.

Albryan took her across the road, well out of earshot of Fish yet close enough that he was in good view. He drew the girl into his arms, and they embraced passionately. Fish felt his cheeks burn as he turned his face away. *This is the "friend" he thinks of leaving me with? His sweetheart?* Something about the whole situation seemed incongruous, yet Fish could not quite put his finger on it.

Albryan broke free at last and began to talk, far too softly for Fish to overhear. The young woman kept her gaze trained intently upon him, nodding at intervals. At last, it seemed that Albryan had no more to say, and the pair made their way back, the young woman now looking curiously at Fish.

"This is Velda Davidz," Albryan said shortly. "You can trust her as you would trust me." He gave Fish a meaningful look in which Fish could not find the slightest shred of his intended meaning. "I need to go," he stated. He cast a quick eye over Fish. "Velda will tend to your wounds."

*What wounds?* Fish began to speak, stopped. He didn't feel any pain. He had barely felt anything during the entire battle, even when—

*Wait.* Fish had not had a moment to calm down since arriving on Brightfeather, and he had allowed the magic to flow through him without checking it in any way. Now, he forced himself calm, quenching his magic, cutting off the channels, shivering slightly as it ebbed through him. Slowly, the whole-body feeling of intense magic firing from every raw, exposed nerve began to recede, and he swayed a little with the sudden realization of pain.

"Are you alright?" The girl reached out a hand to steady him. Fish nodded, brushed her away.

Albryan hesitated, looking between the two of them as if not quite registering what he was seeing. At last he said, "I'll be back sometime this evening," and turned on his heel.

Velda turned towards Fish with concern. "That cut looks nasty." Her eyes roved over him. "Come on. Let's get you patched up."

She had an accent, Fish realized with some surprise, that was nearly identical to Nico's, flavoured with the ruggedness of the Svanlyn mountains. She was not a mage, either; Fish probed carefully, and found only the same not-presence that someone like Nico gave off in the ether.

And now that Fish got a good look at her, he realized why Albryan had been looking between them that way. He and this girl looked uncannily, eerily, alike. It wasn't just the colouring, like it had been with Brialise: Fish was aware that in the Forest of the Morning, one could find any number of people possessed of dark golden skin and black curly hair. This young woman had the same facial structure as his: her nose was just as large and beaky, though without that kink halfway where his had been broken ages ago; she had the same set to her mouth, and the same angular jawline was femininely softened on her, yet still strikingly similar. She was just a step shorter than him, as if someone had designed them as a matched set, and when she raised her eyes Fish saw that they were the exact same yellow-tawny-gold he'd always thought was unique to *him*.

Feeling a little like he'd been dropped into a dream, Fish followed her indoors and up to a room on the top floor. "This is where you live?" he asked, trying to relieve the tension that had risen up inside him.

She looked over at him, a little uncertainly. "I haven't been in Tenna long." She gestured him inside, then closed the door. Fish cast a glance around. The room was comfortable, but did not have the lived-in look of long residence. There was a bed, neatly made, a low table, several cupboards and chairs, a basin and ewer in the corner.

"Did the two of you just come from the battlefield?" she asked abruptly, and Fish turned. She was looking at him uncertainly. Fish wondered what Albryan had told her. He wondered why the young captain had stashed him here with a woman who seemed, at first glance, the same kind of female company that Nico had always sought out in Ülhard.

"Yes."

Something bright flashed across the girl's eyes. "You need stitches," she said. "Let me see your wounds." She moved very close to him, put a hand to his chin and tilted his head so she could see the cut on his brow.

"Nothing more serious than scratches," Fish said.

She scoffed, softly, deep in her throat. "Show me your hand."

Fish realized, only now, that the cut in his left hand had somehow reopened and was bleeding freely. It had never been stitched; Fish hadn't had time for that in the past week, not with flying over the mountains on Brightfeather looking for Baukin's army, and he'd had the thought in the back of his mind that he might need it raw in case he wanted to dig around in Taunus's notebook again. But now it was stinging like the fury of Thrombolis, and he started to worry that Nico had been right about infection after all.

She studied the cut. "You didn't get this in the fight today."

"I get into a lot of fights."

She raised her eyebrows. "Well, there's little point in stitching this now," she said as if to herself. "I'll clean it out and stitch the others." She reached up and fiddled with the collar of his jerkin, which was soaked in blood. Fish couldn't even remember being hit there, but he let her unlace the top and take a look under his shirt. There was a long, jagged cut across his collarbone, oozing blood. The jerkin he wore didn't have neck protection, of course; it had never been intended for close-quarter fighting.

"That one first, I think," she said, and took his right arm. Some blade had gotten him there, as well, on the upper arm above his leather vambrace. It looked to be a clean, shallow cut, and she inspected it carefully before letting him go.

"Any more?" she asked him, and Fish shook his head.

"You need to take your shirt off," she said frankly, and turned away, starting to bustle about the room, gathering things together. Fish picked at the lacings of his vambrace, slowly drawing them off, then undid the rest of his jerkin. His shoulders felt stiff and sore as he shrugged out of the leather. His weapons-belt, still holding a dagger, had to come off before he could divest his shirt. There were large bloodstains on it now, and he regarded it sadly before bundling it up next to the leather.

The girl brought over her enamelled wash-basin, filled with water. "Could you do me a favour?" she asked, glancing over at him. "Do you have enough magic in you to heat this?"

He grinned. "With me, enough magic is never a problem. How hot do you want it?"

"As hot as you feel comfortable with. That's for cleaning your wounds."

Fish frowned, focusing his power over the basin. He had actually never tried something like this before, but now wasn't the time to admit that. How hard could it be? He had studied the intricacies of war-magic before he was ten; heating water was something so laughably basic that he probably didn't need to *learn*.

Something tinkled as she pulled it out of a cupboard, and Fish looked up at the sound. Underneath his nose, the water hissed, boiling with such sudden violence that half of it slopped out onto the table.

Fish pushed away in fright, almost upsetting the table, cutting off the magic at once. His heart raced. He had lost focus for only a moment. The girl moved towards the table, brows raised.

"I take it that was an accident," she said mildly, regarding the mess and the still-bubbling water inside the basin. "Well, no harm done. At least it's hot." She added cold water until the basin was merely hot rather than boiling, then lathered in a bar of pale green soap. She placed a clear glass bottle on the table that looked to contain some sort of spirit. Fish eyed it dubiously, remembering how it had hurt the last time something like that had been put on an open wound, but she only poured out a miniscule amount and used it to clean an ordinary sewing needle and a length of twine. When she was finally satisfied, she turned back towards him. "Sit down."

Fish sank down obediently into the nearest chair, and she dipped a clean cloth in the soapy water and began to wash the scratches. Her hands were deft, and gentle. She was obviously no stranger to this. Fish was intrigued by her, but didn't know where to start. *Why do we look so alike, you and I?* That was no question to ask.

Before he could say anything, though, the girl started to speak. "Are you really one of Albryan's soldiers?" she began. "There's something about you that seems . . . different. And you don't wear their uniform."

"I'm actually a—a mercenary," he told her. "But at the moment . . . I'm looking for an alliance with Qwu'Mallorn. I joined this battle, this morning, on their behalf."

She looked at him quizzically, as if she had a thousand questions to ask, but instead she took his left hand and gently dipped it in the basin, washing out the cut with the soap bar. "You seem rather young for that," she observed. "To be a mercenary, I mean." She stood up and retrieved a towel, carefully patting each wound dry, then handing it to him to wrap around his hand. She washed her own hands, then took hold of the needle. She made him lean backwards, bent over him, and began to sew. The cut on his collarbone was throbbing, and Fish hardly felt the needle go in.

"How old are you, anyway?" she continued as she worked. Her hands were very steady. "Seventeen?"

"Nineteen," he returned, slightly stung. "You're seventeen?"

She arched up to look him in the eyes. It was almost like looking at a distorted reflection, a strangely softened version of his own face.

"I'm nineteen too. At least"—she cocked her head, considering something—"sometime this month, anyway. Maybe even today."

"Today? What's so special about . . ." He trailed off, realizing. It was Thirdmonth the twenty-first.

"It's somewhat of a day of mourning here, apparently," Velda said, "else I would likely have forgotten it as well."

He chuckled wryly. "Now there's something. My adoptive father"—he stumbled only slightly over the words—"he always used to say *I* was likely born this very day. Amidst the—well. The massacre, I suppose you'd call it. In Armour City."

She drew back, looking at him curiously. "So you and I," she finally said, "we look almost like siblings, we were born in the same month of the same year, and even in the same city."

A strange feeling pierced Fish's heart, and he barely noticed as the girl resumed drawing the needle through his flesh. "I thought you were from Svanfeld. You have that mountain accent."

"The brogue." She flashed a quick grin. "I was raised by the Sven monks as an orphan. The town of Lynborder." She seemed to notice the sudden rise of his eyebrows, hesitated, then continued to speak as the needle went back and forth with its small pain. "I was brought there as a baby. Rescued from a group of slavers." Fish twitched involuntarily, and her hand slipped, stabbing him in the collarbone. "Sit still," she admonished. She drew the needle through one last time, and carefully trimmed off the end of the twine. "Now for the shoulder."

She insisted on doing the whole rigmarole with the soap and spirits over again, washing her hands thoroughly and cleaning the needle, and Fish was practically squirming with impatience by the time she returned and started on his arm. But she seemed to have forgotten that she had been saying anything, and after a long silence, he began, "But somehow, you ended up with the Sven monks."

"What? Oh—right. These slavers, they had a whole caravan of refugees from Armour City whom they'd captured one way or another. They tried to cross the mountains and get to Sulshome. That was a mistake on their part." She smiled grimly. "The villagers of Lynborder attacked them, killed them all, and saved us. And the monks took me in and raised me."

"And your parents?"

She shrugged. "Never knew them. Died at Armour City, most likely, or maybe it was them who sold me."

She was silent for a long time, focusing on her task. Fish's heart was beating rather loudly, and the sting of the needle seemed far away, almost as if it were happening to someone else. He was far more aware of the presence of the girl, dark golden eyes intent upon what she was doing, some of her brown-black hair escaping its neat braided bun, soft curls on her forehead slightly dampened with the balmy heat in the room and the effort she was taking with the wound. She held his arm steady in one hand as she carefully stitched with the other, and he was aware of her secure grip, the way her skin tone matched so closely with his that they seemed almost contiguous, made out of one flesh, sculpted from the same hand.

She finished on the wound, washed her hands again, came back and attended to the cut over his eye. She was right in front of his face now, blurred with proximity. Fish forced himself to speak around the lump in his throat.

"Funny," he began hoarsely. "Maybe my parents sold me too. I ended up in the hands of slavers as well. As a babe."

She paused, working the needle carefully through. "But—you mentioned your father—"

"*Adoptive* father," Fish reminded her. "I wouldn't really consider him much of a father, anyhow. He bought me from those slavers. For nothing more than a handful of silver pawns."

The girl's hand suddenly shook violently, and the needle dropped, hanging by a thread from the wound she'd been sewing up. "I'm sorry," she managed, drawing away, "but could you repeat that?"

"Which part?" Fish asked, nonplussed. "The silver pawns?"

"I dreamed of you," the girl whispered suddenly, and Fish stared at her. For a moment they simply remained like that, eye to identical eye, like a pair of deer that had each been startled out of their respective bushes by the other's rustling.

The girl dropped her gaze and turned her head away, flustered. "I'm sorry," she repeated. "What did you say your name was again? Ben?"

"Everyone calls me Fish," he answered automatically, and found the hanging needle with his hand. "Don't you think you'd better finish this? Or shall I find a mirror?"

The girl coloured. "Sorry. Of course." She returned to the stitching, but her hands were no longer steady. Fish bit his lip and made no sound, even when the needle slipped noticeably. Despite his pain and weariness, he felt a strange warmth suffuse his chest. He did not know how to describe this feeling, this pull he suddenly felt towards this stranger who looked so familiar, this intense desire to know her. Love at first sight, perhaps? But this was nothing like the tangled nest of desires and longings he felt towards Nico. Not that kind of love, then.

He wondered whether he should say anything more, but the girl finished at last. "If you like, you can use the rest of the water to wash up a bit," she said, almost timidly.

"I do like." Fish would have given rather a lot for a full bath just then. He stank of sweat and blood, and though he never would have described himself as being fastidious, it was starting to bother him. The girl moved about the room, not looking at him as he scrubbed the sweat and grime from his face, his hair, his armpits. He found the pack he had brought along and unrolled his cloak from it, using it to dry himself off. Rummaging a bit further into it, he found a clean shirt, one of the plain hessian ones that Brother Jakob had doled out. The fabric was a bit too thick for this type of climate, so he left the collar loose to admit more airflow, and hitched up the sleeves until they fastened above his elbows.

Velda came over again to remove the basin. Fish walked with her, glancing out of the lead-paned window. All that had taken longer than he'd thought; the sun was westering outside, turning the gauzy clouds to fiery pennants in its wake. Something about the hue of the sky made him think of Brightfeather, and he wondered how Brialise and the quetzal were faring. He knew that Brightfeather was safe; the five or so miles that lay between them now were nothing to the bond that had been established, and he could sense the quetzal even against the pulsating background in the ether that was every bright soul with the gift of magic.

"Are you hungry?" Velda asked suddenly, bringing him out of his wandering thoughts.

"I'm starving," he replied, realizing how true it was. He tried to remember when last he'd eaten, and recalled only his meagre breakfast, beside the Dreaming Water that morning. And with that, suddenly he felt ready to eat an entire ox.

"A few of us are cooking together tonight," she said. "There'll be a few visitors as well. You're welcome to join, but if you'd rather not—"

"I'll join," he said immediately. "But I warn you, my own culinary skills are not in the realm of what's normally considered edible. I'll do any job that doesn't involve the actual cooking."

She laughed, showing slightly crooked front teeth. "Any good at cutting onions, Fish?"

AS IT HAPPENED, FISH WAS QUITE proficient with a sharp knife and a tub of vegetables. Delourien, at her age, had not had much energy to spare for cooking, certainly not enough to satisfy the appetite of a teenage boy, and more often than not it had been him slicing a selection of mushrooms and leeks from the garden into their pot of perpetual stew. At least, after his arrival, there had always been some kind of meat for it: fish, crab, snails, once or twice he'd even managed to catch a hare. But Nico had taken one look at his attempts on their tiny city hearth, and suggested that they take all their meals at one of Ülhard's many public houses, something Fish could hardly object to.

It seemed that chicken was the dominant source of meat here, unlike the pork of Svanfeld or the seemingly inescapable mutton of southern Vailana, and Fish watched with interest as one of the women brought in a basket of freshly washed gizzards and added them to the skillet. His diligently chopped onions, tomatoes, ginger, some kind of pungent yellow spice and a selection of dried hot peppers made their own way in, at the appropriate intervals, producing a fiery red, spicy stew.

Of the four other boarders Velda introduced him to, three of them were ordinary enough, two Morgein women and one man, all three of them diminutive and black-haired, brown-eyed, olive-complexioned, each with a minor Mage-Gift. The fourth was a bit more interesting: she was not Morgein at all, but from Sanghui, the northwestern corner of the Eastern Continent. The Sang people had traded and mingled with the Morgei for so long that roughly one in four of them possessed the Mage-Gift. In appearance they were almost as dark as true Easterners, though with a rich golden undertone to the complexion that was not so far from Fish or Velda's look. They tended to be tall where the Morgei were short, and this woman, who had introduced herself as Chunhua—no family name, apparently— towered over everyone else who was present. Fish reckoned that she was almost as tall as Nico; unusual enough, for a woman, and he wondered what the rest of her people were like. She had no Mage-Gift, and wore a simple outfit of short-sleeved jacket over pants that ended at the knee, though Fish recognized that the fabrics were at the upper edge of what he and Nico could have afforded in Ülhard even at their most flush. But Sanghui was where silk originated, though she was proving oddly evasive about its actual origins, one of the mysteries of the East.

"My guess is a tree," Fish suggested, when the others at last turned to him. "Sanghui is known for its many hardwoods. Fibres from the bark, or perhaps even the leaves."

Chunhua's dark eyes sparkled with mischief. "That is a guess I've not heard before."

"Surely the production of silk involves magic somehow," Velda chipped in.

The Sang woman shrugged. "Come to Sanghui someday," she said, "and the silk merchants will show you how it is made."

"Tell us now," one of the others begged.

"I am not a silk merchant. I will not divulge their secrets."

"What do you trade in?" Fish asked.

"Leather and furs, from the animals I hunt."

Fish wanted to ask more—he'd always heard that panthers were striped orange in the jungles of Sanghui, and badly wanted to know if it was true—but at that moment, the guests they had been awaiting arrived at the front door.

They were all in the kitchen, which occupied the whole ground floor of the boarding-house, and Velda stood up to bring the pair over. These were clearly Morgein as well, a young woman and a slightly younger man, almost exactly Fish's age if he was any guesser. The girl, by the standards of her homeland, was tall and well-built, though she could not have been more than an inch or two taller than Fish; the young man had about two inches on her, lanky where she was well-rounded. His straight black hair was cropped short, accentuating his narrow face. They caught sight of Fish where he was slouching against the hearth almost immediately, and Velda stopped to introduce them.

"This is Pattin Iscora, and this her brother Kevin. Pattin's at the boarding-house next door, and Kevin's in the army."

People in Qwu'Mallorn did not usually clasp hands in greeting, but instead gave a small bow with their hand clasped over their heart, and both of them did that now. Fish smiled, noticing that the young man seemed to be looking him over from head to toe. "My name's Benjamin Fisher, but you can call me Fish."

Pattin looked curiously between Fish and Velda. "Are you two related?"

Fish felt himself flush at the impertinent question, but Velda answered smoothly, "No. Fish has the Mage-Gift. He's from Vailana."

Pattin shrugged. "That doesn't mean much. Plenty of—of ha— of *Vailanan* families,"—she stumbled over the term so gracelessly that Fish wondered what on earth she had been meaning to call it, instead—"have both Gifted and unGifted members."

Kevin, looking embarrassed, shushed his sister. "That's a nasty cut you've got there," he remarked, and Fish instinctively reached up to brush his hair over his forehead.

"Nothing serious," he replied, and sought to wean the young man away from this topic. "Where are you two from? You don't sound like locals."

The girl answered again. "Our parents have an estate nestled in the Hogbacks, near Quinen." She beamed over at Kevin. "My little brother turned out to have a pretty impressive Gift, and he wanted to do some good with it, so he came over here to join the Army. They sent me along to make sure he doesn't get into trouble—and perhaps to meet a respectable man to marry." She laughed. "Both counts are going terribly, I'm afraid."

Fish was saved from keeping the rest of that conversation going, for just then the others announced that the food was ready. It had begun to rain outside, scuppering their original plan to eat in the garden, so they made themselves comfortable at the long kitchen table instead. They handed out bowls of stew, loaves of crusty bread, and glasses of cider. The cider was somehow as cold as though they'd fetched it from the top of the iced-over Svanlyn peaks, and Fish wondered about that for a moment before realizing that it was something that could well be accomplished with a small, controlled amount of magic. He thought, miserably, of how he'd upset the water in the basin that afternoon. Cooling a glass of cider was not something he cared to try, unless he didn't care very much about the particular glass in question.

Conversation mostly stilled over the food, leaving Fish to surreptitiously eat twice as much as anyone else. The fire of the peppers was just at the edge of what he could tolerate, and he downed glass after glass of cider in an effort to make it seem like he enjoyed this level of spicy food every day, not wanting to look like the hapless foreigner he probably was.

Fish had wondered whether he would feel some miraculous sense of belonging in the Forest of the Morning, some feeling of homecoming and comradeship in this land that belonged to people who possessed the same gift as him. To his remarkable dismay—for he had not realized just how deep his own feelings were on this score—he did not. The people here seemed merely foreigners, with foreign ways. They seemed normal, and chattered about normal things, and Fish was uncomfortably aware that his life experiences had marked him indelibly, set him apart from those who led simple lives.

The one person whom he seemed able to relate to was Velda, and despite appearances, she was fully as foreign here as Nico would be. She followed the conversation and chattered with the others, but Fish could see that there was a barrier, something of shared experience and values that bound the rest together and excluded her. Even the Sang woman seemed to fit in better; she bantered with Pattin in a tongue that Fish recognized as some queer dialect of the Morgein language, and regaled the others with stories of hunting in her jungles.

The meal ended, yet the chatter went on, and Fish began to feel very tired. The cider had run out, and the kitchen was stifling. Quietly, without anyone noticing, he removed himself from the gathering and went to stand in the front doorway, leaning against the frame. The very air smelled stuffy. The rain fell in gossamer threads, as fine as it had been yesterday morning in the mountains when he had bade farewell to Nico.

Something constricted inside Fish's chest, and the air felt heavy in his lungs. The hessian shirt he was wearing chafed against the dull throbbing of his scratches. He wanted Nico like he had never yearned for him before, and he brought his elbows close to his chest to contain the ache that rose within him. It made little sense. They had been separated before, and for longer than a mere day. But somehow their farewell seemed incredibly distant, as though the many miles between lay athwart the bond they shared. Nico was so far away, now. He was the one person with whom Fish had never felt like a stranger.

Save, of course, that night in Friedma Smit's house—and their capture by Taunus—the way Nico had looked at him when he first saw him do magic—

"Hi there."

Fish turned, startled. Kevin Iscora sidled up and took the other side of the doorframe. A friendly smile played over his narrow face, yet something about his attitude made Fish feel off-balance, and he put his guard up.

"Sorry our chatter's so inane," Kevin said. He smiled as Fish muttered a disclaimer. "It's the same with any group of friends, I suppose. Mostly we start to talk about things only we understand."

Fish, who only had very meagre experience of hanging around in groups and chatting with people, remained silent. Kevin shifted and his face turned serious. "But I feel I should apologize," he went on. "About Pattin. She's not usually like that. She had—a bit of a romantic disappointment today."

Fish was lost. "What's there to apologize for?"

"Seriously?" Kevin's dark eyes flicked over him. "She almost called you a—a half-breed," he said at last, quietly. "As I said, I'm sorry."

Fish shrugged. "What does it matter? I *am* a half-breed." *Or more likely than not, anyway.* Armour City had been a giant melting cauldron of half-breeds and mixed families, before Arran started preaching his particularly restrictive way of thinking, or so Fish had always heard. And whether his real parents had sold him or died for him, Fish knew that they were not likely to have had strong ties to Qwu'Mallorn. Not if they had failed to flee from Armour City before the massacre happened.

Kevin looked at him curiously. "Where are you from, Fish? Most of the Morgein families from Vailana came to live here, but you obviously didn't."

People in Qwu'Mallorn certainly did not act bashful about wanting to know personal details. Fish was unpleasantly surprised that he was forced to bend the truth on his first night here, but luckily he had already thought of something that sounded plausible and contained enough real truth so he wouldn't forget it.

"In some places, we were able to hide," he said. "My family lived in Zarath, in the far south. That's beyond reach of the capital. Neither of my parents had the Mage-Gift." He glanced up to gauge Kevin's reaction to this. Fish knew perfectly well that such a thing was possible—his father had been obsessed with blood purity after all—but he didn't know how widely it would be believed. But Kevin only nodded, and Fish continued, "I inherited the Gift from my grandmother, I guess. She was the one who raised me after my parents died. Her Gift was very small, and by the time I was born, I think everyone had forgotten that she could even do magic." Kevin raised an eyebrow, but said nothing. "She and I both hid our magic. She taught me how."

Kevin was nonplussed. "How do you hide magic?"

Fish shrugged. "You don't use it," he replied.

"But how—"

"I couldn't stay there, in the end," Fish said, cutting him off. "Not with my Gift. I made my way to Svanfeld as a mercenary, and now I'm here." He grinned at Kevin. "Hoping to join your Army, in fact."

Kevin regarded him for a while, cocking his head as if listening to something. "That's a strong Gift," he said at last. He chuckled. "Some of the older families in Qwu'Mallorn, they think that having unGifted people in your lineage makes you somehow less Morgein, less magic. You're living proof that ideology doesn't stand up to reason."

Fish had never heard this before, and he could not help a momentary, sardonic smile. *So perhaps Arran's sworn enemies are not truly that different in their thinking, after all.*

Kevin leaned forward, looking out at the rain, and at the closer vantage Fish saw that his eyes, which he had at first taken to be black, were a deep and dark blue. *Eyes like the midnight sky*, he found himself thinking, and quickly looked away.

A sudden fit of giggles erupted somewhere behind them, and Kevin turned. "I have a feeling I might need to get my sister home," he murmured to Fish, and headed towards Pattin.

The party broke up quickly after that, with everyone helping to clear the table and rinse the dishes. At last all the others dispersed to their own rooms, leaving Fish to return upstairs with Velda. It was late, and Albryan had not yet returned. Velda took an oil lantern from the kitchen.

"Do you think you're going to sleep?" she asked him.

"I doubt it." Fish knew there was a bedroll with his pack, and the floor was less uneven than some places he'd slept in the past, but he felt as though he'd left his mind out on the battlefield. He could not stop harrying over the events of the day, over and over again.

Velda led him upstairs, let him into the room, then hesitated. "Stay here for a moment," she said, with a sudden mischievous smile. "Are you alright without the lantern?"

Fish moved towards the wall with the window, and sank down upon the sill. The moon was up, somewhere beyond the clouds, casting a misty light over the street and the surrounding forest. "Yes."

She disappeared down the stairs again, and Fish took the moment to make himself comfortable on the window-sill. It was just wide enough for him to sit comfortably with one knee drawn up to his chest. He cranked one of the tessellated windows open, and gazed out. From this room on the second floor, he could see over the houses on the opposite side of the street to the forest beyond. The soft rain made spiderweb patterns in the tallest yellowwoods, making it look as though the clouds had come down to embrace them. He breathed deeply of the damp, cool air, and gradually, he began to feel calmer.

One might have thought, with his deep coppery skin and black hair, that he was made for summer, but Fish had always preferred cooler climates. Ülhard was a perpetually foggy city, stuck between the sea and the mountains, and temperatures were always low there even in summer. Zarath, also next the sea, got very hot towards the end of summer but was a *hell* of a lot drier than here, and so was Armour City, where thunderstorms came almost every evening at the height of the hottest season, only to clear up and blow out before the next dawn.

In both Zarath and Ülhard, he'd loved the stormy weather, simply because it was so pleasant to light a fire and sit by the window all day whenever the rain or snow was sleeting outside. He could almost see it. Delourien sitting in a chair opposite him with her knitting, Nico sitting cross-legged on the bed opposite him with his sword across his knees, guiding the whetstone across it with firm, slow strokes.

There was movement at the door, as Velda appeared with something in her free hand. She set the lantern down and headed towards him, taking a seat just as he had on the sill.

"There's so many things here I'd never seen before." She proffered the sweet in her hand towards him. "Have you ever had chocolate?"

Fish grinned. "Not my first time, but I've missed it."

"Then I shall have to find some sweet you've never tried before," she teased as they shared out the chocolate.

She stopped speaking for a while, and Fish was reminded of how the silence was with Nico, how the two of them could oftentimes spend an entire afternoon barely saying a word to each other, and yet Fish had never felt that their companionship was lacking. The rich scent of rain curled itself around them, and the taste of cocoa melted in his mouth.

"Fish," she said at last, quietly, and he turned his head. "Can I ask something?"

He nodded, and she took a breath. "What's it like to be in a battle?" she asked, and her voice was softer than the rain hissing onto the gutters outside.

Fish thought about it, of the rush and the blind courage, the berserkness of going into a situation where others were actively trying to kill you, of how it was different than going to murder a man in his house at night, and how it was the same.

"It's like nothing else," he whispered. "It's like you—you lose something of yourself, every time it happens. It takes a while to feel normal again, after." He broke off, shaking his head. "You don't feel afraid when it's happening, but afterwards—"

She nodded as if she understood, at that, and he said no more. But it was not long before she broke the silence for a second time.

"You've lived in a lot of places, haven't you?" she asked, and he nodded again. "What . . ." She paused. "What happened between you and your adoptive father?"

Fish's breath caught in his throat; he knew that the story he'd told Kevin would not work on her. He had given too much of himself away already, that afternoon, not even once stopping to think about it.

*You can trust her as you would trust me*, Albryan Lana had said.

If Fish was here to provide key information on Arran Sylvaissen, there was no point in trying to hide who he was to people who might need to know.

"I'm—Arran Sylvaissen's son," he replied all in a rush, and saw her eyes widen.

"*That's* your adoptive father?"

"I defected from him." Fish grimaced. "That's a fancy way of saying *I ran away.* I was only a child when I left. I didn't know—how things were going to turn out."

She creased her brow. "You ran away and became a mercenary?"

"With one thing and another," Fish replied evasively, "yes. It took a few years, though."

"What do you mean?"

As Fish hesitated once again, he realized that he truly did not want to lie to her. That was strange. He'd never had any compunction about lying to people before, even to Nico. Their whole association had once been based on a lie, or at least Fish's aptitude at concealing truth.

"I've lived by the sword since I was sixteen," he said at last, quietly. "I don't really know how to make a living any other way. And I'm good at it—or at least, I've survived everything that's come at me so far."

"It sounds like a lonely life."

"I have an associate," he said, and swallowed. "Nico. He stayed behind when I came here."

"Nico? That sounds like a Sven name."

"It is." He studied the cut on his palm. It looked quite ugly, red around the edges, yet it had calmed down since that afternoon and only hurt vaguely along with the rest of his scratches. "We met in Ülhard. Midwinter's Feast Eve, the year before last." He laughed softly. "Now that was another fight. The inn got a bit—rowdy that night."

"Not something you started, I hope?"

He grinned at her. "I don't *start* fights."

"I believe that." Her tone was teasing. "I believe that you're the type of person whom fights start *about*."

"That's not fair," Fish protested, even as he began to chuckle. He shifted his position, and winced slightly as aches he'd not even felt at the time suddenly made themselves known, in his hips and all along his back.

"How are your wounds?" she asked.

"They sting."

She frowned. "Let me know if they start to do more than sting. They have mage-healers here. I'm not letting you succumb to infection on my watch." She looked him over critically for a moment, then relaxed and smiled. "They do add something to your appearance, though," she said, teasing again. "In Lynborder, the girls would be all over you." Fish began to flush, and she grinned wider. "But I can't imagine that you've ever had trouble with *that*."

Flustered, Fish stuttered something at random, and she gazed at him curiously. "You blush like you've—*oh*," she murmured. "You've been in battles—killed men—and yet you've never had a girl?"

"The last time I checked," he returned softly, "I don't believe it was a requirement."

She regarded him for a long moment. "No, I suppose it isn't," she said at last, just as softly. There seemed something further behind her words, but it didn't feel right to ask. The rain was still hissing down, and she gazed out the open window even as he did the same. A figure on horseback appeared at the end of the street, hood drawn up against the rain, and both of them stirred as one.

"Albryan," Fish murmured.

She smiled, almost ruefully. "Looks like I don't get to keep you after all."

# CHAPTER XXXV
## COUNCIL

GENERAL THINAS SOVAYA DID HAVE a pair of silver hand-cuffs, and they were so ostentatiously set upon the edge of his desk that Fish wondered if the placing had been deliberate.

It was just the three of them, all alone in this too-tiny room with the eerie light shining down onto the general's desk. Fish knew that the lantern set just above them was somehow fuelled by magic. Its light was like the moon, silver rather than the ruddy yellow of an oil-lamp, and like the moon's light it did not waver nor flicker. And it *hummed* in the back of Fish's mind, contributing to a background of magic that had been far too noisy already.

The general reached out a tentative hand. "May I test the strength of your magic?"

Fish was bone tired; he had spent the last two hours telling Sovaya everything he'd told Albryan already, the general asking many more pointed questions than the captain had. Wordlessly, he offered his arm to Sovaya, who gripped it by the wrist, placing his thumb carefully on Fish's pulse.

Arran had done this often enough, when Fish was a boy, so that Fish knew exactly what was happening. He watched the general's hawkish brows draw together as he tested his own magic against the raw force that flowed through Fish's veins. Sovaya blinked several times, and held onto his wrist far longer than Fish could ever remember Arran doing. But Arran had been familiar with Fish's potential since he was an infant. Sovaya had never tested himself against Fish's Gift before.

At last the general released him, and surreptitiously Fish tucked his hand under his elbow. The feeling of *contact* shivered over him like a cold wind, far too intimate for someone he didn't know.

"Captain Lana has entreated me to trust you," General Sovaya said, leaning forward. Fish did not miss the quick glance he shot towards the pair of silver cuffs. "In the past few weeks, I've received a flood of reports corroborating Arran Sylvaissen's doings in Svanfeld. My men have sensed the presence of blood sorcery, fought with necromes, spoken with bands of refugees. And in the past week, Arran has redoubled his efforts on our borders. The battle that you fought today is not his usual style of border-skirmish." The general looked at the letter that Hugh Anspeare had sent, now flattened upon the desk before him on top of a mess of maps, reports, and ledgers. "According to this, Anspeare is sitting somewhere above Albrecht in command of fewer than a hundred men. A strong defensive position, yet it's not one I'd like to find myself in. Baukin Sylvaissen's armies are rapidly closing in, and the Sven regulars are scattered to the winds."

"That's why he sent me here," Fish said quietly.

To Fish's left, Albryan stirred, pulling a map towards himself. "We could afford to send a battalion," he said, as the general nodded slowly. "Two hundred of our best, practised in battle-magic. If we send only the most magically competent, they could keep their horses going at a steady pace without draining themselves. They could be with Anspeare in just two weeks."

Fish sat up. "That's—more than what I could have hoped for." General Sovaya cleared his throat, and Albryan Lana's bright eyes turned towards his superior officer.

"I am a cautious man by nature," the general announced. "It's one of the reasons I've survived this long. But any military man would be remiss if he did not see the opportunity in this, in the offered alliance. However, there is a complication." He leaned forward, looking intently at Fish. "I am only a servant in truth, bound to obey the authority of the Grand Council of Qwu'Mallorn. To do something like this—to send my men to aid a foreign power—I would require the word of the Council."

"For something like this," Albryan continued, seamlessly picking up the thread where his commander tied it off, "we would have to call an Assembly. A grand meeting of the ruling Councils of our nine regions."

"Surely that will take far too long to organize," Fish protested, dismayed. "The people of Svanfeld are in immediate peril. Ülhard and Von Dharen have already fallen, and the land between the mountains and the sea is infested with necromes. And if Baukin breaks the monasteries—" He stopped, aware that the general was smiling at him gently.

"You are in the ancestral home of magic, Deryck," Sovaya said. "The Assembly does not need to meet in person."

"So you'll call this meeting?"

The general went silent, frowning as he leaned on his desk with his elbows.

"That's the challenge," Albryan said quietly. "Only the Ruling Council of Tenna has the power to call the Assembly. We have to convince them that it's in their best interest to do so."

Fish scowled. "So it's a matter of politics."

"I can have the Council of Tenna meet first thing tomorrow," the general said. "The two of you need to be prepared to speak before them. It could take several days for them to make a decision."

Fish nodded wordlessly.

"I am appointing Captain Lana to serve as your bodyguard and advisor," the general continued. "Anything you need, he will provide; any questions you have, you may ask him."

*And any movements of mine, he will swiftly report*, Fish thought with a stab of cynicism, but he did not protest. Albryan Lana was a friendly face, at least. He looked towards Fish with a slight smile, and Fish found himself recalling their meeting on the battlefield, which felt like forever ago. It had only been a few hours. *You can trust me.* He recalled the sincerity in the young captain's face when he'd said those words.

"We'd best get some sleep," Albryan said, pulling himself out of his chair with what looked like the last effort of exhaustion. "It must be past midnight by now. I'll put you up in my room for tonight."

They took their leave of the general, and Albryan led the way to a regular soldiers' residence at the foot of the hill. Fish was worn out, close to the end of his tether by the time Albryan pushed open a door and lit a candle to reveal a neat room panelled in pale wood.

"Do you have a bedroll?" he asked, and Fish nodded.

"Good. I know I'm going to sleep like the dead."

Albryan helped Fish arrange the roll comfortably on the floor, then pulled off his outer clothes and collapsed onto his bed, rasping a snore even as his head hit the pillow. Fish curled up and blew out the candle. In the darkness, the snoring sounded enough like Nico's to reassure him, even if he couldn't reach out and touch his partner beneath the blankets. He closed his eyes, and weariness chased him down the cliffside of consciousness.

The next thing he knew, Albryan was shaking him awake. Sunlight was streaming into the room, and he squinted up against it.

"Thinas said he was calling the Council first thing this morning," Albryan reminded him. "That could be anytime soon, and we'd best get a wash and breakfast beforehand."

Fish allowed himself to be helped to his feet, took a towel and a bar of soap that were proffered towards him, and followed Albryan in a daze. Their destination was a standard washroom, complete with hot-water baths and polished brass mirrors. The room was empty save for themselves. Fish guessed that it was earlier in the morning than he would ever consider decent.

Hot water on his face and the sting of soap on his stitched wounds did most of the work to wake Fish fully, though, and he washed as quickly as he could. Albryan had already finished in the bathtub, and was shaving his face in one of the brass mirrors hung against the wall.

"Fish," he called as Fish began to towel himself vigorously off. There was a second razor on the basin beside him, and he proffered it. "It's best if you look as neat as possible, and there's some advantage to you looking as young as possible too," he said. "You'll find that men here prefer to keep our facial hair under control. And I don't want the Council to be badly disposed towards you on sight."

Fish hesitated as he took the blade in hand, gazing uncertainly at himself in the polished brass. The razor was very, very sharp, and the steam in the washroom made his reflection uncertain. Fish had watched Nico shave himself a few times, before he'd started to grow out his beard, and a few boys in the Townsguard of Zarath had liked the clean-shaven look as well. But more often than not, men went to the bathhouse or employed a servant to do this for them, and Fish wasn't sure how to begin.

"You've never shaved yourself before?" Albryan guessed before he could open his mouth, and he nodded gratefully.

Albryan gave his own cheek one last quick stroke, dipped the blade in the water, and passed a damp cloth over his face. "All right, just this once, I'll help you. I really don't want you to nick yourself, we can't afford to be late, and this is too important for you to do a cack-handed job." Even as he spoke, he was lathering soap into the basin. "Now stay still," he said, before he began to apply soap to Fish's face. "Don't worry," he said as Fish eyed the blade. "I've done this for countless younger recruits before."

Fish was surprised. "Dare I ask why?"

Albryan chuckled. "I was a drill-sergeant a few years ago. I inspected the recruits every morning, and if any of them had so much as an errant hair on his face, it would be back to the washroom until they learned to do it properly."

"How strange," Fish remarked. The blade now scraping along the bottom of his jawline was incredibly steady, every stroke deliberate and precise.

"I suppose it would seem that way to outsiders," Albryan said levelly. "I was always regarded as the expert. Some Morgein men don't even grow beards until their twenties. I had to start shaving mine when I was fifteen—or risk my father's irritation." He finished with whatever hairs there were on Fish's upper lip, and handed him the cloth to wipe his face. "That's better."

Fish couldn't see much difference himself, though perhaps that was due to the distortion of his reflection in the brass. The morning regimen was not over yet; Albryan handed him a herbal ointment which smoothed the tenderness of his freshly scraped face. At Albryan's suggestion, Fish also tied his hair back rather than letting the curls tumble loose as he usually did.

A messenger from Thinas Sovaya was waiting for them in Albryan's room when they got back. It seemed the general had worked even faster than Albryan had anticipated. "The general says to meet him at the Council Hall in Tenna as soon as possible," the young soldier informed them blandly. "He entreats you both to prepare well."

Albryan grimaced. "I'm not doing this without breakfast," he said to Fish as he waved the messenger off. "Let's get dressed, and I'll arrange us rolls and coffee without the need to visit the mess. I can sweet-talk one of the cooks."

Albryan was as good as his word. They made their appearance at the back door of the kitchen, where a beaming middle-aged woman named Lissia allowed them to occupy a small wooden table, and brought them the promised coffee, along with fresh-baked bread rolls stuffed with nuts and dried fruit. Albryan talked throughout the whole meal; even though Fish was watching him closely, he still could not have said how exactly the young captain managed to eat, drink and say as much as he did, all at the same time.

"Don't use your alias to introduce yourself," he told Fish. "That'll just create confusion. Use your real name. *Deryck*." Fish scowled at the idea that the name Arran had given him was his *real* name, but didn't protest, and Albryan was already moving on. "But you can't claim the last name of Sylvaissen."

Fish nodded. "That's the name Arran took to himself." Albryan paused, and Fish breathed in the aroma of his coffee before taking a sip. It was *good* coffee, easily the equal of the stuff they served in coffee-shops in Ülhard. "I could use *Luzerna* as my family name," he suggested.

"That's a traders' name," Albryan replied, and nodded. "That's fine. Now," he continued, looking Fish directly in the eyes, "you need to get things right the moment you open your mouth. You need to sound respectable, but not *too* well-bred. You can't have any pretensions of still being a prince." He slowed his speech. "I've heard you change your accent several times, very slightly, depending with whom you're talking," he said. "Is that something you can control?"

Fish blinked, amazed. "I can. I—I do."

"Good." That was something he'd never expected to hear. "I don't want you to sound like a commoner, but you shouldn't sound too much like you're from Vailana either." Albryan hesitated. "I don't suppose you know any Morgein?"

Fish grinned. "*Ja'an mallorna ha the'quegvith.* I've spoken it since I was a child."

Albryan regarded him with raised eyebrows. "Goddess," he muttered. "Well. Don't let on that you're fluent, but use the intonations. I think you know what I'm saying."

Fish nodded, returning to his roll. Albryan considered his own food.

"Arran taught you how to speak Morgein fluently?"

Fish nodded again. His mouth was full, and he took a moment to swallow, admonishing himself to be on his best behaviour. "Not just the modern language. I learned the ancient dialects, read the old histories. If nothing else, I was certainly educated like royalty." He laughed shortly, but saw little mirth reflected in Albryan's countenance.

Albryan frowned. "I never thought I'd say anything good about Arran Sylvaissen," he began, "but . . . a good education is a gift in and of itself. And he—he chose well when he named you. *Deryck*. Nothing too specific to his family, nor too modern. A traditional, solid name."

Fish made a face. "Nothing against traditional names in general, but *I've* never liked it."

"Well. With *my* father, I had to find my own education."

"At least your father wasn't a blood sorcerer."

"The best thing I can say about him." The silence following that statement felt far too dense, and Fish looked covertly at Albryan for a long moment, yet picked up no sign of anguish under the freckles which liberally peppered his face. Instead, the young captain moved on, changing the subject yet again.

"You'll be speaking in front of five Councillors," he said frankly. "Their five families have ruled the region of Tenna since time immemorial, and each of them was born to power. Yet the five families are not equal in ranking." He paused. "The first and least of them is Carin Hedgora. Then there's Slovan Formai, the only *patriarch* amongst the bunch. Then Sylvia Anentas and Larichessa Stani, who despise each other. Whatever side either of them chooses, the other will always take the opposite view."

Fish nodded absently, finishing his coffee.

"And then there's the last, the most powerful of them all. Tiralinna Ebraskaia." Albryan paused. "Does that name ... mean anything to you?"

Fish thought for a moment, shrugged. "Should it?" But before Albryan could reply, it snapped into his memory, a fragment from a long-forgotten life. "Wait. That's my—that's Dannine's birth name. *Ebraskaia.* Her mother was some kind of noblewoman. That's her, isn't it? Dannine's mother. On the Council? She sold her eldest daughter to Arran in exchange for her own safety." He vividly recalled Dannine telling him the story. *I remember her, Deryck. I remember her passing me over to the arms of our father. I remember how I cried. I didn't understand.*

A strange look passed across Albryan's face. "It's not like anyone knows the full story."

"*I* know the full story. Dannine and Arran told me. The Ebraskaia matriarch had another daughter safe in Qwu'Mallorn, so she didn't care if Dannine was lost. She had no way of knowing what Arran—" Fish broke off, remembering suddenly how Arran had used that story to illustrate the evils of the Morgein matriarchs. *Be grateful that you don't remember your mother,* Dannine had always told Fish. *She sold you, even as my mother sold me. Only Arran has ever truly cared for us.* Fish looked at the man sitting opposite him, his expression totally closed off, and felt suddenly horribly discomfited.

"We'd best be going," Albryan said abruptly, standing up. "We'll ride into Tenna. I'm sure that Thinas has more to say to us before the audience starts."

"Wonderful," Fish muttered, and heard Albryan chuckle. The sound was unexpected.

"You'll do fine," he said, taking Fish by the shoulder as they went out. "I wouldn't let you do the speaking if I didn't think so."


COUNCILWOMAN TIRALINNA EBRASKAIA was an unsettlingly familiar older version of Dannine, complete with his sister's frown and stony blue eyes. Rather than Dannine's pale gold, her long hair was black streaked with silver, giving her a striking and authoritative appearance. She sat in the exact middle of the table of five, facing Fish directly, so that his every word reached her expressionless eyes first. Though her four fellow Councillors made soft noises of shock or disbelief at intervals, or stirred in their seats, Tiralinna remained completely impassive.

As they had agreed beforehand, Albryan stepped in to lay out the military plan he had concocted with Thinas. He was an excellent speaker, Fish quickly realized, making his point with a directness and simplicity that were enviable. Covertly, Fish made note of his mannerisms.

"This is my proposal," General Sovaya said at last, once Albryan had spoken. The two of them flanked Fish, military men facing a Council of nobly born, richly-dressed women. Even the lone man behind the table, Slovan Formai, seemed effeminate in his dress and bearing. Had Albryan not told him beforehand that Formai was male, Fish might simply have assumed that all of them were women. "In my opinion, we cannot afford to pass up this opportunity. If Anspeare survives, he promises to take the war to Arran Sylvaissen at last—to help rid us of the tyrant we have fought these past two decades. We do not have the manpower nor support to do this on our own—to bring the fight to Armour City." He took a deep breath, and allowed all eyes to turn towards him. "We need this alliance, if ever we hope to end this war in our favour."

A ringing silence followed the general's proclamation. Tiralinna Ebraskaia was the one to break it.

"Thank you, General," she began. "Although the idea of an alliance has merit—"

"Dear child," interrupted the older, white-haired woman to her left, addressing Fish directly and speaking right over her fellow Councillor. Sylvia Anentas, Fish recalled her name, and neither did he miss the anger that flashed across Tiralinna's face. "Your tale is—extraordinary. And you look exhausted. Have you slept since yesterday?"

Fish blinked several times; this was close to the last thing he had expected. "I—not much," he said at last, nonplussed enough that he simply told the truth.

"How old are you?" she asked, and he answered again honestly. "Nineteen."

"So young," Sylvia tutted. "Yet I see in you a beacon of hope for our people." She looked around at her fellow councillors. Seated next to her, Slovan Formai nodded gravely; the two other women looked towards the stern authority of the Ebraskaia matriarch, whose face was set in the same expression Fish remembered his sister wearing just before she would lose control and scream at him.

"How much of this *tale* can we believe?" asked the woman on the far right, with hair iron-grey and a severe profile.

"Thinas has vouched for him," Sylvia rebutted. "I trust in the general. I trust in our brave soldiers. It is they who regularly sacrifice so much just to keep this land safe. I motion that we call the Assembly without any more delay."

"Larichessa is right," Tiralinna interrupted icily. "I do not doubt the general's judgment, only his eagerness to see some progress in this war. There is more merit to waiting, and moving only when we are in possession of all of the facts."

"I would have thought, Tira," Sylvia said with a sly edge to her voice, "that you of all people would welcome a voice from within our enemy's cohort at last. Even if"—she inclined her head—"it is not quite the voice you hoped for."

Glancing at Tiralinna Ebraskaia, Fish found himself impressed. He was no stranger to having to school his face for whatever he wished not to show, but this woman outclassed him in every possible way. She did not move a muscle, nor betray that she had even registered the implication and the challenge in the older woman's words.

"You suppose wrong, Sylvia," she said, every word dropping like a shard of ice into the well of silence that the chamber had become. "Unlike you, it seems, I am not ready to give away my trust to anyone who has not earned it." She sat back, and looked directly at Fish for the first time, a remarkable feat for someone who had been seated right in front of him all this while. "I motion that we dismiss this matter, and imprison this *boy* as we should any foeman who falls into our hands. Until we can interrogate him thoroughly, and establish where his loyalties truly lie."

"I will not allow it," Sylvia returned, just as calmly and so fast that Fish did not even have time to absorb the shock that rattled through him. "I hereby vouch for this boy, and sponsor him into Qwu'Mallorn. And like any foreigner sponsored into our land, he shall not be arrested nor detained without the due process of justice."

As Tiralinna's frown deepened only slightly, Slovan Formai

spoke up. "I will act as second sponsor, granting Deryck the status of diplomat. And furthermore, I motion that we take no further action until we have had time to cool our heads and fully consider all that he has told us."

"If Deryck speaks true, the people of Svanfeld do not have the time we would take," Sylvia returned.

"Patience, Sylvia," Slovan said quietly, and the older woman subsided at last. "Our esteemed colleagues need time to reflect on all this—as do I. I must consult with the rest of my family."

"Very well," Sylvia finally agreed, and Fish's heart sank. "We will arrange to reconvene in five days."

"Agreed," Carin Hedgora said, the only time the youngest Councillor had spoken. Larichessa Stani nodded wordlessly. Tiralinna drew herself up.

"You will not let him wander freely," she said to Thinas, and the general inclined his head in obeisance.

"Very well, then. I will consider whether this gift Arran sent us is poisoned, or whether it is worth *trusting* for all of our fates."

Fish remained rigid as the five Councillors departed one by one, until Albryan took his arm at last and firmly turned him towards the door, directing his steps as they marched outside. Thinas was already gone. Fish could not think of anything to say. "I'm sorry—" he began, looking up at Albryan.

The captain put his hand on Fish's shoulder, forestalling the words that had barely begun to form. "Come, walk with me," he said quietly.

Fish barely noticed his surroundings. Albryan steered him into what seemed yet another grove of the woods that encroached all around Tenna. In Ülhard only the most affluent suburbs could boast of having greenery, but here, it seemed, the forest was always close by.

Passing under the trees and out of sight of anyone else, Fish found his voice at last. "Was that a serious threat?" he asked, unable to keep the edge of real fear out of his words. "Was Dannine's mother really going to consider throwing me in prison?"

Albryan turned to face him. "For what it's worth—no. I think Tiralinna knew that Sylvia and Slovan would oppose that idea, and she wanted to see how far they were willing to go. It was more a test of her fellow Councillors than it was to do with you."

Fish stared at him for a long moment, then turned away with a bitter laugh.

"Sometimes you have to take victory where you can," Albryan continued. "That could have gone better, but it could have gone worse. Trust me. Don't be despondent." Fish turned to look at him incredulously, but there was nothing of pretence in the young soldier's face. "You won over the moderate faction. Two out of all five isn't nothing. Larichessa will always disagree with Sylvia, for no other reason but their long-standing family feud. However, if the rest of the table are united, she'll go along with it. And Carin Hedgora is a nonentity. She'll follow whatever the more powerful heads agree on." He paused, then stated quietly, "We need to win over Tiralinna."

Fish stared at him, aghast. "Win . . . Tiralinna? The woman who was ready to imprison me?"

"It won't be easy," Albryan agreed enigmatically. "But not impossible."

Fish turned away, shaking his head. Not even a full day of being an envoy, and already he wanted to throw it all to the winds. Anspeare should have chosen someone else . . . but there had been nobody else. No-one who had such a personal stake in this fight, who had been raised to nobility, educated in politics, who could read people and negotiate freely . . . who understood what was at stake should he fail.

Albryan was hovering over him. "There's one other thing." His voice was hesitant. "I don't know how . . . how to approach this diplomatically. It's about your Gift." Fish turned back, a chill eating at his guts, and Albryan met his eyes. "I'm going to say this plainly. You told me you abstained from using your magic for eight years, and only recently started again. Your Gift is tremendously powerful, and it's not under control." Fish let out a slow breath as he continued, "You're not grounded; I started to notice it when the Council were arguing over you, and it's stronger now. You're bleeding magic into the ether, and if you get any more agitated, you're going to bleed through on this plane as well."

He was right, and Fish could feel the leakage now that he had been alerted. He found the drain and quickly smoothed it over, tamping down the flow of energy. Albryan nodded.

"That's better. But—those years you missed, when you were an adolescent—they were integral for you to learn to harness your Gift, to coexist safely with it."

Fish's heart sank. "I didn't really have a choice—"

Albryan put his hand back on Fish's shoulder. "I know. Damned if I know what you could have done differently. This is a bad deal, and I'm proposing to help you, if you'll let me. I've worked with lots of young men with powerful Gifts, when they came from families who were common-born. Some of them had similar problems."

"Help—how?"

"Thinas took me off field duty. My sole assignment for the foreseeable future is to look after you. If we're to spend most of our time together, we might as well do something useful. I can teach you what I spent most of my youth learning—how to modulate my Gift."

Fish sighed. His own magic seemed like a hopeless burden, even more so these days than ever before. "All right." He shrugged. "But it won't matter if I have to creep back to Svanfeld in failure."

Albryan's mouth quirked as if he wanted to smile. "About that," he said, turning his steps onto a path that led between the trees. "Follow me."

Fish obeyed, mystified. "Where are we going?" he asked after a while. They seemed to be passing through a network of paths that connected different parts of the town, judging from the small groups and individuals passing by.

"We're nearly there," was all the answer Fish got. The path grew less busy and led up a rise, cresting suddenly into a spacious clearing. They continued onward, to where a screen of young trees gave way to a great house set in the midst of a shady, cultivated garden.

"Aren't we trespassing?" he asked Albryan in a low voice. But the young captain only grinned and led the way straight on, to where a young woman dressed in lime-green robes was sitting on a low bench, absorbed in a stack of papers on her lap.

She looked up as they approached, flicking her long, silky auburn hair out of her face, and made an expression that was not so far from the frowns of Dannine and her birth mother. "Albryan." She shot an intensely curious glance at Fish. "I thought you were in the field this week."

"I was recalled," Albryan replied evenly. "Listen—I wanted to thank you. For allowing me and Velda to spend so much time in your mother's library. I'd hoped that perhaps you and I could work together in future—rather than working against each other."

"I . . . If you wish it." The young woman seemed taken aback. She glanced at Fish again. "Albryan, is this—"

"This is Deryck Luzerna," Albryan said, for all the world as if Fish had just appeared in passing rather than having been tethered to his side for the past morning. Fish moved forward, aware of the girl's interest, wondering what on earth this meant. He inclined his head with his hand over his heart, as he was aware was the proper greeting.

"It is good to meet you, my lady," he said, putting his best manners forward. "May I ask your name?"

The girl smiled brightly. "Mialiné Ebraskaia," she said. "The day is all abuzz with news of you, Deryck. I would love to get to know you."

# CHAPTER XXXVI
# MIALINÉ EBRASKAIA

BRIALISE HAD SPENT LESS THAN a week in Tenna, and already she was leaving.

"Are you sure you're fine to ride?" Fish asked her again, and the girl rolled her eyes. It was very early in the morning, far too early for Fish yet again, but he had felt obliged to see her off. It was as though part of him were untethering. All around them in the muggy morning forest, soldiers were double-checking tack and baggage, yelling to one another, mounting horses. Word was that General Sovaya was sending a large contingent of soldiers into the west of Qwu'Mallorn, to provide better defence against anticipated raids from Svanfeld. Fish wondered how thin the general was stretching his ranks.

"The people here have taken care of me," Brialise replied. "I have seen a healer, and a mind-healer, and both have given their blessing to go. It is not often that such large groups ride from here to the remote west. I will be safer for the soldiers' escort."

She looked up at Fish with the resolution of her decision in her eyes, and he put his arms around her. "If you see my son . . ." she began, when they broke apart.

"I'll do my best for him," Fish said softly. "But I don't know—"

"If I am settled enough, I will send for him," Brialise said.

"But your family—"

"My parents are dead," she whispered. "And my brothers. But I am going to stay, now, with my uncle Liamus and his wife. They will know whether anyone else has survived." She took a deep breath. "I am the last one left. I have a responsibility, Fish. To our lands, our homestead, the labourers who remain."

The young lieutenant, whose name Fish didn't recall, came riding up. "You ready to depart, lady?"

Brialise smiled. "You do not need to call me 'lady,' Gardan." She turned and put a hand on the horn of her saddle. "I am ready."

She rode off bantering with the lieutenant, leaving Fish on his own, the still air forming droplets of moisture to condense in his hair.

Fish wanted to find a mount of his own and ride after her. He wanted to call Brightfeather, who was still languishing at the Border with Albryan's former command. General Sovaya had advised that Fish leave him there for now, and apparently the quetzal was ingratiating himself with the soldiers by hunting, and sharing, a steady supply of antelope. But Fish wanted to fly, to break through the dripping tree-tops that hemmed the warm damp air in around him, to see the sky again. He wanted the steady, solid presence of Nico beside him, like that day they'd flown into the mountains together. Failing that . . .

He wanted to visit Velda Davidz, whom he had only seen in passing whenever she came to visit Albryan. Fish had no idea how she would react if he came knocking on her door, and he had been too preoccupied to try and imagine how he would approach her. Fish had his own quarters in the barracks now, slept alone at nights, and slept uneasily. The army reminded him of the City Guard in Zarath, whilst being just unfamiliar enough to be jarring. Fish had only ever been a regular in Zarath, never an officer, and had never had an entire room to himself.

And magic lessons with Albryan were not going well. They'd had several long sessions with the young captain attempting to teach Fish what he called "grounding"—controlling his magic even under the influence of strong emotion or danger. Fish had picked up the new shielding techniques quickly enough, but as far as he could tell, his Gift wasn't one that could be grounded too easily.

He sighed as he turned, heavy-footed, to go. But the thing that was bothering him the most . . .

"This is how the game is played," Albryan had told him, after introducing Fish to Dannine's blood sister nearly three days ago. "This way, you have a line to Tiralinna Ebraskaia. Mialiné is curious, and she's disposed to like you—as long as you conduct yourself like a nobleman. You remember your manners?"

Fish did remember his manners. He hated manners. He had come to detest almost everything that reminded him of his father, and included in that broad category were court manners, fancy clothes, and personal over-grooming.

He'd resisted as much as he could on the last two. Being made to shave his face *every single day* was nothing less than aggravating, but Albryan had been quick to remind him whenever he delayed a shave or a wash. Fish was used to rolling out of bed and going about his day without so much as combing his hair, but suddenly he'd had to adjust his habits if he was going to succeed in his goals here, apparently. As for new clothes, Fish had tried protesting that he had no coin for such things, to which Albryan had countered that whatever money he spent was coming out of the Council's coffers, since Slovan Formai had proclaimed him a diplomat.

So as Fish trudged back towards his quarters, fully intending to go back to bed and sleep for another four hours—the life of a envoy, at least, was one of leisure—he did not look out of place. The tunic he wore was a deep red linen, which he was well aware complimented his warm-toned skin and dark hair, and the sleeves and collar were edged in gold. He'd bought it to wear to a dinner with Sylvia Anentas and Slovan Formai, the Councillors who were kindly disposed towards him. They had invited him to Sylvia's family homestead, made him meet all their numerous offspring and young granddaughters.

That had been last night.

Throughout all of it, Fish had been on his best behaviour, stifling the hysterical laughter that bubbled just under his skin. Here he was, some nobody who'd been sold into slavery the moment he came into the world, only to be acquired by the most powerful man in Vailana and groomed to carry on his legacy. Now, somehow, he had become a central figure in the game of Morgein politics. Or was it merely a central piece in a game of manipulation and chance?

This piece, however, had things it badly needed to accomplish for itself. The Council of Tenna was meeting again, the day after tomorrow. Fish was running out of time.

He sighed and pressed his eyes shut with his hand, feeling moisture from the air beading in his brows. It was time to take up the pretty girl on her proposition. To allow her to get to know him. It was the last thing Fish wanted, but what choice did he have?

THE MALLORN-ROSES WERE LATE this year. They should have been blooming around the beginning of Thirdmonth, full three weeks ago when he'd arrived back in Tenna. Now, as Albryan led the way into the woods with Velda at his side, they made a riot of white and blazing pink along the path. But the snow had lingered late on the Svanlyn mountains this spring, sending cold winds down along the coast and causing the rains to fall later than usual.

He could tell that Velda had something on her mind. She answered easily enough whenever he asked a question, but her eyes wandered everywhere but towards his face. Albryan had become used to having her full attention, the smiles she would give whenever she saw him, the passionate kisses of greeting. There had been little of that, the past few days.

He took her hand and pulled her to a halt. "We haven't had much time alone together since I came back," he said quietly. He led her off the path, into a glade that was ablaze with mallorn-roses, bright with sunlight. She made soft noises of admiration at the beautiful flowers, and for a while they wandered in the sunshine, holding hands. But a cloud passed overhead, across the bright sun, and a shadow darkened her face.

"Hiram," she said at last, resolutely.

"What about him?" Albryan asked softly.

"I know that you know more of him than I do," she replied. "You escaped from Arran Sylvaissen's dungeons together; you travelled with him for more than a month." Her voice went very quiet. "You know of—of what happened with his daughter. You know more than Hiram would ever tell me, before he was taken from us."

Albryan nodded. The old man was gone, and he had been expecting something of the sort for the past few days now. As succinctly as possible, he told Velda everything he knew. It was not a long, nor complicated story. Nor, he was aware, was it a particularly unusual one. Albryan had met more people than he cared to count, whose families had been torn apart by Arran Sylvaissen's invasion and the subsequent violence. Velda listened intently.

"Twins?" she repeated, her eyes brimming. "But I don't understand—why didn't he . . ."

They had stopped amidst the flowers. "Hiram didn't tell you this, I imagine," Albryan said, "because he felt it would all be too much. That he couldn't offer you any hope, only death. Only the mourning of a family you never had in addition to the one you just lost."

"But now," she said, "now, things are different, once again. There's . . ." She trailed off.

"Fish," Albryan completed. Arriving like a hurricane, this boy had appeared, and he felt windswept, off-balance. Everything in his life had suddenly been disturbed—even the woman he was half in love with. Though the boy was a little rough around the edges, he seemed to have some gift for making Albryan feel protective towards him, responsible for him, as though he were one of Drill-Sergeant Albryan Lana's young recruits. Though Albryan had never had a younger sibling by blood, the army was a collection of brothers, and he had watched over countless young brothers-in-arms before. Fish reminded him of the best of them: smart, curious, maybe a little more bravado than he ought to have. It was hard for Albryan to keep in mind that this boy had been trained in blood sorcery—by his own admission, no less—and had walked a long, broken path of life already, with depths Albryan would likely never touch the bottom of.

"Does it all fit, or am I just trying too hard? Bryan, I feel almost like he and I were *meant* somehow." Velda hesitated. "I've never felt more strongly that I need to be with someone, save maybe—" She broke off and glanced furtively at Albryan. "Save my husband, Emmett."

Albryan swallowed, trying to brush it off, but could not help the prickling at his guts. They'd never talked freely about that, of their past lives. Albryan knew better than to start something he'd regret, yet he could not stop the burrowing shard of hurt. If Emmett had been *meant*, then what was he?

Velda was already continuing: "Yet it's different with him, with Fish. There isn't that—that romantic attachment. I don't know how to explain it, except by saying that he feels like . . . a brother. *My* brother."

Albryan stayed silent for a while, swallowing down the things he did not want to touch. "Fish's magical gift," he began at last, "it might be the strongest I've ever encountered. Stronger than mine, certainly. Now I've met a few who were about equal to me, hard to say which of us was more powerful, but his—" He shook his head. "It makes *me* look like the one with the minor Gift. The two of you—I'm not sure what to make of it."

"So it doesn't fit?" she whispered. "This—me having no Mage-Gift, and him having an incredibly strong one—it's not possible? If we were siblings in truth?"

Albryan shook his head. "I'm not sure what's possible with you," he admitted. "Whether your . . . particular ability is heritable or not.

But if you were just an ordinary, nonmage woman, Velda . . . it could fit." He saw the hope burgeon clearly in her eyes, and his mouth felt dry, for what reason he could not rightly say. "The strength of the Gift doesn't truly matter. Hiram's daughter had no magic, but her mother and her husband both did. Any child of theirs would have had an even chance of inheriting the Mage-Gift, just as I and my brother had. And Caras's Gift is a lot weaker than mine. He'd never be able to wield war-magic."

She was silent, taking in his words like a fern drinking the rain, and Albryan swallowed. "Seeing the two of you together," he said hoarsely, "I could believe it. Hiram told me—that you look like his daughter. The same face and the same eyes, he said, and he claimed your colouring matches that of the man who would have been your father."

The sun shone full upon Velda as she stood with the mallorn-roses at her feet. "I came here looking for a new life," she said softly. "I never dreamed that I would find . . ." She trailed off. "Someone like that. Someone I could be so close to."

"*Can* you be close to him?" Albryan whispered, and she frowned as she looked at him.

"What?"

"Velda, how much has he told you . . . about his past?"

"I know that he was bought by Arran Sylvaissen, if that's what you mean," she replied. "And I know he ran away from that life. It can't have been easy."

"No," Albryan said. "I agree. But he told me and Thinas more than he's told you, and I still have the feeling that he's hiding a lot of it." She continued to look at him quizzically. "I believe that he has good intentions," Albryan said at last. "Fish reminds me of the best of my men, the boys I've trained to become officers over the years. But there's so much hidden in him—so much pain, so much turmoil—that I'm not sure he's the easiest person to know, or to love."

"If you'd been raised by the blood sorcerer of Armour City," Velda returned quietly, "how difficult do you think people would find it to be around you?"

"A fair point," Albryan admitted. "But his state of mind worries me. He has a Gift that's nearly impossible to keep under control, and all I've tried to teach him about shielding and grounding haven't seemed to help much. Perhaps, if he could deal with the things that are bothering him, he'd have an easier time controlling the Gift in turn. I've tried to suggest that he see a mind-healer, but he's pretty resistant to that idea. I know it's not for everyone, particularly those who highly value their secrecy of mind." He passed a hand over his face, then laughed softly. "Fish seems to have this effect," he said at last. "Look at me worrying about the boy, as if he's some green recruit who hasn't experienced life. He's the same age as you, yet there's a lot about him that seems younger."

"What have you got him doing with Mialiné?" Velda asked suddenly, bluntly.

"Elithan told you about that?" he asked. She nodded, then listened with an deeply critical expression on her face as he explained it to her.

"I don't like this." Velda paused. "I don't think Fish is . . . like that."

"Well, then." Albryan could hardly hold back a grin. "In that case, they might be perfectly matched."

FISH LOUNGED ON THE BENCH, staring idly up at the branches of the willow tree as they danced shadows across him. Three days ago, when he'd met Mialiné, she had asked him to "the next high promenade," as she named it, and Albryan had accepted on Fish's behalf without him having any say in the matter. Now, impeccably coiffed and groomed, though aware that he probably showed the signs of the deep exhaustion he felt, he was waiting outside, where he felt far more comfortable than inside the sumptuous mansion she called a house. Her mother was not present, having some other pressing business to attend to, and Fish lost himself in the slow, mesmerizing movements of the tree that arched above.

"Are you ready, then?" A sweet, breathy voice cut through his ruminations, and Fish blinked and looked towards it.

He caught his breath. Mialiné was very pretty, just as Dannine had always been pretty, with long straight hair of a lovely burnished auburn, like autumn leaves, and clear green eyes not so far from Dannine's blue. The gown she wore complimented those eyes, and the gold dust she had applied to eyelids and cheekbones contrasted them beautifully.

"You look . . . amazing," he managed, and she beamed at him.

"You don't look so bad, yourself." She proffered her arm, and Fish took it. The two of them were equal in height, he noticed as she led the way. That made her shorter than both her mother and sister.

Green seemed to be Mialiné's colour, and Fish had anticipated that he would look dreadfully out of place on her arm wearing red. His waistcoat now was a deep seafoam blue, studded with bronze buttons, and the shirt he wore underneath it was of the softest white silk Fish had ever seen. Albryan had helped him dress and clean up earlier that afternoon, saying much less than usual. At the end of it, he'd simply clasped Fish's hand and said, "Good luck."

The trappings of privilege and wealth in Qwu'Mallorn were not so much different from those Fish already knew: a luxurious carriage ride, a picturesque castle a mile or so out of Tenna, beautifully dressed young people holding court in an ancient, open-walled garden surrounded by baskets of flowers and bustling servants. The air was redolent with the fumes of tobacco and perfume, rose-water, vanilla, cinnamon and sugar. There were a *lot* of young men who brushed past, stopping to make small talk with Mialiné, or offering her some light snack or cigarillo. She all but ignored every one of them in favour of Fish. He was intrigued by the lack of chaperones or older adults, and Mialiné was happy enough to explain everything to him.

"These events are for *us*, to get to know our peers. Talk of the future. Perhaps choose a mate." Fish felt the heat rise in his face as she spoke, and distracted her by asking about the food. There were delectable morsels of cheese and sweet pepper, savoury smoked fish, and a baked dessert called *querka*, which consisted of sheets of flaky pastry with shredded quince and honey. Fish thought it tasted like love, or at least what he imagined that real, true, passionate love might taste like, sweet with honey, warm with cinnamon, sharp with anise, bitter with cloves, and with something else in there as well, something surprisingly light and floral under the heavy spices, which lingered on his tongue even as it hovered far out of reach.

Although his surroundings were far too opulent for him to feel fully comfortable, Fish could not fault the Morgein nobility in their indulgences. The light supper was eaten whilst standing about making conversation, and then there was dancing. To Fish's vast relief, Mialiné showed no interest in the latter.

"I'm so bored," she whispered to Fish, who could not stop a grin from spreading across his face. "Want to go someplace we can actually talk?"

Before they left, Fish dared to pinch a bottle of the sweet pink wine they'd been drinking from its place in a magically iced bucket, which made Mialiné giggle uncontrollably. She took his hand, and swept him through the lamp-lit garden into the deeper shadows of a shady grove lit only by silver moonlight.

They wandered the meandering paths, talking of nonsensicalities. She was easy enough to hold a conversation with, like anyone who had been bred and raised to high society. She had a talent for dancing around any topic that either of them might find uncomfortable.

Dannine, Fish recalled, had never mastered that skill, at least not as long as Fish had known her. She had been oft tongue-tied and prone to sulky silences, and she had hated hobnobbing with the lesser nobility who had replaced the "old blood" of Armour City. It was their older sister, Ceazyn, who'd had the gift of charisma, and continually exercised it.

Mialiné got around to talking about her work, the magical defence of the Border. "It takes a whole team of us," she said. "The magical net needs to be maintained daily." She laughed. "But I wouldn't have thought you'd want to chat about the technicalities of magical construction."

"I don't." She did not seem in the least bit wary of him, but Fish had an inkling that asking complicated questions about the workings of their defences might seem like he was fishing for information, to some. "Why don't we find a place to sit, and open this?" He held up the bottle.

"Capital idea." She led him back towards the garden, to a private alcove shaded by foliage. Someone had stacked cushions in there, and it was softly lit with the same kind of magic lamp Thinas Sovaya had in his office. There was even a little table with earthenware cups and plates.

Fish sank down to the cushions, bemused, whilst Mialiné poured them both a cup of wine and daintily took a seat beside him. She took a long draught, and Fish did the same, steeling himself for whatever he might have to ask this night—or do in return. She sat back, staring at him. Fish's head spun.

*This isn't working.* It wasn't a surprise. Fish had no idea how to seduce someone, and with her he couldn't even imagine that he might *want* to. He would probably have a better chance trying to sweet-talk Albryan Lana. But Mialiné was crouching forward, gazing at him, and their faces were close to meeting, making him wonder if—

"Mm." Mialiné leaned her face away, and tucked an errant strand of hair behind her ear. "Didn't think this would really work, but I suppose I had to try. The problem is, I don't think either of us are looking at something we want here."

"W-what do you mean?"

She crouched back towards him, the cushions sinking under her weight. "I mean that I find the idea of lying with a man abhorrent, Deryck. And I think you feel much the same about women."

Hidden in the shadows, Fish could feel himself colouring. "I'm not . . ." he began. He shook his head to clear it of the wine, and drew his knees towards his chest. "I didn't set out to—"

"You want something from me," Mialiné interrupted. "I'm not simple. You want me to talk to my mother and get her to change her mind about General Sovaya's plan." There was something almost forlorn in her face as she drew back, and Fish didn't say anything for a long moment. He had put up shields against other people's interest for long enough that he could recognize that she was doing the same. Yet there was a crack in her armour, a fissure he might be able to wedge open, though he wasn't yet sure what was fuelling it.

He reached for her hand, sighed deeply, and flung his own shields to the winds. "Listen," he said, "it's the very depths of stupidity for me to sit here and pretend that you don't remind me of—of my adopted sister."

There it was, in the open. Fish instantly knew that his guess about Mialiné's fissure had been correct. She swallowed, and her eyes watered.

"You're not really curious about me," Fish continued. "You want to know about your sister. You want to know what kind of person she is, whether she'll ever come back." He shook his head. "I'm sorry that I only have bad answers to all of those questions. Arran Sylvaissen was not a—a good parent."

A tear splashed down Mialiné's cheek, smudging the gold dust. She nodded.

"If you want me to tell—"

"No," Mialiné said resolutely, putting a careless hand to her face and wiping the gold into streaks that Fish thought looked almost like feathers. She stood up and went over to the table, grabbing the open bottle of wine and refilling her glass. "I don't want to hear it. Not now. Not tonight." She turned back to him. "This genuinely wasn't just about Dannine." She took a sip of wine, and seemed to be steeling herself. "I want something from you, in return."

Fish looked up at her, alarmed by the grave tone in her voice. "Please tell me it's not a child."

"Goddess, no!" Mialiné sank back down to the cushions beside him.

"I am the only child remaining to my mother," she said after a little while, looking straight ahead and dangling the cup from her hand. "I have responsibilities. Obligations. One of those *is* the continuation of the family line." Fish nodded to show he understood. "There are other ways, though. Instead of taking one of these oh-so-charming young males as consort, I could marry a woman."

"Marry a—" Fish lost his voice. "You can do that?"

"It's unorthodox, but not out of the question. Someone of the right temperament, from a high house—a younger daughter, unlikely to ever inherit. She'd bear children, and instead of having any myself, I'd simply adopt hers into my family."

Fish cleared his throat. "Sounds a little like you already have someone in mind."

She smiled mysteriously. "I do. She's beautiful, well-spoken, smart, loves children, and is the fourth daughter in her household. She's perfect. She's recently had a child of her own, which is why she wasn't here tonight. It would mean I already have a potential heir the moment the marriage takes place."

"So what's the problem?" Fish asked, nonplussed.

Mialiné's smile vanished. "Mother."

Fish blinked, trying to piece together the puzzle. "She won't allow you?"

"She doesn't respect me, nor approve of my ideas." There was a bitterness in Mialiné's voice. "She's already planned out my entire future for me—and she can be narrow-mindedly determined sometimes. I think you know." Fish nodded. "I think, sometimes, that she doesn't even believe that people like me could exist—people who find the idea of being with the other sex this horrendous, this unnatural. She doesn't understand that I couldn't just close my eyes and 'go through with it' for the sake of the family. It wouldn't be true to myself. The very notion is just too disgusting. I could take a consort and have our marriage be largely a business transaction. That's been done. But the physical aspect of the relationship would never happen. It's far too *wrong*—and where would be the point in that?"

Fish nodded slowly, feeling for himself the truth of what she said. Before tonight, he had never contemplated what it would truly be like to bed a girl, and he realized now that the idea seemed as alien to him as bedding a stone statue. "I understand how you feel," he said, softly, "but what can *I* do about it?"

"A chance for a chance," Mialiné replied with a toss of her head. "I want a chance at glory, Deryck. A chance to prove myself. Once I have that leverage, I can change the trajectory of my life. I can make Mother listen to me. When General Sovaya's men ride to battle in the mountains, I want a group of us women to go with them. I want to ride with them. Lead them."

Fish hesitated, taken aback by her words. Mialiné continued.

"I can't make Mother approve of your plan," she said, "but I can give you a chance to convince her. I can arrange the meeting. I can tell you exactly how to win her over. She's as curious as I am, and I know that she's been *dying* to meet you all by herself, one-on-one."

"I have a feeling," Fish said, quietly, "that the general won't like this." From all he'd seen in Qwu'Mallorn thus far, women stayed at home and got to rule the roost, but only men were afforded the dubious privilege of adventuring.

She raised an eyebrow, and held out her hand. "So what do you say?"

Fish leaned forward, grinning, and clasped it. "Deal."

# CHAPTER XXXVII
## PRINCESS

"ARE WE CLOSE YET?" THE MERCENARY woman asked, and Nico carefully lifted his head, sighting over the ridge to the mountain slope where the necromes prowled.

"We should be within a day's walk of Von Dharen," he returned, speaking softly. He was fairly sure that they lay out of earshot, but it always paid to be careful.

"At last." Josephine scooped her braids behind her head, twining the errant locks back into place. Nico kept his eyes on the slope. A human commander had arrived, mounted on a horse, with a kerchief over his face and a floppy hat pulled down to cover his forehead. *Another boy from Ülhard?* Nico wondered to himself, and tightened his grip on the loaded gun Josephine had let him carry.

"Commander. Mounted," he said shortly, and she nodded without a word. She was all competence, now, with not much trace of the jovial demeanour she wore at other times. Nico had been eaten up with curiosity to meet the "experienced mercenary" Anspeare spoke of, and intrigued to find a young woman not so much older than himself, with cool-toned dark skin that spoke of Eastern ancestry somewhere in her recent lineage, and a swagger and charming smile that could rival Fish when he badly wanted something.

"Do you think we can sneak past them in the dark?" she asked, keeping her voice low.

Nico scowled. It was late afternoon. This little knot of necromes numbered only half a dozen. Yet they had made their camp—or possibly more accurately, their *den*—directly athwart the only route that he and Josephine could realistically take down to the town. Were the two of them to turn back now, they might have to scout along the cliffsides for days before finding another reliable footpath.

He fingered the musket gun. "We might be better . . . taking care of them now. Before nightfall."

Josephine wrinkled her nose before answering. Full summer was almost upon the mountains, and the air was dry and drowsy as the hillside baked in sunlight. In this weather, the ripe stench of necromes, walking dead men, could be detected from nearly a mile away. Nico wasn't sure how their commanders stood it. This one had muffled himself in his kerchief, but stood his ground as the living corpses slouched around him. His horse, clearly picking up the discomfiting stench, jerked against its reins and danced backwards. Josephine laid a hand on the silvered hilt of the sword she carried by her side. "You need to get them in the head, right?"

"Decapitation works best." Silently, Nico readied the long-barrelled musket. "I can get the commander. Take him by surprise."

At her nod, he crouched down and sighted along the barrel as he held the musket steady against a rock. Josephine had let him practise a little on the way up from Anspeare's camp to the Beerstana Pass, but this would be Nico's first time trying to kill a man with it. He'd never had much taste for archery, but he'd heard that aiming a firearm was a different thing altogether.

Josephine's gun was the latest in this sort of weaponry, with a trigger that struck a tiny flint which set fire to the powder that propelled the lead bullet. Nico had been fascinated by the mechanism, never having seen a firearm up close before, and he took his time making sure he was ready before touching his finger to the trigger. To her credit, Josephine was silent, for once. The swaggering mercenary could rival Fish for volubility at the best of times. It was one reason Nico had been enjoying her company so much, these past few days in the wilderness.

The gun spoke, just as the horse decided to sidle away again.

The lead ball missed the commander by more than a foot, crashing into a rock beside him and shattering into pieces. Nico swore. The horse reared up on its hind legs with a loud whinny, and all six necromes turned growling towards where the two of them lay. In just a moment, the human commander regained control of his horse, and with a yell turned its head towards them. Nico scrambled back, reaching for his sword.

Josephine grabbed the gun from him. With a speed and efficiency that Nico would never have believed possible, she took a cartridge from her bandolier, ripped it open with her teeth, emptied it into the flash pan, then quickly crammed the rest of it down the barrel with the bullet and struck the butt of the gun against the ground. With the rider fast approaching and only moments to spare, she lifted the gun to eye height, sighted, and fired in less than a single breath.

The commander fell from the saddle, spurting blood as the bullet hit him square in the chest, passing right through his armour at a distance of less than five yards.

Nico felt a twinge of jealousy, but there was no time to dwell on it—the necromes were hard on their commander's heels. This time, at least, Nico knew what to do with them. "Strike for the head!" he reminded Josephine, leaping into the fray even as he put action to words, making a savage, sweeping stroke that took the nearest creature's head clean off.

The battle was short and sharp; luckily, the necromes took no note of tactics that would be obvious even to the most battle-inexperienced men, and generally attacked haphazardly, flinging themselves at any who dared cross their path. Nico had taken care of three of them already when he heard Josephine cry out, and turned to see her stumble as her right leg gave way beneath her. Even in the uncontrolled movement, she lashed out at the creature attacking with the hand that still held her gun, striking such a blow that its head burst open like a rotten fruit, spilling gore as it fell to the ground.

Had Nico not been in the midst of red battle-anger, he might have retched; instead, he raced to her aid, dispatching the one remaining necrome with an efficient swordstroke to the back of its neck. Sheathing his filthy sword, he approached Josephine and supported her weight, dragging her towards a nearby overhang, away from the gore and the stench.

"Let me see the wound," he said urgently.

"It's all right. I know about the poison." Josephine sank to the ground, showing him where her trousers had been rent along her thigh. The wound was a deep, ugly scratch, clearly inflicted by the necrome's long fingernails, yet Nico could see no trace of the congealed black blood which would inevitably spell disaster.

"We need to wash it. There's soap in your pack, right?" Nico's voice shook, and he swallowed hard, trying to get it under control. He did not want to lose a companion like Josephine, and especially not to the kind of death-undeath that those afflicted by necrome blood would experience. If she died here, Nico would have to separate her head from the rest of her corpse for his own safety, and that was a proposition he did not relish.

"Take me someplace nicer first," she begged, and Nico reflected that she could not be in *that* much trouble if she felt capable of making jokes.

"Can you walk?" he asked, and she nodded vehemently.

"It's just a scratch."


THEY WENT AS FAR AS THEY COULD before the arrival of dusk, a good distance away from the carnage. Nico found a small overhang in the midst of a grove of bushy thorn trees, and built a fire so that they both could heat water and wash. He did not feel comfortable until the black gore had all been scrubbed off.

Josephine went behind a protruding boulder to take off her pants and tend to her wound, which Nico found passing strange. Given the way she'd behaved thus far, teasing Nico endlessly about being a "brogue boy from the sticks" and only laughing when he made ribald suggestions back, he would not have thought the mercenary woman to be bashful about showing skin. She returned with a cloth bandage showing under the ripped fabric of her trousers, and stretched herself out beside the fire with a soft groan of pain.

"That wound is going to be a problem," Nico said quietly. "The princess is very likely holed up in her castle somewhere. We might need to climb walls, and we *will* need to move fast."

Josephine hesitated. Finally she said, "You'll go in on your own then. I'll find a hideout higher up and keep watch over your escape route. We discussed this, remember? Whether it was worth risking both of us, or whether we should leave a lookout? Now circumstances have decided it for us."

"I don't like it." Nico scowled. "I'd rather get you to safety—"

"You don't have time for that. They could move the princess at any moment. This doesn't change our mission." She regarded him sombrely. "We came to fetch Princess Katrina, and that's what we're going to do. This is more important than either of us."

Nico scoffed. "This maiden's life is worth both of ours?"

"That's not what I mean." She paused. "People are counting on us. On our alliance with Anspeare."

Nico scowled deeper, and crouched over the fire, feeding it more kindling.

"You really don't like Hugh Anspeare, do you?" Josephine said.

"The first time we met," Nico replied stiffly, "he threatened to hang me, and then threatened to sell my partner to the same tyrant king *you're* trying to depose."

Josephine's mouth quirked. "Par on course for a mercenary's life."

"I'm not a mercenary."

"No." She cocked her head. "You're an assassin, Anspeare told me. You've no conscience, and will kill in cold blood as easily as swatting a fly. You've no morals, nor code of honour. You're a menace to society."

Nico shrugged, even as he felt anger chew at his heart. *It was never my choice. I did the jobs that found me, the ones people would pay good money for. I never trained for this.* Out loud he said: "I've never killed anyone who didn't deserve it in some way. Guildsmen. Minor nobles. Corrupt politicians. You're dreaming if you think any of them are innocent."

A half-smile hovered on her lips. "So that's why you don't like Anspeare."

"Seems to *me* that everyone's bending over backwards to oblige this man just because he was born into the right family," Nico said shortly. "You're hoping he's going to be salvation for Vailana, but he's just another petty tyrant. Exchange Arran for Anspeare, it's still just another king. Vailana once had an independent Council."

Josephine was quiet, and seemed to be thinking. Finally she said, "You're not wrong. But there's a difference between Arran and Anspeare. One of these crazed tyrants can perform *magic*, and wipe out the whole city should he ever feel the need. The other can't."

Nico began to retort, then recalled Fish and the fear he'd felt in some of his partner's blackest moments, and curbed his tongue. Josephine continued speaking.

"I can barely remember Armour City before Arran," she said frankly. "They executed my father when I was nine, and all I remember since then is being afraid." She shook her head. "I just wanted to leave after that. To go somewhere—anywhere—else. That's more than half the reason why I followed in my mother's footsteps. The very first chance I got, I left for Wilderland to fight a bandit incursion."

Nico avoided her gaze, knowing exactly how it felt to be afraid, to flee a place that had once been home. He still didn't fully understand. Fish was of nobility. Dispossessed perhaps, which was yet another thing he had in common with Anspeare. The two of them shared a background which Nico could never fully touch, and the more time Fish spent with Anspeare, the less Nico had seen of the impish, carefree young man he'd come to know and love.

Jo, though—Josephine was as common as grime on a city brick wall. Nico was grateful for his own privileges, things she clearly shared: he was grateful he'd been taught to read and reckon numbers and to use a sword. He was grateful he'd been encouraged, as a child, to spend time in the monastery library, reading and dreaming romances of times long-forgotten, no matter how poorly those dreams had proved to stand up to reality.

"We get Anspeare his precious princess," Josephine was saying, "and he gives us some semblance of order and justice again. Perhaps not ideal, but leagues and leagues better than what we have now. He helps us crush the blood sorcerer once and for all; he gives us a Council again, a working government with checks and balances. He can't rule alone, not without the consent of places like Kerath. He has to make *some* compromises, and after I've talked to him, I think he will."

Nico only grunted. Josephine fell silent, and did not speak for a while. At last she said, "You'll go, tomorrow night?"

Nico sighed, and stared into the fire. "I'll go."

THE LORDLY DWELLING ABOVE VON DHAREN had not been built for defence, to say the least.

"That's where they're keeping her," Josephine said with certainty, crouching down in the bushes beside Nico and placing a hand on his shoulder to keep herself steady. They had made their laborious way up a high cliff overlooking the mansion at a distance of less than three hundred yards. As they watched, a knot of soldiers in the dirty-white colours of the blood sorcerer's army appeared on one of the decorative parapets set around a handsome pink sandstone tower.

"If she's even still alive," Nico growled.

"She is. She has to be. With the rest of her family presumed dead or missing, Katrina is the key to ruling Svanfeld."

"Does this *blood sorcerer* even care about that?" Nico returned, but she ignored him.

Turning his attention back to the little castle, Nico considered. "That wall would be easy to scale," he said, pointing it out. "That's a blind spot for any of the guards, down there in the shadow of the cliff."

Josephine nodded towards a tiled courtyard on the other side of the mansion. Obviously intended for grand receptions, a small flight of steps led up to the tiles from a manicured garden. It seemed almost directly below them where they sat, though shady bushes obscured a full view. "I'll try to get as close as I can to that yard. That'll give me a vantage over the front of the building. If you run into trouble, try to run towards me."

"This is where we part, then," Nico said. "I need to backtrack and go down *there* in order to get close to the wall." He nodded towards a little ravine which led almost directly towards where he was to go.

Josephine clasped his hand in farewell, then stiffly pulled herself into a crouch that was obviously painful as she shuffled towards her chosen perch. Nico frowned as he set off in the opposite direction. A healing scratch, superficial as it was, should not be paining her this much a day afterwards.

Nico kept the bushes between him and the mansion as he hiked towards the ravine, where he would be shielded from view. The people who had built this place had not been concerned about invaders from the mountains, nor the sea. Svanfeld had been at peace for a long time. The mansion seemed only lightly held, though Nico guessed that half a garrison could likely disappear in the enormity of the sprawling dwelling.

At last he reached the bottom of the ravine, and arranged himself at the foot of the wall. It was full night now, though the moon shone high above. Nico remembered a job in the city, not so long ago, the last time he'd had to climb a wall. The last job he'd done with Fish.

Nico had managed to shelve all thoughts of his partner in the past few days, had not allowed himself to dwell upon any of it. What Fish was doing. When he was to return, and if he would bring the aid that everyone was hoping for.

He was not about to lose himself now. Josephine was counting on him.

This wall was not half so challenging as ones he'd scaled before. He merely looped a length of rope around one of the rounded crenellations adorning the walkway above, and slipped over in no time, sidling away into the shadow of the house. In short order, he found a door that the guards had left unlocked. Evading them upon their rounds, he entered and passed into a pitch-black corridor, feeling his way along.

Hugh Anspeare had given him a detailed description of the mansion's interior rooms, for which Nico was now grateful. The first place to look for the princess was in her own room, which Anspeare had taken pains to describe to Nico how to find. It was close by. Not pausing, Nico made his way through the corridor. His eyes adjusted to the darkness before long, and the silence of the night signalled to him that it was safe to move around.

He reached what he thought—or fervently hoped—was the right door, and paused for a moment, listening. The mansion was quiet, more so than felt comfortable for a dwelling that had been built for distinguished guests and grand occasions. He could hear no sound from within the room beyond.

Nico took a bent hairpin from his pocket and carefully inserted it into the lock—only to find it already turned. Frowning, he reached for the handle. The door swung open to reveal a luxurious lady's bedroom lit by a single oil lamp against the wall. There was no-one in it.

Nico scowled and crept inside, pulling the door shut behind him. "Princess?" he called in a low voice. "Princess Katrina?"

There was only more silence. Nico lit the row of candles on the mantelpiece, and inspected the room. It had clearly been inhabited, recently enough that Nico could detect the faint fragrance of activity. Female clothing was strewn haphazardly across the floor. He passed over a pair of underwear which looked to have dried-out stains of woman's blood, and the chamberpot had obviously been utilized in the past few hours. Yet the princess herself was not to be found. Nico ransacked the room, checking in each cupboard and under the canopy bed. The narrow window was shuttered, and had clearly been that way for some time.

It was late at night. Likely the princess had already been fed, and nobody would come to check on her until the morning. It was the perfect time to make an escape.

Grinding his teeth, Nico left the room as quickly as he could, dashing down a dimly lit corridor. He had not gone far when suddenly an armoured figure appeared from the shadows to face him, drawing its sabre.

*Shit. Shit shit shit.* Of course there would be guards about. Nico's luck had just run out. Not having the space, in the narrow corridor, to draw his own blade, he parried the swordstroke with his vambrace, pushing forward to unbalance the enemy fighter. To his surprise, it worked better than he could have dreamed. The warrior stumbled back with a cry of surprise, dropping his sword. With the visor of his helmet drawn down, Nico could only see his eyes, blue and wide and filled with—*fear*?

He advanced, and the enemy soldier tried to get up and run. Nico caught him easily, pinioning both his arms. "Let me go!" came a high, panicked voice from within the visor.

Holding the armoured figure securely with just one hand, Nico reached out the other and drew off the helmet. A young woman's face glared up at him, incandescent in defiance. Golden hair was gathered into a tousled knot behind her head. She struggled wildly against him. Not a fighter, Nico knew, if the blood sorcerer's army even allowed women to fight alongside them. Somehow, he doubted that.

"Stop fighting me, Princess," he growled. "Hugh Anspeare sent me. I'm here to rescue you."

She froze, looking up at him as tears spilled out of her eyes. "Hugh?" she choked out. "He's alive?"

Nico dared to relax his grip on her a little, and was about to answer affirmatively when he heard it, unmistakably. Guards were approaching. He turned, instinctively drawing two of his daggers.

There were two of them, no match for Nico when his bloodlust was up, but just as he crossed blades with the foremost, who was unwisely trying to swing a sword in the enclosed space, he heard the princess scream in warning. Yet two more guards came at him from the opposite direction, and Nico lost himself in a blur of steel. He set the wall to his back, and fought with the same single-minded determination that had preserved him on the streets of Ülhard.

It was to his advantage that the blood sorcerer's soldiers did not seem to realize that they had too little room for swordfighting. One man bashed his sword hand against the wall and dropped the weapon. Nico was on him in a moment, drawing the dagger across his throat and throwing him into the path of his companion.

Nico whirled, taking a hit against his shoulder. He no longer wore the light leather armour of a true assassin, and the blade glanced off the dull metal pauldrons Anspeare had equipped him with, granting him time enough to come in under his assailant's guard and stab him swiftly in the neck. Turning yet again, he stayed an oncoming swordstroke with his other dagger, but the force of the blow caused him to drop the blade.

The back of Nico's neck prickled, and he leaped away from the other swordsman, who was closing in behind him. Backing into a corner, he held off the first, who came at him with renewed determination. In the shadows beyond, the princess stirred. Nico saw that the dagger he had dropped was lying on the ground before her.

The princess seized Nico's dagger and threw herself upon the swordsman closest to her. Flushed scarlet with rage, she screamed as she sank the dagger into his back. He yelled in pain, twisting around. The soldier Nico was grappling with turned in shock, letting down his guard, and Nico finished him off the same as he had done the others. The princess raised Nico's dagger for a second try, her face and stolen armour spattered with red. Though completely unskilled, in her blind anger she struck true. The blade sank into the side of the soldier's neck, and a gush of blood spurted from the vein that Nico knew was hidden there.

The last foeman collapsed, and neither Nico nor the princess spoke for a long moment. Katrina was breathing heavily, staring down at her kill. At last Nico cleared his throat.

"You'd best retrieve that dagger. You might need it again."

Katrina flushed, and bent to work it loose from the man's neck. Blade and hilt were both coated in sticky blood. Nico wordlessly handed her a kerchief he fished from his pocket.

"I'm not sorry," she said, her voice shaking. "He killed my uncle. These others—they killed my aunt, and my cousins, and even the servants. All I could do was watch."

"Far be it from me to judge," Nico said quietly. "I've killed many men. None of whom murdered a family member of mine."

She turned brimming eyes on him. "Are my father and mother truly dead?"

"Your father is." Nico did not see any point in delaying this. "And, they say, your eldest brother. Prince Rolf."

A fierce kind of hope flared into her face. "But my mother? My younger siblings?"

"They're alive, all of them. Two girls, and an ten-year-old boy, right? I've seen them."

Katrina's expression turned from desperation and hate to a kind of relief that Nico felt deep in his own bones. "They said they were going to take me to some man called Baukin Sylvaissen," she said, and her voice was oddly flat. "Tomorrow. I didn't care whether I lived or died. Not after what—what they said he was going to do." She choked out the next words. "And how much they were going to enjoy it, when he let them *watch*."

Nico swallowed. "We need to leave, and quickly," he said. "I'll protect you, but there could be more guards on their way already."

"You said that Hugh was alive." Something in the princess's voice was different this time, and Nico thought fleetingly of Fish as a pang passed through his heart. "Say it again."

"He's alive. He sent me," Nico repeated impatiently. Distant noises came to his ears, and he grabbed her hand. "They're coming. Stay close to me."

He led the way as they both dashed towards the front door and the courtyard, as he hoped like hell that Josephine had found a good place to settle herself. The pursuers were hard on their heels, and when they reached the yard, it seemed that more and more men came boiling out of all the doors of the mansion like ants. Nico drew his sword and engaged with the first who came at him. Anspeare had said that Baukin Sylvaissen's human soldiers carried muskets of their own, but none were in evidence just yet, thanks be to all the gods in the Sven pantheon for that.

Just as Nico felled his first foe, a crack louder than breaking ice in the dead of winter rent the air. Swordsmen all around him ducked and swivelled, staring around uncertainly.

"Get down!" Nico made for Katrina, pulled her against the courtyard wall, pushed her to the ground and crouched over her, shielding her body with his. His heart pounded with the wrongness of turning his back to an enemy during a fight, but as another gunshot ripped through the air, shattering into splintered pieces on the courtyard tiles and eliciting loud yells and cries of pain, he mastered the feeling and did not turn his head, not even to glance behind himself. Josephine continued to fire from the cliffside above, a single bullet at a time, reloading steadily with her accustomed speed. Nico heard the sickening crunch of a lead ball punching through plate-armour, and thud of a heavy body to the tiles.

"Fall back, you idiots!" he heard someone yell. A couple more gunshots sounded in the silence, then ceased. Nico raised his head.

"Come on," he said, standing up fully and pulling Katrina with him. "They'll be back, and maybe with their own muskets. We have no time to waste."

JOSEPHINE MET THEM ON THE PATH, wan with exertion. She had left a trail through the brush that was painful to Nico's eyes. *City-bred mercenary*, he thought to himself, but Josephine's skills were not those of woodscraft. She had never had occasion to learn them.

"That was incredible," he said at once, but she only nodded. Her eyes fell on the princess, and Nico's heart gave a sudden twinge at the beatific joy and relief that appeared in them.

"Princess Katrina," she said. "We're going to do our best to get you to safety."

But despite her words, and despite the rock-hard determination that Nico knew she possessed, it soon became clear that Josephine could not make good on that promise. Nico took them up a steep trail by the light of the moon, winding back towards the place where they had massacred the necromes yesterday. But after less than an hour, Jo was having trouble keeping up. Her injured leg seemed excruciating to put any amount of weight on, and she went slowly, breathing hard in pain, leaning heavily on a stick she had wrangled from a dried-out strangler vine.

It took them the whole night to make the ascent, and rosy dawn was creeping through the shrubland by the time Nico espied the ridge where they had sat yesterday. That was a powerful defensive position, nestled as it was right over the trail. Josephine had long since given up protesting that nothing was amiss, and she let Nico help her along as they made their way. Nico felt ill, and kept glancing back over his shoulder. Several hours ago, they had discerned the faint sounds of pursuit on the night breeze: the barking of dogs, yells of men, a stray gunshot.

Finally, they reached the ridge. Josephine released Nico's arm, and sank down where she could sight over the rocks and bushes, putting her weight on her uninjured leg.

She looked up at Nico, and caressed the barrel of her gun absently. "I'm staying here."

Nico's heart lurched. "They're coming," he reminded her, as it hammered in his chest.

Josephine cocked the gun, leaning the barrel over the ridge. "Then I'll be ready for them."

"And I'll be with you," Nico promised immediately.

"No!" Josephine turned to glare at him. Katrina stood frozen as if arrested in flight, still holding the dagger which Nico had not taken from her. "Nico, if the princess doesn't make it, all this will have been for nought. Not just our mission—the whole war."

"Then I should stay," Nico said. "I'll hold them off long enough for you both to get to safety."

"Are you insane?" Josephine demanded, and her eyes were so hard that Nico stepped backwards, abashed. Seeing him retreat, she softened a little.

"Nico," she said. "Listen. Don't let your muscles do the thinking here. You know this wilderness; I don't. You found the trail down here. I'm not even sure where to start looking for it, and I don't know what to do or which direction to go if I'm ambushed. The princess *has* to get back. Otherwise all this will have been for nothing. And besides"—she waved the musket at him—"I've been practicing with this thing for years. You've had—what? One shot that you failed to make? Tell me, how does it make sense that I go and you stay? I've a better chance than you at actually getting them, and you've a better chance than me at getting back."

"Your wound," Nico argued. "It's infected. You need to get back soon to have it attended to."

Josephine's eyes lingered on him for a long moment. Coldness had evaporated from her expression now, and she spoke softly when she rebutted, "That's a risk I'm going to have to take."

"Jo—"

"*Go*, Nico," she whispered. "Once I've taken care of these bastards, I'll follow you at my own pace."

She met his eyes with hers, devoid of any emotion but urgency, and Nico subsided in surrender even as the wrongness of it burned inside him.

"You don't have much time," she reminded him, nestling the barrel of the gun against the same rock Nico had used previously.

"No," he agreed at last. He turned, feeling like a coward, and did not look at Katrina. "C'mon, Princess."

She followed him without a word, sparing only a brief glance back for the mercenary woman.

NICO HEARD NO GUNSHOTS. EITHER he and Katrina were travelling faster than he had anticipated—and he was doing everything in his power to make sure they did—or Josephine had not needed to use the gun.

Or—

Katrina was physically fit, taller than Josephine, and well-dressed for the terrain they traversed. Though occasionally she fell behind, she never asked Nico to slow nor wait for her to catch up. They spoke little, rising at dawn and sleeping after darkness fell on the mountain, half dead every day with exhaustion. They dared not use the road to ascend towards the Beerstana Pass, but Nico knew exactly where he was going.

It was late afternoon on the third day when they stumbled from a grassed slope down to the main road, nearly collapsing right in front of the gate which sat locked, barred, and manned across it.

He heard yelling, calls of recognition, and at last the sound of gate-bolts sliding open and mailed footsteps approaching. Two burly guardsmen led Katrina away reverently, allowing her to dangle from their shoulders. The guard captain approached Nico where he sat numbly in the dirt, and stretched out a hand.

"Let's get you cleaned up and fed, soldier."

Nearly an hour later, having satiated his immediate hunger with a bowl of porridge, Nico wandered into the dusty yard and stood blinking. Something was obviously different about the outpost. The men seemed jovial, contrasting sharply with the bitter mood Nico had observed when he and Josephine had begun their descent to Von Dharen nine days ago. There was bustle instead of apathy, conversation and laughter in place of resigned silence.

Had the arrival of the princess truly meant that much to these men? Somehow, Nico doubted that. And the yard seemed fuller, somehow. More men were about. Perhaps Anspeare had sent reinforcements, but where could he have found more fighters to send?

Had he finally located General Vanya and the remnants of the Sven army?

A young man in plate-armour passed across his view, leading a horse, and Nico could not refrain from staring in surprise. The man was clearly not Sven: he was darker than Fish, short like Fish, and even had the same curly hair. Nico took note of what he had somehow not registered before. The garments the man wore under his plate were *green*, not the blue of the Sven military, and the long cloak which hung from his shoulders made him seem like nothing so much as walking foliage.

Nico stared around. The green soldiers were everywhere, outnumbering the beleaguered guardsmen of Svanfeld. There were new horses, fresh horses, beautifully bred animals done up in fine leather and green barding, and some of the men were even stringing up a green flag with some kind of silver standard embroidered upon it.

He caught hold of the next soldier who passed by him, and did a double-take. He had just grasped the arm of a young *woman*, unfamiliar to him, with a thatch of black hair and lively black eyes. She was not attired as a common soldier, but wore a practical travelling outfit with well-heeled boots, breeches and a comfortable robe that came down just below the knee.

"Yes?" she asked, and Nico had to blink several times, again, as he recognized the same musical tones in her voice that the waif, Brialise, had always spoken with.

"What's going on?" he managed.

She smiled. "Qwu'Mallorn has come to join the fight."

Nico let it sink in as she walked away. *Fish?* These were Mage-Gifted soldiers, like him. Nico could hardly credit it. And where was Fish? Had he come too, to bask in the magnitude of his triumph? He looked around, his heart beating suddenly very loudly, scanning each face that passed. Too many had the boy's colouring, but Nico did not find what he sought.

"Are you Nico Klavbert?" a female voice sounded from behind him, and he turned. An attractive young woman with auburn hair and a green outfit was approaching him. "Hugh Anspeare said you'd be arriving here shortly. I have something for you." She reached into a pocket at her belt and took out a scroll of parchment, bound in twine.

Heart in his mouth, Nico unfurled the scroll. Even were it not for the frank address of "Partner" and the flourishing signature at the bottom, he'd have recognized that expansive scrawl anywhere.

*Partner*, the first line read, *they didn't execute me after all. I'm alive and well and I have so much to tell you.*

Keeping his eyes fixed on the paper as he moved beneath the eaves of the guardhouse, Nico nearly collided with Katrina, who stood there watching the proceedings in the yard with as much awe as he himself had been doing.

"Can you believe it?" she asked softly. Nico only nodded absently, scouring Fish's simple and all-too-brief words. At last he turned to her, and found that she was already watching him.

"I'm safe now," Katrina said. "You've done your duty by me, Nico. Now it's up to you to decide what you do next."

Nico looked at her, his heart too full of conflicting emotions to say anything. She shifted her gaze, looking west towards the wilderness.

Nico took a deep breath, folded up Fish's precious letter, and tucked it into his shirt, beneath his armour and just over his heart. He reached out, and clasped Katrina's hand. "You're too right, as usual, Princess."

THE ARRIVAL OF THE MORGEIN SOLDIERS turned out to be a blessing in more ways than one. They had brought a string of pack-mules up from the monastery, of which Nico was able to purloin two for his journey, lading them with water and provisions. Instead of striking out into the wilderness immediately, a squad of mage-scouts rode with him along the road for the first half-day, turning back when Nico reached the point at which he would have to locate the track he had used to take himself and Josephine down towards the coast.

The rugged mountainside seemed almost like an old friend, now, and Nico travelled through most of the night, stopping only to let the mules rest once the waning moon made its appearance in the sky. He snatched a few hours of sleep, and awoke early the next morning.

Firstly, he checked for any sign of Josephine's trail, any indication that she might have followed them after all. The surety that she had not cramped his stomach with worry, and he pressed on as quickly as the mules would allow. Less than half the day was gone before he reached a landmark, a giant boulder no more than a few hundred yards from where they had left her. There he strung the mules to a sprawling thorn-tree, taking from his provisions only a canteen of water, double-checking that all his weapons were in place.

The ridge was empty but for torn-up cartridges and a lingering aroma of gunpowder and rotting meat. Insects chirped in the new grass, and the sun shone bright from a clear sky. A warm breeze swished through the pockmarked boulders.

Not far from the ridge was an overhang large enough to shelter from the rain, and that was where he found her, motionless and curled into her bedroll with her trusty musket lying an arm's length away. Nico's heart sprang into his mouth, but before he could close the few strides towards her, Josephine stirred, tossing violently back and forth as though caught in a restless dream. Her eyes opened; she stared directly but did not appear to see him, and muttered something unintelligible before slumping back down.

Nico strode forward and opened the canteen, pressing it against her lips. "Drink," he commanded, and there was sense enough left in her to obey. The moment she drank, she seemed to revive, sitting up and steadily sucking down the rest of the water.

Josephine had two cartridges left, tucked neatly into her bandolier as though she had finished a job well done. Her sword was not at her side; Nico cast around, and spotted it leaning against a boulder, crusted in dried blood. By the look of it, she had efficiently taken care of their pursuers, then curled up in her bedroll to sleep before setting out. It was in that bedroll that she had, seemingly, succumbed to fever. Her own canteens were dry; she had clearly been unable to rise and refill them at the nearby stream.

Josephine finished the water with one last gulp, and lay back weakly. She still didn't seem fully aware of his presence. Nico could see moisture beading on her brow, though it was not at all hot in the crevice where she lay. He sat back for a moment to consider. It had been fewer than five days. Whoever held the command in Von Dharen was likely only now hearing that the princess had escaped, and perhaps was sending more men into the mountains even as they lingered here. He decided that he did not have the time to administer any of the simple medications he had brought with him. They would not do much good anyway, not when she was so far gone. And the Morgein soldiers back at the pass had a mage-healer with them.

Nico crouched over her. Josephine only moaned weakly and shook her head.

"C'mon," he muttered. "We have to get you out of here." He pushed the folds of her blankets aside and reached for her leg, to examine the wound. The flesh felt hot even through the fabric of her trousers.

"No!" She pushed away from him with what seemed the last of her strength. Nico froze. The look in Josephine's eyes was unmistakeable. She was half delirious, Nico realized, but her fear had its roots in reality. He recalled suddenly how she had refused to let him tend the wound before, and realized now that it was not—never had been—a show of strength, nor stubborn pride.

"Jo," he said softly, "look at me." Her eyes were half glazed, but they locked directly onto his, which Nico took as a good sign. The infection had not overcome her yet.

"I need to get you back to the pass, and quickly," he continued. "You need help. That scratch's not going to heal on its own. Maybe—maybe you've heard this before." He broke eye contact even as his voice faltered. "But I won't hurt you. Not the way—" His chest constricted, and he had to force the next words out. "Not the way I was once hurt."

Nico had never told anyone this story, and he was not about to divulge it now. Even that smallest of confessions—that *hint*—was more than he had hinted to anyone ever before. "Please, trust me."

He met her eyes, and though they shone with fever, he could tell she had understood. At last, Josephine nodded. She let Nico check her physical condition, unwrapping her from the soaking bedroll. The leg was by far the worst of it; she had acquired a few extra bruises and cuts, but nothing serious. Nico attached her sword to his own belt, slung the musket over his shoulder, and lifted her into his arms. She weighed no more than Fish did, being a bit more slender where he had muscles, and Nico had carried his partner out of difficult situations enough times to know where to grip and how to distribute the weight.

Once she was sitting firmly on a mule, he strapped her into place, and left Von Dharen and the rotting stench of necromes behind.

There was no sign of pursuit, yet Nico pushed himself to make haste. They rode the rest of the day and half the night, Josephine slumped over the mule's withers for most of it. By the time the new day dawned, they had covered more than three-quarters of the distance. Nico made her drink as much honeyed water as she could hold, and by the time they reached the last high ridge before the pass, to his astonishment, she was showing signs of reviving. She was riding the mule now, not just being carried as a passenger, and when the guard tower astride the pass loomed on the skyline, he saw relief appear beneath the sheen of fever-sweat on her forehead.

A new flag flapped above the tower today, gaining momentum with the dry early-afternoon breeze. Josephine squinted towards it. "What—" She flicked her mule's reins, prodding it into a trot.

"Wait—" Nico began, but Josephine had already pressed her mount to the top of the ridge. She stood and stared, her eyes going wide and her mouth open. The tricolour flapped in the wind, three shades of forest green, and the embroidered banner unfurled as she stood there and showed itself proudly, emblazoning the silver tree on dark green against the sky for all the world to see.

"They came," Jo breathed, and there were tears running down her face. "We were right to hope. Magic to fight against dark magic."

# Chapter XXXVIII
## Magic

"D AMN IT, FISH, *FOCUS*! It's not just yourself you stand to hurt here! You could hurt others, as well—but maybe you don't care about that—"

There was a ringing silence following this outburst. Albryan broke off, putting a hand to his forehead in obvious dismay.

"Of course I care about that," Fish whispered through gritted teeth, even as something resonated with Albryan's frustration in his own chest.

"No, I'm sorry," Albryan said remorsefully. "I shouldn't have—but the danger involved here—" He looked at Fish, the concern so obvious in his eyes that Fish suddenly thought of what it might be like, to go up like a human torch, a pure scorching burst of power that left nothing but ash behind. Would it hurt? How many would he immolate alongside himself?

"I'm sorry," Albryan repeated. "Shut off the magic, and we'll talk."

Fish took a deep breath, and prepared to reverse what he had been trying to do. His magic flared painfully, making him gasp and bite his tongue. From where he sat cross-legged on the floor, channels of power reached towards the reinforced silver bars that had been built into this starkly empty, windowless wood-panelled room. The channels should have been clear, flowing harmoniously. They were not. Discharge flared along them, a sickly lugubrious green on the earthly plane, even uglier on the eldritch one, fissured black and blood red, angry and twisted.

"It's not . . . working," he said, suddenly frightened. "It's not shutting off the leakage. I—I don't understand what's happening."

In a trice, Albryan was there before him. Fish could feel the *conduit*, the way the pure energies passed through the young captain without touching him, dispersing harmlessly back into the ether seemingly without any effort on his part.

Albryan took both his hands, and Fish sighed in relief to feel the magic redirected—away from him, away from anything it could damage on the earthly plane—back into the ethereal plane, where it belonged.

"I don't quite understand, either," Albryan said softly, and Fish looked up to meet his eyes. "You have so *much* energy—I can't comprehend where all of it is coming from. I thought perhaps you were doing it deliberately, but now I see you're not." He paused. "Something we did seems to have triggered some kind of instinctual reaction in you. I don't know what, nor how you've managed to channel so much through yourself."

Fish only shook his head, concentrating hard to not let himself begin to cry. Bleakness and frustration burned in his chest.

"Can you see what I'm doing?" Albryan asked.

It was a distraction from his own anguish. With their close vantage, when Fish looked at Albryan on the other plane, he could see it now. Though magic flowed all through and around him, Albryan Lana had built something within himself to protect and encase his own body, something that functioned like a dam wall, holding just enough magic back and allowing the rest to overflow to the ether. He nodded.

"Do you want to try again?"

Fish focused intently on trying to imitate what he saw. But the "wall" he was trying to build was powerless against the onslaught of the forceful current that possessed him. The dam kept eroding, battered by the sheer force of magic, wisping away even as he built it up. The frustration came again, and anger flared—

"That's enough." Albryan's voice was calm, the voice of a teacher, as it normally was. "I thought you were being lazy. But I see now—it's like you're trying to carve filigree with a longsword." He took a deep breath, and released Fish's hands. Magic was still leaking from Fish, though not nearly so much, and he sat numbly as Albryan contemplated him.

"We need to find some way for you to build your own technique," Albryan said at last. "You need to draw off more power into the grounding structure. But not today," he said, even as Fish began to droop. "I think we've both had enough." He stood up. "Are you coming to dinner in the mess?" he asked as he went around the room, dismissing the shields and the last traces of magic.

Fish averted his eyes. "I think—I need some time alone before that."

It was past noon outside, and Albryan clasped his hand in farewell the same as usual, as though Fish hadn't nearly immolated himself, half the barracks, and Albryan to boot during today's session.

"You're still flaring, intermittently," he warned. "Not a lot, but it might affect the unGifted. Try to relax, to damp it down."

Barracks had seemed very empty since the soldiers had left to aid Anspeare, with Mialiné and her sorceresses in tow. Most of the remaining troops were being deployed somewhere along the Border, though Albryan had stayed, and Fish wondered why. He would not be surprised to hear that Thinas Sovaya still did not trust him enough to wander freely, despite the day he'd spent talking of his childhood to Tiralinna Ebraskaia and the way she had come out on his side at the Council the next day, making the entire military venture possible. The general had not been happy to defer command of his soldiers to Mialiné, and even Albryan had questioned the idea before finally conceding that politics was a game of compromise.

Fish sighed, tossed curls that were soaked with sweat out of his eyes, and pulled a cigarillo from his trouser pocket. Like many of the finer things in life, tobacco was more readily available in Qwu'Mallorn, and the quality was far better than the stuff he used to smoke in Ülhard. Fish rolled the cigarillo in his fingers, put it to his lips, and then, on a whim, snapped his fingers together. The magic that was still sparking from him translated into a brief flame, and the cigarillo was lit as he inhaled. He probably shouldn't do magic so close to his own face. He didn't care. But even Albryan usually had to blink and call on reserves for the reservoir of power that was required to spark flame, and Fish savoured the tiny victory as he let out a long, shuddering breath with the cigarillo smoke. He made his way over to a nearby tree, and leaned against it, closing his eyes and willing himself to relax fully. If he could relax, he could find the source of the leakage that was flaring—

"Fish?" His eyes flew open to see Velda standing before him. He straightened up. They had seen each other often enough in the past month, yet always Albryan had been there, almost like a buffer set between the two of them. It had been like that last night, when they'd met for a light dinner at a bakery and Fish had dared to ask how she and Albryan had met. Both of them had muttered something about the mountains and Velda's deceased husband and son—that story, at least, she had told him—and changed the subject, Velda lamenting that Mialiné had already introduced him to *querka*, and Albryan starting to tell one of his many ridiculous military stories.

"If you're looking for Albryan—" he began.

"I'm not." She smiled, and started towards him. "I came for you."

"Don't touch me," he warned, putting his hands up in front of himself to dissuade her. A look of hurt flashed across her face, and instantly Fish felt remorseful.

"Look—I'm spilling magic," he explained quickly. "The un-Gifted don't have any defence against it. I could hurt you if it gets any worse. Seriously hurt you." He sought her eyes with his own. "It's better if you leave."

"Are you sure?" she asked quietly. "Because you don't look like you want to be alone."

Unexpectedly, shamefully, Fish felt moisture well up in his eyes. He stared at the ground. "I . . ."

"I came looking for you," Velda interrupted gently, for all the world as if she knew that changing the subject would distract him, "because I have something for you."

"For—?"

She nodded. "Come over to my rooms. I'll make some tea. I was going to ask you both, but"—she gave a quizzical half-smile—"I think perhaps it's time I talked to you alone."

It was a stiff walk to Velda's quarters near the middle of town, but Fish was glad for the respite. She said little as they went, and Fish, gratefully, felt the magic fade even as they walked.

"Let me do that," he said, when she crouched beside the hearth to light a fire under the teapot. The faggots flared up with the slightest touch of his hand, and he was gratified by her admiring exclamation.

For someone who had grown up in Svanfeld, where magic was unknown, it was surprising how little she seemed to fear it. Fish eyed her as she bustled about with the tea. Perhaps Albryan had never had occasion to scare her, like he'd done to Nico. Of course, that day when he met Taunus again, that day had not been one of Fish's gentler displays. He swallowed. Anyone would've been shocked. Nico had never rejected him because of it. Not even when he'd been hit by backlash, or when he witnessed Fish's magic destroy another person's sanity.

Velda interrupted his train of thought once again, proffering a steaming cup towards him where he sat on one of her free-standing chairs. "Is it safe to hand this to you?"

Fish reached out and took it from her. "Now it is."

"So," she said, sipping her own tea almost nervously, "I know we haven't known each other long. But I've enjoyed spending time with you." She hesitated. "I'm not sure when you're going back to Svanfeld."

Fish grimaced. "When the general thinks it's a good idea." Hugh Anspeare had vowed that if he managed to stabilize his position in the mountains, he would come south and lay siege to Arran Sylvaissen in Armour City. Fish knew that Thinas Sovaya was hoping that might soon occur, and in the meantime, he clearly wanted Fish somewhere he could keep an eye on him. Fish could not be ignorant of the threat his Gift might pose, but the other side of the coin was that if something happened here, he might be the only one in possession of the raw power that was needed to fight off someone like Dannine.

"Well," Velda said, "before that time comes, to make sure you don't forget that you met me . . . I made something for you." She put down her tea and took something that looked like a package of cloth from a nearby table. "I noticed you've mostly been wearing the same hessian shirt whenever you come here." She handed it to him.

Fish could not rightly say why he had kept wearing the plain shirt Brother Jakob had given him at the monastery, even now that he had demonstrably finer, better-fitting clothes in his wardrobe. Perhaps it was to remind himself that Nico was still somewhere out there, awaiting his return. Perhaps he felt it more fitting to wear such clothes around Velda, given her obvious common birth and mountain accent, though she seemed to have seamlessly adapted herself into Morgein fashions.

An odd feeling rose in his chest as he unwrapped the package. It wasn't styled like the tunics of Qwu'Mallorn. The pattern was something he'd seen before, like the shirts they'd worn in the little village below the Beerstana Pass, common to workmen and the like all across Svanfeld. But the fabric—that was much finer than anything he'd seen up north. Raw silk, subtly patterned like the coat of a wild cat, and she'd done up the cuffs and collar with decorative patterns in gold silk thread.

"Do you like it?" she asked. "I thought of making it colourful, but dyed silk is *expensive.*"

Fish attempted to swallow a lump in his throat. "You shouldn't have," he began. "I'm not—"

"Chunhua wrangled me a substantial discount on the silk," she interrupted, "and before we go down that road, Fish, you *are* worth it. I wanted to celebrate what you accomplished with the Council, which by all accounts is the most anyone's gotten them to do in years."

Fish vividly remembered the first time that Nico had given him gold. They hadn't really been friends yet, he'd still been using Nico as free bed-and-board whilst he figured out what to do with himself in Ülhard, but he'd helped the assassin out of a tight spot and Nico had given him half his total earnings on that job. Outside of his excitement to actually be receiving that amount of money—the Townsguard of Zarath had paid in silver, not gold—Fish remembered the sudden rush of belonging, the thought that perhaps Nico might be thinking of keeping him around for more than just the chores he'd done around their room.

It was the same feeling now, the same golden happiness that ignited in his heart, and for once he was at a total loss for words.

"I knew you'd like it," she said, as he looked up at her, eyes brimming now with a fresh nest of emotions. "Go on, try it on. I'll turn around."

"There's no need," Fish laughed. "It's nothing you haven't seen before." He shrugged off the hessian shirt, and carefully donned the new one. "It fits perfectly. How did you figure that out?" He was astonished.

She smirked like a cat in cream. "You left a shirt in my room, remember? With those leathers you seem to have forgotten."

"Oh—" Fish had completely forgotten, what with everything, and truth be told he probably did not need those old leathers anymore, and the shirt had been ruined anyway.

"Well, I tried cleaning it, but the bloodstains wouldn't come out. Then when I was thinking of sewing something for you, it occurred to me that it was still there, so I took it apart for the pattern."

Fish wanted to close the space between them and hug her, but something sounded alert in his body. He was leaking magic again. He felt a touch of fright. He wasn't even *calling* the magic; it seemed to be responding to something external, as though a presence outside of himself were drawing it forth.

"Fish?" She stepped closer to him, and he stepped backwards. "Is something the matter? You can tell me—"

"No. You don't really know me," Fish said in a low voice. His heart was beating frantically. What if he had lost all control of the Gift at last? "You've spent your life with—with ordinary people. Normal people. I'm not like that."

She raised both her brows. "I think you'd be surprised just how strange *normal* people can be," she said softly.

Fish shook his head. He was too agitated; he knew that the magic must be spilling from *somewhere*, and he tried desperately to tamp down on it. His right arm was afire, prickling with the sensation.

"Fish—" She reached out and touched him, and Fish flinched as if he'd been slapped, shoving away from her so fast he knocked into a chair, which went flying. A forgotten cup of tea fell to the ground, clattering away somewhere behind him. Fish took no notice. He stood gaping, disbelieving what was right in front of his eyes.

Velda stood calmly in front of him. She should have been in pain, should have been burned. She should have been crying, scream-ing at him to leave. She was none of those things. She stood like a rock, rooted in the maelstrom of magic that had spilled all around her, and none of it could touch her.

"You—you're not hurt," he faltered. He reached out, imagining only that somehow she was hiding from *him* what he had once hid-den from everyone else—magical ability. But nothing stirred in the ether.

*Nothing* stirred. Fish stumbled back as his legs gave way beneath him. She was absorbing the magic, somehow. She was a hole in the world, something that he'd been taught could not exist, and yet she was standing right in front of him. "You—" he began, and could get no further.

Velda sighed. "This is ridiculous," she muttered. She approached him, and Fish drew back yet could not take his eyes from her. Firmly, she took his hand and interlinked it with hers. Fish could only stare dumbly. Magic was leaking from him, spilling out visibly into the material world, pure white laced with sparks of golden foxfire, and her touch was—*somehow*—absorbing it all.

"That's not possible," he managed at last.

"So I've heard," she returned dryly, and Fish looked up to stare her straight in the eyes, noticing again how much they were like his own. The same shape, the same colour . . .

"You and I," he whispered. "Why do we look so much alike?"

He expected her to turn her head away; to mutter a disclaimer; perhaps to shake it and smile sadly. Instead, she looked directly at him, and her gaze was steadfast.

"I think . . ." she began, "I think that you're my brother."

It had hung between them since the moment they had met, unspoken, hovering in the ether. Neither of them had dared to put it to words. Neither had dared to hope too much. Saying it out loud was different, and Fish was nearly overwhelmed by the sense of anguish that shot through him at her simple words.

He sat immobile, hands threaded through with hers, still leaking magic yet hardly aware of it, her incredible ability soaking it all up like a sponge, and listened as she continued to speak. Listened to her tell, at last, how it was she came to reside in Qwu'Mallorn. Of her meeting with Albryan and an old man named Hiram Lynstream, survivor of the massacre in Armour City—husband to a Mage-Gifted wife, father to a lost daughter, grandfather to twins who were due the very night of the fall—

"If you look like her," he said at last, numbly, "then I look like her, too. And the rest of the family—dead on the streets of Armour City, and her father—captured and thrown into jail. She was all alone. What—what happened to her? If both of us ended up in the hands of slavers—"

Velda's eyes were as wet as his. "There's no way of knowing."

"Knowing?" Fish shook his head. "It all fits, don't you see?" His voice was shaking. "Arran wouldn't have—" His voice threatened to break, and he forced it steady. "Arran would not have wanted you. You don't wield magic, you don't feel any different in the ether than any other person without the Gift. If both of us were there, he would have paid the silver for *me*, for the child with the Gift, and he would never have given *you* even a passing glance. You would have meant nothing to him, and he would never even have told me . . ."

"Truly?" she whispered.

"Truly. Arran never asked the slavers about my parents. He encouraged me to think the worst of them. That they sold me, that they were unworthy. He wanted me to hate them, and to love *him*."

They sat there for a while longer, neither of them saying anything more. The magic flowed through Fish, ebbed palpably, and soon he became aware that something felt different. He felt—grounded. As though something within him had centred itself. The magic wasn't quiescent, but it seemed that now it was flowing the way it should be—into the ether.

"Velda—" he began, but suddenly they were interrupted by a loud knock on the door. A woman's voice echoed his, calling her name, though far more abrasively.

Velda started as if surfacing out of a waking dream. "Oh—I'm sorry." She put a hand to her forehead. "I promised Pattin I'd go with her to the night market—"

"It's all right," Fish said quietly, standing up with her and touching her shoulder. She smiled at him, then turned to open the door.

"Velda! You never came to fetch me!—oh." Pattin's eyes swept over Fish. "Hello." She seemed unsure for a moment, then smiled. "Look, are you two *certain* you're not related?"

"Pattin, please." Kevin was with her in the corridor, Fish realized, lounging against the opposite wall. He grinned tentatively at Fish. "Hi there. Been a long time."

Fish had seen Kevin about, in the past weeks, in the mess, the barracks corridors or the washroom, or riding by on his way to train recruits, but they hadn't exchanged much more than terse words of greeting or a friendly wave. There was still something about the young soldier that unsettled him, something in his demeanour that Fish couldn't quite put a finger on.

Fish cleared his throat. "So you're all going to the night market?"

"Tonight's my last night off," Kevin said. "After this, I'm joining the border-patrols."

"You should come with us," Pattin said brightly to Fish.

"You should," Kevin chimed in. "You're dressed for it already.

And I haven't seen you much about town."

"I haven't had time," Fish returned.

"Don't you have time now?"

Despite himself, despite all he had gone through that afternoon, Fish realized that he did want to go. He was curious as to what the nightlife in Tenna was like. Fish had good memories of carousing in Ülhard, of laughing with Nico, of drinking ale with Stonetooth Skimmer. His heart constricted. He doubted there was much carousing happening in Schooner Street tonight.

He nodded, giving a hesitant smile. "I'll come."

PATTIN'S COMPANY WAS EXHAUSTING, though Velda seemed to take it in stride. She drew the talkative girl off as they wandered the various stands, leaving Fish and Kevin to trail behind them. Fish proclaimed that he was starving, and Kevin stopped at a stand where a rotund man was grilling long skewers of lamb topped with a sizzling sauce. The smell was mouthwatering. Kevin insisted on paying the few coppers for the meal, and they ate as they walked, Fish taking pains to keep his new shirt clear of the grease. Fresh from the coals, the meat was delicious, but only half-stilled his appetite. Nearby, a middle-aged woman was hawking fresh-baked loaves of bread with flowers and herbs baked into the crust, and someone else was offering hot meat pies.

"You must have practised a lot of magic today," Kevin observed after Fish insisted on stopping at his fourth food stand.

"Huh?"

"I'm always ravenous after I exercise my magic," Kevin clarified.

*That would explain it.* Fish looked around for the girls, and found them chatting over sweets nearby. Velda found his eyes and looked at him with all the regard of an older sister. "Alright?" she asked, and Fish felt his heart constrict.

"I'm really tired," he murmured, and Kevin stirred beside him.

"Let's go for a drink, you and me," he suggested. "We can sit down for a bit. I know a place that serves excellent cider, and strong mead."

The mention of those things reminded Fish that it had been rather a long time since he'd last gotten decently drunk. He had taken a swig of that distilled booze on the lakeside with Nico sitting next to him, and woken up the next morning with a fuzzy head and no memory of what had happened after that. "I could certainly go for some mead," he said, and Kevin grinned as though Fish had just made his night.

Velda smiled as she bade him farewell and to enjoy himself, and Fish looked on with a twinge of regret as Pattin dragged her away, exclaiming over a display of woven shawls she had just spotted. Fish was left alone in the crowd with Kevin, who kept his hands crossed behind his back as he led the way through the bustling lanes towards an inn which stood just on the edge of the encroaching forest.

"Do all the soldiers come to drink here?" Fish asked, spotting several young men in military uniform lounging in the taproom.

Kevin nodded. "The officers have a private chamber, though. But I'd like to sit outside, tonight." Fish murmured his agreement. It was close to midsummer, and the air felt still and clammy. Kevin led him into the yard, where small groups of men were sitting around at benches and tables. There were clusters of women amongst them, yet fewer than Fish would've expected. More than half the soldiers seemed to be enjoying each other's company, and were ignoring the women completely. That was odd. Fish recalled the street walkers and good-time girls who haunted such establishments in Ülhard. If you knew where to go, there could be the occasional boy for hire too. Fish wondered what the equivalent was in Qwu'Mallorn, and where one needed to go to find those elusive men for whom they had that special word—*ak'a'jana*.

Some exotic nocturnal flower was opening to the night, and Fish breathed in the heady, cloying perfume. The seats Kevin found for them were close to the flower, which trailed in long vines over a half-crumbling wall in the deep shadows of the garden. Despite the seclusion, a serving-girl immediately appeared to take their order.

"So did you join the army after all?" Kevin asked. "I've seen you around with the officers, but nowhere else." When Fish hesitated, he laughed lightly. "Don't worry, I know better than to ask. 'Classified,' isn't it?"

"Sorry," Fish murmured. The serving-girl arrived back, forestalling the need for conversation as they both tasted the spiced mead. It was stronger than the stuff Fish was used to, and vibrant with cinnamon and cloves. He looked around, seeking for a fresh topic of conversation, and spotted a familiar face. Even from a distance Fish recognized Albryan's grizzled lieutenant, Erion. He was with a much younger, much comelier man, draping his arm about his companion's shoulders in a way that looked a little beyond brotherly. Fish tried hard not to stare. Things were different in Qwu'Mallorn indeed. Hugh Anspeare's second-in-command, Cedric, had never been so close with the men he commanded.

"Looks like some of the boys have come off duty," Kevin remarked, and said nothing about the physical affection that would have been unheard-of in Svanfeld and Vailana.

Their conversation turned towards trivialities: the weather, trinkets at the marketplace, whether a piece of chocolate from the bar was worth the price. Fish relaxed, and began to enjoy himself. It was innocent, companionable. He remembered a time when it had been like this with Nico, before they had taken that damned job with the damned Guilds and things had changed between them. Some forlorn part of Fish wondered how it all might have fallen out had he truly been a nobody—a boy from Zarath with no notable past and no reason to alarm anyone with the forceful magnitude of his Mage-Gift. He would not have had to mask it in Ülhard. He might have been able to tell Nico ages ago.

The serving-girl reappeared with more mead. Fish had lost count of how many times this had already occurred. He was relatively clear-headed still, though a rather disturbing warmth was starting to make its way through his guts into his chest. There were a *lot* of men in this drinking hole, including the rather good-looking one sitting in the chair just next to him, leaning close towards Fish as he made conversation, and just that morning Fish had been pent-up enough that the usual ritual had left him still feeling dissatisfied afterwards, like a brimming chalice that was being filled even as it sought to drain itself.

Kevin was not someone he had to see on a regular basis. Fish didn't really mind if the young soldier thought ill of him. He wondered idly what would happen if he were to tell Kevin that he found him attractive. Would that be the end of their association, or would Kevin be kind enough to point Fish towards some other young man who might reciprocate that attraction?

"Hmm?" Fish looked up, aware that Kevin had just asked him a question, though having no idea what it had been. "I'm sorry, what?"

"I said . . ." Kevin began again, clearing his throat, "that perhaps we could go someplace more . . . comfortable?"

Fish half-smiled. "I'm perfectly comfortable here," he returned, not sure what Kevin meant.

Kevin had an expression, now, as though something had not quite gone right for him. He shifted in his seat. "Look, Fish," he began, and to his surprise Fish saw a spot of colour appear in each of his cheeks. "If I'm doing things wrong here, please tell me. I'm not sure what's normal in your—your culture."

*What the hell is going on with this man?* Fish stared at him, noticing suddenly how intent Kevin was upon him, whole demeanour poised as if to reach out and embrace Fish, one of his legs thrust just far enough inside Fish's personal space to discomfit him, his hand stretched out along the table as if he would have liked to put it on Fish's hand—

*Oh.* Realization hit Fish like a physical blow, and his whole world tilted sideways. *Really?* It was this easy for—for someone like him . . . to find someone, in Qwu'Mallorn? And it didn't have to be someone he paid?

Fish had been called a few things in his lifetime, but "slow" was not usually one of them. He had been far more accomplished than any of his adoptive siblings, not only in magic but also at everything else. Languages, history, military theory, sword-fighting. Pursuits of the mind came to him as easily as pursuit of the blade, and Fish had never found himself feeling particularly frustrated over anything he *couldn't* do. He had talent and skill for anything he set his mind to.

Except, it seemed, *talking* to his best friend about his nascent feelings. Or getting Nico to actually open up in turn. Or realizing when someone was trying to catch his attention—

"You—you're not doing anything wrong," he stammered. He reached out and laid his hand, deliberately, on the other boy's.

A jolt went through him as Kevin smiled, bit his lower lip and looked at Fish with what, he now realized, had been romantic interest all along. At the same time, something inside Fish tugged at him, rebelling. This wasn't right. This didn't feel right.

But it was almost midsummer; the night tasted sweet and cloying as nightshade, and Fish wanted someone to draw his formless longings from him like poison from a snake bite. It wouldn't mean anything. It would just be a little harmless fun, with an attractive boy who wanted nothing more than the pleasure their bodies could create together. So why did it taste so much like betrayal? No-one else would know—no-one who mattered, anyhow. Fish could do whatever he liked, and have the freedom to walk away at the end . . . to walk back to his partner. Who wouldn't know a thing.

It wasn't Kevin he truly wanted, Fish knew that well enough. But the young soldier was handsome enough, wasn't he? He had an easy smile, hands that looked like they knew their way around the hilt of a sword, eyes the blue of the midnight sky. So what if this wasn't quite the lover he'd been picturing? Women might not want to take a lover who could prove inconstant in the long run, but it made no sense that Fish should feel the same; there was no chance of the handsome young soldier leaving him pregnant and mired in scandal afterwards.

But it would be his first time. And he didn't want to admit that to this personable, worldly young man who was the next thing to a total stranger. Fish didn't feel completely safe—not the way he had felt that afternoon with Velda. There was a part of him that wanted to put his hand away from Kevin's and onto the dagger at his belt.

Fish's instincts nudged at him to clear his head, but he ignored them. He didn't want to sober up. He felt just tipsy enough, relaxed enough to accept whatever Kevin might want to do to him, numb enough to blunt the sharpness of any pain that might result.

Kevin reached out his other hand and gently cupped Fish's face, far more intimate than anything Nico had ever done. He could feel sword-calluses on Kevin's fingers, rasping through the stubble he had grown by neglecting to shave the past few mornings. "For a moment there, I thought maybe you weren't interested," Kevin said.

Fish swallowed. "Why go someplace else when the forest is right there?" he breathed. Kevin followed his line of sight to the deep shadows under the trees, and grinned broadly even as the colour rose hotter in his face.

Kevin reached into his pocket, pulled out the silver for the mead they'd been drinking, and placed the coins on the table. The serving-girl was nowhere to be seen. He got to his feet, just a touch unsteadily, and reached out a hand to Fish. "If that's how you want it," he whispered, eyes sparkling.

Fish's heart pounded in his chest. He took the young soldier's hand. "Lead the way," he said, trying to affect a casual anticipation that he did not in the least feel. His mouth was dry, and the lightness in his head could not counteract the leaden weights that had settled in his stomach.

He leaned heavily on Kevin's arm as he stood up. It was pleasant enough to be pressed up against the lanky young man, to feel his hand, warm and steady, entwined with Fish's own. No-one else seemed to notice them, nor to care. He swayed a little as Kevin walked them out. On the dark forest path into which the young soldier drew him, he stumbled a little more. Kevin stopped, and looked down at him in the gloom.

"The mead hits hard, doesn't it?" he said, and Fish nodded wordlessly. Kevin's hand was at his cheek again, and Fish started just slightly before accepting the contact and leaning into the touch. They were all alone in the starlight, facing each other. Fish closed his eyes and steeled himself, awaiting the kiss.

"Fish—listen." He opened his eyes. Kevin was staring at him in the darkness, indigo eyes inscrutable. "There's something going on with you, and it isn't just the mead."

Fish felt hysteria rise in the back of his throat. *Of course there's something going on with me, everyone who ever cared for me has abandoned me in some way or another, and I want to feel loved, I don't care whether it's real, just show me something painless, something easy, damn it!* His tongue felt like lead in his mouth, and he couldn't speak.

"Before this gets any further," Kevin continued, "maybe we should both sober up. I didn't mean to drink this much—or to make you this tipsy."

"It doesn't matter," Fish insisted. His tongue rasped in the bottom of his mouth, and he caught Kevin and pressed up against him. The two of them were not much different in build, but the young soldier had a leanness to him that Fish liked, and arousal spiked in him like a knife blade, right and wrong at the same time. "Don't you want me?"

Kevin growled a soft curse in Morgein, and Fish found himself suddenly moving in reverse, until he backed up against the trunk of a tree that must have been enormous. He kept his gaze trained upon the young man who held him, hoping but not daring to ask that he would be gentle when it came to the physical joining.

But even after that burst of urgency, Kevin did not seem to be lost in the grip of uncontrollable passion. He put his hands on Fish's shoulders, and regarded him, leaning very close. Fish caught his breath, his stomach full of slightly-sick excitement, his lips parted and his breathing heavier than usual.

Suddenly Kevin turned away with a soft groan. "I . . . I think I'm going to retch."

Something inside Fish untethered itself, making a giggle bubble up from within his throat, and before he knew it he was laughing hysterically, doubled over and wheezing, as Kevin sank slowly to his haunches with a look of misery Fish knew all too well.

In the midst of this ridiculous moment, the sudden comedic un-ravelling of an encounter he had both relished and utterly dreaded, Fish was completely unprepared for the *thing* that washed over him, eroding the solid ground he stood on and bringing him to his knees with a strangled gasp, clutching at the grass in disorientation.

"You're drunker than I am," Kevin laughed, sitting back.

"No." Fish felt more sober than he had all evening, and dread wound itself suffocatingly into the fibres of his being. "That's not what this is. Can't you feel it?" He looked at Kevin, who was regarding him now with puzzled bemusement. "No," he whispered to himself, "no, you wouldn't." He stood up, just as another lurch throbbed all through him, and he fought to keep it under control. Some instinct in him called out to Brightfeather, and he felt the presence of the quetzal in the back of his mind, reassuring and earthing him in the midst of the sudden cacophony that raged through his senses.

"What's wrong?" Kevin asked, frowning.

What could he say? Fish didn't know precisely what was about to happen. "Danger," he gasped at last, giving voice to the warning which rang throughout his body, singing of discord unleashed in the ether, of silver, brimstone, darkness and blood. "I—I think we're under attack."

# CHAPTER XXXIX
## BORDER

DANNINE FOLDED HER ARMS AS SHE watched the men work, scowling in impatience. Before her, the magical Border flared as if aware of her presence. She knew that it was not aware, not in the way a human mind would be, but this magical work of the Morgei was complex and sometimes unpredictable, and she knew there was a possibility that it would find a way to alert someone, anyhow.

Many of the sorcerers who usually monitored the Border from within had gone off to Svanfeld, honouring this new alliance. The border patrols were spread thin, too. Dannine rocked forwards to view the nine dead guardsmen stretched out at her feet. They were Thinas Sovaya's reserves, and made no match for Dannine's magic and her soldiers' silver swords.

The Morgein soldier she had spared was managing not to scream as Dannine's sergeant, Hal Stoliden, carefully worked the point of his dagger into the back of his neck. Dannine couldn't be sure if it was bravery. The Mage-Gifted reacted in strange ways to having a silver collar bound about their throats. The soldier was handcuffed and ankle-cuffed in silver, his arms bound to his torso with rope, his legs trussed together, keeping him from wriggling. Impassively, Dannine watched as blood pulsed from the back of his neck, just above the silver collar. Stoliden was careful to carve the wound exactly as she had instructed. He was by far the most competent in this, and the only one Dannine trusted to be at her side this hour.

Stoliden's men finished digging the last hole along the hundred-yard stretch she had mapped out. One of the men fell back with a curse as suddenly the flaring Border reached for him. They had to work carefully; the holes needed to be close to the root of the magical structure, and every now and then, as though it knew precisely what they were about, the liquid wall of magic would "splash" towards one of them at random. Were it to touch him, that would signal the end of his life.

She motioned for them to commence placing the substance she had spent weeks beforehand preparing. Silver dust and gunpowder did not readily mix, and both materials had to be joined in such a way that each retained their unique properties. The black powder to produce the detonation; the silver, of course, to nullify magic. It was a mark of how strange alchemy could be, that the substance which the soldiers now poured into the freshly dug holes was not a powder, but a viscous, grainy, dull grey liquid.

"It's done, Mistress." Stoliden stepped away from their captive, his long knife scarlet to the hilt. Dannine handed him a tin from her belt, containing a similar but fundamentally different substance. This was a smooth, metallic, free-flowing liquid—it contained silver, yes, but its essence was woven together with dark magic. Stoliden handled the stuff carefully, cautious as always when it came to sorcery. That was smart. He would very likely not survive the experience if so much as a smear landed on him.

The wound at the back of the Morgein soldier's head bled freely, yet when the substance was poured down to mingle with the blood, it did not flow with it. Instead it coiled into the wound, attracted inexorably to the source of magic within the man's body. Stoliden caught his breath as they both watched it work. The Morgein soldier was completely immobile; his breath came in harsh gasps of pain, and the sergeant's heavy knee between his shoulder-blades kept him in position. This was crude, but it would do the job. There was no need for the surgical precision with which Arran usually bound his victims to himself.

As the silver tendrils settled in the open wound and dug their way deep into the Morgein soldier, he began to scream.

FISH DIDN'T TURN UP ALL THROUGHOUT the evening, not even for dinner. Albryan checked, and detected him a mile or so away, in Tenna. He was well attuned to the boy's signature by now, and could pick him out easily even within a thicket of lesser presences. His power shone like no other, and the things he could do were nearly as disturbing as Velda's abilities.

The mess was quiet tonight, and Albryan brooded by himself until Thinas Sovaya walked in. Most of the few officers present came alert, saluting or nodding at their general. It was rare enough to see him here; Thinas usually took meals privately, in his own quarters or office. He collected a plate of food and a cup of strong tea, and came towards Albryan, taking the vacant seat just opposite him.

"Albryan," he greeted.

"Sir."

Thinas looked towards the empty space next to Albryan as though wanting to ask what had become of Fish, but he didn't say anything more. Albryan sipped at his own tea. The general seemed deeply preoccupied. At last, Albryan asked: "Any news from the mountains?"

"Mialiné is proving herself a surprisingly competent commander." Albryan knew that it cost the general something to admit that. He'd been taken aback at Fish's plan himself. The idea that Mialiné and her highborn sorcerers might *want* to do more than the perfunctory when it came to defending their homeland had been news for many. "They fought a small battle recently. Casualties were satisfactorily low."

Albryan had known Thinas Sovaya for nine years, since the day he'd been a recruit standing next to Elithan on the practice-ground, watching as the general closely inspected this new group of boys who'd joined up. Thinas had personally handed Albryan his first ring of rank, mentored him after that, and appointed him secretary and then spy. They had worked together for years, yet Albryan still could not truly say that he knew his superior officer well. There was always a separation. Generals were not meant to cultivate close friendships with their disposable underlings. Albryan had learned why that should be, the hard way. It was near impossible to send men out to die when you knew them too closely.

He was about to ask a second question when there was a sudden thud at the side door of the dining-hall, followed by a frantic scrabble as if someone were grasping desperately for the handle. Thinas turned to look, as did everyone else, as a young soldier stumbled through the doorway.

Albryan frowned. The soldier was of the regular rank-and-file, though as he lifted his head, Albryan recognized his face. A sergeant, recently promoted: his name was Giolon Finnas. Curiously for such a warm night, his cloak was drawn about his shoulders, the hood obscuring most of his face. He was chalk white under tanned skin, and as he lurched forward towards Thinas, Albryan saw blood drip from somewhere beneath that cloak to the ground.

"General," he rasped. Thinas was already rising to his feet, and something sounded alarm in Albryan's heart.

"What is the meaning of this, soldier?" Thinas demanded. Cautiously, Albryan rose from his own seat and approached Giolon. "Are you not meant to be on patrol at this very moment?"

"My squad were all wiped out." Giolon gave another step forward. "They're at the Border, sir, we have to go—"

"Steady on, soldier." Albryan reached out and took his arm.

He felt it in an instant, like a lightning strike. The wrongness, the corruption. The blight. Giolon started, made eye contact, and all at once everything changed.

To Albryan's magical senses, Giolon Finnas was no more—the one who stood before him was a dread presence he knew all too well. *Dannine.* She filled the mess hall with her dark fire, and Albryan released the young soldier's arm and stumbled back without thinking. Tendrils of darkness spread out from the heart of Giolon's being like the tentacles of a burst jellyfish, reaching for his Commander-in-Chief—

Albryan's first instinct was to defend Thinas. Light ripped from his hands, controlled magic that cut right through the darkness. Recognition and hate flared in the young soldier's eyes. With a guttural growl, he turned on Albryan.

Albryan had been ready for this moment all along, prepared to face the visage of truest evil again, sometime in his future. He had not expected it to come in the form of a young man he'd mentored personally, advancing upon him with hate etched into twisted features that had once been familiar. Yet even as his heart dropped, he knew that there was nothing he could do—no way he could save Giolon without sacrificing himself, Thinas, and only Goddess knew how many other good soldiers. He threw out a bolt of clear, pure magic, which met the disoriented mass of darkness in a clash he knew was unequal. This was not Dannine Sylvaissen—not truly. She was only appropriating the young sergeant's power, and nothing he did to Giolon would hurt *her*.

Giolon staggered backwards, and critically, Albryan hesitated, wondering if perhaps there was some means of saving him after all. But the unmistakable cruelty of Dannine Sylvaissen appeared on the young soldier's face. He turned, and with a savage grin set fire to the whole room.

Everyone else, all the other officers, had enough time to find their own defences, to throw up shielding against the gouts of flame that ripped through the wooden room, immolating roof and rafters. Albryan desperately set his own shields in place. Dannine did not allow Giolon that salvation. Beset by his own fire, the young sergeant's body burned, sending a wave of sickening stench towards Albryan. But even as he fell, wasting away, Albryan could have sworn he saw relief appear briefly in Giolon's eyes.

Instinct carried Albryan onwards, out of the burning room with the rest of them, helping damp the flames as they threatened to encroach the rest of the barracks as well as the great tree which had always brooded over the low building. Someone was coughing in the silence as the fire hissed away, and Thinas, standing right by him, was looking decidedly shaken.

It did not take the general long to recover, however. "Adakas, Thornas, Giradon." He turned towards his officers. "Something is clearly very amiss. The three of you, rouse whatever soldiers you can find this night. On duty or not, I don't care. Prepare for an invasion of the town."

Faces around Albryan turned grim, but these were senior and disciplined soldiers. No-one questioned orders nor uttered their personal thoughts. "Evanos," the general continued, "go to the house of Julissa Cattenna, and bring her to me. We need to find out if her sorcerers have detected anything from the Border." The lieutenant thus addressed looked dubious, but nodded.

"The rest of you, find horses and prepare to meet me at the foot of the hill. I'm personally getting to the bottom of this. Not you," he said sharply, as Albryan moved to join his peers.

Albryan began to protest, but fell silent at the look his superior officer gave him. Thinas waited till the others had all filed away, then rounded upon him.

"You knew," he said quietly. "How?"

"I—" Albryan felt bile rise in the back of his throat, and the smell of ash was suddenly suffocating in his nostrils. "Sir, you don't understand—"

Thinas's eyes went hard. "Then explain it to me, Captain Lana."

VELDA WAS AT A LOOSE END. Pattin had, in fairly short order, found some young suitor to dally with, and the bustle and noise of the market seemed suddenly at odds with Velda's mood. She wandered beneath the nearby trees, then wandered further into the forest, thinking about what had happened that afternoon. About Fish. Above her, the stars gleamed like a nest of bejewelled mysteries, divinely untouchable.

She slowed and turned her head as a soft sound came to her. A fitting sound, somehow, here beneath the twilight of the swishing trees, though she could not imagine where it was coming from. Lute music. Clear, precise notes twinkled through the branches like raindrops, and she found herself moving in their direction.

Before she knew it, she stumbled across a grassy clearing, and stopped abruptly at the edge, feeling like an intruder. The mysterious player was Elithan, though somewhat unusually, he was alone. He sat upon a fallen tree-trunk, lit by a softly pearlescent glow which Velda realized was coming from within himself. He was intent upon the movement of his hands across the strings, but as she watched, he trailed off and looked up as though discerning her presence in the shadows.

"Hello?" he said, and Velda came guiltily forward.

"I'm sorry. I didn't mean to intrude, but I heard you playing—"

"No matter." Elithan smiled and set the lute aside, standing up. Velda watched in fascination as the light surrounding him dispersed, flowing into a lantern which she knew could double as an oil-lamp, if the bearer were so inclined. Elithan neatened his curly hair with a muscular brown hand before turning to her.

"You play beautifully," Velda said. "Your music . . . it does something to the listener. Stirs the soul."

The handsome soldier grinned broadly, ducking his head as though to remain humble. "That's something," he said softly. "The last time I had such glowing admiration, it was from my eldest."

"Your eldest child?" Velda asked curiously. "How many do you have?" More often than not, whenever she had come across Elithan, whether it was on his off time at barracks or about in town, he had had a small child attached to him. Albryan had mentioned "daughters" more than once, but remained reticent about whatever arrangement there was with a mother. And Elithan was clearly not married, nor courting any specific woman.

"Four." He smiled. "Ambrizete, the eldest, she's eight. Calice is five; Enya three. And my youngest, Elissa, she's just had her third-moon naming ceremony."

"And how many does Albryan have?" The question slipped out before Velda could help herself. It was something she did not have the courage to ask Albryan directly, nor could she bear yet another explanation of how different the Morgei were when it came to such customs.

Elithan paused, looking down at her in the starlight. At last he answered, "None."

"Can you be sure of that?" She meant the question to be light, teasing. She wasn't sure she succeeded.

"The magic gives us many advantages," Elithan replied inscrutably. "For myself, a child doesn't come unless we *both* wish it. But Albryan's different from me. For him, children represent family, love. And I know he's never felt that kind of connection with anyone." He paused. "Not until you."

Velda didn't know what to say. Elithan was looking at her with something almost like accusation. Warmth edged her stomach as she took in what he appeared to be saying. She knew that Albryan was a devoted lover, a loyal one, and that their attachment meant more to him than just a frolic in the forest. But the true depth of his feelings eluded her.

"My birth family is vast," Elithan said, still regarding her with the same expression. "I have an older brother and sister, both born, like me, before my mother was married. And then she found my *alf*-father, and gave me"—he paused for a moment as if in thought—"three younger brothers, and six sisters."

Velda raised her eyebrows, confused by the abrupt change in subject. "Where do they all live?" She'd seen no evidence of such an extended family around Elithan.

"They're fisherfolk. I was born and raised in a small hamlet near the town of Quinen, miles away from here. Most of my family can barely perform any magic, but I was, as they say, destined for greater things." He sounded almost sorrowful. "Our lives have drifted so far apart that I barely know what to say to my parents and sibs when I see them." He shifted, folding his arms. "Albryan is as much family to me—no, perhaps even more, in a way—than what they are. I see what he's done for you, the risks he's taking, the things he's hiding." He paused again. "I hope you see it, too."

"I do," Velda began at once, but before she could get any further, a twig cracked sharply in the darkness beyond the clearing. They both turned at once towards the sound.

A shadowy figure came into view. A chill touched Velda's spine, and she caught her breath in tension before the figure moved into the circle of light cast by the lantern, and she recognized the face of Elithan's lieutenant.

"Erastes," she said in relief.

Elithan, however, frowned and stepped slightly in front of Velda. "Lieutenant. I thought you were running checks on the patrols tonight."

Erastes said nothing, which was odd. There was not enough light in the lantern to discern his features clearly, but to Velda's eyes he looked drawn and grey. She did not know Erastes well enough to tell whether this was out of habit for him, but something ignited foreboding in her heart.

"Why are you presenting magic, Erastes?" Elithan asked sharply. He had unfolded his arms, and his fists hung tense by his sides. "Explain yourself."

Instead of speaking, Erastes drew himself into a stance Velda recognized as readiness for battle-magic.

She could not tell who struck first: whether it was Erastes sending out the first bolt of power, or Elithan. But the unleashing of hostile magic had an immediate effect on her. Velda knew, by now, that benign magic was not enough to move the implacable power. Even the occasional sharp flare from Albryan or Fish, though she always felt it stir in what they called the ether, was not sufficient to draw her ability forth. But danger signalled in her mind as the copper taste of magic filled the air, and she reached out with pure, raw instinct, no thought but to defend herself and Elithan from whatever madness had taken hold of his lieutenant. Light flowed out from her hands, soft as Elithan's glow had been, and yet this was steel and silver to his golden magic.

The moment the light touched him, Elithan staggered to his knees, throwing his arms up as though to shield his face. Erastes reacted even more violently, cringing back until he seemed nothing more than a frightened boy. He curled in on himself, and as the light passed over him, she saw it: the same kind of blight Albryan had once carried, nestled deep within the young mage-soldier's soul. But where Albryan's had merely begun to encroach upon the source of his magic, Erastes was consumed by the black growth. The golden branch-patterns of his magic were diseased, rotten. The anguish which radiated from his soul threatened to buckle Velda to her knees.

There was nothing she could do about it, Velda knew, unless she could restrain and touch him.

In the cold glow of the light, Elithan stumbled to her side and stared at his hands.

"You're doing it," he stammered. "Right now. On *me*. That's—real."

Velda's attention was on Erastes. "It's real," she hissed. "And if you can restrain *him* somehow, I can heal him."

"Heal—" Elithan's eyes went towards his lieutenant, who now appeared to be slowly recovering, standing up straight. "What's wrong with—" A look of horrified realization came over his face, and he put a hand to his forehead. "No," he whispered. "Bryan *told* me—"

Erastes drew his sword, the metal ringing harshly against its sheath. Elithan seemed to come back to himself all at once. He seized Velda, dragging her behind him even as she was still nullifying the magic she could tell he wanted to use. But she had almost no control over the ability, not like this—not when she could barely tell which of the two of them was preparing to strike—

Elithan pushed her back, roughly, and sprang at Erastes in the same movement. Velda hit the ground on hands and knees to see him rush the younger, shorter lieutenant, grabbing hold of his sword arm before he could strike with the blade. A terrible realization hit her: Elithan had no weapon. He had not expected danger to strike this night.

Furthermore, she realized as they grappled together and Erastes snarled in his friend's face, eliciting terrible memories of the necromes in the mountains: whoever was controlling the young lieutenant was after *her*. They had to be: Elithan had no particular quarrel with the servants of blood sorcery. But Velda had an unheard-of ability, one that had sent the princess Dannine of Armour City fleeing home to her father in shame. An ability that could nullify even Arran Sylvaissen's dark sorcery. It made sense that he would want to kill her for it, and with the thought her power shone even brighter, damping all magic around for a radius she could not tell how far—

Erastes struggled furiously against Elithan, then suddenly stepped back in what looked like a practised manoeuvre, ripping his arm backwards. Elithan's hand lost its grip, slipping along his wrist, and the blade came down and made inevitable contact, slicing clean along his palm. Elithan cried out, his face twisting in pain and betrayal. Erastes swiftly kicked his feet out from under him, pivoted neatly, and drove the sword through Elithan's unarmoured chest.

Time slowed, turning to treacle. Elithan's body fell and hit the ground. Velda wanted to scream, but dread froze all sound from her and she could only whimper. She was still on the ground; the world had gone black in just a fraction of a moment.

Some instinct propelled her to her feet, and she came face-to-face with Erastes—or the man who had once been Erastes. No remorse nor recognition was left in his eyes.

"I'm not here to kill you," he rasped. "Not kill you, under no circumstances, no," as if it were an order that had been burned into his soul. His eyes glowed with deep-buried madness. "Come with me."

She turned to run, but in a trice he was on her, twisting her arm painfully behind her back. She cried out and tried to rake his shins with her feet, but he kicked them out from under her and bore her to the ground, pinning her down.

"Stop struggling," he growled in her ear. "I won't kill you, under no circumstances, but I'm allowed to hurt you if I want."

She went rigid. Would this always be her fate, manhandled into captivity, forced to comply because someone else was ruthless and stronger than she was? She smarted with frustration. It didn't matter that she could fell the works of the mightiest sorcerer, not when she could be physically overpowered and dragged off like some—some slave—

Silence fell save for the rasping of his breath in her ear. When next Erastes spoke, Velda didn't believe that anything of him was left. It was too unlike the quiet, almost bashful young man who had kept her talking about horses for a solid hour the day she met him.

"Now, maybe I should give you a taste of what will happen if you dare fight against me again." His breath was hot against her neck, and he gave a laugh dry as desert sand. "Your lover's being taken care of. No-one's coming to save you. And I have all the time I need for your punishment."

VELDA WAS NOWHERE TO BE FOUND, nor was Pattin. Fish paced the half-empty market stalls in frustration, wishing he could sense her the way he could Albryan—or any other person who had the Gift. And whose presence was familiar to him. For the first time, Fish cursed the fact that Pattin did not fall in that category.

"She must have gone home," Kevin said, trailing after him. "It's getting late. Both of them probably have."

"Can't you find your sister?" Fish demanded.

Kevin blinked at him. "I've never been able to do that." He shrugged. "Look, most likely Velda's back in her room by now. That's only logical."

Fish's gut told him different, yet he could not substantiate that feeling. Something hovered at the edge of his magical senses, and the presence of Kevin was a distraction. "Tell you what," he said at last, turning. "You head back to barracks, see if you can find out what's amiss. I'll find her."

Kevin hesitated. "If something is going on, Fish . . . shouldn't you be talking directly to the officers?"

Fish floundered, then rallied. "Look . . . I'm not a regular soldier," he said at last. "I've worked more closely with the sorceresses. On the magical lines of defence." That shut Kevin up, and Fish forced a smile. "I just need to set my mind at ease about Velda, and then I'll be going"—he cast around for only the briefest of moments before he recalled the name of the woman who had replaced Mialiné—"to Julissa Cattenna's residence. It's on the same side of town, miles away from the barracks." He hoped that was true; Fish didn't actually know where Julissa Cattenna lived, but it was a fair guess: the nobles mostly had their residences and mansions on the eastern fringes of the city, almost directly opposite where the army was stationed.

Kevin didn't look quite convinced, but he nodded at last, and left without another word. Fish let out a deep breath he had been holding to himself all this time, and called out to Brightfeather. The quetzal was already in the air, winging towards his position.

"Velda," he whispered aloud. Something wasn't right. Fish could almost physically discern the stench of blood sorcery, and it disoriented his magical senses. After reawakening his Gift and training with Albryan, Fish could now recognize the distinct difference between clean, natural magic and what his father and adoptive siblings used. The taint. He shivered. The sacrifice.

That thought seemed to lead somewhere, a tether to the real world nearby. Fish walked to the edge of the market square, where the town gradated into the same forest where he and Kevin had sat heedlessly drinking, not even an hour ago. But the taint was a nest of cobwebs, too splintered and chaotic for him to pinpoint properly. And chunks of it seemed to be disappearing, drawn by some inexorable force into a yawning, implacable abyss . . .

Fish's heart jumped into his throat, and his mouth went dry. The abyss. The hole in the world. His twin in nothingness. He could sense *where* the magic was disappearing from the world. That break in the fabric of reality was nearby . . .

He started off immediately, hastening between the trees, heart pounding as he broke into a run. If that break in the world was Velda, then she was in direct contact with a creation born of blood sorcery.

He felt it long before he saw anything, causing him to slow his frantic footfalls and flick a spare dagger from out his sleeve. His heart beat with danger as he passed into a clearing. A body lay in the shadows, but Fish took barely any notice. Two figures struggled at the edge of the clearing: a mass of dark magic, and—

The mass of darkness resolved itself into a man. Fish had almost expected to see the face of his father again, but this was a young Morgein soldier, freckle-faced and tow-haired. Though there was little physical resemblance, Fish found himself thinking of the young prisoner he had interrogated in the mountains.

The man had the harried look of someone who had just been interrupted in the middle of something forbidden. He had both Velda's arms twisted behind her back. With his other hand, he was holding a sword to her throat. Fish could tell by a glance that he was using most of his strength and focus to keep her restrained. Tears tracked down her cheeks as her eyes met Fish's, yet she seemed—as yet—unhurt. Something swam around her in the ether, manifesting only as a weak grey light on the earthly plane. Yet Fish felt it beat against his magical senses, strong and unwavering. Experimentally, he tried to touch his magic, and found that he could not. He started, realizing the depth of her ability. That afternoon, she'd been a hole in the world, passive, absorbent. What she was doing now was active, defensive. Waves emanated from her, nullifying any magic that dared come near.

It had not saved her from being physically overpowered and captured, but as he stood there, Fish could see that the dark mass that was the young soldier was very slowly diminishing, being drawn off into the ether bit by tiny bit. What this portended, Fish couldn't tell.

"Deryck," the soldier hissed, as though the name itself were a malediction.

"In the flesh," Fish returned. He knew those cold, implacable eyes. No matter whose stolen face they stared from, he had been the chosen heir to Arran Sylvaissen for long enough to recognize him anywhere. He knew that look, though never before had it been directed at him. Fish remembered a conversation with Nico, weeks ago. *I hope he can't do that to people.* He remembered his own flippant answer, and felt sick.

"When last did we see each other like this?" the soldier went on, taunting. He leaned his face into Velda's neck as vainly she cringed away. Anger cramped in Fish's stomach—and shame. He remembered too well. He'd spent half his life running from those memories. Arran's puppet raised his head. "There was a girl then, too, as I recall. A pretty little thing, younger than this one. Do you remember what we did to her?"

Fish's knuckles trembled around the dagger he was half-concealing at his side. He dared not break, not now. It had been the second ritual sacrifice, out of the three which were required to bind him heart and soul to Qwu'Horya. The sacrifice of blood. He gripped the dagger harder to stop his hand from shaking. It had been the first time Fish had ever killed someone. He had been eleven years old. He felt the hard edge of steel cut against his hand. Blood spilled into his palm, cooling, grounding.

"I'm unarmed," Fish lied, refusing to acknowledge his words, seeking to distract him, looking right at Velda. She knew that Fish kept several daggers hidden beneath his clothes. She'd seen them on his belt and strapped to his wrist. Not only the very first time they'd met, but just that afternoon. *It's nothing you haven't seen before*, he repeated to himself, wishing he could transmit the thought directly into her head. His fingers curled lightly around the hilt of the blade, finding their grip. "You have something I want. I'm willing to trade."

The soldier snickered. "What could you—"

The bait was taken. Moving fluidly, Fish threw the dagger.

Arran's puppet saw it coming, and moved aside. But in doing so, he loosened his grip on Velda, which Fish had counted on. She twisted in his grasp. As Fish had guessed he would, the soldier held back from cutting her throat, and Velda flung herself free.

Fish reached out and seized her hand, pulling her towards him, and time stopped. Magic flared from him as it had before in her presence, being inexorably drawn forth, and it met the waves of not-magic that she was emitting. The eldritch and the earth joined together, and the edges of reality shattered around their linked hands.

Velda turned to look at Fish, staring in disbelief, in *recognition*—and let go. Both their powers blinked suddenly out, fading into the ether as though they had never been. The connection was lost. They were just a boy and a girl, standing alone against an implacable horror that loomed in the background. Arran's puppet was readying himself already, gathering his dark power.

Impulsively, Fish grabbed Velda's hand, and this time he held tightly to her, reaching for all the reserves of the magic he possessed. His power drew forth the force of hers, and reality parted like an earthquake splitting the ground in two. The apex of that parting pointed directly toward the soldier who was inhabited by Arran Sylvaissen's presence.

In the moments before it reached him, Fish saw sight and life dim in the young soldier's eyes, knew that Arran had abandoned his slave to his fate. No mortal body could stand up to the might of the abyssal energy that fractured between Fish and the girl who was his reflection yet opposite. The soldier fell limply, almost softly, to the earth.

Velda let out a long, gasping breath, and Fish felt the withdrawal of tension, the easing off of her power even as his own retreated. Reality annealed itself, resolving into the plain mortal world in which he stood blinking, wondering just what the hell had happened and knowing that he did not have the time to figure it out.

Velda began to tremble violently, and her knees gave way beneath her. Gently Fish helped her down, crouching before her and taking both her hands. "Are you all right?" he asked softly, urgently.

"Yeah." She nodded emphatically, and let him slip an arm around her. She was shivering violently, though the night was balmy and the sweat of exertion was smeared on her brow. "Fish, what—what's going on?"

"I think," he said, "that Arran Sylvaissen wants you, for some reason—and tonight, he's seized that opportunity." She nodded weakly, and Fish knew that she must have already thought that out for herself. "It's probably because of what you can do—what you just did with me," he continued. "We shattered reality." She looked at him without comprehension. "We opened some sort of door to a—a higher plane. A different world."

"A different world? What does that mean? Like—the world of the dead?"

"Perhaps." Fish stood up, and resolutely she stood with him. "But we don't have time, not tonight. There's something more. I don't think Arran's given up on catching you. I don't think this soldier was the only one."

"Fish." She suddenly looked panicked. "Just before you came, he said—he said Albryan was 'being taken care of.'"

Fish paused, searching the ether. Spots of confusion were manifesting there now, something that did not bode well. There was a feeling of apprehension, as if something enormous were waiting to fall. Yet even against this background noise, he easily picked out the bright, familiar presence of Albryan.

"Albryan's all right," he told her, smiling slightly at the obvious relief in her eyes.

Something creaked behind them, and Velda stepped back with a cry. Fish turned to see Brightfeather, great serpentine flying thing that he was, winging down towards him. He grinned in relief. In all this, he had nearly forgotten about the quetzal, but now he could get to the bottom of everything so much easier.

"Do you want to come flying with me?" he asked, still grinning. Velda's eyes went as round as moons.

"That's your quetzal?"

"The same." Fish nodded proudly.

She half-turned, looking back at the bodies in the clearing. Tears brimmed in her eyes again.

"These men," she said, "they were soldiers. Albryan's friends. They were both good men."

It was then that the looming *thing* in the ether finally gave way, collapsing like a dam wall. Fish felt it resonate all through him, and Brightfeather flapped and squawked as the backlash hit him too. And at last, Fish understood what was going on, and anguish ran all through him as he discerned the whole of Arran's plan.

"Fish?"

"Dannine," he whispered. Her silver presence sliced through him like a spearblade in the absence of the magical Border. Cold. Angry. Fish knew that there was no escape this time, not from her. Not if he wanted to keep Velda safe. Her face was a mask of confusion now, as she gazed from him to the quetzal.

"I have to go," Fish said. "I'm the only one who can stop her."

"Stop—who? Dannine? Your adoptive sister?" Velda came forward. "I'm going with you. I defeated her before; I nullified her magic. I can protect you."

Fish forestalled her immediately. "No. No way."

"Fish, you've seen—"

"I am not letting you risk yourself," Fish said flatly. "Not against *her*."

Velda reached out, seized Fish's hands with both of hers, and interlinked their fingers. Again, Fish felt something tremble along the edges of reality, where his magic and her not-magic met.

"Can't you feel this?" she demanded. "Don't you think we were meant to stand against the darkness together?"

Fish took his hands away, cutting off the magic she drew forth. He would need all his reserves and more, before this night was done. "If we were meant to stand against the darkness," he said softly, "then I was meant to ward you so that you can bring the light."

"Fish, no—"

"I'm expendable," he said harshly. "You're not. And you—you're *good*. Kind. Pure of heart. I was raised for battle, trained for the kill. You weren't. If I survive this—"

"Take me with you, and you will."

"And what if *you* don't?"

She stood blinking at him, not giving a retort, and Fish turned away without waiting for her to find one. Brightfeather bowed his head, chirping softly. Fish transmitted comfort to the quetzal as he took the saddle. Dannine would certainly be on quetzal-back too, one of the mounts who had been Brightfeather's nest-sibs and play-mates. Just as Dannine had been to Fish.

The quetzal straightened, preparing for flight. Velda ran forward.

"Fish!" she yelled.

"I am *not* taking you," he repeated.

"Then take my words," Velda called up. "You're not expendable. Not to me. And what we did—that power we brought forth—that's never happened with anyone else."

Fish paused, feeling the vibration of Brightfeather's tension beneath him.

"We were meant to be *together*, Fish," she continued. "Don't die. Please."

Death had always felt closer to Fish than life itself. As a child soldier, as a runaway, as a swordsman and assassin, only a step away, breathing down his neck with a cold caress. He took a breath and felt the stirring of air through his lungs, ready to risk itself once again. He could feel the impatience thrumming through his blood, eager for it, as though a violent end was all that his body desired. He looked down at her.

"I won't," he promised, and signalled Brightfeather. The quetzal spread his wings and crouched down, preparing for flight.

# CHAPTER XL
# FLIGHT

ANNINE WATCHED FROM A SAFE distance as her weapon tore a hole through the Border. Eldritch interference flared green on the other plane, and the whole magical structure shrank back as the essence of silver ripped through its fibres. They were wholly severed. They could not find each other again.

"*Ready!*" Stoliden gave the cry, and the soldiers formed up behind Dannine as she casually sat her quetzal.

The Forest of the Morning was home to nearly all who possessed the gift of magic, but as she winged up into the air, Dannine felt a distinct presence, bright as the caress of the noonday sun even against the background of a thousand other burning souls. *Deryck*. Exhilaration flowed through her, dark and thick and flammable as tar. She already knew all of it, of course. Arran's puppet had been placed well, bearing witness to almost all that transpired. Deryck offering an alliance to the Morgei, betraying Arran openly now. "We won't interfere," Arran had told her, when learning of it. "This plays into our hands. Deryck will be surprised, dismayed. He will try to protect the people who rely on him." He'd placed a hand on Dannine's shoulder then, and his voice burned now in her mind. "Defeat him, daughter. If he stands in your way, annihilate him."

Dannine had gorged herself on life force, augmenting her natural magic with the lives of a dozen victims. She was strong with the dark goddess. She would not fail. Deryck was only the beginning.

The quetzal spread out its wings against the carpet of night, above the shadowy trees, and as her soldiers marched on the hapless town, Dannine followed the tether to her quarry unerringly.


Since the moment he started talking, Thinas's eyes had not left Albryan's face. Not knowing what else to do, Albryan told it all. The only thing he downplayed was the extent of Velda's ability. Guilt riddled him as he spoke, yet he stood straight as he explained his reasoning.

There was a long silence, in which Albryan tried to read the verdict in his general's eyes. The burned-out room continued to smoulder in the sweltering night. Coals glowed red-hot in the settling silence.

Thinas held out his hand. "Your rings," he said in a deadly calm voice.

Albryan didn't respond. His heart hammered in his chest.

"Your *rings*, citizen Lana," Thinas repeated.

Had he expected anything different? Even so, Albryan tried to dissemble. The military was all he had known since he came of age. He was one of the most competent soldiers that the army of Qwu'Mallorn had ever reared. Thinas knew his quality. Surely this could not be his decision. "Sir, please—are you asking—"

"I asked for your rings of rank," Thinas responded in a voice of stone, "because you are hereby stripped of your position in this army. The trial for high treason can wait until we have resolved this crisis you have brought upon us."

Numbly, Albryan slipped the four bronze rings he wore from his arm. His hands were steady when he handed them over; for that much, he was proud.

"After tonight," Thinas said, and Albryan could hear his voice quavering slightly, "you will no longer be welcome in this compound. You will relinquish your quarters, your weapons, your uniform, and all the symbols and privileges of this army."

Albryan nodded, not saying a word.

"In the morning, a tribune of your peers will hand you over to the Council—"

Something flared inside Albryan at the mention of the Council. "What should I have done, then, according to you?" he demanded helplessly. "Leave someone dear to me to the whims of politicians? What would you have done?"

Thinas's expression softened, but only slightly. "If there was a conflict of interest, soldier," he replied, "you should have chosen one or the other."

Neither of them said anything for a long moment. There was dread and darkness in the air, not just from what had happened here, but something more, something happening even as Albryan's world was collapsing. Thinas felt it too; Albryan could read it on the general's face, in his worried scowl.

"It's the Border," Albryan said hoarsely, certainty spreading through him as familiar aberrations exploded in the ether. "It's Dannine Sylvaissen. She's doing the same as she did in the western borderlands, and perhaps worse. Perhaps a full-scale attack on Tenna."

It was just then that one of Thinas's remaining captains came riding up. "General!" he called frantically. "I met with a group of scouts from the Border. There's been a serious breach, and they spotted the enemy marching on Tenna. Hundreds of men, by their estimation. An invasion force."

Thinas turned away from Albryan with awful finality. "Lend me your horse, Adakas," he said. "Are our troops massing for battle?"

Albryan's head spun. They were coming to pass, all the nightmares he'd ever had, and he was powerless to move. He had been dismissed. The ether churned with as much chaos as his mind, making him want to scream. Adakas spared Albryan nothing but a cursory glance as they turned away. He was no longer welcome in their comradeship.

Something crystallized inside him, heavier than lead, harder than steel. If the army, his once-sworn brothers, no longer wanted him, Albryan had other people to protect. Dannine knew what Velda was, had seen what she could do. Albryan had a bad feeling. Velda—who pulled magic back to the ether—and Fish, who pulled it in vast quantities from the ether into the mundane world without even meaning to.

Arran Sylvaissen had once had Fish in his power, bought him and paid for him and raised him as his own. Doubtless he had been aware of the boy's potential, known all along what a powerful blood sorcerer he might have made. The notion of it sent a knife of foreboding along Albryan's spine. Would Arran have any interest in Velda's power? It was something that had needled at him for a long time, and now it was upon them. Would he realize that she was likely the born twin of the boy he had once groomed to fight for him?

Albryan was suddenly afraid. Whether it was for Velda, for Fish, for what Fish might do, for what both of them together were capable of, and why—he couldn't say. Something felt *wrong*, beyond the sickness and shame that curdled in his stomach. Albryan didn't know, could not know, whether Velda was in danger. He could barely pick out Fish in the roiling disorder of the ether. Dannine Sylvaissen was *somewhere*, but not in the position Albryan would have expected were she marching with her soldiers on the town. That was enough to give him pause. If the enemy's true purpose was to invade Tenna, why would Dannine not be leading the invasion force?

Unbidden, Albryan's feet had already begun to move, carrying him away from the smouldering ruin. If nothing else, he had to make sure Velda was safe—from people like Tiralinna Ebraskaia as well as Arran Sylvaissen. What had he been thinking, bringing her here? They would leave Tenna under cover of the chaos, as soon as possible. And Fish would help, Albryan knew. They would all leave together.

He reached the stables, one of so many places he'd felt truly at peace, at home, here amongst the beasts he reared and trained for battle. The bustle of the moment, men grabbing mounts at random and riding off in pairs and groups, felt surreal. No-one noticed as Albryan quickly tacked up one of his favourites, a chestnut mare with white socks, and two others that he fixed to her saddle with long lead ropes as he mounted up. He paused on his way out, his chest aching with emptiness, considering his situation. He needed weapons, and Fish's possessions were still in the room he'd been assigned.

Albryan stopped at the officers' residence. All was in darkness as he broke the minor spell that warded Fish's door. That was against etiquette, but Albryan reckoned Fish would forgive him; the boy had never been much for regulation himself, and had constantly invited Albryan into his room, not seeming to like the solitude either.

The pack Fish had brought on his journey from Svanfeld was still packed; Albryan heard the clink of coins in the bottom, spotted a mass of clothes and leathers inside. He closed the pack and shouldered it. Fish's sword was placed neatly in a weapons-bracket against the wall, and bits of armour were strewn about the room, rather less neatly. Albryan gathered them all.

Then it was into his own room, where he grabbed his own sword and daggers and armour, the hunting bow he was proficient with, and nothing else. As he stepped into the still-dark corridor, declining to use any magic to light his path, he wondered fleetingly where Elithan found himself this night. Perhaps he had woken from sleep to find the whole place in furore and fuss, and likely was already marching with the rest to meet their enemy head-on. Albryan paused as a pang shot through his heart, threatening to buckle him to his knees. That was where he should be. By Elithan's side. Fighting side-by-side with his brothers.

*Get going*, Albryan told himself harshly. *Move. That's no longer your place, and you have others relying on you.*

No-one came to stop him as he stumbled out into the yard. No-one watched as he rode away, heading straight towards Fish's presence, refusing to let himself look back.

THE QUETZAL WINGED INTO THE SKY, and Fish spotted her immediately on the midnight horizon, approaching on the wings of her own mount. It seemed as though this should be a momentous meeting, that they should be parrying with words before their blades and magic met, but all Fish felt was an urgency to get it done and over with.

Fish was ill-prepared for battle: his magic had been drawn off all day, practising with Albryan, in all that had happened between him and Velda, even in the after-effects that lust and alcohol had left in his body. So much had happened that he felt close to exhaustion, only the necessity of this moment keeping him aloft. He wore no helm nor armour, only his usual boots and the light silk shirt Velda had given him, and the only mundane weapons he had were two more silver daggers.

Against this, Dannine was armoured all in silver, lancing through Fish's magical senses, and she burned with unmistakeably augmented power, complete in her preparations.

But there was no avoiding this. Fish directed Brightfeather onwards, and the quetzal obeyed, flying straight ahead like a thrown dart.

After a few moments, Dannine's quetzal reacted, turning, banking far to his left. Fish watched in surprise as she inscribed a wide half-circle around him. It wasn't like her to turn away from a direct confrontation. She passed him towards the town and banked low, as though searching for something on the ground.

Fish's heart went cold. Velda was down there.

Dannine recovered from the arc and winged up again. As she did so, she produced a bolt of magic that glowed with pure, crystal-white light against the blanket of night sky. An unmistakable signal.

*No.* Fish's guts crawled with horrified realization. He should never have left Velda on her own. She was vulnerable down there, helpless against the enemy soldiers Dannine had just signalled.

Dannine was already swivelling back towards Fish, her intent as obvious as the anger which built around her in the ether. It was too late for regret and recrimination. Fish reached for his magic, clumsy with startlement.

The quetzals met and wheeled, screeching ear-splitting defiance towards each other. Fish could see his sister's face, passive beneath the silver gleam of her helmet, devoid of emotion in a way he did not remember. Brightfeather was larger and bulkier than Dannine's quetzal, yet Fish could feel that his mount was reluctant to engage. His plumage was different from the other quetzal's, more lustrous and varied, with accents of purple and gold along his crest and wing-joints. It was like the contrast between a hen and a cockerel, and Fish felt a sudden realization.

Dannine tossed a quick bolt of magic which Fish easily deflected, recognizing it instantly for what it was. The prod of a weapon only to draw away—the test. She wanted to probe his abilities before committing herself to a blow.

Fish positioned himself and Brightfeather between Dannine and the town, standing as defender. Brightfeather discouraged the other quetzal with a series of sharp shrieks, baring his considerable beak when she attempted to sneak past him. Dannine continued to take the offensive, eager for battle as ever she had been. Fish deflected blow after blow, all different energies and angles, as though she were testing his reflexes. Yet Fish knew she had far more power than this.

Even as that thought flew through his mind, Dannine sent a fireball towards him, fiercer and stronger than any of her previous attacks. Fish fumbled at the defence, and overspilling magic jarred him, rushing through his body and setting his teeth on edge. The past few weeks, he had been growing used to Albryan's way of doing things: calling his magic in an aura of calm, bringing forth a pure and passionless haze from the ether. The *emotion*—anger, loathing, defiance, resentment—that Dannine had laced throughout her magic burned like slag in the back of Fish's mouth. Brightfeather winged upwards in alarm, and Fish sent a white-hot whipcord of retaliation towards Dannine, only to see it dissipate in the sharp haze of her gleaming silver armour.

Yet another realization struck him. The only way he could realistically stop Dannine was to curb her quetzal. Brightfeather's presence filled the back of Fish's mind at that thought, almost hissing in warning. Fish read the emotion—the *love*—as clearly as though the flying serpent had communicated it in plain words.

"We won't hurt her," he responded, a sudden idea piercing the darkness of desperation. "We'll save her."

Linked as their minds were, Brightfeather could read Fish's idea without having to ask him—and Fish sensed his immediate approval. They wheeled back, narrowly dodging yet another flare of magic. The attacks were coming faster now, and Fish built a shield around himself and Brightfeather, absorbing Dannine's energies. Just for a moment. He only had a moment to get this right, for Dannine would soon divine what he was truly about.

Fish built a lasso, weaving it quickly from fibres of magic, making it strong and unyielding and designed to block the bond between quetzal and rider. He wasn't sure whether he could in fact get that last part *right*—Dannine's bond with her mount was different from his with Brightfeather, a bond of master and slave. But that wasn't truly important. Dannine battered him with a magical attack designed to shatter the shield he had thrown up. He could feel it weaken under her onslaught, ready to break, but a moment before it did, he quickly dismissed it, deflecting her attack and throwing the lasso in the same movement. Her power thrummed past him, making the hair stand up all over his body, screeching past Brightfeather's exposed neck-feathers. The quetzal squawked in alarm, yet held his position. The lasso flew, wrapping itself securely around the form of the young female quetzal.

She rolled in the air, taken by surprise. Fish held on. Dannine instantly reacted—but to Fish's surprise and horror, she began to laugh.

Before he could let go, before he could set the power aside and dissipate the connection back into the ether, she reached out and touched it with the full might of her own magic, sending a powerful and malicious flare along the fibres of the woven bond. Fish recoiled in horror, trying to let go, but it was too late. Dannine's flare of power hit him and entered him, passing through his body like a gout of flame.

A properly constructed grounding—the dam wall Albryan had shown—could possibly have saved him. But Fish had never learned to do that properly. He'd struggled with shielding, with containing backlash, even when he was a boy. He hadn't grasped what Albryan was trying to teach him until that very afternoon, and somehow Velda had helped him—but he didn't quite understand *how*. Desperately, he tried to build an inner shield, tried to deflect, resisted the oncoming, consuming power with all his might.

The pain of her magic, fuelled by bitter hate and burning desire, tore through him. Against his own expectations, his quick, flimsy inner shield held, deflecting the worst—the damage on the mortal plane. He would not be physically burned, but his own magic was ripped into disorderly fibres as her power smashed the connections into chaos. Still, he would escape alive; the harm was not permanent.

But the moment that burning energy left his body, Fish felt it meet something else—something solid and earthly, which soaked up the rogue magic like a desiccated sponge and had no way to deflect nor shield against it. *Brightfeather*, he realized, and instinctively, desperately, tried to gather the overflowed magic back towards himself. But it was far too late to reverse what was already done. The incinerating horror of Dannine's power bound them all together, and Fish felt it pass through the bond he shared with Brightfeather, burning in anguish.

A white-hot blade of energy ripped through both quetzals like a boning knife through a supine fish. Silhouetted sickeningly against the indifferent night, they writhed and contorted like speared serpents. The lancing white outline of the female quetzal, bent in the throes of her agony, burned itself into Fish's eyes just before Brightfeather's wings came up, obscuring his vision as the quetzal, limply, began to fall from the sky.

DANNINE CLUNG TO THE QUETZAL'S back. It had happened fast—the force of her magic ripping right through Deryck's being and overspilling into both the feathered beasts, destroying their bodies from the inside out. Her quetzal keened as it fell, a thin and broken sound, emanating from its beak along with the acrid stench of smoke. There was nothing more left here for Dannine. The price of the feathered creature's life, though high, was well worth paying for the victory.

She leaped from the quetzal, letting its broken body fall where it would, and funnelled all her magic into creating a cushion to land.

Hal Stoliden and his knot of men on horseback had followed her instructions to the letter. They were waiting, dismounted and holding their loaded muskets at the ready, with her precious quarry. Hal himself held the best of their horses for Dannine to ride. A poor replacement for a flying mount, but it would have to do. The greater part of Dannine's army was spread out between here and the broken Border. There would be little chance of anyone being able to follow them unmolested from Tenna.

Dannine was surprised that the girl had been so lightly protected; one with an ability such as hers should have been counted as either unfathomably precious or inconceivably dangerous. But as her eyes took in the figure of the young woman they pushed forward, her plain garb yet proud poise, the stubbornness in her eyes that out-weighed terror, she realized the truth, and wanted to laugh. Albryan Lana had told no-one else of the girl's precious ability. He'd kept all this to himself. Whatever he and Deryck had been fomenting to-gether, the matriarchs of Qwu'Mallorn were not a part of it.

"A poor protector, in the end," she observed dryly, inclining her head as, far in the distance, Deryck and his stolen quetzal hit the trees and crunched to the forest floor. The girl raised her gaze to Dannine's.

"He's not dead," she said steadfastly, straining against the silver bonds that encircled her wrists. The silver did not impair her ability in the least—she was nullifying Dannine's magic even as they spoke—but it was a sensible safeguard against whatever unknown powers this one might still possess. "I know he's not, and *you* know it too."

Dannine considered her. "No," she said at last. Deryck's magical force was so bright, so glaring in the ether, that she would know if that glare had been dimmed, as though the sun itself had been blacked from the heavens. "For now, anyway. I flung him from the sky. He's lying injured somewhere, dying even as we speak. Broken."

A savage joy flitted through her at the thought, even though Deryck was no longer her all-consuming obsession. Dannine was past that.

The girl's eyes filled with tears, but she blinked them away before they could fall. Dannine swung into the saddle of her horse, and Stoliden passed up the girl to sit in front of her. Dannine had to reach around her to control the reins, but she preferred to have her father's prize where she could constrain her every movement. She flicked a dagger from her belt and held it to the girl's throat, putting a hand in her thick, curly hair to turn her head. The girl's face was impassive, and her dark eyes burned defiance. Dannine gripped her close, and their faces were very near when she spoke.

"Just remember, should you entertain any thoughts of running away—" She slid the point of the dagger up to touch the girl's lower lip. "You don't need a tongue to serve my father. Nor your eyes."

The girl's eyes glittered like gemstones, yet her voice was remarkably controlled. "I understand."

Without any more ado, Dannine flicked the reins, forcing the horse to a trot, then into a canter. Stoliden barked the order, and his soldiers mounted and followed, creating a protective formation around Dannine as they rode. Trees flew by as they hurtled along the forest path. The attack on Tenna would cover their flight, but without her quetzal, Dannine was pressed for time. With the girl so close to her, she could not even touch her magic, and would have to rely on her nonmage scouts to ward the way ahead.

THE TUMBLE TOWARDS THE FOREST FLOOR took forever. Fish knew that Brightfeather was dying, and instinctively he reached out, trying to share his power, like he had done that day with Brialise, a day that seemed now impossibly long ago. But their magic was not the same. The quetzal was of the sky and earth, eternal, and Fish was fire and blood, fleeting, mortal.

He should have been able to channel his magic to save himself, to build a cushion beneath their falling bodies and the unyielding, merciless ground. But the damage Dannine had caused was still in full effect. The threads of his magic slipped away like strands of silk, leaving his body too fast even to grasp onto, let alone build something so complex. All focus fled his injured, agitating mind, and magic flared uselessly into the ether as he continued to fall.

He was going to die here, entangled with the quetzal's charred corpse. They were falling too far to ever survive.

If he had one overriding regret—

Fragile feathers and bony wings enfolded him, and Fish felt something encircle him on the ethereal plane as well, something as strong and enduring as the earth itself. "No—" he began, comprehending. "I'm not worth it—"

*I die.* The thought was composed not of words, but Fish understood as clearly as though Brightfeather were talking to him in plain language. *My death, certainty. You—wingsib. Little featherless brother. A chance, you have, to live. A chance, I give you.*

*No*, Fish responded, *No, it's my fault. I made the mistake. I failed* you. *It's not fair—*

*"Fair" matters not. Be still, hatchling.* Something tugged at the edges of Fish's consciousness, seemingly drawing him into sleep. He didn't want to sleep. It wasn't right that he should be spared any suffering. He struggled against the force that had him in its grasp, but its hold upon his mind was as sure and strong as that of a mother hawk's talons around her nestling.

*I didn't know you could do that . . .*

*I do many things beyond your reckoning. Hold on, little brother. Hold on. It approaches, a rough landing.*

IN THE MIDDLE OF TENNA, ALBRYAN stopped the horses and stood unable to move, or react, as the quetzals danced. The ether went dark with the massed power of the two combatants. Around him, civilians of the town crept from their houses to find out what was going on, gaping in awe as gouts of magic tore across the sky.

Albryan watched, horrified, as both quetzals flared with wild magic and fell from the sky, leaving wisps of charred feathers in their wake as they hit the forest canopy. His heart beat frantically, yet he could still sense Fish in the ether, bright as ever, which couldn't be if he had died. There was still hope.

Around him, there were anxious exclamations, frantic questions. Albryan wasn't sure whether these people recognized him as a soldier by the sword and armour he had hastily donned, but they seemed to look automatically towards him. He took his mount in hand. "The best you can do," he called levelly, using every ounce of military experience he possessed to make his voice calm yet carrying, "is to stick together, and find safety. Put magical defences around your homes, and *stay put* this night. The enemy is coming, but your soldiers are ready for them."

Before his voice broke, and before anyone could question him, he rode off. Fish might just have saved them all from Dannine Sylvaissen. But he had done so at an inevitable cost—and Albryan could only hope it would not include his life. Was Fish lying injured somewhere, broken by the fall? Or had he succeeded in saving himself? Urgency drove Albryan onward, through the town and across the market square, into a clearing he remembered occasionally visiting with Elithan. Sometimes, his friend would sit here on clear unclouded nights, practicing—

Albryan pulled the horse up so hard that she reared on her hocks, the two mounts following nearly colliding with her. The trailing lead ropes entangled with his stirrups, making him swear in frustration as he half-fell from the saddle. He pushed away, forgetting all about the horses, falling to his knees as his feet gave way beneath him.

All of Albryan's nightmares were coming true this night, though this one he'd never even dreamed before. Elithan. *Elithan!* The thin strand that had bound Albryan to sanity these past few hours gave way, and he sank beneath the weight of his own despair underneath the uncaring stars.

A time later, he came back to himself again, and discovered to his own surprise that he was still alive and rational. The reality of what he had discovered flayed his chest to an open wound, yet he still breathed. Blood still pulsed through his veins, animating a body that barely seemed to belong to him. Nearby, the horses he had brought were grazing peacefully in a corner of the clearing.

A few feet away from Elithan's corpse lay that of his lieutenant, Erastes. Albryan remembered all too well the celebration they'd had. Erastes's promotion. Elithan's joy. *What the hell happened here?* The sickening taint of blood sorcery lay thick in the clearing, and when he touched Erastes, Albryan recoiled, sensing the same evil that had eroded Giolon Finnas's very soul.

Though the two men lay some yards apart, someone had clearly taken pains to treat them both with gentle respect after death. It was incongruous. Their eyes were closed, not staring, their hands neatly folded over their chests. Elithan's lute was laid carefully by his side, the thing that had caught Albryan's eye when he rode by, and by the side of Erastes had been placed a bloodied sword which could have inflicted the wound in Elithan's breast. Someone had tried to clean the blade, a little, and soaked up some of Elithan's congealing blood in a cotton handkerchief that looked oddly familiar. And, he saw as he inspected the bodies closer, they had laid a single mallorn-rose between the clasped hands of either man.

Albryan's heart ripped at the implication. Where was Dannine?

He reached into the ether, and found a horrifying confirmation. She was moving *away* from the town. He groaned in anguish. The army marching on Tenna—Giolon—these were nothing but distractions. The thing Arran Sylvaissen truly wanted was *Velda*, the girl who could undo even his foul sorcery. She had been here, in this clearing. Albryan felt certain of it. Elithan had protected her from a blighted Erastes. Fish had tried to protect her from Dannine—

*Fish.* Albryan stood up, dazed, and sensed him instantly in the ether. *Not dead. Still hope.* He held onto that tendril of hope, of life. The boy was not far away. Albryan pushed between the trees, coming into an area of dense undergrowth. Thorns ripped at his shirtsleeves, tangling vines of mallorn-roses sprawling beneath his boots. He smelled an acrid aroma of burning feathers, mingled with the rich earthen scent of upturned clay.

The quetzal had made its own crater as it hit earth, upturning the turf for several yards before finally coming to a standstill against the foot of a giant ironwood tree. It smouldered gently as it lay, sending wisps of smoke into the still air. It was curled around something like a protective mother might curl herself around her child, and Albryan sensed the remnants of a magic foreign to him, an energy low but strong, enduring as the earth itself.

He approached the smoking ruin, and carefully lifted a bony wing to find Fish, curled up and breathing gently, the way he had once slept in his bedroll on the floor of Albryan's room. He bent down and began to lift the boy, and Fish started as if waking from a sleeping-spell and struggled in his arms.

"Wait," the boy whispered, and the depth of loss in his eyes threatened to break Albryan's heart all over again. He fixed on Albryan's face. "Bryan?" He squirmed, and fell to hands and knees as Albryan let him go. He turned to look at the quetzal, at the quietly simmering corpse.

"No," Fish whispered in a broken voice. Albryan approached him, sank down and took his shoulder, turning him around, away from the sight. He drew the boy into his arms as he began to cry. He held Fish tightly, as the sobs racked the boy's slight body with such violence that Albryan feared he might break apart. And before he knew it, Albryan himself was crying too, clinging to Fish as the gulf beckoned, threatening to open beneath him.

"I should have known," Fish sobbed, unwittingly echoing the voice of self-beration in Albryan's head. "I should've guessed. They took her. They came for Velda. I lost her. I've lost your regard. I'm so sorry."

"Don't be silly," Albryan whispered, clasping him tighter. "This is more my mistake than it could ever be yours." Shame tore at him. If he'd been a better soldier . . . But the way the Council had treated Fish suggested what they might've done with Velda, and Albryan knew in his bones, now, that he would have done anything—made any impossible choice—to prevent that.

Familiar sounds, clinks and footfalls, came through the trees, slowly approaching. Albryan felt despair take hold. Not even this grief could go uninterrupted. Evil would not give them even that small reprieve.

Fish sprang to his feet, smudging the tears away. Albryan followed his gaze dully between the trees. It didn't take an experienced soldier to realize what was going on. The invading enemy had reached Tenna on foot at last. Hundreds of men, perhaps half a thousand, were marching towards the town. He and Fish, as luck would have it, stood right in their way. The torches they carried pierced the night, bobbing between the trees, and the light glinted off drawn swords and silver armour.

They weren't making an effort to keep quiet; Albryan guessed that was part of the battle plan, to sow fear that would begin ahead of the violence. Horns sounded, and a battle-chant went up, as though the pack had smelled blood.

A look that Albryan had never seen before passed across Fish's face. Suddenly he understood, with cold surety, that this boy had once belonged to Arran Sylvaissen. Had been raised by him; trained by him. The ether began to quiver softly, as though vibrating in resonance with something it was attuned to. Albryan scrambled to his feet and backed precipitously away.

Fish turned himself into a defensive position, grounding his feet and slowly beginning to move his hands as though turning a lever. Albryan's eyes widened in disbelief. The ether itself was moving *with* Fish, as though the whole fabric of magic itself were obeying him. It massed behind him as slowly he turned himself into a strange stance, hands held inches apart and vertical, emotion sliding off his face like mud in the rain.

Albryan didn't recognize the arcane gesture Fish made, though he knew that it was not a symbol of blood magic. It chilled his blood nonetheless. Calling power through gestures of that ilk was an older way of battle-magic, with far more risk to the spellcaster. The sheer weight of the ether around Fish stirred Albryan's heart with horror. If he lost himself in *that*—

The enemy approached through the trees. The front rank, marching ahead, spotted Fish and let out a cry. Time slowed to treacle. Fish looked serene, the only time Albryan had ever seen him so calm whilst performing magic. His eyes were unfocused, as though he were looking through the real world to the ethereal one. There was no panic, no desperation, as slowly he locked together the fingers of his right hand.

Albryan felt it happen, lifted a hand to shield himself in an instinctive, futile gesture, as the air above the army began to shimmer with an unearthly light. The soldiers were all in silver armour, but nothing could prevent Fish from magicking the very air they breathed, pulling it from their lungs with a strength of magic even Albryan had never imagined that anyone could wield. Fish flared with magic, lit by it, consumed by it. He was nothing but a vessel, a conduit for eldritch power to flow directly into the mortal world. He was allowing the magic to run wild, relinquishing his hold upon it, merely pointing it in the direction he wanted then abandoning all control.

The entire vanguard went down, six ranks deep at least, over two hundred men by Albryan's estimation. They gagged and choked, robbed of air to breathe by the twinkling haze, and fell dead for their comrades to stumble over as momentum carried them a few yards onward before the horror set in.

Albryan's heart felt as torn and ragged as wet paper in a windstorm, and he wavered between going over to Fish and forcefully slapping some sense into him, or taking the boy in his arms and giving what comfort he could for the dreadful weight of the ability that had been gifted to him at birth.

Either would have been fatally dangerous. The boy was lost in his magic. The dying force of so many men darkened the ether, depressing Albryan's spirit. Still the force continued to flow. Then, very slowly, Fish moved, began to reverse the gesture, and Albryan's world narrowed to a point.

The enemy soldiers were no longer advancing. Halting over the bodies of the vanguard, they had come to a complete standstill. There was rampant confusion and fear; Albryan could taste it in his mouth. A few more men began to choke and gag, as they blundered into the outlying webs of the spell.

Fish stood upright, alone, and those who caught sight of him cowered back. The magic around him was visible even on the earthly plane, a sticky, glowing white like cobwebs. The webs undulated gently around him, as though stirred by currents of the unknowable void. Slowly, he moved to dismiss them.

Fish moved with precise, agonizing slowness, shifting his body back from its unnatural contortion into a neutral stance. Albryan felt the texture of the ether, saw the sheer *weight* of what it was that Fish had to reverse. The boy's muscles shuddered physically against it, pain streaking his features as he pushed back with all his might.

He didn't give in, didn't collapse nor make a mistake. Albryan breathed again. The massed power stopped flowing, leaving only the groans of dying men and confused yells all throughout the surrounding forest. Fish swayed on his feet and fell heavily to his knees.

Albryan ran to his side and lifted him with a hand beneath his shoulders. The enemy were regrouping. Whether Albryan could hold them off, he didn't know. What would be their chances of surviving a surrender? The blood sorcerer's men were not known for taking prisoners. Fish had killed over two hundred men in the space of ten minutes, and Albryan's being still rang with the horror of it, yet there were at least two hundred more now realizing that the immediate danger was past.

"We have to run," he said, urgently shaking Fish. The boy only shook his head.

"No—they're here—"

Albryan thought, at first, that he was delirious with exhaustion, speaking only malformed imaginings. But then the drum of hoofbeats sounded through the earth, and he heard a clarion, familiar war-cry, raising his head before remembering that he was no longer to answer it.

The cavalry of Qwu'Mallorn streamed past, led by Thinas at their head. Albryan realized that they must have seen most of it; he had been so focused on Fish that he probably would not have noticed the Goddess coming to life just behind him at the time. As the charge passed them by, a burly soldier skidded to a halt, positioning his horse so as to protect them. He reached down a hand to Fish.

"Come on, soldier," he called. "I'll get you both safely out of here."

FISH HAD SAVED THE TOWN of Tenna, just as he had once saved Albryan and his men from certain defeat. Qwu'Mallorn was safe, for a little while longer at any rate. The would-be invaders had been wiped out, yet the taste of victory was ash in Albryan's mouth.

Thinas knew full well that Fish had been the difference, yet he could not protect him nor Albryan from the wrath of the Council. They had been given one chance, the general casting a meaningful look at the horses Albryan had taken from the stable and pointing out that the Border was still broken before turning his attention away. The battlefield stewed in exhaustion, and funeral pyres began to reach to the starry sky even as they rode into the night.

Elithan had once written a poem, stringing words together as he adjusted the strings of his lute. *All your life will be up-and-down like this. Take joy in your triumphs, yet in your defeats do not succumb to despair.*

Fish, who was riding ahead, turned in the saddle to look back. Albryan saw his own despair and sorrow reflected in the boy's face. But for the both of them, there was also the urgency, the unyielding pain and bitter comfort, of shared hope.

They passed the shattered Border, leaving crystal-slices of jagged magic keening their wounds up to the sky, even as the sun rose golden over the rolling plains of Vailana.

Book 3 of the Forest of the Morning trilogy

# Goddess of the Dark

Coming 2025/6

Keep updated at www.thepinkhydra.com

# Chapter XLI
# Blood

"WE SHOULDN'T BE DOING THIS," Albryan said, and the dagger in his hand shook. "It's wrong. It's—dark magic."

"Do you want to find out where she is, or not?" Fish slipped off the last of his clothes, and arranged himself rather awkwardly on the bedding they had agreed to sacrifice. This was going to be messy; there was no avoiding it. "We have to be sure. *You* said so." Albryan did not look at all happy to be reminded of this fact. "I'll be all right. You know how to do field healing, don't you?"

Albryan tried to speak, failed, and licked his lips. The hand which held his dagger was still trembling. He crouched near Fish, not looking at him. "I've helped stanch the wound, when men were injured on the battlefield," he replied hoarsely. "I can't take the pain away, nor replace your blood. I can make the wound knit, a little, and clot the blood enough to encourage scabbing. I can discourage infection from taking hold. And I can replenish your magic if this spell draws it off."

Fish grinned. "Sounds like a good deal to me. I'm sure I've never been in such gentle hands before." He showed Albryan where the cut was supposed to go. "Starting from the bottom of the ribcage—across the side here—a hook towards the back helps with the direction of the flow. If you can twist the knife."

Albryan shook his head violently, and the rest of him shook even worse. "That's not—that's not a good idea, Fish. That's where your guts are. If you end up disembowelling yourself—"

"That's what *you're* here for," Fish returned.

Albryan was shaking so badly, now, that Fish wondered whether he was about to have some sort of seizure, and he didn't answer.

Fish sighed. "Give me the dagger," he said at last, impatiently. This wasn't Albryan's accustomed style of magic, and Fish supposed he should have known better to start with. This was blood magic, though not the kind where you needed to have a bond with the dark goddess for it to work. But tracking people was difficult at the best of times, particularly when something was preventing them from being found, and it wasn't enough for them to locate Dannine's signature. They needed to be sure that Velda was with her. They couldn't afford to walk headfirst into a cleverly constructed trap.

But for this, they needed blood for the spell to work, needed a sacrifice, and Fish had vowed long ago, promised himself, sworn by everything inside him and the earth all around him and the stars and the sun and the moon in the sky, that he would never again hurt another for the purpose of gaining power. So it had to be self-mutilation, or nothing.

This much was true, at least: his own blood was a much stronger, more efficient source of power than some nobody off the street would be. Arran had recommended draining at least one whole non-mage being for a spell such as this; Fish did not need to drain nearly as much out of himself. A tenth part, perhaps. Maybe even less.

Fish had learned, long ago, to regard his body as something superfluous to himself, merely a tool to accomplish whatever needed to be done. That lesson had never completely sunk in: he still craved pleasure and close affection, still shied away from unwelcome touch. Years of living away from his father, amongst normal people who treated these as harmless human indulgences, had given Fish a taste for things that could blunt anguish, like strong drink and tobacco. Arran's teachings had been austere, allowing little pleasure save for the slaking of bloodthirst. Affection, sex, narcotics, the affectations of rank and splendour—Arran Sylvaissen did not indulge in these things, but wielded them as torments and punishments.

"I take it you're not going to do it then?" he asked frankly, as Albryan wordlessly handed him the knife, pale under his freckles. Fish tested the weight and grip of the dagger in his own hand.

"It's going to be awkward," he continued softly, "but at any rate, if I do it myself, at least that won't confuse the direction of the magic." His gaze flicked towards Albryan. "But if we want it to work, you're going have to hold me in this position. Otherwise I may not be able to reach."

Albryan shook his head again, and Fish tensed in frustration.

"The dirtier the cut is, the more blood I'll have to lose," he said in a low voice. "If you don't help me here, Albryan, I'll be injured worse than if you did."

Albryan raised his eyes at last, and they looked at each other for a long moment. Fish was still impatient; he wasn't sure why this had engendered such a strong reaction from a man who'd been in battles and killed countless soldiers with far harsher violence than he was about to inflict. "I'll hold you," Albryan finally agreed, as though he'd conquered something inside himself.

Fish nodded. "Pass me a pillow," he said, and Albryan obliged. Fish shoved it under his head, holding it in place with his left arm. His head was elevated now, so he could see what he was doing. He squirmed himself into the best possible position, tracing the line of power across his flesh with the very tip of the dagger. The point of the blade, as it danced across his bare skin, felt almost pleasurable. His heart was beating loudly, but he could not afford to entertain ideas of how this was going to hurt. Else he might start trembling as badly as Albryan. His grip on the knife was secure.

"Hold me in position like this," he said to Albryan. "Don't let me flinch."

Dusk was falling outside. Albryan and Fish had stopped for a few nights at an abandoned homestead which sat in a grove of blue-gum trees upon the plain. Armies from both sides had been back and forth across the farmstead in the past decades, rendering it feasible to raise nothing but more warfare in these lands. A crow croaked outside the empty window, sitting on a dead branch. Albryan's hands felt warm and comforting as he gripped Fish, shoulder and thigh, pressing him gently to the ground and holding his body firm.

"That's it," Fish breathed, dancing the knife blade across his flesh once again. He reached for his own magic, and felt Albryan's presence already there, bright in the ether, pushing gently against him, ready to augment his strength and provide energy for the healing process. There would never be a better time. He drew forth the magic until it pulsated beneath his skin, filling him with throbbing sensation, then sank the knife into his own side without so much as a quiver of hesitation. Blood welled up, thick and red, and it spilled wetly across his skin as he sliced unerringly.

As Fish had hoped, the sensation of surging magic lessened the sensation of pain. It was not a numbing: Fish could still feel everything, every nerve-string in his body accentuated by the raw lightning that magic always engendered in his veins. Yet the flood of power transmuted the pain into something that was more like ecstasy. Fish's head swam with the shock of losing blood, and he held on to that power, clinging to consciousness. And before he was fully aware of it, the power of his blood joined with the power he drew from the ethereal plane. Pleasure twisted inside him, lifting him into its embrace, and he no longer inhabited the dark, fleshly cage that was his body. His luminous spirit lifted itself into the winds, and even without the quetzal whose loss still knotted his soul, Fish *flew*.

Other novels by Emmylou Kotzé:

The Broken Knight

Forest of the Morning


Short stories:

"What Makes a Man . . ." (Cloaked Press, Fall Into Fantasy 2024)

"No Deal" (White Cat Publications)

What Happens In Camp

"Home on the Hillside" (Inner Worlds #6)


Poetry:

"Approaching Storm" (On Spec #129)

Amphipolitan: Skirting the Transient City

Caged: Poems of a Shattered Reality

# About the Author

Emmylou Kotzé is a poet and writer from Mangaung, South Africa. The name of her birthplace translates as "The Place of the Cheetah," which may help explain her lifelong fondness for mystic felines. The major artistic influence on her life as a child was the TV show *Xena, Warrior Princess*, which showed the ideal of a woman who can kick ass, solve problems, and break hearts wherever she goes. Since then, Emmylou has had a burning passion to write the lives of unconventional heroes in historical settings in all their passion, power, guts and glory.

"Forest of the Morning" is a narrative that has undergone many branching-offs, retellings, and alterations over the years. Originally a saga titled "Elfmage," about a long-lost elven princess reclaiming her kingdom, it all started in 2006 with Velda and Hiram. Albryan was added in 2008 as the love interest, and Dannine as the principal antagonist. In 2009, when a young assassin named Nico entered the narrative along with his handsome, flippant partner Fish, the story began to gain direction.

# About Pink Hydra Press

Founded in 2024 to make a space for new, queer, and weird speculative literature, Pink Hydra Press is the only organization of its kind in Africa. The genre/lit magazine The Pink Hydra has published short stories and poems from dozens of international authors. The book press is just starting out.

If you enjoy stories with a touch of the weird, or if you're an author who loves writing books and poetry infused with weirdness, come visit us at www.thepinkhydra.com.

We publish a variety of genres, but we are particularly interested in queer science fiction and fantasy, stories written by and about women, stories which challenge the current status quo, and spicy romantic and erotic stories.

Many heads. One mission.

www.ingramcontent.com/pod-product-compliance
Lightning Source LLC
Chambersburg PA
CBHW051551100726
47898CB00001B/52